SCARECROW

Also by Calvin Hernton

Sex and Racism in America
White Papers for White Americans
Coming Together
The Cannabis Experience (with Joseph Berke, M.D.)

SCARECROW

By Calvin Hernton

DOUBLEDAY & COMPANY, INC.
GARDEN CITY, NEW YORK
1974

Portions of this work have appeared in 19 *Necromancers From Now* edited by Ishmael Reed, and in UMBRA Anthology (1967–68).

Library of Congress Cataloging in Publication Data

Hernton, Calvin C
    Scarecrow.

    I. Title.
PZ4.H559Sc [PS3558.E695]   813'.5'4
ISBN 0-385-09547-3
Library of Congress Catalog Card Number 73–14049

To John A. Williams

The author wishes to express his appreciation
to Panna Grady.

For about three months I was in the power of spirits, having a dual existence, and greatly tormented by their contradictory and unsatisfactory operations . . . They tormented me to a very severe extent, and I desired to be freed from them. I lost much of my confidence in them, and their blasphemy and uncleanness shocked me. But they were my constant companions. I could not get rid of them. They tempted me to suicide and murder, and to other sins. I was fearfully beset and bewildered and deluded. There was no human help for me. They led me into some extravagances of action, and to believe, in a measure, a few of their delusions, often combining religion and devilry in a most surprising manner.

—HENRY M. HUGUNIN, in *Spirit Possession*

Be careful therefore that as ye drive out devils from the bodies of others, so ye banish all uncleanness and evil from your own bodies lest ye fall beneath the power of those spirits who by your ministry are conquered in others.

—MONTAGUE SUMMERS, from the rite
of the Ordination of Exorcists,
in *The History of Witchcraft*

It is the business of writers not to accuse or to prosecute but to intercede for the guilty once they have been condemned and are undergoing punishment

—CHEKHOV

SCARECROW

CHAPTER ONE

Wednesday, September 8

1

Scarecrow was a writer who had published a book which had marked, or would mark, the fateful turning point in his life.

He had thought the truth would be appreciated. But when the book appeared it was blasted by everyone. One reviewer called it "the product of a deranged mind." Yet the book had made Scarecrow, if not famous, then infamous, and most of all, rich. Within three years of publication, he had made nearly half a million dollars. Of course, the Internal Revenue Service had taken its toll. Another heavy sum went for his divorce settlement. Still, yesterday he had gone to his bank and withdrawn a bank draft for more than a hundred thousand dollars.

2

Now he was in his two-room studio apartment standing in front of the mirror. It was two A.M. Wednesday. He had not slept all night. He was tired, dog tired, from the labor and strain of the last couple of days and nights. But it was because of this very labor, this very strain, that his mind would not be at peace. An hour ago he had taken a bath and massaged his skin in the milky liquid they had given him at the hospital. Yesterday, after leaving the bank, he had gone to the hospital to see about the sores which had suddenly appeared all over his body. Now, in the mirror, which extended from the floor to the ceiling, the reflection of his gangling body, splotchy with sores and greasy with the milky liquid, glistened before his eyes. When sunrise came he would put on his clothes and go down and get a taxi that would take him to the pier. He was leaving his country.

"My country?" he thought. "This ain't never been my country!"

Yet it was the only country he had ever known. He had been born in it. It was his grandmother's country. His father's country, whoever he was. It was his uncle Beechum's country, Juanita's country, and the country of all the people he had ever known. Yes, it was his, or it had been his. He had gone and fought for it, killed for it in Korea. And he had hated his countrymen more than the people he had been sent to kill, for it was they, his countrymen and women, both here and over there, who had put a hurting on him at a tender age that would possess and come back to haunt him throughout his living days. There, in Korea, in the blind heat of this hurting, he had turned on one of his countrymen, Sergeant Orville Handson, his own sergeant, and filled him full of lead. They knew he had done it and not the enemy, as he had reported. They must have known. Why else would they have sent him to "psych" and given him a medical discharge. But now he had killed again. No later than last night he had slaughtered, in the eyes of his country, the most precious and tabooed thing that a black man can lay hands on.

No. It was not his country any more. And now this morning he was certain that it had never been.

3

Last night. Not this night, not Tuesday night, which had crossed over into this morning. But *last* night, which had been Monday night. About ten o'clock, he had been sorting out his stuff and packing, mostly books, manuscripts, notes, and a few clothes, when he heard a key slip into the lock of his door. He was in his robe on his knees, sweating from the sorting and packing. He stood up, tightened the robe around his waist, and remained standing there in the silence listening to the *click-click* sound of the key working in the lock. He knew who it was. Only one person had a key to his apartment. His wife. But she could not get in, for the inside chain was hooked, and Scarecrow just stood there. He had not seen her or heard anything of her in six months. A year and a half ago he had moved out of their plush six-room apartment on Ninety-Seventh Street between Columbus Avenue and Central Park West. He had returned to his old neighborhood downtown on the Lower East Side of New York. Shortly after that, his wife divorced him and sent him the papers. Without a word, without protest, he paid the settlement. Anything to get her off his back. He had never wanted to live up there among those sissified middle-class people anyway. He was glad to come back to his old stomping ground, where he had struggled to become a writer, and had made it. Then six months ago she had appeared before his door, crying and so nervous and jittery that her upper and lower teeth knocked together uncontrollably. Their daughter was with her parents in Boston, she said, and she could not go to them in her condition. What about all the money he had given her? She still had it. But she needed someplace to hide out, to get herself together. Besides, she pleaded, she was missing his loving, dying to be had in the way that only Scarecrow could have her. She edged her way inside the door. Just for a few days. She would not get in his way. She knew he had other women and she would not make trouble. After all, they had once loved each other, and they had brought a child into the world.

She kept her word. She came and went on her own. If they happened to be there at the same time she kept to herself in the smaller back room. Scarecrow treated her like a dog. He completely ignored her. He brought his women in as if no one had a key to the place but him. He moved about as if she did not exist.

Except when she begged from time to time for him to make love to her. He hated her. He did not make love to her, he fucked her, he screwed her, he used her, he dick-whipped her, and she ate it up, she took all he dished out, and he had a whole lot. After about three weeks she disappeared, no note, not a word, nothing.

Now here she was again, having unlocked the door, with her white arm reaching around inside trying to unfasten the chain.

"Open the door, Scarecrow. I know you're in there, and I know what you're up to."

She knew! She had found out. But how? He had told no one. Of course, Dr. Yas knew, it was he who had made the arrangements. There was Wantman Krane who was going with them, and Maria; and he had told his best friend, David. But they all were to have kept their mouths shut; especially, he had cautioned them, if they should run into his wife or any of her so-called friends. Yet he knew, as he stood there listening to her, that it was impossible to hush up the grapevine on the Lower East Side. You might as well go to the moon first. He unfastened the chain.

"Thank you," she said, coming out of her coat and flinging it across the room onto the couch. "Now what's this I hear about you leaving the country?"

Scarecrow did not say anything. He had nothing to say. Looking at her standing there, he was momentarily taken aback at how beautiful she was. But he had grown to despise her, and when you despise a person you think of them as ugly, no matter how attractive they might be in fact.

She moved across the room, stepping over several boxes, and leaned back against Scarecrow's huge desk, which was littered with papers, books, and other junk. "I've got news for you," she said. "You might as well stop this packing. You aren't going anywhere. You aren't leaving the country." She banged her little fist down on the desk, gropped, stammered. "I . . . I . . . I mean, you aren't running away with that . . . that . . . woman!" she screamed.

So that was it.

4

"Listen," he said. "I'm grown. I ain't married to you no more. I can do anything I please and you ain't got nothing to do or say about it."

She started crying and biting the tips of her fingernails. "You just want to destroy me. You want to hurt me. Both of you!"

"Both of who?"

"You and that woman."

"Baby, why don't you just go!"

But she was not about to leave, and she reiterated her assertion that Scarecrow wasn't going anywhere either. She knew what had gotten into his head: Black Power, Black Revolution, Black Consciousness, Black Is Beautiful, Black This and Black That! Yes, Scarecrow had suddenly gotten BLACK. It was like a disease, an epidemic among the militant blacks that infected them with a blinding hatred toward *all* white people, and especially toward white women. When she knew, and the blacks knew too, that just a few years ago white women had been the sole supporters of those so called "Black Militants." Now, after these same blacks have slept with all the white women they wanted to and have been loved by them like nobody else has ever loved them—now, they were going around hating and denouncing these women. And for what, for whom? For their so called "beautiful soul sisters," who wouldn't give one of those niggers the time of day before all of this black racism became fashionable.

She stepped toward Scarecrow with her little fist raised. Well, he wasn't going to get away with it. Not this time. He had already embarrassed her family with that book he wrote exposing their personal life together. Her family trusted Scarecrow and Scarecrow betrayed that trust, betrayed their marriage, when he wrote that obscene book. Now he was going to run away with a black woman! No good. How did he think she—

"There was never any trust between me and your family," Scarecrow cut her off. The only reason her family tolerated (and he emphasized *tolerated*) their getting married was because she was pregnant and her family was scared that their grandbaby would come out black like Scarecrow. If they'd known that the child was going to come into the world white like their daughter, his wife's family would have never given in to their marriage. Like every other white dog in the country, her liberal-ass family was racist through and through. It was the thought of a black man getting into the drawers of their precious white daughter that drove her father wild. It seemed to him that his wife and her family should've been glad he was going away!

Scarecrow's hands had begun to sweat.

His wife shook her head from side to side, her long hair swung back and forth. She had always been afraid of the man she married, but it had been this very fear that had drawn her to him, and so it was now. "Racist!" she confronted him with the word. The country was racist, sure, it was racist. How did Scarecrow think he got famous? He made it off of black and white sex! If America wasn't a racist country Scarecrow wouldn't have made a dime off of that book he wrote about them. If it weren't for her, and all the other white women he'd slept with, he couldn't have even written that sonofabitching book. If it weren't for white women and racism Scarecrow'd still be writing nickel and dime articles for fly-by-night tabloids!

Bullshit! Scarecrow strode across the floor toward the bathroom. He wanted to put some distance between her and himself. He was not aware, however, that this was what he was doing. His back was to her now and he spoke in toward the bathroom, the door of which was open. His voice echoed in there, making a hollow chamberlike sound.

"I'd have written that book anyway," he declared. It went all the way back to his childhood. He had discussed it with his friends David and Ish long before he knew his wife was alive, and she knew it too. That's what's wrong with all these liberal-ass honkeys. They think black people don't know anything about their own fucking experiences in this country, they think black people don't know nothing about this country, until they come along and tell us. Fools! If any white person had helped Scarecrow

6

with the book at all, it had been Scarecrow's only real white friend, a man, a southern cracker from Arkansas. *What the—!*

Scarecrow had suddenly spun around and what he saw assaulted him. There she was, naked, her skirt lying on the floor circling her bare feet. Goddamn. A man looking in through the window would have fainted from the sheer force of her physical beauty. But a gloom, a dread, a seething hatred rose up in Scarecrow. He felt haunted, as if this had all happened before. Then he knew where she had probably been for the past six months. She's been in the nuthouse again. He remembered himself being in the nuthouse in Korea after he'd killed his sergeant, and later in New York when she, his wife, had torn up his war novel, and he had tried to commit suicide. Now, as if in a trance, as if somebody else was looking out of his eyes, he saw her approaching, sauntering nakedly toward him, ethereally, as though she was walking on air. It was the way he had seen her that first time he had slept with her. It was the same way she had floated nakedly toward him.

He hadn't even known her name then. Her name was Beautiful, her name was Sustenance. Later, after that first time, he had found out that she was a psychologist working on a doctorate at Johns Hopkins University. She had been twenty-one years old at the time. A damn genius. Her father was a Harvard philosopher, a colleague of Paul Tillich. As the days and nights and weeks and months passed, she continued to float nakedly unto him. He had immersed himself in her body and her oils and her spirit and her mind and, yes, her whiteness. He was in love—or better yet, he was released from hatred. The suffocating maladies of his past were conquered and laid to rest within his tormented spirit. Then she got pregnant and the trouble started with her father. But they were married anyway. They moved into the plush apartment uptown. The child, Oriki, was born. His wife was disappointed and angry, because she had wanted a black baby to hurt her father with. Subsequently she stopped floating unto him. Next the book was published and their life together became a living hell, and she floated on air toward him nevermore.

Now, nakedly, she was floating again. As though his eyes were a slow-motion camera, he could see every minute movement of her muscles and limbs as she moved toward him. His perception of her now, however, was not as it had once been. He saw her not as an angel or a lovely young goddess, but as some demonic seductress, a floating white siren of incarnate evil. He moved backwards away from her into the bathroom where, like a siren indeed, she pinned him up against the washbasin.

"I've been a mean girl again," she chanted. "I've bruised you. Take off your robe and let me soothe you."

Somehow he maneuvered clear of her. "Don't touch me, get away."

But she fronted him and hatefully stared him in his eyes. "What's the matter? You scared to touch me? Your daughter is white. Why are you so paranoid about me now? I've been your wife, your lover! I'm a honkey but I've been *your* honkey. I've been out there just like you, with you, by your side, and I've suffered and fought just like you in every way. I turned against white people, even my father, for you, for us! Man, I'm a *black* white woman. I've even begun to hate my own whiteness. Because you and all the others drove me to it."

Sure enough, Scarecrow noticed that she had begun to bob and weave her shoulders while she spoke, and shuck about on her feet, just like a black person. He hated her all the worse for it.

"Go Away Don't Bother Me!" he shouted.

"All right," she said, but made no move to leave. "I'll teach your precious daughter to hate you. Prick! I'll teach her to hate your black guts! I'll change her name. What's a white baby doing with an African name anyway! I'll teach her to *be* white, to *think* white. I'll teach her to hate every nigger she sees. You aren't going to run away from me with that black bitch and get away with it. You hear me!"

Scarecrow heard her all right. Yet he heard nothing but noise, senseless, agonizing cacophony resounding and bombarding in his brain. His hands, or somebody's hands, reached out and

8

grabbed her throat. A hurting had broken loose inside of him. A heat had risen in his chest and he felt he was suffocating. With his hands clasped around her frail neck he wheeled her bodily around and slammed her against the wall. The plaster cracked from the force with which he slammed her. Again he wheeled her around by her neck, slamming her this time against the bathroom mirror in which, by chance, his eyes caught sight of a weird and telling scene. *There, in the mirror, in wretched rags with sticks for arms and legs, stood a scarecrow with his scrap-iron fingers clutched around a toothless wrinkle-faced stringy-haired hag.* GO AWAY DON'T BOTHER ME! he screamed. But there was no sound. For he himself was within the mirror, and he had gone into a dream.

4

He had just been born. Something covered his face and he saw dimly through a haze. He was without understanding and feared what he saw. He wanted to run but he was a baby and could not get up. Old black women dressed in potato-sack garments with bandanas around their heads and aprons covering their loins, stood there pronouncing words of omen.

"Lawd, child, born with the caul over his face. Gonna see varmint and belong to the haunted."

His fear grew unbearable as the sundry assemblage of noses, mouths, eyes, teeth and undulating tissue swarmed about him. He trembled. He screeched in terror. But he bore that terror, for there was nothing that he could do.

"Po thing, fraid of people awready."

His mother told him that God had been his father. God, she said, sent the babies down into the forest and the mothers went among them choosing the ones they wanted. They were walking along that fine spring day. His mother was tall and beautiful. Scarecrow reached to her knees. He loved her so much. He loved the closeness of her substance. Then he overheard her telling her friends that she wished she had had a girl instead of him. He felt betrayed, deceived. His mind started spinning and his eyes went glassy. If his mother had wanted a girl, why hadn't she chosen one when she went to the forest instead of choosing him! From that day hence, little Scarecrow took unto himself his mother's hurt. It was he who now would forever want a girl, a daughter, a sister, a woman thing.

After that incident Scarecrow slowly began to realize that he and his mother were different, not that his mother was a woman and he was a little boy, he had always known this, but that his mother's face was the color of the moon whereas his face, and indeed his whole body, was black like the stuff that billowed out of the stovepipe and got all over everything whenever something went wrong with the fire. He soon formed a habit of staring intensely at his mother when her head was turned, and often he would forget himself and stare at her while she was looking at him. "What you looking at me like that for, boy!" she would shout at him; but then again he would not hear her sometimes and she would slap his face in order to make him take his glassy eyes off of her. Scarecrow loved his mother; he was not aware of it but he grew to want her in a way that he could never have her, and while he loved and wanted her it made him hurt because he could not be what she wanted him to be, and he also hated and loathed her. As time went on, no matter how much she scolded him or how hard she slapped him, and although he never knew exactly why, he could tell that his mother had gotten to be scared of him, which caused him to stare at her with even greater intensity.

Later his grandmother became his mother. She told him what she knew about his father. His father was a hustler, a moonshine runner and a gambler. He had been gunned down by gangsters from Memphis, Tennessee. Scarecrow not only loved his grandmother, who was as black as he, but he *liked* her, even after she gave him the most severe beating he ever got from her. He and his grandmother were great companions, they were comfortable in each other's presence, and Scarecrow knew that she was not scared of him, not even after he had danced with the scarecrow who had come alive on top of the hill, and not even after he rode on the back of the big bird, after which it seemed that more and more people got to be scared of him, especially the little black girls his own color who always made ugly faces at him and ran to beat the devil.

His grandmother told him many strange and wonderful things about where they had all first come from and why they, she and him, looked the way they looked. They were not from this land but from a faraway place across the wide and deep waters. "Whare we's came from, me and you used to be royalty"—she would emphasize the word *royalty!* "We's pure stock, and our folks wus ristocrats. They wus cravers of wood and forgers of iron and some of dhem wus high priests and medicine men and knowed all the wisdom like how to cure the sick and make it rain. Yo mamma is not like us, but it's not her own fault, it wusn't my mother's fault either, Lord knows she couldn't help what old massa did to her. But you got royal blood in your veins. Tis true as I'z sitting hyear telling you. And it's gon come busting out too; just you wait and see, show as the Lord willing, you gon be something more than just another nigger." Then she would embrace him preciously and add, "You awready is."

They, Scarecrow and his grandmother, lived first with a grand-uncle named Uncle Beechum in a backwoods southern place called Tallahoma, Tennessee, where there were very few Negroes and what seemed to Scarecrow like a whole lot of redneck white folks, during the late 1930s. It was night by the fire. Outside, from a distance, came the roaring hoofbeats of horses. Whoever they were, they were riding to beat the wind. His grandmother went to the window and peered out. She Screamed. Little Scarecrow ran to the door to see, but his grandmother grabbed him and slung him under the bed. She bolted the door, dowsed the light, dropped to her knees and began to pray.

Lying under the bed, totally at a loss for the meaning of the dark, Scarecrow heard the horses as they thundered up to the house. The reflection of a cross on fire shone through the shades

11

into the room against the wall. Something landed *thump* on the porch like a heavy bale of rags. The horses raced away. His grandmother unbolted the door and ran out.

"Oh, my Jesus! Oh, my Jesus! Oh, my Jesus!" She cried Jesus' name three times.

Scarecrow had come to the door. Sensing that he was there, his grandmother wheeled around and flung him back inside the house.

"Dontchu come out here!" she shouted.

But Scarecrow had seen it. His uncle Beechum hanging from the burning cross. His body was roasted and mangled. The *thing* was lying on the porch. The words of the horse riders echoed in Scarecrow's brain: *Teachchu Niggurs T' Mess Round Wit Our Women!!!*

Back in the house he felt an amorphous undefinable hurt thrashing inside of him, and he wanted it to leave him alone. That was when he first dissolved into mirrors and discovered the land of Go Away Don't Bother Me.

Meanwhile, his grandmother had come back into the house and was calling his name and searching for him.

"Gramma, it's me. I'm right here. Can't you see me!" he yelled out to her and waved his little black hands. But his voice was dumb and his body was stiff as a rod.

His grandmother's eyes grew large and she screamed again. She took up the scrubbing brush. She slapped him across his face, she shattered the mirrors to pieces. She grabbed him by the shoulders and shook him.

"Boy, don't you ever let me catch you at that again," she warned. "If you keep turning your eyes into glass, folks will think you done lost your mind and they'll put you away."

Scarecrow always tried to obey his grandmother because she never deceived him. But the world was so deceptive and violent that more and more he had to seek refuge within the uncharted regions of his own psyche. He had been born during the Great Depression, when President Roosevelt gave his fireside chats and assured the nation that there was nothing to fear but fear itself.

He and his grandmother were then living in Chattanooga, Tennessee. Cold days they stood in front of the welfare supply house along with a whole lot of other hungry and freezing black people and watched the white folks go in and come out with potatoes and beans and fatback meat. Scarecrow had grown bigger now, a big boy for his age, and like the old black sisters had predicted at his birth, he saw deeply into many things. He grew to hate the white women, they were actually teen-age girls, who gave out the rationings at the welfare, because they made all the black people wait until the white folks took away everything. He screamed at one of them once and she refused to give his grandmother any rationings, even though there were some left that time, and he got mad at his grandmother because she went away mumbling about being a pilgrim in some damn weary land. More and more he lived in the land of Go Away Don't Bother Me. It was lonely there. He created his own friends and playmates, and created, out of the rags of the scarecrow on the hill overlooking the big red house in which they lived, a sister and named her "Rita." But the white boys from across the railroad tracks tore up his sister, ripped her to pieces, and did a terrible thing to Scarecrow himself, and he was unable to distinguish what they did to him from what they did to his sister. By this time he had learned to enter into the land of mirrors without the actual presence of a mirror. With his grandmother's old trunk he made such a grand funeral for his sister that the house would have burned down had it not been for the grace of God.

Soon he was going to school. On the long way to and from school there was a little white girl who, on one occasion, asked him where did colored children go to school, since she never saw any in the school she went to. Some policemen saw them playing. They took Scarecrow home and forced his grandmother to strip him and beat him naked like that, for playing with a white girl. During the long torturous beating Scarecrow had fled into a dream. His hands were around the throats of every white woman he had ever seen, around the very throat of the little white girl herself.

It was during the occasion of this beating that Scarecrow's puberty, his manhood, came into being and spilled there on the floor.

5

The realization came to Scarecrow's wife. She felt tears burning her cheeks and warm water leaking down her legs. She had made one last attempt, one final appeal. She had looked helplessly, mercifully into Scarecrow's eyes. But his eyes were solid glass and showed no sign of recognition. That was when she gave up the ghost, she knew it was over. She went under offering no resistance whatever.

Scarecrow did not know how long he had been standing there before the mirror with his wife's throat crumpled in his hands. He knew all life had gone out of her by the way she hung limp from his strong hands. Finally he released his grip and her body collapsed on the bathroom tile. There! He had done it. She would not teach anybody anything. He stepped over her and walked back into the main room. Momentarily he stood there staring at his packing and things as if he did not quite know what it all meant. Yes, he was leaving the country, he was putting everything behind him. He turned around and walked back into the bathroom, something was out of place. Then it hit him. *You too,* he thought, as he gazed calmly down on her. He went back into the room and sat down in the chair before his desk. He lit a cigarette and took a few puffs. He looked at his watch; it was six o'clock Tuesday morning. Damn it, he had to finish packing, he had lots to do today. He crushed out the cigarette and went about packing. When he was done he stacked the crates and bags by the door. There was also some garbage to be taken down and placed in the backyard. *Why not put her in with the garbage!* No. She was small but she would weigh too much for garbage. The thought of his wife as garbage sent a flash of irony through his mind. He had to do something with her, he just couldn't leave her lying there. Where had she been the last three months? Who had seen her?

14

Had she told anyone she was coming to see him? For all anyone knew, she was missing, disappeared again. God knows where she was. But what was he to do with her! He had a few more things to pack. He'd go down and get another carton from the streets, and while he was out he would think about it.

He took the garbage down. After he put the plastic bag in its proper place, he walked up First Avenue to Houston Street, turned right and strolled East, passing fish markets, bric-a-brac shops, secondhand furniture stores, Puerto Rican bodegas. He had seen a few discarded cartons, but they were either too dirty or too large. He stopped for the red light at Houston and Avenue B. On that corner, across the street, on the south side of Houston, he saw a luggage store. He knew the store, it was run by Jews, a man and wife, short, fat, squatty and always busy as hell. The man, the husband, was outside taking away the iron gates from the windows. It was windy on that corner. He pulled up his coat collar around his neck, walked across Houston Street and stood in front of Sam's Luggage Outlet. There were suitcases, footlockers, trunks, handbags, and all sorts of luggage.

He wasn't standing there a minute before Sam grabbed him under the arm. "Thinking bout traveling, need some luggage? Come inside. I got anything you need and you can't beat our prices, my boy."

Scarecrow took his arm out of Sam's grasp. "After you," he said.

"No, no," said Sam. "Customers always first." He ushered Scarecrow into the small, junky, luggage-smelling store.

Luggage was everywhere. All over the place. Stacked ten feet high. The aisle down the center of the floor was no more than two feet wide.

"Well, what'll it be? Trunk? Got some nice three-piece Samsonites, slightly damaged, good as new, reasonable price. Martha, come out here. Got a customer."

Martha, who looked just like Sam, came out from behind a dingy curtain which covered a hole in the rear of the place.

"Good morning," she said. "Windy out. Gonna have a hard

15

winter. Well, what'll it be, my boy?" She adjusted her thin-rimmed glasses on her nose and took Scarecrow by the arm.

"I'd like a footlocker."

"Got just what you need," said Sam, rushing toward the back.

"They're up here, Sam," said Martha, rushing toward the front.

Sam about-faced and pushed Scarecrow up the aisle toward the front where footlockers were stacked to the ceiling.

"What about this one? Strong, waterproof, good lock, sturdy," said Sam, as he slapped the footlocker impressively.

Scarecrow said he liked it. Wasn't choosy. He asked how much it cost.

"How much you got to spend?"

"Aw, man, just tell me how much the price of the thing is."

"Cheap. You can have it for a song and dance. How much can you afford?"

"I got five dollars."

"What you think, Martha?"

"Aw, awright. Let'm have it. He looks like a nice lad."

With tax, explained Sam at the cash register, it came to five fifty-five.

Scarecrow put it on his shoulder and was halfway up the block when he turned around and came back. "What's that trunk worth there in the window?" he asked Sam, who said it was worth twenty-five dollars but that if Scarecrow wanted it he would make him a deal.

Scarecrow left the footlocker there in partial exchange and forked over fourteen dollars and forty cents, which meant that he paid nineteen ninety-five for the trunk. He lugged it back down the street, up the stairs, and into his apartment. *Back down on the street with the trunk on his shoulder, he had not been himself, but was again the little boy as he had been long ago in Tennessee, flying a kite made from newspaper and old sticks; and the heavy trunk became the kite that drifted high into the crystal sky, and as the kite rose higher Scarecrow, the little boy, was also lifted up into the horizon. Then he experienced that the newly purchased trunk (which was the kite) was also his grandmother's old trunk in which he had put the rags of his sister Rita and set on fire, but it was he himself, Scarecrow of rags, instead of his sister, who was suddenly burning up the sky, and the trunk and the kite had turned into the huge and strange bird from the sea on whose back he now soared away into the hottest regions of the flaming sun.*

Once he had gotten back to his apartment with the trunk, he sat down on top of it and rested. When he had caught his breath he went into the bathroom and brought his wife out and put her in it. It wouldn't work. The trunk was large enough but it was not nearly long enough. He could break her bones. No. He could chop her up. No. Wait a minute. *Wait a minute.* Yes. That was it! He had been making it up as he went along. Now his mind made a leap, a sort of revelation came to him. He'd chop her up, pack her parts in the trunk, along with some manuscripts and a few books on the bottom, and check the trunk in at the dock with the rest of his things. Then what? Better put some mothballs in too. Then what? He knew. He'd throw her overboard. How? Well, he could do it at night. He could pick his opportunity. He didn't have to do it all at once. She'd be chopped up, in pieces. He could get rid of her piece by piece, night by night, and no one would be the wiser. When he got to Europe, all he would have in the trunk is what he left with, books and manuscripts and mothballs.

He went back down and purchased from the hardware a hacksaw and a heavy-duty Yale lock and also, on second thought, a butcher's blade. He'd put the saw and the blade in the trunk too and dispose of them in due course. He passed the local A&P Supermarket and another idea came to him. He went into the market and strolled down the aisle to where the paper towels and toilet paper and Kleenex and napkins and plastic bags were. There were no individual bags so he got a carton of six and started away. It was a good idea. He could put two or even three of the bags inside each other and that would reduce the chances of breakage or anything like that. Then, without thinking, a familiar televi-

17

sion commercial appeared in his mind as plain as if his mind had turned into a camera. He had gotten a carton of the large extra-duty garbage-size bags. He now went back down the aisle and picked a box of a dozen assorted plastic bags of various sizes, the ones equipped with the zipperlike stay-seal edges at the opening. He saw the commercial of two housewives in their spic-and-span kitchen marveling over how meat, milk, and any other things you put in the bags were utterly secured by the zipperlike seal; even when one of the wives held a bag filled with boiling-hot tea up-side down and shook it, the bag remained sealproof. Once the bags were sealed, nothing could get in, nothing could get out, they were airtight. Also, with the smaller bags he could cut up his wife's corpse into individual parts, such as a hand, a foot, a lower arm, and so on, and put them in separate little bags which could all be put into the larger garbage-size bag, which he would then put into the trunk as one total bundle. He worked several hours, in the bathroom, in the bathtub, sawing, cutting, chopping, washing blood down the drain, dissecting, laboring in total con-centration. His mind was dedicated, his body moved like clock-work. Once, however, he became self-conscious and he faltered. He leaned against the wall and mopped his brow. He could hear his own panting. Leaning there, with the pieces, the blood, the dead-white head lifeless with staring eyes and wet blond hair—he felt haunted, as though he was reliving an experience he had lived before but which had been misplaced in his mind. He thought he heard a name being called. Not his name but somebody else's name. Sounded like a whisper. *Bigger.* He jerked around. There was no one, nothing. Again, while carefully placing the parts into the large garbage-size plastic bag and lifting it into the trunk, flashes came to him of what he had done with the rags of his sis-ter Rita. He had put them in his grandmother's old trunk. That's what it was, he thought, a coincidence, nothing to get jittery about.

When he had finished, when he had cleaned everything spotless, he took a bath. That was when he discovered that his body was covered with sores. Some sort of rash had broken out all over him. Well, he would just have to forge onward. He had dressed and phoned a taxi. The driver had helped with the trunk and the other things. He had been driven to the pier, had checked everything at the dock, had gone to the bank and then back acrosstown to Bellevue Hospital. The day had been long and laborious. While riding to the pier, the full awareness of what he had done blossomed in him like an instant-blooming flower. He had a *secret* that put him beyond the station of ordinary men in society. But he had never been ordinary. What applied to other men had seldom applied to him. Now, however, he was not merely beyond society, he was beyond himself. Anything could happen. Suddenly he was possessed with the urge, the desire, the temptation, to tell somebody. At the pier, when everything had been taken out of the taxi, he had tipped the driver and said, "Guess what?"

"What?" replied the driver offhandedly.

But Scarecrow had checked himself.

6

Now it was Wednesday morning, and he was anxious. Soon he would board ship and sail. He had been up most of the night, unable to sleep, pacing the floor, pausing for long periods of time to gaze into the mirror. So many things had gone on in his mind. The sores, for one thing, bothered him. At the hospital a team of doctors and interns had examined him, and one of them, the older one with spectacles, had told him that they did not know what was the matter. The doctors had given Scarecrow a bottle of milky liquid and instructed him how to use it, saying that he should see a specialist as soon as possible.

But the sores were not what had lured him to spend so much time before the giant mirror. As a matter for future reference, he had not been in front of the mirror but inside it, in the land of Go Away Don't Bother Me, an indopsychic region where time and biography knew no boundaries. The mirror was his way of reflecting.

At various times during the course of the night he had held his daughter, Oriki, in his arms. He had talked to her and kissed her and bounced her up and down on his knee as though she were actually there in the flesh. And in her flesh, all over her flesh, he had been reminded of his daughter's mother, whom he had killed. But he had killed, not her, but the likes of her many times before. Yes, in his heart, in his mind, in his life, there had been much violence. He had been raised on violence. When he and his grandmother moved to Chattanooga, after the lynching of Uncle Beechum, they lived in the big red double-tenant shingle house with another uncle named Sims, who had a daughter whom he beat night and day. Sometimes while Uncle Sims was beating his daughter, whose name was Florina, Scarecrow would feel as though it was he who was being beaten. The sounds would come through the wall into his room and he grew to hate his uncle. He spent many hours daydreaming about how he would kill Uncle Sims one fine day. The same was true with the people who lived in the house next door, Mrs. Frazier and her son Billy, whom she beat, and her husband, who beat her. Night and day. The screaming, kicking, knocking over of furniture, the cursing and yelling.

The very first day in Chattanooga, Scarecrow was standing on the porch and a group of boys gathered around. They were dirty and ragged and flies swarmed about them. The biggest one said he was Junebug, and he told the names of the others—Lawrence, Stockdale, Buggle, Billy, and a boy with a very long head.

"Dhis hyere iz Mule Head," said Junebug, slapping the boy on his head. They all laughed, including the boy himself. They were standing in the yard, and Scarecrow was up on the porch.

Junebug said, "U'm dhe leader. I kin beat anybody. I been in dhe formatory five times for stealn and fightn."

Scarecrow had never seen the likes of such boys before, and he laughed.

"Whatcha laffn at, black mudderfuckar!"

A lady came out of the house across the street. She wore a torn and ill-fitting dress and had a broom handle in her hand.

"Oh, oh! Mule Head, hyere com yo mama!" exclaimed one of the boys.

"You nasty, filthy, horse-headed bastard! You ate the baby's food agin!" yelled the lady, advancing with the broom handle.

Mule Head threw his arms over his head and started running around in a circle there in the street with his mother chasing after him.

"Motherfuckn bitch, donchu hit me no mo with dhat broom!"

"You little bastard, I catch you, I'll kill you!"

"Kiss my ass, whore! Keep yo cunt shat you won't git so damn many babies to fed."

"Don't you talk to your mother like that, you longhead sonofabitch, I'll kill you!"

The boys were standing off to the side, laughing and poking one another in the ribs. Several grown people passed. Except for getting out of the way, they did not pay much attention to what was going on.

Mule Head's mother slipped and fell. Mule Head picked up the broom handle and started hitting her with it.

"Sam!" she yelled, running toward the house.

A handsome coal-black man wearing a suit appeared in the door. Mule Head's mother stationed herself behind the man and began yelling at Mule Head. "Low-down sonofabitch, hit your own mother, send your ass to reform school!"

The man said, "All right, Robert, knock it off."

"Fuck you, too, pimp!" shouted Mule Head, and swung the broom handle at the man.

The man slapped Mule Head to the ground, picked up the broom handle and stepped back inside the house.

Mule Head lay there in the dirt, kicking and screaming, "Black motherfucker, knock me down! You ain't none of my daddy. My daddy's a white man. U'ms yellow, light skin. My Mamma's light skin. Black coon like you slap me down! U'm gon shoot you when I grow up, kill yo black ass! Wait and see!"

21

Mule Head's mother came out of the house and lifted her son in her arms. He clung to her.

"My poor baby, don't cry, Mamma loves you, my poor darling," she said, and carried him inside.

The rest of the boys gathered back around Scarecrow. He had never heard any of the words that Mule Head and his mother were saying, but somehow he knew they were bad words. In his grandmother's book, to run from any grown person was worse than sassying them with words, and that boy had actually *hit* his mother.

Scarecrow felt ashamed and alone and he wanted to go back in the house.

Junebug said, "Com back hyere, black mudderfuckar!"

Scarecrow turned around and walked to the edge of the porch. Junebug grabbed his shirt collar and jerked him down on the ground. The rest of them gathered around, grinning. One of them smelled like do-do; it was the little fat one, Billy. Buggle, the blackest one, had yellow caked on his teeth.

They were suddenly all over Scarecrow, lifting him up and carrying him somewhere. Stop. Put me down! he yelled. But to no avail. When they did put him down, they threw him down, hard against the ground, in back of the house in a field with weeds and debris and stuff. Junebug sat straddle of him on his chest and pressed both of his arms to the ground. His face was slapped and he started struggling and kicking, but another one pinned his legs down.

"Awright, Buggle, make'm eat it," said Junebug.

He did not know what it was they were trying to make him eat, but he knew he was not going to eat it. When they could not force his mouth open, Buggle spread it all over Scarecrow's face. It was do-do, dog's leavings, and it stunk worse than anything he had ever smelled. Why! Why were they doing this? What was the reason? He couldn't make sense of it. He hurt so inside that he had no words to express it.

"Hey!" a voice called. "What yall doing out there? Why, you low-down dirty rats!"

It was a lady, actually a teen-age girl. She chased the boys away. She lifted Scarecrow in her arms, wiped his face and kissed him. "You must be my nephew," she said. "I'm Florina. I'm your Uncle Sims's daughter."

7

All night long Scarecrow had been wandering in the mirror of his past. As a child, violence was everywhere and there was no escape, except into the world of Go Away Don't Bother Me. Yet he knew this morning, oh, yes, he knew, that he had not escaped the violence. He had merely become that violence. After the white boys ravished his sister, he too found himself among the black boys when they went hunting for white boys in the endless game of retaliation between them. Many nights he remembered beating and getting beaten, himself standing over some fallen white boy and sending the iron of his belt buckle down again and again into the white flesh—and feeling strange in himself, as though he was standing off somewhere far away watching it all happen. He knew now too that in the boundaryless land of the mirror there were boundaries nevertheless, boundaries accented and marked off by acts and thoughts of mindless violence. Standing now within the mirror, he experienced it all so clearly; the fat red-faced white woman spitting on his grandmother and his grandmother drawing out her rusty knife to cut the woman's throat, and the big white men dragging his grandmother off the bus and beating her, and he strangling to unconsciousness an innocent, yes, *innocent*, little white girl there on the bus unnoticed during the commotion, and all the while thinking that he was standing in the school yard with hundreds of other black children, their bodies erect, their faces turned upward, reciting the Pledge of Allegiance to the flag flying gallantly in the wind.

Indeed, the confusing thing about mirrors is that sometimes one cannot tell which image is the real thing and which is the reflection. Often what is seen in the looking glass of experience is not the true reflection of the self but is a distortion put there by estranging elements of time and biography. What is more confusing and dangerous is when an *inside* figure appears in the mirror and begins to move first!

But the main problem for Scarecrow this morning was: *Scarecrow, are you running away?* He had lived in New York on the Lower East Side for seven years. He had been a part of the life there; the jazz, the bohemia, the poetry readings, the pot smoking, the wild parties and free loving. He had lived and loved among the poets, painters, folk singers, writers, all struggling to become something, to become somebody. And he had found, no matter how many he had lost, a few lasting friendships. And the women. Oh, God. He had lived in a world of flesh. Now he was cutting that flesh loose. He had found Maria.

Such was the nature of the mirror into which he was now staring. Some people believe that a person's background, his ethos, his past, is what determines his future. Some believe that cats and other animals can see ghosts and spirits. Scarecrow did not know about all of that. But he knew one thing. He was leaving. It was now time. His grandmother always said that if your right arm offends you, cut it off.

CHAPTER TWO

Wednesday, September 8 (the same day)

8

He was on the street now. He had not taken a taxi immediately, he wanted to walk a while and take a last look at the neighborhood. New York was such a crowded city, thousands of people were already rushing around. Scarecrow wanted to see the sights, hear the sounds, smell the smells and feel the feelings of a place he knew he would never see again. Finally, after walking several blocks, he hailed a cab.

If he knew Maria, she had been at the pier since before sunrise. But he did not know Maria. The first and only time he had made love to her was two weeks ago when she left her husband, Simon, and moved to Harlem. She said she wanted to be among her people, black people. Maria was an attractive woman, black as the night; she was tall with slanted eyes, her hair was jet silk and she wore it long down her back almost touching her buttocks. She talked fast and had eccentric ways. Scarecrow had been shocked, intrigued, and then all the more excited, to discover, when he made love to her that first time, a red she-fox tattoo on her belly. Although he had been in her presence from time to time through having been friends with her husband, Scarecrow had had no real intimate contact with her except on one or two occasions.

Secretly he had always admired her. But neither of them had ever said or done anything to indicate their desire for each other. Only once: Maria had been arguing with Simon while Scarecrow was present. She had picked up an empty beer can and thrown it not at her husband, but at Scarecrow, who was sitting in the kitchen minding his own business.

If Scarecrow knew little about Maria, she knew nothing about him. He did not love her, not as a person; he wanted her now because she was a black woman, a beautiful black woman; it was her blackness that had turned him on. But he was certain that he would get to love her as a person, as an individual, for she opened up a yearning in him, a need, that had been aching in him all his life. Until she had come along Scarecrow had never been with a black woman, really black, except for the whores in his hometown Chattanooga, and as far as he knew he was the first black man Maria had ever had. So they were both on the rebound from the white world. They were going to make it, they were right for each other.

9

The pier was a busy place, hundreds of people were milling and rushing about. Scarecrow was composed, he eased comfortably through the crowd. Then he sighted David, his number-one friend, who was waving to him, edging his way through the crowd, a big wide grin on his solid black face.

"My main man, Scarecrow! What took you so long? Wow!" David swung around, gesturing at the crowd. "Look at all these people!" He took Scarecrow by his arm. "Come on, my man, Maria's about to incite a Black Revolution waiting on you."

Maria had spotted them. She knocked and bumped people aside, some of whom turned around and stared at her. She was wearing black stretch pants, a black turtleneck sweater, a black mohair jacket, and silver slippers; her long black hair encased her handsome oval face as if to shield it from the elements.

"Sweetie!" she leaped upon Scarecrow. "What have you been

doing I've been waiting over an hour The ship's ready to sail I'd begun to worry kiss me."

"Look," David said. "There's your ship, the *Castel Felice!*"

The ship looked a mile long and it was swarming with people.

Maria said, "Well let's don't just stand here Let's get aboard David and I have been aboard already It's a luxurious bourgeois ship strictly high class kiss me."

They pushed their way through the crowd on board the ship. David got up close to Scarecrow and told him that Rex Temple, the novelist, was on board somewhere. Then he lowered his voice to a whisper. "There's a party going on down there in Dr. Yas's cabin. Gary's down there to see you off, and Marlina is too. I thought you ought to be prepared."

Maria jerked Scarecrow's hand. "Come on What you procrastinating for There's a party."

10

They descended several flights of stairs and edged their way through a series of narrow mahogany corridors. Then Scarecrow heard familiar voices. A rich southern drawl called out, "Scarecrow! You ol' dog you!"

It was Gary, a poet, from Arkansas, who had advised Scarecrow on the writing of his sex book by supplying intimate knowledge. His redneck cracker's face seemed whiter than usual and his big protruding eyes were larger than Scarecrow had ever seen them before.

"Well, Ma-an, hi you feelin'?" said Gary, grinning.

"Great," replied Scarecrow, feeling suddenly scared, at loose ends, but he maintained his composure.

They were just outside of a cabin. Dr. Yas, the huge Jew and renegade psychiatrist, reached out with his deformed hands and pulled Scarecrow inside. The small cabin was crowded to the full.

"Hey, baby!"

"What kept you so long?"

"Yeah, we thought you weren't going to make it!"

27

"How does it feel?"

"Have a drink!"

"He don't drink any more, so pour it on him!"

"Let's lock the door and have an orgy!"

That last remark was made by Wantman Krane, notorious poet of the Beat Generation. "Man, can you believe it!" he exclaimed. "We are on this ship. On! This! Ship! We are going to make it. Good-bye, America!" Krane spun around in the crowd and raised his arms up toward the ceiling. "Goddamnit, let's sing it, Good-bye America!"

They all started singing, all except Scarecrow, making it up as they went:

> Good-bye, America, Good-bye
> Good-bye, shitass country, piss on the-e-e-
> Piss on CIA, piss on LBJ, piss on FBI
> Good-bye, America, Good-bye-e-e!

"Haw! Haw! Haw!" guffawed Dr. Yas over the voices of everyone else.

Krane said to Scarecrow, "You ain't met my sweet pussy, have you?" Then to a woman, he said, "Come here, baby, I know you've heard about him and here he is in the flesh. Meet Scarecrow."

He said her name was Hellos. She was tall with a reddish-white complexion, her build and the texture of her flesh radiated carnality, but it was something about her face that made Scarecrow want to stare at her. He was whirled around however by Dr. Yas, who introduced him to several of the people who had come to see him off. Then from behind someone put their hands over Scarecrow's eyes. He knew her touch, it was Marlina!

She was standing on the bed. Forgetting about Maria being there, or in spite of her presence, Scarecrow reached his hands around back and squeezed the voluptuous white woman, who bent over and showered his face with Scandinavian kisses. A cheer went up in the cabin as Scarecrow received slaps on his back. Marlina

28

yelled above the noise into his ear that she had brought him some going-away presents. She climbed down off the bed, took his hand and started through the crowd. Maria was standing in the doorway, blocking the way and sending hostile beams from her orientally slanted eyes. Marlina ducked under her arm, but Scarecrow was forced to brush up against Maria as he passed, and she did not give way much. Marlina led Scarecrow down a flight of stairs and then through the corridor, which was packed with people.

"Here's your cabin," she announced. "And this is your closet. I put your things in there." She stood back, beaming at him. "Well, go on"—she nudged him—"get them out, see what I have for you."

Scarecrow was taken aback. "But how did you know where my cabin was, and how did you find it, in this maze of a ship?"

She placed her arms around his waist and let her hands slide down on his hip. "Ships are like men," she said. "No matter how old-fashioned or modern they are, they're all laid out basically the same."

He faced her, held her close, and kissed her. He felt the pulsing of her heart beneath the softness of her breasts, and thought of the years they had been friends and lovers. She had always catered to his every need and demanded nothing. Be it sex, love, money or a shoulder to cry on, he could always call on Marlina and she would be at his mercy. She lived far away from the bohemia, noise and rat race of the Lower East Side, far uptown in a large spacious apartment. She never intruded on Scarecrow unless she knew she was wanted, yet he was forever welcome in her house, for love, something to eat, money, or just someplace to hide out and get away from it all for a while. *But someone was standing in the doorway.*

Scarecrow turned and cheerfully said, "Maria, this is Marlina, an old friend. Marlina, Maria."

Marlina extended her hand but Maria refused to shake it, standing there in the doorway with coldness in her eyes.

Quickly Scarecrow said, "Look what she brought."

It was a bottle of Russian vodka and a leather shaving kit filled with lotion, soap, toothpaste, hair oil, cologne, shaving equipment, the works, all very expensive imported stuff. Marlina was smiling, Maria just stood there, fuming.

Holding the vodka, Scarecrow threw one arm around Maria and the other around Marlina. "Let's go back to the party."

He got them out of there fast!

11

The party was over. Passengers crowded the decks and there was barely room to stand. Red, green, pink, blue and white confetti was flying everywhere. Scarecrow whispered to David and Gary that if they should see his wife, they should not let on that he had left the country. He thought this was a good move. Then the three of them embraced, David and Scarecrow kissed.

"Take it easy, my man. I'll miss you," said David with tears in his eyes, and left the ship.

The ship was cleared of everybody who was not sailing. Maria slipped her arm around Scarecrow's waist and they wrestled their way through the crowd to the railing. How strange the people seemed standing there on shore! David, Gary and Marlina were among the crowd. Maria had the last of the vodka and she drank it freely from the bottle. Her eyes were aglow, her face lit up. She kissed Scarecrow, licked her tongue out at Marlina; then she laughed loud and long, just like a proud sassy black woman, thought Scarecrow.

Happy Castle! was what the name of the ship meant in English. "This is your Happy Castle," Marlina had told Scarecrow upon her leaving.

Now he felt the vessel moving. He looked down at the people standing on shore. David, Gary and Marlina were slowly going away. Scarecrow gave them one more wave, threw them the last kiss.

12

Scarecrow, Maria, Krane and Hellos, along with Dr. Yas, stood at the railing. Silence was among them. There was New York, receding in the distance, its skyline towering in the brilliant glow of the sun. And they were leaving America!

Scarecrow looked down at the water, the white foam spewed out from beneath the ship. Somehow the white foam reminded him of the bones and organs of his wife locked in the trunk below. He thought the sound of the foam spewing out from beneath the ship were the sirens of his wife's remains. Lifting his eyes from the water he gazed back across the ocean at not just New York but at his entire native land, and he could no longer hold back his tears. He was leaving his daughter, whom he loved more than anything on this earth. He did not love her because she was white; he would have loved her no matter what color she was; his need for a daughter was his need for the love of any woman—a mother, a sister, a lover, a daughter; it was all the same for Scarecrow. The last time he saw his daughter she stood before his typewriter and punched the keys at random, for she could neither read nor write; but she went on punching the keys straight across the page without spacing until she had filled several sheets on front and back with as many lines as the sheets would hold. Scarecrow smiled warmly to himself, as he could still visualize the lines on the pages.

bdjikmzpowyujfklmcnbz;pe/28kfm5./zndjfp½;aywh
wujncmlorkjsmv.zpljht8ikwsqz.mbnkiu7uolfgnkve

She had stapled the pages together that day like she had seen her father do, and then she brought them to him.

"Why, Oriki, this is fine. But what is it?" inquired Scarecrow.

She had cocked her little head and said, "It's my book. Read it to me, Daddy."

Scarecrow loved his daughter because she was a female thing. Ever since he had heard his mother say she wanted a girl instead of him, his soul had been haunted by a chasm, a feeling of ontological loneliness, between his being man and woman being woman. In and through his daughter Scarecrow had realized an intimacy the meaning of which went deeper than the mere love a father might have for his child. By having Oriki he had bridged the chasm, had destroyed the loneliness that separated him from womankind. By her being his, he had merged himself ultimately with the entire *female species!* This is what his daughter meant to him. This was what all individual women meant to him. The loss of Oriki would be a sore in his heart forever.

13

Toooot! . . . Toooot! . . .
BROOOMMM! BROOOMMM!

Krane, who had been mumbling to Scarecrow all the while, pried his way in between Scarecrow and Maria at the railing. "Those boats are cutting us loose," he explained, putting one arm around Scarecrow's shoulder and the other one around Maria's waist. "Those sounds," and he imitated the sounds, *"Toooot, Toooot . . .* BROOOMMM, BROOOMMM. They mean we're in international waters. See, the tugboat turns around and heads back, the pilot boat steers aside and waves us past. Hot jig a-damn! We're on our way!" He squeezed Maria and slapped Scarecrow on the back, flap!

Maria said, "I share your enthusiasm but I can do without the jig a-damn massage."

Awkwardly Krane took his arm from around Maria and motioned to Hellos, his companion. "Come up here, baby. What you standing back there for anyhow?"

Scarecrow glanced around. Passengers were roaming about, many of them had drinks in their hands. Scarecrow saw Dr. Yas —his hands out in front gesturing like an orchestra conductor —talking to a stranger. Krane went over and joined them, leaving Hellos alone at the railing with Maria and Scarecrow.

Maria turned to Hellos and said, "I'm Maria We were never properly introduced."

"They call me Hellos," she whispered, without a trace of expression on her face.

"Why you whispering What's the matter you Got a cold or lost your voice or something?"

Hellos did not reply.

"You think you're going to enjoy the boat ride?"

Hellos did not respond.

Scarecrow was wearing his dark glasses. Through them, out the corner of his eye, he saw that Hellos was the same height as Maria, who was almost as tall as he was. But Hellos was more stoutly built than Maria; she was not fat, yet somehow she appeared to be more carnal or voluptuous under the flimsy blouse and skirt she wore. The blouse was pink with a brown wool sweater thrown around her shoulders, the skirt was brown and fitted rather loosely and yet not very loosely—it was a short skirt. From her shoulder hung a knitted bag on a leather drawstring. Scarecrow was staring at her pelvis, which was broad and looked extremely accommodating for nestling perfectly up into her and making love. He saw that she had big reddish knees. It was her face, however, that was most striking. Her hair was brown and thick, it lay flat on the mold of her head and wandered down the sides of her profiles and hung in fluffs about her neck. Her cheeks were barely red, her lips were petite and moist, her eyes seemed to never blink. That was it. Her goddamn eyes!

Maria turned to Scarecrow and, imitating Hellos, whispered, but loud enough for everybody to hear, "Some mighty creepy people on this boat ride They *call* me Hellos What she mean Is that her name or isn't it kiss me sweetie."

Without waiting she cupped Scarecrow's face in her hands and kissed him, running her fingers through his Afro hair, wiggling her body and sighing. Over her shoulder Scarecrow saw that Hellos was staring at them, staring at him! Then she walked away.

Instantly Maria withdrew, and exclaimed, "Look at the ocean sweetie We're like the ocean free!"

Scarecrow heard himself saying, "It's not too good to be too free."

"What's the matter with you Is that redneck rubber-ass honkey woman getting next to you already!"

"Who, Hellos?"

33

"Hell yes Hellos Who do you think I'm talking about Mrs. Roosevelt I saw her staring at you and you giving her the once over Once over nothing You were *eyeing* her all over!"

That's because there is something about her that haunts me, I can't quite get it together but there's something out of whack about her and it gives me a weird feeling. That was what he started to say, but instead he said, "Relax, baby. You don't have anything to fear from her, or from any white woman any more. It's you and me from here on in."

"Well how am I suppose to feel You come on this boat with your white friends and they ignore me or glare at me like sycophants or paw on me like that Krane character which is worse or wave their deformities around in my face like what's his name Dr. Yas I mean They're your friends and—"

"David isn't white," said Scarecrow.

But she went right on, "I know you had a lot of honkey women running after you down there on the Lower East Side You're a Man That's one of the reasons I wanted you and got you but I must admit that Marlina woman caught me by surprise A genuine European accent She's no beatnik she's a real blue-blooded Viking and she had the nerve to oil on you right before my eyes Where did you find her and in front of all those people and now There's this dreary-eyed Hellos beaming at you like pitiful I know it was all too fast and crowded but how am I suppose to feel You never introduced me to any of them I mean and me being the only black woman in the crew when I know honkey bitches think you're their noble black stallion How am I suppose to feel!"

She had worked herself up into a tantrum, just like a little girl, thought Scarecrow, and his heart went out to her. He took her in his arms and kissed her long and passionately. She mellowed in his embrace, completely surrendered herself to him; and he felt her lithe body firm against his body, her legs and hips and crotch pressing tightly against him. The urge to have her, to mate her, rose up hard and big in his pants. But he was not himself, he had not surrendered to her completely as she had to him, and a nagging feeling was lurking somewhere in his being. He released her and looked into her face. Her slanted eyes reached out for him, almost pleadingly; the blackness of her face was radiant.

"I'm going to love you, sweet woman," said Scarecrow. "I'm going to love you to the ends of this earth." And to himself he wondered if what he had said was a declaration or a plea.

Maria said, "I'm sorry but I want us to be happy and you well you seem bothered about something distant Are you in one of your moods?" She touched his face with her long slender fingers, said, "Are you melancholy about leaving I'm not I hope I don't ever have to go back."

He took her hand from his face and held it in his. But his mind wandered. Goddamn it, why can't I keep my thoughts on this woman! For he, at that very moment, felt haunted by the bones of his wife down there in his trunk. The severed head and the white face flashed through his mind. By killing his wife he had thought the way was absolutely clear; but were her dead bones now to stand between him and Maria more obstinately than when she was actually alive. He had to get rid of those bones, the sooner the better.

He released Maria's hand, turned, looked out to sea, and said, "It's just that I've never been at sea before."

"Well I be damned!" exclaimed Maria. "I haven't ever been on a boat ride before either but it's not doing me like it's affecting you Why are writers so obsessed with the sea anyway It's just a lot of water plain old H_2O all right I'll leave you to it let it wash over you and cleanse you Dig it I'm going and get inebriated but I'll be back sweetie kiss me."

He kissed her and she left him there. His eyes followed her, lingered upon the silver-slippered, high-heel, sassy black woman's stride of her tall and slim body, until she was out of sight. But his mind had not followed her at all; something uncontrollable within him, something about being there with her aboard the ship like they were, had stolen his consciousness away from present time and present being, and sent it hurling back into the past. Like a man under hypnosis, he turned around and faced the sea. His eyes were glassy as he gazed down into the shimmering water.

14

Although he had been born with a veil over his face, and the old black women had murmured ill fate over his cradle, he had not always belonged to the haunted. Yet it had happened soon enough, as if destiny herself had ridden down out of a black sky and possessed his tender soul. That night, Christmas night, he had not been able to sleep. He had heard his grandmother stir beside him where they slept together in her bed. He had his own room, but due to circumstances of those times which drove rich people to jump from buildings and poor people to die of starvation, his grandmother had rented his room to a lodger for two dollars a week. Mr. Moss was the lodger's name. A short stout black stub of a man who collected rags, tin cans, iron, and all sorts of junk and discarded wood and planks, and baled paper for his livelihood. People called him Junkman. Had times been better and had he not been black, with the diligence he put into collecting junk, he could have easily been a lawyer, a doctor, a businessman, or anything he might have set his mind to. But the Great Depression, the black plague of want and scarcity, reigned over all. And now on this night, Christmas night, the night of his seventh moon, Scarecrow was awake when his grandmother crept out of bed and came back into the cold room carrying some apples and oranges and walnuts and sticks of peppermint candy in a red makeshift basket, and placed it before the fireless fireplace. All year Scarecrow had been a good boy, as good as Junebug, Billy and the neighborhood would let him be. His grandmother had promised that if he was good, Santa Claus would bring him the huge walking female doll he had seen in the window of Sears, Roebuck. For Scarecrow was an incomplete child, and he yearned to have a sister. Oh, how pleased his mother would be when he presented her with the great girl doll! But now, on this night, he had seen through the veil.

"Grandmomma," he said.

"Boy, whatchu doing wake?"

"Grandmomma," he cried.

His grandmother knew him well, and now she did not attempt to deny what she knew he had seen. She was his Santa Claus. She had always been his Santa Claus. The big fat man in the red suit with the long white beard and the puffy red cheeks was a pimp. It was time Scarecrow knew the truth. Circumstances no longer permitted him to be a child. Santa Claus had to be *paid* and his grandmother had no money for the walking doll. Instead, she hoped the fruit and nuts would suffice, that was the best she could do. Scarecrow felt no anger against his grandmother; yet, while she hugged him close and tried to soothe him, he felt mortified through and through, and with all his might he hated that fat man in the red suit with the ugly white beard. He could not understand why you had to pay money for presents at Christmas. You paid for things all through the year, he could understand that. But at Christmas, the season of Cheer, Peace on earth and Good Will to mankind—why did children have to pay for presents at such a time! The fit tore him loose from his grandmother's embrace; he ran heedlessly out the back door and willy-nilly across the field up the long ascending hill to suddenly face the scarecrow standing on the pinnacle of the mound. He had always known the scarecrow was there, he had seen it every day since he and his grandmother had moved to Slaton Street into his uncle Sims's red house. But now he felt an innate affinity to the makeshift heap of rags and crossed sticks. He stared up at the thing, for it was far taller than he. His eyes were burning from crying; he wiped them with the back of his fist and just stared up at the thing, unmindful of the snow beneath his bare feet and the cold winds lashing his body and face. He *stared* at it! Then he noticed a piece of sharp ice hanging from the breast of the scarecrow, an icicle sticking in its very heart. His little hands were

37

now nearly frozen; but, moving as if in a trance, he approached and seized the icicle. He felt the cold shoot through his hand, up his arm, and then all through his body. But he held on to the icicle and drew it out, and flung it up toward the sky. The icicle whirled in the blackness of night like a rod of pure white flame and streaked the sky. Up, up, up, it went; and finally out of sight, it never came back down. Amazed, he gazed up at it until all was black again. Presently he felt a touch on his shoulder, a hand. Thinking it was his grandmother come to fetch him from the cold, he turned to tell her what he had seen. But it was the scarecrow himself, moving, dancing before him on legs of sticks and rags.

"Whose little black boy is you?" said the thing.

"I'm my grandmomma's little boy."

"What is your daddy's name?"

"I don't know my daddy's name."

"Why are you crying?"

"I wanted a sister for Christmas."

Taking Scarecrow's hand into his own, the scarecrow began to sing and dance very slowly round and round in a circle. *Your name is my name, my name is your name,* he sang while leading Scarecrow in the dance. *I Am Anthropomorphic. Angel and Devil of the Fields. Conceived in Man's Fear. Ancient as Pestilence and Bird and Crop. While Men Slumber and Children Deride and Bird Eschew and Crop Prosper, I Stand Sorcerer. Sacrificial in Man's Stead. Body and Spirit. I Scare and Crow of the Fields.*

Round and round they danced, boy and scarecrow, scarecrow and boy. What a spectacle they were on top of that hill as the moon spewed her yellow beam down on them like a golden spotlight.

I, Proxy, ordained by Puritan's Madness, Fixed by his Cursed God and mocked by his Vaunted Wretchedness, stand alone in Alien Rags; Eschewed by Creation's Beauty, Unrecognized and Denounced by She in whose womb I was given the birth of Life, by She whose rejection my Heart has borne the Bitter Ages of

Death! Oh, Exorcise the Vex of Evil Sunday and unlock the Rid-dle of my own Hood and Man and Womankind!

Then the scarecrow instructed little Scarecrow to stretch forth his open hand to the black sky in which the icicle reappeared and once more the night lit up with a pure white flame that eventually landed into Scarecrow's awaiting hand. He then turned on the scarecrow, utterly possessed by some unknown power, and began to uncontrollably stab the scarecrow with the icicle until at last all the rags of the scarecrow lay at his feet. Out of those rags, after many days and nights of clandestine labor, Scarecrow made himself a girl doll, six feet tall, and she became his one and only sister.

It was not long after the scarecrow incident that Scarecrow rode on the big bird. He had discovered it in his grandmother's garden in their backyard while doing his chores. It was a huge bird larger than a big dog. It was wet and Scarecrow surmised it had come out of the sea, which was over the steep hill which rose up from their backyard. He began to pet the bird and suddenly found himself astride it and the beast flapping its huge wings, taking him up above the trees and away to God knows where. Scarecrow had thought he was dreaming again, but when the neighbors came out of their houses and gathered around and he saw his grandmother with the broom, swinging it up at him and yelling for him to stop his foolishness and come down off that bird, he knew it was really happening. He grew frightened because the big bird had begun to climb upward into the sky and Scarecrow wanted the animal to let him down; and in his fright, images of the scarecrow came into his mind and what the scarecrow had said to him that Christmas night, and he felt himself changing into the scarecrow, whereupon the big bird began to shake and flutter its body furiously in the air and Scarecrow was thrown from astride the huge beast; falling, he landed safely amid the leafy branches of the tall oak tree in their front yard with but a few minor scratches and abrasions on his body.

As time went on, the boys in the neighborhood delighted in making Scarecrow imitate the scarecrow. Walk like the scarecrow!

Talk like the scarecrow! "Do the scarecrow for us!" they would say. All the while they would be making fun of him, poking and picking at him and harassing him. But when he, in his role of scarecrow, would scowl and growl at them like the scarecrow, they would grow frightened and run for their hides.

As he grew older, even into manhood, people remained afraid of him; they tried to cover it up but he could always tell. Some of them, especially women, the very women who said they were "drawn" toward him, later would actually confide in him that they had been and were afraid of him. His wife had made such a confession. Some of his friends even told him this. But nobody was ever able to say precisely what it was about him that frightened them, yet they swore they felt afraid in his presence. All except one man, who thought he was a train and went about the neighborhood making the sounds and moving his feet and legs as though he were actually a train. That man—a wretch of a creature who wore ragged coveralls and an engineer's cap and black boots worn out at the toes and heels from dragging and trudging his feet—that man, who was known as Train Man, who was pitied, shunned and whispered about by grown folks and who was laughed at and imitated in jest and thrown rocks at by children— that man, Train Man, was unable to move his head, which was paralyzed in a fixed position to the left. If he had to look to the right he had to move his entire body in that direction in order to see. Some whispered that he had had a stroke and gone out of his mind. But Scarecrow's grandmother said that he had murdered his wife for her money and put her body under a train to cover up for his crime and that on the night of her funeral her ghost had returned and slapped Train Man's face to the position in which it was now fixed—other grownups corroborated her story.

Although he never looked Scarecrow in the face, he was the only person on Slaton Street who would stand and talk to Scarecrow without signs of nervousness or fear. And unlike all the rest, Train Man never made Scarecrow the victim of any kind of harassment. On the other hand, Mr. Moss, the lodger, the diligent Junkman, never failed to harass Scarecrow. He poked him when his grandmother was not looking, made ugly faces at him, and threatened to bale him up in a bale of rags and sell him to the rag factory, where he would be thrown into a vat of burning acid. Then there were the men at the steel foundry where he worked during summers in between school terms.

Mr. McFadden owned the steel foundry. He was a rich white man in whose house Scarecrow's mother was a domestic servant, and who had gotten Scarecrow paroled from going to prison for burglarizing a parking lot along with Billy, Junebug and Mule Head—so Scarecrow was obliged to work in the foundry even though it was living agony every single day. Mr. McFadden employed some hundred and fifty men, half of whom were blacks, and they harassed him constantly.

"Boy, you ever git a good piece of ass?"

"Yeh, Scarrycrow, com'on, tell us bout the last time you got some cunt."

"Fuck! Dhat boy ain't had his dick wet since the last time he got caught in the rain!"

"That ain't so. Is it, boy?"

"Hell it ain't! Bet if a bitch gapped open her ass and showed him her cunt, he'd run away like *she* was the scarecrow!"

"Aw, piss on you, nigger. Dhat boy don't fuck round wit all dhem nasty clap pussy bitches you horse round wit. He's young. He gits that tender meat, donchu, boy? You ever busted a virgin?"

"Virgin, my ass! He's a goddamn virgin!"

"Aw, naw!"

"Hit ain't so! Com'on, boy, show us hi big yo peter is!"

"Yeh!"

"Damn right. Let's see!"

"Shee-it! Dhat boy don't *git* no ass. He *gives* it away!

"No Kidding!"

Aw, ha, ha, ha, ha, ha, ha!

They would be sitting on empty barrels and crates and on the floor in the bathhouse, where they ate lunch. There would be

Robert and Henry and Mason and Mr. Peterson and Big Moose, who had the foulest mouth of them all and who bothered Scarecrow the most and of whom all the others were afraid, and Jake with his missing front teeth and whose wife was always putting him in the "dog house," as they called it.

Sometimes Mr. Peterson would make them leave Scarecrow alone. Mr. Peterson was a light-brown-skinned Negro who knew the other men well, but he kept to himself most of the time, silent, withdrawn. When he did say something he spoke slightly above a whisper, barely opening his mouth. He stayed drunk all the time, even on the job, and yet he never staggered, his every move was deliberate and always under control. You had to get to know him to tell he was drunk, there was a red film in his eyes and sweat dripped from his face without ever seeming to bother him. Although the others would talk and sort of joke with him from time to time, their words and attitude toward him were guarded with caution and respect, even the white men. Scarecrow liked Mr. Peterson and secretly wished that such a man could have been his father. Behind his back the men whispered that Pete was not a man to "fuck with," and said he carried a gun hidden somewhere on his person, and he had been known to use it.

"You niggers knock it off. That boy don't care about that nonsense you talking. He's got more important things to think about. Anyway, he's got a girl and she ain't no wretch like you niggers mess around with. I know. I've seen him with her. Now leave him to eat his lunch."

"I knowed it, goddamnit!" one of the others would say, but carefully. "Every time we git dhat Scarecrow going, Pete's got to butt in. That's awright dhough. One of dhese days Pete ain't gon be round and U'm gon to catch dhat boy wit his drawers down and ram my big black dick up his natural asshole."

"Yeah, Pete, hi com you always taking up for Scarecrow?"

"Shee-it! I don't blame Pete. I'd take up for him too iffen I wus conning him out of all his money." That would be Big Moose, he always said "shee-it."

In a throaty whisper, Mr. Peterson would say, "I'm getting all your mammy's money, that's whose money I'm getting. The boy knows I pay back every red cent I ever borrowed off him. Now I'm telling you niggers for the last time, leave him be to eat his lunch in peace."

That would be that, at least for the rest of the day.

Scarecrow used to see Mr. Peterson on Ninth Street, the main street for Negroes in Chattanooga, almost every Sunday when Scarecrow would be taking Juanita to the movies. Juanita was Scarecrow's first sweetheart. She was a very very light-skinned girl with long black hair that hung down over her shoulders, and she was extremely tall for a girl. Mr. Peterson would be standing somewhere alone on the street, looking as if he were about to fall asleep. He never made any noise or cursed or anything like that, he never spoke loudly as other drunks did. When Scarecrow and Juanita would pass him, he would nod or maybe he would sort of reel toward them and say, "Good afternoon, Mr. and Mrs. Scarecrow."

He would smile like he always did by lifting the right corner of his thin mouth slightly up toward his cheek; sometimes he would move toward them and ask, "Fifty cents for a shot? Give it back Friday."

Scarecrow used to notice that deep within his eyes, behind the alcoholic film, there was somebody looking out at them, somebody who seemed to have been thinking something rather sad but also very warm. Every Friday Mr. Peterson returned the money he had borrowed, and he always gave Scarecrow a half dollar extra.

Although he worked with them and was one of them, black like they were, Scarecrow never felt that the men accepted him, and he felt estranged among them. They worked hard but they never received enough on payday to pay back the money they had "dough-balled" from Mr. McFadden during the week. Their lives were weekends of drunkenness and getting beat up and getting thrown in jail and being robbed and catching venereal disease and stabbing somebody and gambling and playing the numbers and shooting up some gin house and MOTHERFUCKER, WOO, WEE, DIDN'T WE RAISE HELL SATDAYNITE!

And they never seemed to care. Scarecrow wanted to scream at them. Of what he did not know, but he felt guilty all the time he was in their presence.

The other men, the white men, he hated them with all his heart.

"Nigger, what you washing yo face fur? You so black, can't tell when it's clean or not!"

"That nigger done washed his black face so much till it shines like coal, ain't that right, nigger!"

If Scarecrow did not say "Yassuh" to everything they said and did to him, he was kicked or "accidentally" tripped or made to do two days work in one. Then they discovered that he was attending college.

"What they teaching you at that college, nigger? You reading bout Li'l Black Sambo!"

"You thank you better 'n these other niggers cause you got your black ass stuck up in some nigger college, don't you, nigger!"

"Nigger go off to college and git educated, first thing he thanks he's good as a white man, first thing he wants to do is put his black dick in a white woman. Is that what you going to college for, nigger!"

Although he worked at McFadden's for four summers, two while in high school and two while in college, he was never really there. He shielded himself from the hard labor and from the vulgarity of both blacks and whites—he withdrew into the world of Go Away Don't Bother Me. He was two selves, he was there and he was not there. Another part of him lived and moved within the mirror of his mind; and in that mirror, even as the men harassed and hurt him, he was daydreaming of their deaths. So, when he received his "GREETINGS" papers from Uncle Sam, realizing his education would be interrupted, he was nevertheless relieved. His professors offered to fight his being drafted, since he was an excellent student and was obviously being drafted because he was black. But Scarecrow forbade them to intervene.

His mind was made up. By going into the Army and serving his time, his future education would be secure under the G.I. Bill, and he would not have to break his back working on any job where he would be harassed or demeaned.

But the Army turned out to be worse than McFadden's factory. Immediately after training he was sent to Korea, where he came under direct supervision of a white man from North Carolina, Sergeant Orville Handson, who had an unmitigable hatred for Negroes. He got so many black soldiers killed by giving suicidal combat orders that the Negroes would have fared better had they been fighting on the other side. Handson's tongue was incapable of pronouncing the word "Negro." Even after he was reprimanded by the commanding officer of the company to refer to the black soldiers as "men" or "soldiers" or at least by their names, he still persisted in calling them "niggers," "coons," or, while in the presence of an officer, "Nigras." Even some whites hated him, for he was a fat, redneck, blotchy-faced southern cracker dedicated to nothing but meanness and bigotry. But when it came to blacks, he swore to their faces that the only people he hated more than niggers were the "gooks." He killed Koreans, not merely soldiers but innocent men, women and children, with the greatest of psychopathic zeal. He delighted in winging the women and little girls in the arm or leg or shoulder or some other nonfatal part of their bodies, and he would ravish them, after which he would slaughter them by driving his bayonet repeatedly in the private parts of their bodies. Then he would drop grenades upon their dead remains and blow them to bits.

It was after such an occasion, involving Handson, Scarecrow and three other soldiers, that Scarecrow lifted his submachine gun and leveled it directly into the fat blotchy face of the sergeant. Throughout the six months of fighting, as far as he knew, Scarecrow had killed only two or three Koreans, to save his own life. But in his mind he had killed Sergeant Handson a thousand times over, for to Scarecrow, Handson had become the embodiment of every white person who had ever offended him or any

45

other member of his race. When he squeezed the trigger of his machine gun and the bullets riddled Handson's face, the other men, one white and two black, leaped to their feet, for they all were resting on the side of a hill among the foliage. But the three drew up short and just stood there, because it was already too late, and they were as relieved as they were amazed. However, they had to restrain Scarecrow after what seemed like an eternity of machine-gun fire into the Sergeant's face, which was no longer a face but a blown-away pumpkin filled with a hundred blood-spurting bullet holes.

When he came to himself, he stared down at the mess and whispered, in the exact voice of Mr. Peterson, "The enemy has finally killed the Sergeant." His glassy eyes were mazed with red streaks, as though they were indeed the alcoholic eyes of Mr. Peterson himself.

15

From aboard the *Castel Felice* Scarecrow could see nothing in sight but water; the sky was a dull gray, tinted with the red glow of the setting sun. Standing there at the railing, the wind whistled in his ears and chilled his face and shoulders. Looking straight ahead, the ship rising and falling with each thrust of the engine, Scarecrow was sailing into distance and darkness. He thought of his wife's bones in the trunk in the hold. He had to keep alert for just the right opportunity, for he could not run the risk of anyone seeing him lugging the trunk to his cabin.

That had been a mistake. He should have never allowed the trunk to be put in the hold, he should have earmarked it for his cabin. But he had not really planned this thing, it had not been premeditated, it had just happened, and he had made it up as he went along. There must be hundreds of trunks, not to mention other cargo, down in the ship's hold. Would there be workers down there, an attendant perhaps? Would the hold be locked? Yet he felt optimistic. He had been lucky so far, indeed, he had been lucky all of his life. His grandmother had taught him that he was supposed to be lucky, his African ancestors were witch doctors and artisans, and had he not been given the legacy of the scarecrow from the scarecrow himself, all of which meant that he was subject to forces, both malignant and propitious, that ordinary men were not. Yes, he would wait and choose his moment. He would just have to wait and see, and deal with whatever happened when it happened.

CHAPTER THREE

Wednesday, September 8 (the same day)

16

"So here you are! What you standing out here all by your lonesome for? Contemplating the sea, eh."

It was the poet, Wantman Krane. He had two mugs of beer. Handing Scarecrow one of them, he said, "Damn women and Dr. Yas in there yaky, yaky, yaky. What's the matter with these women we got with us anyhow? Hellos got her mouth all pushed out and being a general drag. I know what's the matter with her, she's off her rocker. But that girl with you, Maria, she treats me like she hates me or something. I ain't done anything to her."

"Maybe she's not used to you yet."

"Shit, you don't have to get used to anybody to treat them like a human being!"

Scarecrow wanted to say that Maria didn't like white people. Instead he tapped his mug to Krane's and said, "Here's luck."

"Yeah, cheers! What am I so sad about anyhow? It's great to get away from America. I have no regrets. Except my mother, I ain't seen her in years and she's dying from cancer." He slapped Scarecrow on the back and pointed out at the ocean. "Hot jig a-damn! What's more beautiful than the ocean, containing everything, breathing, living, decaying, regenerating metaphysical omnipotent ubiquitous being. And here I am! Part of the entire wonder of the reachless vastness of the cosmos. One small fraction of all life-force is me, here, now, present in the eternal unfolding refolding expansion of consciousness. Hot jig a-damn!"

Interrupting himself, Krane drank the rest of his beer, spilling some down his chin in the process. "It's a magnificent thing to comprehend how vast and interminable the universe is," he went on, stretching his arms to indicate the vastness of the universe. "And to know and feel that in all of this endlessness I am and you are—and that everything as it is and was and will be, no matter how big or fractional—is infinite and significant in this particular moment right here in time and space. Ain't that right, man?"

Below his full head of red unkempt hair Krane's face was sunken; his dull-white skin was dry and cracked at the wrinkles about his eyes and near the corners of his mouth. He stood about five feet eight inches; he wore a dull-brown jacket which was unbuttoned; his yellow corduroy pants were uncreased, his plaid shirt was open at the neck revealing the reddish crop of hairs on his chest. He was about thirty-five years old, the author of three volumes of poetry which he says have been ignored. Yet he enjoyed a lively reputation because of his constant brawls and physical fights with other poets and his antics and heckling tactics at poetry readings. Now his lips were wet with beer, and there was excitement in his eyes.

"But what if we were not here now? Would that make any difference? Would the absence of the presence of our flesh and blood negate the existence of our *being!* If you look straight out yonder across the ocean where that red ring from the sunset is coming down, if we sailed straight out there, we'd be heading for the Arctic Circle! You see, the sun is setting behind us, and because of the ocean and the way light rays are refracted upon the horizon the red ring is cast to our left. We're sailing east. That's north straight out there that way. Europe is straight ahead. But as far as the ocean is concerned, we're sailing at a southeast slant. Shit, man, I'd like to build a *bridge* across the ocean, ha, ha, what

50

you think of that! Oh, hell, I'm out of beer. Let's go inside where the rest are, it's chilly out here. Come on."

Krane threw his arm around Scarecrow's shoulder, and as they started toward the bar, he said, "Lots of fine young pussies on this ship. I like young chickens, don't you? The younger the better. And it's going to be a long voyage. Look at *that* one! E-e-e-O-o-o-W! Hot jig a-damn!"

The girl's face was oval-shaped. Her hair was jet black and thick like a horse's mane. It was parted in the center of her small round head, where it lay flat on her skull and fell down on each side of her face to where it was gathered into a ponytail at the back of her neck. Her eyes were gray and ever so sleepy-looking under thin, distinctive black lashes. Her mouth was small, her lips fine. She wore a red blouse, black skirt, pink knitted stockings and a white sweater. Her breasts were full, bra-less beneath the sweater.

A crowd was at the entrance of the bar, people squeezing in and out. The threesome, Krane, Scarecrow and the girl, waited their turn. Krane maneuvered himself next to the girl and said, "Hey, sugar, what's your name? You look French."

She looked up at Krane out of her sleepy eyes, she just looked at him. Finally, as though with great concentration or, rather, with absolute abandonment, she said, "I'm from New York."

"Oh, yeah!" Krane got around in front of her and blocked her from entering the bar. "That's where I'm from too, the Lower East Side. You ever been down there? Where did you live in New York? You're beautiful. They call the Lower East Side the East Village. It's a swinging neighborhood. Lot of artists, writers, folksingers, beatniks, hippies, dope heads and people who dress like you live there. I'm the poet, Wantman Krane. Ever heard of me? Maybe you ain't read none of my shit, but you *must* have heard of me. Are you sure you ain't French? You got that French aura about you."

The crowd at the doorway thinned out and Scarecrow stepped inside. The sudden warmth caused a mist to settle on the lenses of his tinted glasses. He took them off. It was not a very large bar but it was bulging with people. Straight chairs and several plush couches lined the walls, which were solid glass panels covered by crimson drapes that hung to the floor. There were more tables scattered throughout, around which people sat in expensive-looking comfort chairs. Behind the counter, which was to Scarecrow's immediate left, a man in blue was busy mixing and serving drinks. Neon lights flashed on and off: LIDO BAR. The sound of conversation, laughter and the tinkling of glasses blended into a steady issuance of noise. Every type of face was among the crowd, every kind of hair-do and all manner of clothing. Presently Scarecrow was hit in the face by a balled-up piece of napkin. He looked and saw Maria with one foot on a chair propping herself up above the heads of the crowd, waving to Scarecrow, no, she seemed to have been pointing. Her mouth was working but it was impossible to hear above the noise. Then Scarecrow felt a hand on his shoulder. It was a strange, haunting feeling, the hand on his shoulder.

"Hey, baby, what you going to do? Walk right by and not see me?"

He turned and saw that it was Dr. Yas, which explained the hand. "How do you expect me to notice anyone in this mob?" he said.

Dr. Yas gestured at the crowd. "Haw, haw, haw! It's a gas." Then, pointing three deformed fingers in the direction of Maria, he said, "Well, look, baby, everybody's over there in the corner. Go on over and I'll bring you a drink, since I'm already on line."

Scarecrow told him all right but that he wanted orange juice. He arrived at the table and Maria took his hand, pulled him down and kissed him. "How is it out there sweetie?"

"Chilly."

Scarecrow spoke to Hellos but she just gazed at him. Then Maria nodded toward someone standing there holding a drink and smiling at Scarecrow.

He turned. "Rex!" he exclaimed. "Rex Temple!"

Clutching Scarecrow's hand, his flushed white face a big glad smile, Rex said, "You son of a bitch."

Scarecrow explained to Rex that David had told him he was on board earlier this morning and he was going to look him up but that he had not gotten around to it yet.

"You son of a bitch."

Scarecrow wanted to know where Rex was headed and why he hadn't told him he was sailing the last time they saw each other. But that had been more than five months ago and Rex hadn't known he would be sailing then himself. But Scarecrow! What was *he* doing aboard the *Castel Felice*. Whereupon he sent a strong, but good-natured punch to Scarecrow's stomach. Scarecrow had never quite figured out why so many writers went around acting like boxers, and some of them even tried to write like boxers box!

He recovered from Rex's blow and Dr. Yas returned with the drinks on a tray, some of the liquids sloshing over. Referring to Rex, Dr. Yas yelled out, "Dig it, baby, this is going to be one far-out voyage!"

From the tray Scarecrow got his orange juice and set it in front of him. Dr. Yas was drinking a thick yellow liquid but it was not orange juice. Rex threw down the last of his present drink and picked up a glass full of pure scotch. Hellos took a glass of white wine. Maria had a bloody mary. Dr. Yas proposed a toast, "Fuck the Lower East Side. Fuck New York. Fuck LBJ. Fuck the war in Vietnam. Fuck America. Fuck to live. Haw! Haw! Haw!"

The glasses went up, all except Scarecrow's. Almost everybody in the place had turned to stare at the boisterous Dr. Yas, who, sloshing beer down the side of his bearded mouth and waving one hand in the air, yelled out, "Y-e-a-h, b-a-b-y, like psychedelic!"

Hellos tugged at Scarecrow's coatsleeve. Speaking slightly above a whisper, she asked, "Where is Krane?"

Scarecrow paused momentarily as if to recall where Krane was, and studied Hellos' face. Her eyes were blue, radiant, and although they were perfectly still as if in a trance, as if lifeless, strange energy seemed to have been dancing within them. She wore no make-up, yet her cheeks glowed with a natural sort of redness, or pinkness. Her nose was keen but not too keen, and she had broad, sensuous lips like the mouth of a sultry Negress. There was about her face an inner mysteriousness, and Scarecrow was unconsciously leaning toward her, closer and closer.

But before anything happened, whatever it might have been, Maria forcefully jerked him around. "Sweetie! Where is Krane?"

He turned back to Hellos and told her that Krane was outside. Hellos took her wine and left, making her way through the crowd in high heels, like a bird might do, the flimsy skirt revealing the richness of her behind. How did Krane get this woman, where did he find her, who was she, what was it about her that made Scarecrow's blood boil? And he gazed after her until she was out the door.

Rex pulled his chair close to Scarecrow and started talking to him.

Concernedly, but to no one in particular, Dr. Yas asked, "Where's Hellos going?"

"What do you care!" snapped Maria. "Why is everybody eye-balling that flabby-ass woman Who is she anyway!" She drank heavily from her bloody mary.

Rex was telling Scarecrow, "That's why it has taken me twenty years to produce another novel, because America has no literary tradition which is rooted in anything except commercial value, fad value, or racist propaganda known as the plantation tradition. America tries to turn every writer, successful or unsuccessful, but especially the successful one, she tries to turn them into whores. She has little use for great writers, I mean *great* writers and not just popular ones. This is why I'm leaving, I can't write in that country, and I got a new novel to get done."

Rex Temple was a short, stoutly built man of about fifty years with a chubby face which always appeared rather flushed. The first time Scarecrow met him was at a party, a literary party given in honor of LeRoi Jones back during the days when Jones was high up in the beatnik literati—Rex moved around with a bottle in his hand. Scarecrow discovered that he was a novelist who had written a very famous book, *Harvest*, a long time ago and had not written anything since. The next time he ran into Rex was in a New York bar well known as a writers' hangout. Again Rex had his own bottle in his hand. Looking at him now, with his glass of scotch in one hand and gesturing with the other, he appeared to be what he was, a writer who drank constantly. Despite his drinking, however, he always radiated an inner sobriety. In this way he reminded Scarecrow of Mr. Peterson. He was saying, "Twenty years ago I won the Pulitzer. They tried to turn me into a prostitute and I wouldn't let them, and I have had to pay the price. Now they say nobody remembers me. Damn," he held up his glass, "I need a refill."

Everybody needed refills but no one rose to get them. Scarecrow reached over and patted Maria on her ass and said, "Baby."

Reluctantly she got up. "All right hand me the goddam tray Funny every time you want something it's *b-a-a-aby*," she said to Scarecrow.

As she squeezed out of the group Dr. Yas slapped her behind. "Atta girl, Maria."

"Keep your damn hands to yourself Kike And what's that poison you're drinking?"

"Pernod and water, good for what ails me."

"The gas chamber is good for what ails you!"

"Haw, haw, haw!"

17

After supper Maria and Scarecrow steered clear of the others and came up on deck. Night had fallen.

"Guess what sweetie I saw two Negroes in the dining hall the only blacks I've seen on ship One looked African the other was thoroughly dressed up You know suit tie shined shoes haircut no mustache one of those kind of Negroes *N-e-e-groes* who wants to impress Mr. Charlie that he is not like the rest of us niggers."

High in the black starless sky a full moon shone, pure gold. Somewhere, Scarecrow thought, a lonely dog must be baying in the night. He heard Maria talking and was aware of her there beside him, but somehow the moon and the night and the thought of a baying dog made him think of his wife's bones, yes, he had to do it soon, he would throw her bones into the sea and they would be gone, lost forever in the deeps. Thinking of her bones, he thought of his daughter. *Oriki!* Oh, God, could he forget her, could he live without his most precious thing? (for she was the completion of what was lacking in him, being his mother's man-child instead of her darling daughter.) Completely unmindful of Maria now, he reached inside his coat pocket and brought out Oriki's photograph.

"Did you see him sweetie sitting a couple of tables behind us with two cute little girls Hey sweetie! You listening to me What's that you got Let me see."

He handed her the photograph.

"Goddamn it's a naked white baby!"

"That's my daughter, Oriki."

"Your daughter? Why this is a white cracker baby if I ever saw one Don't look nothing like you Don't favor you at all Why nigger black as you you'd get your balls cut off being seen with a baby like this Why I bet you were thinking of that honkey wife of yours too standing here beside me wishing they were here instead of me But—shut up don't deny it—it wouldn't do you any good anyway because I got you now and you're not going to get away from me I mean like it would be good for both of us if you'd forget about your past life with all them Vikings and tore up that blue-eyed picture of your honkey daughter and While I'm on the subject if you have any notions about making that Hellos bitch you better forget them too I hate that bitch already I hate all of them cracker black-dick maniacs trying to take black women's men from us If she continues after you I'm going to get tough—after all I mean I'm nobody's fool."

Not only her words but the force of her breath against his face as she spewed them out made Scarecrow hurt in his chest as though *his* breath was being crushed inside. Hot flashes went to his brain and, without fully knowing what he was going to do, he turned on Maria with his hands raised. But, at that precise moment, they both were halted by the sound of vibrant music and singing.

"It's a jukebox."

"It's The Supremes!"

18

It was a huge room at the extreme end of the ship in the rear down by the poopdeck. There was a bar, some tables and chairs, a center space was roped off for dancing, but the crowd had spilled out onto every inch of the floor. By the time Maria and Scarecrow got there The Supremes were through and another record was playing, Ray Charles.

Standing just inside the door, Maria and Scarecrow looked at each other and then they broke up with laughter. Teen-agers, hipsters, hippies, swingers, soul sisters and brothers, young people who got high, older people who dug the scene, girls in multicolored pants and sweaters and knitted stockings and skirts above their thighs, all were there.

Instantly the rhythm of the place and the mood of the crowd fell upon them. Syncopated psychedelic lights flashed on and off. Scarecrow and Maria stood there popping their fingers and dancing, *boogalooing*, in their tracks. When the record was over, they worked their way to the center of the floor.

"Hey, baby! What took you so long?" Dr. Yas threw his arms around both of them and squeezed their ribs with his hands. "Ain't this a gas! Just like the Lower East Side. Haw, haw!"

In the crowd they tumbled from the swift rocking of the ship. Dr. Yas was flung loose from Scarecrow but both he and Scarecrow held on to Maria, who was now in between. The ship made another dip. Swaying, Scarecrow reached out reflexwise and caught hold of whoever was there. It was Hellos. The four of them swayed with the crowd. Hellos let out a soft, joyous scream, "Wheeeeeeee!" Scarecrow saw that tiny crystals of water were hanging in her brilliant but lifeless eyes.

Dr. Yas put his great hands up in the air and tried to pop his fingers. "Inner space and outer space, baby, is all one space, like psychedelic!" He reached out and swooped up a girl.

The girl went into an epilepticlike motioning of her limbs, her head thrown back, her breasty chest heaving and vibrating, her knees jerking up and down, her buttocks bouncing with the rhythm of her movements. Dr. Yas in his baggy pants with his hands up in the air, pranced and gyrated, his flabby belly jolting up and down.

Maria got on the floor and Scarecrow started dancing with her. Her lips were slightly parted, her eyes were barely open, her face was a calm mask of animal lust, her jet-black hair came undone and rode the air as she wiggled and jiggled her pelvis to the polyrhythmic music with incredible control.

Then there was Hellos, dancing in a semicircle, not jumping or heaving but weaving and swaying in and around Maria and Scarecrow.

Maria's dress was of expensive crepe, one piece from neck to knees, with a wide thick black cowboy belt around the waist that rested on the expanse of her hips, which were moving like pistons on a fast-moving train. The dress had crawled up to her thighs and clung to the curves and in the crevices of her body like wet cloth.

Hellos was still prancing, swaying, weaving and sashaying in and around Scarecrow and Maria, her short skirt swinging loosely above her large white knees and her voluptuous pelvis undulating as if to another music not there but off in the distance in another period of time; her knitted bag hung from her shoulder and her face was set softly, with the whites of her eyes staring blankly at Scarecrow.

Somebody yelled, "WHOOOOOO Weeeeeeee!

Scarecrow ambled between the two women, one black, one white. He wiggled his shoulders to the *in*-beat of the music. His arms hung loose at his sides. He threw back his head and strutted proudly, first in toward Maria, who had a mean, sexy no-expression look on her beautiful, sweaty black face. Then he strutted back toward Hellos, who, he noticed, was now both smiling and weeping serenely. Bending over, letting his head hang as his arms flopped around freely, Scarecrow did the dance of the scarecrow.

When they shut down at three A.M., the farthest thing from Scarecrow's mind were the bones of his wife. Since he and Maria both had cabinmates, they could not retire to either of their cabins. They went around in back of the place, where there was a lone bench with a watch light glowing softly above it. Scarecrow unscrewed the bulb.

19
EXTRACT FROM SCARECROW'S JOURNAL

I am keeping a journal of this voyage. It is not for publication. It is my own private record of my thoughts, feelings, and whatever strikes my fancy to write about. To begin, I want to say a few things about Dr. Yas.

He is sixty-one years old. I don't know much about him personally. I met him on the Lower East Side, New York City. But before I met him I knew of his reputation and had read one of his books, plus several articles by him in psychological journals. From what I have gathered, he first practiced medicine for twenty years. Then he turned psychiatrist. During the last ten years he has become famous. Rumor has it that in connection with his switchover to psychiatry, he went insane, and that a woman was involved. Whether this is true or not I do not know. Anyway, he is a huge man, six feet four inches tall. Don't know how much he weighs but it's got to be more than two hundred pounds at least.

He has plenty of hair but when he bends a little you can see a bald spot in the mold of his head. He is a Jew. His face is covered with a long shaggy beard of which he is proud, since some say he looks like the poet Allen Ginsberg. He wears old-fashioned rimless glasses and dresses in the same suit all the time. But here is the extraordinary thing about his appearance, if you wish to use that word. On both of his hands the third fingers are only half developed and are webbed to the fourth fingers, so that he has but three real fingers on each hand. I understand that his toes are like that too. He calls himself an existential psychotherapist specializing in schizophrenia and claims that madness is not necessarily a disease but is often an attempt to cope with a disease, that schizophrenia is as old as mankind, and that the most accurate therapy for certain kinds of disturbed persons is not to prevent them from going insane but to allow them the freedom to go mad. These along with other such claims and his unorthodox style of life have not only made him famous but controversial. Outstanding people have been his patients, movie stars, writers, millionaires, government officials, and so on. Four years ago he left his suite of offices in midtown Manhattan and moved to the Lower East Side among the struggling artists, bohemians, blacks and Puerto Ricans. Right now he is on his way to join up with a group of European intellectuals and psychiatrists (or "antipsychiatrists" as they call themselves and the leader of whom is the noted R. D. Laing) who have invited him to collaborate with them in a long-term project on the study of schizophrenia. Now there is something going on with or between Dr. Yas and Hellos. Although he tries to be cool, he is nevertheless definitely concerned about her. I do not know what the nature of his concern is but I am going to find out, because I have to.

20

EXTRACT FROM SCARECROW'S JOURNAL

I am sharing a cabin with three young men, white. The first one is dark-complexioned with black hair and a boyish face; the second is tall and blond with an air of effeminacy about him; the third is tall, red-faced and evil-looking. When I came in earlier this afternoon they looked at me with a start. It was the first time they had seen me. The first one (whom I shall call "Number One") said "Hi." The other two ignored me. When I entered the cabin they were talking lively, then a cold silence fell over the room, and I felt their stares when my back was turned.

CHAPTER FOUR

Thursday, September 9 (the second day)

21

Fire was between them. They did not take time or even think to undress. As soon as Scarecrow had turned off the light, he and Maria tore into each other. When his hands encountered the hot nakedness of her body underneath the sweaty crepe dress, his lust grew more fierce than it already was. So fierce that in the struggle to enter her wet tightness he shot between her thighs. All the while he had been struggling to enter her, Maria had moaned and groaned like a virgin in pain, for she was yet too small for him. But when Scarecrow came the way he did, prematurely, Maria moaned in even more agonizing disappointment. "Oh no no no no I wanted you in me," she cried. Then she was delighted beyond the intense frustration of her letdown, for although Scarecrow had spent his seed outside her womb, he was yet firm and throbbing, only now slightly less hard, less ferocious, and he instantly slid into her, this time softly, gently, warmly, expanding again as hard and big as before, even more so; and Maria felt her womb, her very insides, opening up to him, yet containing him fastly, whereupon, like Scarecrow had done, her issue uncontrollably broke and flowed in a continuous stream of almost unbearable ecstasy for what seemed like an eternity. And as he rode her and held her and caressed her and kissed her, a spontaneous flow of words spilled from her mouth. "Oh my god god god god you got my god forever forever fuck me FUCK me black fuck me NIGGER oh GOOD nigger GOD man BLACK man oh, oh, please, please . . ."

Scarecrow was too lost in rapture to catch everything she uttered. But somehow the word "nigger" struck a blow and for a fleeting moment his stride was halted, his body flinched and his thrust began to subside. Only to be reawakened by the realization of the Blackness of their love, which electrified him like a thousand stars shooting through every muscle, tendon and pore of his body. Oh, yes, the BLACKNESS of what they were experiencing, each for the first time in their lives, drove them on and on, until at last they fell away from one another, and the night-black waters of the moonlit ocean heaved and thrashed about the hull of the ship, and the sounds were atavistic drums in their ears.

But no sooner had they fallen apart than Maria took off the dress, which was gathered up around her neck, and Scarecrow felt her clutching at his shirt and trousers. Both of them, naked and black in the black night, saw how beautiful their black bodies were and they gazed upon one another in a wonderment akin to that which only the innocent are capable of. Maria bent low and took Scarecrow's blackness between her elegant black fingers and pressed him to her face and kissed him and hugged him and cried and worshiped him in her great Negroid mouth until finally he flew away, and still she continued until he did not know any more if she was loving him or hating him or if he were alive or dead; and it was he this time who cried out for mercy. Like a sentinel she rose from her knees and stood before him, the yellow moon shone on her proud black frame, for that is the way she stood, wide-legged, bold, and looked down at him with the triumph of a monarch. The sheer power that radiated from her being made Scarecrow unable to restrain himself from looking at, from facing, the all-consuming source of that power; for his head was level with her belly, and he saw the tattoo of the red fox quivering just above her womb, and further saw the lips of her womb themselves quivering. Then she reached and drew his face down, down, and he took the throbbing rosebud of her nature, which throbbed like he had throbbed, into his mouth. Backwards she fell to the deck, but he stayed with her, for she held his head viced between her thighs as she issued unto him again and again, moaning, groaning, arching her back and buttocks, stretching her limbs, the muscles in her legs and ass and whole body taut with tension to the point of breaking. Scarecrow surrendered. He went out to her. He loved her so much, she was so beautiful, that he now worshiped her and gave himself to her with such utter loss of ego that his being merged with her being and he found in that merging a more complete self than he had ever imagined it was possible to experience. And he made her break, her floodgates burst, and the flood fluids oozed out like thrusting gales, screaming and leaping in spasms of total release and utter fulfillment.

When they returned to reality (or was it unreality?) they found themselves sitting naked on the bench. The sun was rising, like a ball of flame its fiery beams glistened upon the ocean. The ship rode the waves straight into the face of the sun, leaping and plunging as if its belly was being scorched by the iridescent waters. Maria and Scarecrow were breathless as they huddled together on the bench.

Finally Maria broke the spell. "Goddamn them!"

"Who?" Scarecrow snapped to consciousness. "Who you talking about?"

"All those Viking bitches that done had you that's who I hate the thought of you making love to them I hate your wife She gave you a baby I want to give you a baby We'll have lots of children Goddamn those white whores! You ever made love to them like you did to me? Tell me about them What did you do to them Was they good as me?"

Scarecrow was taken aback. How could she talk like this? What had come over her? How could she have any doubts after the way they had loved! He raised her chin to kiss her.

Maria pushed him away. "I want to know!" she shouted, and told him that his body had been contaminated by sleeping with white women and that she could not rest until Scarecrow told her everything, especially about how it was with his wife. She said the fact of him having slept with white women made her feel that the women were lying with her and Scarecrow when they made love. "All of them!" she declared. "All over us all over *me* when we fuck together."

Something inside of Scarecrow began to recoil. He had had flashes of complete understanding of Maria while they were making love. But now? What the hell was happening? He took her hand, cleared his throat, and spoke to her in what he meant to be a reassuring tone, saying first that she was talking crazy. Secondly, his wife, *ex*-wife, might have been a lot of things but she was not a whore. Then he came to the main point, that every time he made love, no matter with whom, it was sacred to him. You understand, *sacred*. And with Maria it was the most sacred of all. She should stop worrying about other women, black or white. It was her and Scarecrow from here on out.

"What about that Hellos?"

Goddamn it, Goddamn it, he cursed to himself, hiding his emotions. "What *about* Hellos!"

"I asked the question You tell me All I know is there's something mighty screwy about all these people on this boat ride and you too Scarecrow but That Hellos is screwy as hell and I don't know what's behind it So you tell me."

He knew Maria was right, he was as intrigued about Hellos as she was. But for some reason he could not admit it to Maria, he did not know why but he just couldn't. "Nothing! Nothing about Hellos!" he snapped, thinking what the hell was Maria trying to do anyway? Why was she so hung up on the fact that he had slept with white women. That was in the past. Why couldn't Maria leave white women out of their relationship! He was dogged in his thoughts, trying to ease his own guilt by shifting the blame to Maria.

Maria sucked air between her teeth. "All right," she said and nestled in his arms. "All right sweetie I believe you kiss me."

Scarecrow kissed her long and, he hoped, convincingly. She pulled him down on her again and whispered, "One more time sweetie like this on this boat ride in the broad open daylight to remember."

The long night of continuous lovemaking had taken its toll on Scarecrow's stamina. But during the night he had come to love Maria beyond all restraint, and, as he lay wiggling upon her hot naked body, slowly but surely his loins began to throb once more with the fire of potency. However, no sooner did she feel him rising between her thighs than Maria started wiggling violently against him, yet she clung to him fiercely, she was pulling him toward her and pushing him away at the same time. All the while she gyrated her sex and grunted like a wrestler. Yes, she was wrestling, she was fighting! During the struggle they tumbled off the bench and Scarecrow pinned her to the deck. Still, she prevented his entrance by tightening her legs beneath him. She was a strong woman, Scarecrow felt the strength of her body almost matching his. He did not want to fight, he wanted to make love with tender abandonment. Yet Maria would neither let him submit to her nor would she succumb to him. He actually tried to surrender but Maria got one hand free and landed a burning slap to his face. Goddamn her! Scarecrow was full of himself now and his sex was big and hard as all hell and ready to burst. In one violent motion, holding her arms pinned to the floor, he raised the lower part of his body upward so that his knees were fixed in between Maria's tightly pressed thighs, and then he spread his knees outward with the utmost force, sending Maria's thighs akimbo, whereupon he slid back down on her, and before she could tighten her legs again, he rammed himself up in her like a ferocious bull. Maria screamed. Scarecrow didn't give a damn. He had gone mad wild. He was going to fuck her to within an inch of her goddamn nymphomaniacal life! On the other hand, after she had screamed, Maria recovered instantly from the brute thrust

67

of him entering her and began again fighting and squirming and grunting and pumping and grinding, forcing Scarecrow to become more violent in order to remain in her. Something other than their Blackness was driving Maria now, something more powerful than sex or love or lust, something more desperate than their being man and woman even. But he was the stronger, and he rammed her and rammed her, and gripped her long hair with both hands, bending back her angular black neck until her mouth gaped open and she went *Aw, Aw, Aw, Aw.* Like a jockey riding an untamed stallion, Scarecrow rode her and rode her and rammed her, until at last she broke and mellowed like a lamb. He was in her up to the hilt now and he pressed the hairy mound just above his penis hard against her rosebud, which itself was standing erect. Again she let out a scream, which simmered down gradually to a prolonged continuous groan. They were together now, completely in unison. Up to this point both of them had stared determinedly into each other's eyes. Now their eyes were closed, and a fierce, violent and yet somehow mellow locking rhythm of their bodies consumed them. All the while Scarecrow was visited with an imminent consciousness; even as he rode her into ultimate satiety, he was haunted with the feeling that he would never be man inside of this particular black woman again. He did not know, or was unable to fathom, the full meaning of their outlandish copulation on Maria's part. But he knew that in their brutal fornicating Maria had ceased to be a black woman and had become a universal thing; she, in her mad glorious self, had at last transcended race and color and had become pure, holy, unadulterated *pussy.*

When it was over, Scarecrow suggested that they leave before someone discovered them. But Maria did not want to leave, she didn't care who discovered them. Finally she did agree to leave and Scarecrow would walk her to her cabin. Again she clung to him, saying that she did not want to part from him for one moment. All right, all right, but at least she could go to her cabin and change that funky dress she had on. To this she also responded negatively. She liked the feel and smell of the clothes she had fucked in.

Before Scarecrow could recover from that remark, she took his hand and led him down a corridor. Suddenly she pushed him. He stumbled into a room, she shut the door, the lock clicked. Scarecrow looked around and saw that they were in the ladies' room. Beside the usual stuff there were ironing tables in there also. He turned back around to question Maria as to what they were doing in the ladies' toilet. Lo! There she stood buck naked, the flimsy dress lying in a heap on the tile around her bare feet. Her face was tilted up toward him, her eyes were dreamy, her lips were quivering, her legs were apart, and her arms were outstretched.

"Take me," she whispered.

Scarecrow blinked his eyes and both hands went to his ears. Images of his wife as he murdered her in his bathroom flashed in his brain, and he heard the sound of her dead bones rustling in his trunk that was stored in the ship's hold. *He had to get that trunk, he had to get rid of those bones!* He took his hands from his ears, but the sound of the dead bones persisted. Backing away and shaking his head negatively, he shouted softly, "No! No! Let's get out of here!"

Stepping over the dress, Maria moved toward him with her hand raised, ready to strike. "Do it to me nigger I want you to do it to me here and now," she said, approaching, her hand still poised to strike.

Scarecrow had learned karate while in the Army. His instant reflex was to defend himself in that manner. But as he warded off Maria's first attempt to hit him, he checked his reflexes and did not strike her—instead he sought to grab and hold her. She outflanked him. Quick as lightning, she got behind him and grabbed him with both arms around his waist; before he knew what was happening he was standing there naked from the waist down, with his trousers and underpants down around his legs.

He looked like a fool. He felt like a fool. Anger shot through him. On sheer instinct, he wheeled around and with the ball of his open palm shot a blow straight between Maria's tiny breasts to her chest. It was a sharp rabbit punch and it knocked the breath out of her. She gasped and sunk to her knees. But she quickly recovered and locked her arms around Scarecrow's legs. He tussled to get free but she kept grabbing and holding him. They were struggling in earnest now. Not only was he hampered by Maria clutching after his legs, but the way his clothes were gathered around his ankles made it difficult for him to maneuver away from Maria, who hustled after him on her hands and knees. Scarecrow tripped and fell forward upon Maria and flattened her against the tile floor, face down. She tussled to get out from under him and he struggled to hold and subdue her, but she kept tussling and would not be still beneath him. Her small slick naked buttocks were against Scarecrow's vitals, and as she fought to get from underneath him she felt his body growing hard in between the sensuous mounds of her backside. Scarecrow was aware of this also, and he hated both Maria and himself for what was happening. But—the more he struggled to subdue her, the more she fought back—he found his excitement growing, and greater the anger and hatred boiled in him. Back on the bench Maria's violence had caused Scarecrow to become violent. Now she was doing the same thing again. *Why!* Why did she want to fight instead of make love? Damn her! Damn her! He did not know if it had been an accident or if he had done it deliberately. All he remembered was that when he entered her she screamed to the top of her lungs. But it was too late, Scarecrow did not hear her, he could not hear her, for he had entered the land of Go Away Don't Bother Me—his eyes shone like mirrors. A mixture of guilt, hatred and anger galvanized his body into a blind instrument of sensuous punishment and sadistic rapture. He would hurt her and brutalize her, and goddamn it, she would once and for all stop fighting him. But in his state Scarecrow was not aware that, after the initial shock, Maria had begun to wiggle beneath him, not fighting but responding, and now she was pushing herself up to him beneath the furious weight of his hot sweaty pumping body.

70

Afterwards, he could not look at her at first. Something dark, like a dark secret, had happened between them. He loathed her, he loathed himself. Yet another dimension had been added to their love. Sometimes nothing draws two people closer than the secret knowledge of some dark thing between them. But Scarecrow did not want it to be dark, he wanted it to be beautiful. He loved her now in a newer, deeper and more intimate way; but at the pit of this love there loomed another kind of darkness, the darkness of anxiety, of guilt. Finally, when they were in the corridor he kissed her and, still avoiding her eyes, told her goodnight and that he would see her later on during the day.

But Maria would not have it. She accused him of calling her "B-a-a-a-by" again, and wanted to know what he had up his sleeve. She pointed out that it was not night and she was not ready for Scarecrow to leave her. She suggested that they go to Scarecrow's cabin, pointing out that she had five cabinmates but he had only three and the chances were that they had gone to breakfast.

Scarecrow frowned.

She started crying. Like most men, Scarecrow could not stand for a woman to cry, it got next to him. But he noticed that although she was crying like a baby, an evil look was in her slanted eyes. Then, hugging him closely and sobbing all the while, she said, "Please sweetie I don't want this feeling to leave me I may never have it again Let's just go to your cabin Let's just go and see."

"Maria, for God's sake," he pleaded, "I'm tired. I ain't no iron man, I ain't no satyr, I'm *tired*. Anyway, this is not the end of the world. We got all of our life before us."

"If I was a white woman nigger I bet you wouldn't be tired!"

"Goddamn you!" Scarecrow jerked free of her and started away at a fast pace, with Maria trailing after him at an equally fast pace.

When he reached his cabin Maria rushed past him. "See see," she said, standing in the cabin, "Nobody's here They're gone We got it to ourselves sweetie."

"But suppose they come back. They'll catch us," said Scarecrow.

71

"Fuck em!" She was climbing up the ladder into Scarecrow's bed. "Maria, that's not my bunk!"

She jumped down from where she was and quickly mounted the ladder leading up to the bed across the room. "Come on let's sleep together," she said. "Don't know why you wanted us to have separate cabins in the first place."

She was at the top of the ladder and was crawling into the bunk; her nakedness was exposed to Scarecrow as he stood by the ladder looking up at her. He had never seen a woman's genitals from such an angle before. If she had been completely nude it might have been different, but seen from this angle underneath her flimsy dress, it was at once repulsive, vulgar and yet somehow exciting to him. He undressed and climbed up. "We'll sleep," he said.

Maria had other notions. She kissed him, petted him, caressed and did a hundred other little love things to him.

"It's no use, Maria. I told you, I've had it for now."

"Get on top of me," she said, scooting under him and pulling him on top of her. "Hit me," she told him. "Go on, slap me."

"What! *Hit* you!" exclaimed Scarecrow, repulsively. Yet, in an estranged way, he felt attracted by the idea. He rolled off of her.

She pulled him back on top. "Hit me nigger," she said in a harsher tone than before. "I'm not asking you I'm ordering you Beat my ass Beat my ass Go on nigger you know you want to All niggers like to beat their women Who am I Who would you like to fuck? Your mother! Your grandmother! Your—"

Scarecrow socked her in the jaw, not with his hand but with his fist, hard. And at once he was appalled at himself; again hatred and disgust seethed in him against Maria. "Get out of my bed, woman!" he shouted. "I'm nobody's nigger, I'm a man. Get out before I kill you!" Yet he knew she was not going to leave. He knew it! And deep inside he was wondering if he really wanted her to leave. He would fight the feeling, he had to, how would he face himself if he did not fight this thing? Maria was coaching him into going somewhere he had never been, and he was stricken with an inner fear, of which he was terrified.

Maria knew no fear, she was determined, she knew what her goal was. She held him tightly upon her and wiggled her naked body against his. Sweetly she whispered in his ear, "Think of your wife You hate her but you still would like to fuck her not make love to her but FUCK her the lily-white Caucasian cracker bitch And Hellos you know you want her Think of how fine and white and voluptuous her flesh is her big succulent tits her juicy pussy all waiting for you to put your big black hot rod in That's it sweetie my sweet black beautiful man yes yes yes sweetie Oh! Sweetie! And any other bitch you want you love you hate some nameless white—or black—bitch who done you wrong and you couldn't do anything about it until *Now! Now!* You have her in this bed beneath you naked and at your mercy Oh! Darling! Darling! Love me make love to me you strong beautiful virile nigger you do it to me to me do it to *me!*"

22

When Scarecrow woke he was alone. He could not remember when Maria had gone. He looked around the cabin and at the other bunks; only one of his cabinmates was there, Number Three, the red-faced one, asleep in his bunk. His face held the same evil expression as when he was awake. Scarecrow wondered whether or not Number Three or any of them had come in the cabin while Maria had been in bed with him. He wondered what time it was. He must get up. He would take a hot shower and massage his body in the milky liquid, like the doctor had instructed. Then he would dress and go look for Hellos.

Before he woke he had had a dream. He dreamed he and Maria were making love, not in his bunk in his cabin, but on the sea. He did not know how they were able to lie afloat on the ocean and make love but somehow it was happening. No. They were not actually making love but they were trying to. Trying, because, similar to what had happened in reality, Scarecrow had been un-

73

able to have an erection. But unlike in reality, where he had been tired and did not want to make love, in the dream he really wanted to and he could not rise to his own desire. He was in agony with a burning lust that he could not fulfill because his sex was all wrinkled and dried up like a dead twig. All the while Maria was pleading and crying for him to love her. Then Scarecrow had felt a presence other than himself and Maria on the ocean. He looked up and saw far in the distance a figure coming closer and closer into view. It was Hellos riding on a tremendous wave; her teeth were fangs and the strands of her hair were flaming serpents. A huge pot boiling with the bones of his wife was before Hellos and she was stirring in the pot with the tail end of a ragged broom. Scarecrow realized the cause of his impotency with Maria. Hellos, the sea witch, had put a fix on him. He started swimming toward her, he would destroy her, and he and Maria would be lovers forever. But suddenly he grew frightened, for as he neared Hellos he saw in her face the face of his dead wife, and within this face was another face, the face of Juanita his childhood sweetheart, and within her face he saw yet another face, which was the face of the little white girl with whom he had played and for whom his grandmother had been forced by the police to beat him unmercifully. Then he realized that sprouting from the shoulders of Hellos, with her face of many faces, were the head of a red fox, plus the head of his grandmother and the head of the huge rag doll he had made out of the rags of the scarecrow, and called his sister Rita. He began screaming but no sound came from his mouth, and although he was executing the expert movements of the swimmer he was sinking down down down.

It had been this dream that had awakened Scarecrow. What did the dream mean? Maria had seduced him into potency by preying on his vulnerability. But how much of the dream was reality and how much of the reality was dream, Scarecrow was unable to sort out. He knew, however, that, as in the dream, Hellos had been a part of the reality. But the reality had also been a sort of dream, a fantasy. Scarecrow could not go on with that fantasy; as in the dream, he must now confront Hellos in the flesh. He *had* to, for he now felt and feared that Hellos constituted some kind of ominous portent for him and Maria.

Since he did not know her cabin number, he went to the main lobby and scanned the passenger registry. There were more than a thousand passengers on board the ship, and he went through the list twice, but Hellos' name was not there. How could that have happened? He felt haunted. He left the lobby and went to Maria's cabin. He wanted to tell her how much he loved her, to pledge himself to her forever. He wanted to confide in her, to tell her it was Hellos and the image of that little white girl that had initially aroused him. There were some cackling females in Maria's cabin but Maria was not there. Again he felt haunted.

In the corridor he saw Dr. Yas coming out of his cabin. That French-looking girl with the sleepy eyes was with him, the one Wantman Krane approached yesterday; she was wearing a red sweater that was too small for her breasts, a tight black miniskirt, and red knitted stockings, her hair-do was the same, she held an armful of fashion magazines.

Before Scarecrow could ask Dr. Yas where Hellos lived, Dr. Yas pounded upon him. "Hey, baby, glad I ran into you, we're going to have a session tonight. Krane and Hellos and Reggie here are going to be there. We're going to connect in the Lido Bar round leven tonight, and then we'll go over to the other place, you know, where we were last night. Yeah! How bout last night! Why don't you come along and bring your woman, dig. You know Reggie, don't you?"

Scarecrow nodded. The girl merely peered at him and leaned against the corridor wall. Scarecrow asked Dr. Yas if he knew where Hellos was.

Instantly Dr. Yas's entire manner changed. "I've been looking for her myself. So has Krane," he said, staring at Scarecrow.

"Do you know her cabin number?"

"45-B. But she's not there."

Dr. Yas was still looking straight into Scarecrow's eyes and it made him nervous, for now Scarecrow saw that the fat hippie-dippie psychiatrist could have an overpowering presence. Scarecrow shifted his stance and said, "Well, I just wanted to see her. I went to the lobby and her name was not on the registry."

"I am aware of that too," said Dr. Yas confidently. "It is unusual but nobody is perfect. She's probably not the only passenger they overlooked."

23

Scarecrow went straight to cabin 45-B. A girl wearing a negligee opened the door, she was the only one there. She was young, pretty and had a beautiful head of short curly black hair. She talked with her face, flicking her eyebrows, shifting her large brown eyes, manipulating her firmly cut mouth. She said her name was Kaisa, and that Hellos had not been in the cabin all night, and she had no idea where she was at present.

Before he reached his own cabin he spied some teen-agers milling around in front of the door. They were dressed in zip-up jackets, tight-fitting trousers, open-neck shirts; Scarecrow recognized one of them as his cabinmate, the tall red-faced evil-looking one, Number Three. They saw Scarecrow approaching.

"Make way," announced Number Three, who spoke with a heavy Georgia-cracker accent. "Here comes my loverboy Negra cabinmate!"

They all parted and Scarecrow walked into their midst.

Number Three said, "Negra cabinmate, where's your Negress?"

Scarecrow walked up to the door. Number Three was standing in front of it. "Excuse me," said Scarecrow.

Number Three did not move. He said, "Negra cabinmate, we done inteegrated the cabin, what about the bunks!" He smiled a nasty cracker smile.

"Excuse me, please," said Scarecrow once again.

Number Three reached in his pocket and pulled out a pair of dark glasses. He was grinning. He put the glasses on and ambled his face close up to Scarecrow's. In a raspy imitation of Louis

Armstrong's voice, he said, "Well, yeh, daddio, like you my ace boon coon!" And he sprayed Scarecrow's face with fine saliva.

His buddies sniggled in the background.

Scarecrow did not flinch. He took a deep breath and coughed up a mouth full of spit. He walled it around on his tongue for a few seconds. The grin on Number Three's face disappeared, his eyes grew large. With all the breath in him Scarecrow heaved the mucus into Number Three's red face. This was the moment Scarecrow had been preparing himself for. When Number Three made his move, Scarecrow was going to knee him in the groin and at the same time bring his knee upward into Number Three's nose, and also at the same time landing two quick karate chops to both sides of his neck. But Number Three just looked dumbfounded as the spit landed in his face; then he threw his face into his hands and backed away. Scarecrow pushed him aside and walked into the cabin.

Time he got inside the cabin he heard the alarm sounding.

BRRRRING! BRRRING! BRRRING!
CLAAANG! CLAAANG! CLAAANG!

The Captain's voice came over the public address system. ATTENTION ALL PASSENGERS ATTENTION ALL PASSENGERS THIS IS A FIRE DRILL . . . FIRE DRILL . . . ATTENTION . . . PLEASE PUT ON LIFE JACKETS AND PROCEED TO YOUR RESPECTIVE FIRE STATIONS . . . ATTENTION ALL PASSENGERS . . .

Scarecrow got a life jacket from the closet and put it on. Meanwhile Number Three came in. Scarecrow watched him. But Number Three merely got his jacket and went back out, not remaining in the cabin long enough to put it on.

In the corridors passengers were pushing and grumbling and pretending that the ship was actually on fire. Scarecrow had no idea what fire station he was supposed to report to, so he followed the crowd in his corridor.

"What a time to call a fire drill!" complained one lady. "I was in the shower, all I have under this robe is *me!*"

"At least you got an excuse. Look at me with not a sign of make-up, and my hair in these rollers, I must look *terrible!*"

"Mommie, this thing *hurts.*"

"Keep that life jacket on, Johnny. You hear me, put it back on!"

A man in back of Scarecrow yelled out, "Women and children first!"

A man up front yelled back, "Speak for yourself, brother!"

People were such fools, thought Scarecrow. Then the idea dawned on him. He turned and started going in the opposite direction from the crowd. It was rough going, people kept telling him that he was going in the wrong direction, so he stopped and leaned against the corridor wall until they had all passed. Then he rushed to the opposite end of the corridor, went down a flight of stairs and came to a door marked HOLD. The door was not locked, he opened it, another flight of stairs led down into the ship's hold. He wondered if anyone was down there, an attendant perhaps. He had to try it. It was the first opportunity he had gotten and it was a good one, in that everybody, he hoped, was going about the business of fire drill and the interior of the ship would be vacant.

Cautiously he descended the stairs. In the hold at last, he peered about for anyone who might be down there. No one, nothing, stillness. There were hundreds of trunks, bags, crates and all sorts of other junk. How in hell was he going to find his trunk among all the rest! Where would he start? He peered around. Maybe they used some kind of system of storing, like trunks in one place, footlockers in another place, and so on. He looked for trunks. It was impossible, he could not be that lucky! He saw it. It was the first thing he caught sight of, not with the rest of the trunks and footlockers and baggage but sitting all by itself, in clear view on top of two huge crates marked SOUTHAMPTON IRON WORKS. He ran down the aisle to where it was. He reached up and worked it out a bit from the crates, he wanted to be certain it was his before he pulled it down. It was. Carefully he pulled it off top of the crates and, turning, eased it onto his back. It was not heavy, he'd make it if his luck held out. Going as fast as he could but careful not to trip or fall, he made his way back up the stairs, then around a corner and up the second flight of stairs. He was now in the corridor of the ship. Momentarily and bent over with the trunk on his back, he stood still and listened. The ship was absolutely quiet except for the humming of its various parts. He moved ahead, almost trotting. That's when he lost his grip on the handle and the damn thing slid off his back and landed on the floor with a loud resounding noise! He jumped around. He felt naked. Had there been somewhere to take cover he would have hidden. But in the corridor there was nothing but walls and floors. He waited for someone to come, for someone to respond to the noise. Nothing. He raised the trunk up on its end. Bending over forward, he reached around and pulled it onto his back again. He was thankful that his cabin was on a corridor one floor above the hold. He entered the cabin and set it in the center of the floor. No. That would possibly cause curiosity. There was a space between the door and the foot of his bunk, he pulled it down there. Yes, it looked natural at the foot of his bunk. He still had on his life jacket and he was wet with perspiration from head to foot. He grabbed a towel and dropped it instantly, because his hands were cramped from having held the trunk. He worked his fingers back and forth. There, that was better. After he wiped his face and tried to compose himself, he ran on tiptoe through the corridor in the direction in which the passengers had gone.

He found them in a place called the Veranda Lounge, which was four times the size of the Lido Bar and about twice as large as the place with the jukebox where they had danced the other night. He eased his way among the passengers until he was standing in front of an entire wall of transparent sheet glass. It was oval-shaped like the nose cone of a space capsule. Through the glass, down on the afterdeck below, which extended out from under the Veranda Lounge into a perfect V, he saw members of the crew lowering lifeboats, rolling up hoses, and going through the motions of the fire drill. He was resting now, his breathing had almost returned to normal.

He watched the crew complete their rehearsal. Then the fire drill was over. Scarecrow turned to leave as the rest were doing, and there she was, Hellos, standing a few feet away, just standing there, *gazing* at him. He made a start, she had frightened him, seeing her unexpectedly, and she looked ghostly, unreal, as if she were an illusion. Unconsciously his hand went out to touch her, to see if it was really her. But now he knew it was her and he drew back his hand, which had begun to perspire heavily. Looking at her, he realized that the picture he had in his mind was nothing compared to Hellos in the flesh. She was the most beautiful creature any man had ever seen or dreamed of! Even the knitted bag hanging from her shoulder enhanced her charm. No! It was not charm. It was more than charm; he did not know what it was, magic maybe; whatever it was about her was enough to drive a man crazy if he could not possess it. And he found himself taking her face in his hands and kissing her. But, although her mouth was warm and succulent, she did not respond, she just stared at him out of those gazing eyes. Then Scarecrow raised his fist. A fury raged within him. He wanted to destroy her, he wanted to blot this thing out, whatever she was.

"I've been looking for you," he said.

She did not respond. She just stood there gazing at him.

Scarecrow slapped her, *Whap!* "I want to talk to you!" he shouted. People turned and looked in their direction. Furies of heat were imploding inside Scarecrow.

Hellos did not flinch. A knowing and fleeting smile shone on her face, and then she was the same as before. "I want to talk to you too," she said in her characteristic baby whisper. She turned around for Scarecrow to untie her life jacket in the back. He took off his jacket also. Then she took his hand in hers.

Walking with her was like walking with an angel. She carried her body delicately as if she did not wish to excite anyone with her being; walking as if something inside her might break if she stepped too lively or too rhythmically, yet there was an easy elusive rhythm to her style, a sensual melody, as if she was not walking but *floating*. They were standing inside her cabin before Scarecrow realized it. There, in the cabin, Hellos placed her hands together as if to pray and then whirled around extending her hands outward as if to beckon. "Oh, I met the most beautiful person last night!" she exclaimed; yet her voice was ever so soft. "You will never believe it but he's a divine," she went on. "He's crippled, some kind of invalid from birth, so tiny and divine. He has not set foot on land in fifteen years. Would you believe it? He's been traveling all those years all over the world, and he knows so many wonderful secrets. I spent the night in his cabin listening to his secrets as he sat perched upon my knee. Fantastic! He is the only divine I have ever met who does not have an ounce of Satan in him."

Was she crazy? Was she trying to put him on? Or what? "I didn't come with you to hear about some cripple," said Scarecrow. "I want to know about *you*."

Serenely she whirled round and round in a circle, and serenely she said, "I am crippled. You are crippled. We all are crippled. I know about you. I know *everything* about you. And you know nothing about me. But we have a world of time ahead of us, and in time you shall know what I know."

Scarecrow noticed how her skirt flared out about her beautiful white thighs as she whirled around, and when she stood still how it fell down like a curtain over her behind and lay there loosely, so that the dimples in her buttocks were discernible. She was earthy without being vulgar, sexy but not lewd, voluptuous without being flabby. Hating himself, he could not resist her. He took her in his arms and pressed her close; her stomach slanted away down to her crotch and perfectly fitted the structure of his own

81

body; she was made for loving, she was tall and pliant in his arms. But although his body ached for her, his mind was confused, and he pushed her away.

Taking the bag off her shoulder and laying it on the bed, she told him the following story. At one time she had been an airline hostess, flying from New York to Budapest twice a week. Then her mother died in a plane crash. Her mother was Irish. Hellos did not know anything about her grandparents, except for her grandmother, who, she said, had been burned at the stake for communing with dark figures in the south of Ireland. After Hellos' mother died in the crash, she gave up working as a hostess. She could not take it any more. Then, too, her father began suffering extreme paranoia about the mother's death. The father was of German descent, of the old Protestant fundamentalist stock, but in reality he had never been religious in his life. That is, until the mother died in the crash. Then he went senile and became extremely religious and superstitious. He, the father, lived in Elyria, Ohio, where Hellos had been born, on a farm, and he wrote her three letters every day after the mother died, warning Hellos about how sinful it was for man to fly; nothing but evil would ever come of it. If God had wanted people to fly, her father insisted, He, God, would have given man wings.

Her voice trailed off. She slumped down on the bunk, folded her hands in her lap, and then said, "Have you ever eaten the testicles of a hog? It was a ritual in our house but I did not like it. It was repulsive. I don't know why, but I just couldn't eat those things. Then one Thanksgiving my father got drunk and made me eat them. I was six years old. Have you ever seen them lying on a plate! I cried and pleaded, and my mother did too, but he made me eat them anyway. I bit into one of them and vomited in my plate. Father took his belt and beat me. 'Eat!' he said. I've hated my father ever since."

She threw back her head and started crying, not like a grownup but like an enraged baby.

"Easy, easy, childhood is a rough time for most children," Scarecrow heard himself saying. "But we must not let those things cripple us for the rest of our lives." He looked quickly around the cabin, for at that instant he felt as though it had not been him who had said those words.

"But I am not strong," Hellos whined. "And I cannot be calm." Then she told him that she must not have hated her father as much as she had thought, because she resigned her job and went to live with him. But it had been too late. Her father was not only senile, he had lost his mind. Plus he suffered paralysis from the neck down. Two weeks after Hellos had returned, the father died in an institution from a brain hemorrhage. Stricken with guilt, she had gone to New York and taken a job as a social worker. But she could not work, she was lost. Within a single year both of her parents had died. So she took to drinking. "I was depressed all the time. I thought of suicide constantly but I am incapable of killing myself. Someone else will have to do it for me. The main thing, I felt old, useless. That's how I came to the Lower East Side and met Krane. But I do not love him, I never did, I let him use me, I let them all use me. There are other things that I cannot tell you in so many words. But they'll be revealed to you as we go on. We are going to go on, you know."

Scarecrow sat on the side of the bed and put his arm around her. But for some strange reason he was still frightened of her. No. Not of her, but of *something!* He could not put his finger on exactly what that something was, though. While she had been talking, he detected a tension in the barely audible and hypnotic way she spoke, which lent to her otherwise serene countenance an underlying chaos. But from what she had just told him he supposed that that was natural.

"Now get out," she said, rising, pointing at the door. "And don't approach me again until you have broken off with Maria."

What! Scarecrow sprang to his feet. He didn't believe he had heard right.

"Keep your voice down," she said, opening the door, stepping back from it and pointing outside. "You must be strong and you must be calm. Break with that evil woman and I'll be yours; understand, we are destined. Now go!"

24

He had not gone out of Hellos' cabin of his own free will. He had wanted to have it out with her; after all, had not this been his purpose in the first place! No, he had not gone of his own volition. There had been something in her finger, some strange power in the way she had pointed at the door, which had commanded him to leave, and he felt that he had been banished, or *driven*, from her cabin.

He went up on the deck feeling as though he was strung out on top of a precipice with only the void before him. But he had faced the void before, he had experienced the wound of his mother's wounds, and although he had been affected, he had not been afraid nor had he been uncertain. Now, however, certainty eluded him and fear pricked at his emotions. Yet he felt as though he was on the brink of a tremendous leap, and once having made that leap he would have no other course but to ride it through to the end, whatever the end might be. Perhaps this was what Hellos had meant by saying that things would be "revealed" to him. But what things? And the dream, Scarecrow's dream of Hellos with the faces of his wife, his childhood sweetheart Juanita and the little white girl, and the heads of his grandmother and the scarecrow and the fox sprouting from Hellos' shoulders. Did the dream have portent for reality, or did reality have portent for the dream? And what did she mean by saying that she knew "everything" about Scarecrow? She was a liar. Yet she reminded him of someone, or was it of something? But he did not know her, they had only met aboard the ship. How could he possibly know her? If he knew her, he did not know that he knew her. One thing he knew for sure is that he would not stand up and sit down at the same time, he would not be tied into a knot; he would strike out first, he would explode.

Up on deck he mopped his brow and wiped his hands, for he had begun to sweat profusely in Hellos' cabin. He knew what his sweating hands meant, it happened whenever he was in a situation that threatened him, made him nervous, anxious, fearful. Damn it, who did Hellos think she was, giving him an ultimatum to break with Maria! He had killed once in order to free himself from the hurt that had been put on him during his childhood, and he had done it as much for Maria as for himself. He would never break with Maria, now that he had found her, never!

Darkness found him still on deck, leaning against the railing, staring out at the waters. It must have been getting close to suppertime, he thought, and he had not made up his mind what to do about Hellos. Unconsciously he reached into the breast pocket inside his jacket for his daughter's photograph. It was not there. He must have left it in his cabin, yes, in his other jacket. Loneliness swept over him and he yearned deeply for his daughter. But that was over, it had to be over.

He stood there staring out at the darkness. Some young ladies came by and looked at him with guarded interest. Then Maria appeared.

25

"Sweetie—"

Before she could say anything else, Scarecrow had her in his arms and was kissing her, not a sex kiss, but a kiss of deep affection. He loved her so much that he was grateful to do so. His love for her was almost desperate. When he released her he told her so and complimented her on how sweet she smelled. Then he realized that she was wearing a solid white fur coat. He marveled at it but wondered if she was not too hot in it, inasmuch as it was a humid night.

"No," she said. "Kind of chilly to be out anyway I'll take it off inside Where were you sweetie when the fire drill happened?"

A lump lodged in his throat. He was not afraid of Maria, but what was he supposed to tell her? Well, darling, I went to the hold and brought my wife's bones to my cabin so I could more easily dispose of them. Perhaps someday he would tell her, he would tell her everything. And why bother her with Hellos now? Why break the spell of being so close to Maria right now when he had missed her more than he had realized. He merely told her that his station was in a place called the Veranda Lounge. She said hers had been in the ship's hospital and that she saw one of Scarecrow's cabinmates there, the little one, Jim was his name, he seemed like a nice fellow, kiss me, sweetie.

He kissed her and told her about his run-in with Number Three.

Maria backed off and looked at him incredulously. "Is that all!" she exclaimed. "I wish I'd been there I'd have well I'd have done more than spit in his face!"

She looked as if she was ready to kill a tiger, and in that big fur coat. Scarecrow laughed good-naturedly and suggested that they go to supper.

"Oh no," she said. That was one of the reasons she had been looking for him, everything's changed, she found out at lunch. Where was Scarecrow at lunch? There's a new seating arrangement and definitely more orderly, since the dining hall won't hold all the passengers at once. So the passengers had been grouped into shifts, with assigned seats at assigned tables with individual waiters for every table. Maria and Scarecrow had been assigned to the third shift. "And wait till you see the people at our table sweetie They are a *circus* They've been asking about you sweetie I put you in the corner I know you like corners I told them at lunch you were taking your beauty nap but that you'd be there tonight What time is it sweetie?" She seemed anxious.

"Eight-thirty."

"Oh God it's time Come on If it's one thing I can't stand it's being tardy for supper."

People were already in the dining hall and more were coming, but everything was quite orderly. Inside the door Maria pulled off her coat, she was a few steps in front of Scarecrow.

WHAT THE HELL IS THIS!!! Scarecrow faltered. His brain vibrated as if he had been clobbered with a baseball bat.

Maria didn't have a damn thing on. No! Wait! She had on a dress, no, a robe, no, a gown, no, it was a *garment,* a magnificent one at that. It looked African. Without revealing any drawstring or elastic, it gripped her tightly around the upper part of her waist just beneath her breasts and hung, no, it flowed down the entire length of her gangling body and swished ever so gently against the floor. It was not a tight-fitting garment; it hung loosely, running the length of her body down to her feet, which were clad in what was obviously a pair of authentic African sandals that revealed the tips of her bare toes. The garment was multicolored, subdued crimsons, threads of black, mysterious orange, a little purple here and there, and it was multiweaved; the three-inch hem at the base of the garment was a vibrant red with heavy-duty zigzag stitches. Scarecrow did not know what kind of material it was but he could tell it was the finest in the world. A cryptic slit ran from the hip down to the floor, revealing only at certain measured instances the ebony smoothness of her bare leg, it seemed. She wore tight gloves up to the middle of her forearms which were subdued blue, almost velvet-black, and which were cutaway at her hands, leaving her long feline fingers free and agile. Her hair was rolled round and round on her perfectly formed skull and came to a long rodlike aggregate in the center of her head and stood up erect like a shiny, stately black phallus. She looked superb, impeccable, perfectly groomed.

But that was *all* she had on! From her long sensuous Modigliani neck down to where the garment clung beneath her breasts, she was stark naked. Her shoulders, her stately neck, her chest, her breasts—were bare. Maria's breasts were a little like a preadolescent girl's, but they were upright, even her nipples were upright, testifying and witnessing the indisputable maturity of a grown woman.

A rumble went through the dining hall, then dead stillness, then a mighty storm. One man looked around. Three people

87

looked. Then ten, thirty, fifty, a hundred, everybody! A child fell out of his chair!

Scarecrow rushed to Maria. Let's get out of here and put on some clothes, he whispered, forcefully.

Maria said she had on *her* clothes and that Scarecrow looked overdressed to her.

Scarecrow crushed her arm in his hand. He wanted her at least to put the coat back on. Maria was not cold, it was hot, Scarecrow had said so himself. But how did he like her outfit which she said was called the Afro-ensemble. She had made it herself. Didn't she look great? Well, yeah, Scarecrow had to admit that, but why hadn't she spoken to him about it beforehand! Maybe tried it on so he could have gotten used to the idea, and braced himself for the dining-hall mob.

"Fuck the mob They're all honkeys Who cares what they think This is for us black folks For you and me sweetie Shit niggers always talking about getting back to Africa to our roots Well let's get all the way back! Anyway," she cajoled him, "it's my new thing sweetie." She wrenched her arm free and strolled away.

The dining hall was in pandemonium. Whistles. Yells. Coos. Sighs. Catcalls. The works. Scarecrow himself felt naked! He put on his dark glasses and followed after her to the table. A man got up and slapped Scarecrow on the back. A redheaded youth rose and said, "Well, whatayouknow, here's the man who's older than me but yet younger! Aaah, ha, ha!"

Scarecrow assumed the youth was talking to him but his eyes were riveted on Maria. The youth wore thick horn-rimmed glasses.

The talk about the dress lasted for ages, eons. Maria ate it up. A bearded youth down at the far end of the table completely ignored Maria. And that made Scarecrow angrier!

Finally, the round-faced girl, sitting next to the redheaded boy, said, "Why didn't you come to lunch? Maria said you were sleeping. Were you really, or were you seasick? She's been telling us about you. My name's Sue." She extended her hand.

Maria introduced Scarecrow around the table. She started to

rise. Scarecrow jerked her back down. He tried to put her coat around her but she wouldn't have it.

Giving Scarecrow what he no doubt thought was a "man's handshake," tight firm grip and all, the redheaded youth, who became known as College Joe, said, "Maria says you're a writer, says you're keeping a diary of the trip."

"It's a journal," Scarecrow told him. "And I'd rather call this trip a voyage."

College Joe said, "Diary, journal, trip, voyage, it's all the same to me."

Scarecrow had the impulse to say, Fuck you! He said, "You're probably right."

He noticed that the redheaded pregnant girl at the table was staring at him, then at Maria, and back at Scarecrow, again and again. Her big mouth was hanging open.

Sue asked Scarecrow if his journal was poetry. Scarecrow frowned. Sue said that Maria told them Scarecrow wrote poems. Maria explained that she did not mean that Scarecrow was writing his journal in verse. Sue apologized and wanted to know if Scarecrow would recite any of his poetry for them. Scarecrow did not memorize his poetry. Sue could not understand this, since she used to have a boy friend and he recited his poems to her all of the time, hee, hee. The girl was pitiful, thought Scarecrow, but he told Sue that the boy friend must have loved her dearly.

"Aw, shucks." Sue waved at Scarecrow, blushing. "Nothing like that. We were just high school sweethearts. Now com'on, one li'l bitty poooem. You must know one."

Maria said, "Really darling he never memorizes any of his poetry I know He's never done it for me He doesn't believe in reciting from memory It's one of his *principles*." She leaned over and kissed Scarecrow.

Scarecrow felt mortified. People were still gaping at them. "Maria, let's get out of here," he whispered, raising her coat to her shoulders.

She brushed the coat away. "Relax sweetie we haven't eaten yet and I'm completely famished."

College Joe cleared his throat and said, "This here diary you're keeping, you going to put me in it?"

Motherfucker, thought Scarecrow. He said, "I do not know you."

"That's easy," he snapped. "I'm twenty years old. People say I act older, look younger, ah, ha, ha. I'm from Newmount, Arizona. I'm studying engineering at the Smithwelliam Institute, eh, that's in Maine. I'm a junior there. My father runs a thriving business, construction. I'm on my way touring Europe for my first time. My name's Robert Gentry, Robert Oliver Gentry, but people call me Bobby, that's my nickname, my mother gave it to me, ah, ha, ha. Now you can put me in your diary."

Ignoring Gentry, Scarecrow faced the pregnant redhead, who was transfixed and had been staring all the while at him and Maria with her big mouth hanging open. He said, "BOOO!"

The redhead snapped out of it with a start. Then she feigned laughter. The others joined in like puppets. The plain one, Sue, reached over the table and tried to pull off Scarecrow's dark glasses. He leaned back out of reach.

"Aw, com'on, let us see your eyes," she drooled. "Why do you wear them anyway? Do you wear them all of the time?"

Scarecrow turned to Maria. "Suit yourself, I'm getting out of here," he said.

Maria leaned over and whispered, "If you get up from this table I'll be stark naked before you can move two steps."

Scarecrow froze in his seat. He fumed. He felt annihilated. He hated Maria. She had been putting on airs all night. She never used words like "famished" or "darling" before. He hated them all.

The food came. Lamb chops, broccoli, boiled potatoes, soup, tea, coffee, ice cream, and other dishes. Scarecrow did not eat. Gentry ate like he talked, dogging his food into his mouth and smacking his lips. Sue ate very nicely and self-consciously, she had a line across her moon face for a mouth. The pregnant redhead stuffed food into her huge mouth as though she were feeding two people already. Her lips would have been monstrous on a Negro. They were painted with thick red lipstick. She had big football eyes which were overly made up with black mascara. Her hair was swirled up on her head like a red balloon. As she gobbled down the food, she kept a running conversation with Maria about how delicious or horrible it was.

Sitting there, Scarecrow felt he must look like a grizzly black gorilla with sunglasses on.

CHAPTER FIVE

Thursday, September 9 (the same day)

26

Finally, when they had finished eating, Maria wanted to go straight to the Lido Bar where they were to meet Dr. Yas and the others. Later they all would go to the other place where the jukebox was and have a party. But Scarecrow dragged her out on the deck. There he confronted her. "Woman, what the hell's gotten into you?"

"That's exactly what I want to ask you," asserted Maria. "I do things to please you and you jump all salty and embarrass me in front of those people You sat at that table and acted like I wasn't there I searched for you all day and couldn't find you and when I do find you you act like you're not glad to see me You act like you're *ashamed* of me!"

"That's a lie," said Scarecrow. "I'm in love with you. You're my woman."

"Then why do you treat me like you do! I left my husband for you and you treat me like excess baggage on this boat ride I make love to you I do all kinds of things to please you I dress up nice so you'll be proud of me and you go around acting like you're ashamed of me You act like I embarrass you shit! There's something wrong with you nigger something wrong with you You don't even try to protect me All I feel like is your goddamn baggage! That Krane's been aggravating me You ought to make him leave me alone He's your friend You *are* embarrassed of me because I'm black Aren't you! Don't deny it I know I can—"

He cut her short by grabbing her coat collar and jerking her face up close to his. "Bitch," he said between gritted teeth. "I want you to go to your cabin and put on some clothes. Now! I'll wait for you in the bar."

He flung her against the railing. She got herself together and went below. Scarecrow walked to the railing and held on to it. He was trembling from anger and frustration.

. . . so now, Scarecrow, you begin to see what kind of woman Maria really is. But what kind of woman is she? He knew she was emotional. For a year he had been around her and her husband. He went to parties with them, he laughed with them, he spent many hours in their apartment. There was nothing to it. Time passed. Scarecrow began to notice her more and more, cooking, washing, coming out of the bathroom, bending over, laughing, the way her dress clung to her body, the way she smelled, her underclothes lying around or hanging on the clothesline. He began to entertain the idea. But no! Maria was the wife of Scarecrow's friend, a white man, a Jew. He had to be careful about that, he had to watch his motives. Time passed. But he could not get her out of his mind. He imagined that she felt toward him like he felt toward her. But suppose it was merely his imagination and she felt nothing. So he continued to act natural. When she was dancing with him and rubbing her thighs against him and breathing in his ear and touching his neck with her lips, Scarecrow acted natural. Then one night at a party he was acting natural and Maria's husband was in the other room and she tumbled on the bed where Scarecrow was sitting. He found himself kissing and fondling her, and lo!—she was on fire for him. A few days later he called their house to tell Simon that he had found a buyer for one of his paintings, and Maria answered the phone, Simon was not there. Before Scarecrow could tell her why he was calling, she told him that she had been expecting his call for weeks, and she arrived at his apartment in a matter of minutes. Then she left her husband. She told Scarecrow she was going to leave him anyway, because she was "sick and tired of living with a honkey."

Now he had her. He knew it wasn't going to be easy, he was no romantic. But, man, you should have refused to bring her with you! But he had killed for her! Besides, he liked her, he desired her, damnit, he *needed* her. Hell, he even liked that *Afro-ensemble* she had on tonight. She had nerve, beauty, intelligence. And most of all, she was black. She was one of the first black girls to go on the Freedom Rides. Scarecrow knew of her bravery in Birmingham; the police had jerked her off the bus, put her in jail and beaten her. She organized the inmates into a hunger strike that lasted for sixteen days and got worldwide attention. It was Maria and her husband who got all those artists, writers, and other people on the Lower East Side, and marched in front of them to City Hall when that cop shot and killed the Harlem youth, which sparked the rioting during the long hot summer in the northern ghettos. Maria was a woman, a black woman, Scarecrow could look up to. Face it, he was deeply in love with her, and he did not want to lose her. But, man, you don't *know* her. What was she going to do next? Something was wrong with her. It seemed to Scarecrow that Maria had blushed when he got violent with her, it seemed that she liked it. Yes, she had been violent the other night when he made love to her, she had forced him to be brutal to her. Goddamn, she was always doing something to rile him up. He had other things to contend with. He missed his daughter, there was that Hellos, and in his trunk down in his cabin were the bones of his dead wife. Tonight maybe?

27

The fox is a nimble furry animal belonging to the canine species. Unlike the common dog, however, the fox can never be tamed. It is a wild animal that defies domestication. The she-fox is the most cunning creature in the animal kingdom, it lives and sur-

vives by its wits, its trickery, which is not a trait that is learned or
acquired through experience. The slyness, or the craftiness, of the
fox is an *instinct* as strong and persistent as the sex drive.

When Maria left Scarecrow at the railing and went below she
was furious. She had wanted to look great for Scarecrow. She
hungered for his attention. So she had worn the *African-ensemble*,
not for herself, not to be a spectacle or show for others, but for
Scarecrow alone. If she drew attention from others, that attention would surely be a compliment to Scarecrow, for she belonged
to him, she was his woman. But Scarecrow had been ashamed of
her, he had rebuked her. The sonofabitch! He had treated her
like her father always treated her, even as a baby. Oh, how she
hated her father! But Scarecrow had made love to her, he had
touched her. Yet she had had to force him to do so. By rebuking
her, Scarecrow had not only made her furious but he had hurt her
to the core. As she crept through the corridor, hugging the fur
coat close to her body, she wept, as she had done many times before when her father had similarly rebuked and rejected her as
a little girl. Standing alone back up on deck, musing over how he
had first met Maria, Scarecrow would never know what craftiness was going on in her mind, which was as quick and facile as
her lean and nimble body.

She had been born in Louisiana, the town of Union. Her parents were middle-class Negroes of high social pedigree dating
back to the Reconstruction period in the South. Her mother was
white as a white woman, her father was pure black. The father
had married the mother and entered into her social circle, which
was mostly of Caucasion blood, and through his own stamina,
plus the aid of certain influential members of his wife's family,
he had achieved success, symbolized, in one instance, by becoming the president of a most renowned Negro university. Maria
inherited all of her father's traits—cunning, intellect, endurance,
drive, ambition, handsomeness. But she never received his love.
He never held her in his lap, he never spanked her, he never kissed
her, he never played with her, he never *touched* her, not even

when she cried and threw tantrums and kicked at him and screamed for his attention.

So now as she crept through the corridors of the ship on her way to change her clothes, she was her father's rejected little girl. And being rejected, she was the prowling fox in her fur, as she had been that night on the Street of Dreams when she was but a mere six years old. Scarecrow was mistaken in assuming that the fox on Maria's belly was a tattoo. Maria herself, in thinking that it was a birthmark, was equally mistaken. In Union, Louisiana, a stretch of some four blocks marked what was known as the Street of Dreams. Although Maria's parents lived in a great house in the better part of the town, their house was but a short distance from the Street of Dreams. It was a notorious street of many strange and sundry happenings; there were drunks, beggars, prostitutes, cripples, witches, pimps, thugs, taverns and dark houses in which nameless deeds were perpetrated day and night. A dense forest hovered at the end of the street in which other more sundry perpetrations were rumored to have occurred. People who went into the forest and who were fortunate enough to return, for many were never seen or heard of again, babbled in strange tongues about two-headed animals, fauns and snakes and weird ceremonies of the dead. It was said that the ghost of the evil sorceress, Madame Laveau, dwelt in the thickets of the forest amid a hundred shrunken human heads. Both her father and mother had summarily warned little Maria never to traverse as far as the Street of Dreams, let alone the dark forest. But on *that* night, hurting and weeping from her father's hatred and rejection, Maria, the six-year-old, entered into a dream in which she crept out of her bed and went prowling along the forbidden street. At the end of the street loomed the great dark forest and the child heard a voice calling unto her, to come into the forest, and at its edge a luminous figure of a woman robed in silver costume appeared with a red fox at her side. "Whose little girl are you and why are you weeping?" inquired the figure, to whom the child replied, "I am your little girl and I am weeping because my father does not love me." Then the figure clasped the little girl to its breast and kissed her fully on the mouth and stroked her and lay down with her nakedly until her tears turned to strange ecstasy and her hurt was healed, and the red fox kept watch while they drank a brew that burned the bowels and put the head in a state of dream. "Seven Moons And Seven Suns Shall Ye Know My Face And Honor My Sign," spoke the luminous figure!

A mere six years old when this dream happened to her, Maria would never come to grips with whether it was really a dream or whether it had actually occurred. But from the night of the dream onward she found herself being drawn to the Street of Dreams in wakeful hours of the day and at nights too, whenever she could manage to slip away from the tight scrutiny of her parents. Often she went to the Street of Dreams as though in search of her father, her *true* father, for her father at home could not possibly have been her real father. First of all, the cruel coal-black man was too old to be her father. His coldness toward her is what inevitably led her to notice how old he appeared. But she had no idea that he was chronologically as old as he actually was. "Old" to little Maria meant that her father was mean and cold, and it meant her hatred for him. Later when she had actually confirmed her notion of his age with her mother, she was shocked to discover that the man had fathered her when he was sixty-five years old!

Many times when Maria wandered along the Street of Dreams, among the strange and forbidden people (forbidden by her parents, especially her father), she would saunter down to the edge of the dense forest and just stand there as if in a trance, and the dream would return to her and smooth her innermost longings, longings for which at that time she had no names. Denizens of the street grew used to the little black girl wandering among them; some would give her things to eat and pet her; painted women and drunken men slobbered kisses on her face; white women always fondled and cuddled her and eyed her wantonly. Maria loved the Street of Dreams, she felt warm among its sundry inhabitants, and often she cried alone wishing that her father would make her feel like the people on the street did. It was on her thirteenth birthday—seven years after the dream—that she fled from her own birthday party, crying and mad and outraged because her father failed to return home, to Union, for his daughter's fruition into seed and blood and womanhood. It was four A.M. when she fled from the house—she and her mother had waited and waited; the father was in New York on business and had promised to come back in time for the party, but he did not show, he didn't even phone or send a telegram. Then she stood, a tall gangling girl, in the shadows of the edge of the dense forest, weeping fitfully, helpless and so alone in the world, with her angry fists balled and stuffed doggedly in the pockets of her slacks and pressed firmly against her throbbing groin. Once more she entered into the dream but, unlike all the other times, the figure that reached out to gather her up was not the Madame Laveau, ju ju sorceress of silver, but a man, a black man, a derelict, ugly, filthy and bent on rape. Little known to him, however, he was but a would-be rapist, for the sight of him suddenly transformed the hurt and docile Maria into a thing unknown even to herself. She tore the derelict to pieces, ripped and clawed and chewed him to bloody meat and near death, before passers-by pulled her off of the poor wretch—then they fled screaming screams of horror at the unbelievable sight of what they had seen. Shortly thereafter, Maria discovered the image of the fox just below her navel, which she interpreted as a late-developed "birthmark," which would lend itself to lucrative use when she would later become a part-time striptease dancer in the nightclubs of Greenwich Village.

By the route she had taken, in order to get to her cabin, Maria would pass Scarecrow's cabin. Nearing his cabin she caught sight of someone she immediately recognized, Hellos, moving away from Scarecrow's door in that floating manner in which she walked.

Maria approached her. "What you doing lurking around my

man's door for witch!" she shouted, clutching at Hellos' large protruding breasts, meaning to rip them to pieces.

But Hellos floated out of reach, as she brought forth an object from the bag she carried and began waving it around in front of Maria. "Get back, bitch, touch me not," Hellos chanted. "I know what you are. I can *see* you," she said, as she fled through the corridor, and Maria was unable to pursue her.

She then turned and tried Scarecrow's door. It was locked but someone from inside opened it.

"I'm Maria," she said to him.

"Yes, I know. I'm Jim, your boy friend's cabinmate."

They talked for a while and Jim went out, leaving Maria in the cabin alone. Furiously she searched for Scarecrow's journal. She wanted to see what he had written about her. She'd bet he'd written about Hellos, or about his wife, or some other white woman aboard ship. She didn't trust him all the way. But she did not find the journal. In her search, however, she came across the photograph of Oriki, Scarecrow's daughter, and the shaving kit that that woman, Marlina, had given him as a going-away present. Using her canines, she bit into the kit with the force of her rage and slashed it to pieces; thinking that the bottle of milky liquid Scarecrow used for his sores was part of the package, she smashed it along with the rest of the kit's contents. She felt better now.

In her own cabin she changed clothes and went to meet Scarecrow and the others in the Lido Bar. On her way she heard singing and guitar playing. She went in and saw Dr. Yas among the crowd of listeners. She sat on the floor beside him and started shaking her head and clapping her hands to the music.

28

Before Scarecrow left the deck and went into the Lido Bar, he was approached by one of his cabinmates, Jim, the timid one who had let Maria into the cabin. Cautiously he approached Scarecrow at the railing. After introducing himself, he told Scarecrow that he had been trying to get up the nerve to speak to him about the incident Scarecrow had had with Number Three, who, incidentally, had moved out of the cabin. Jim had been embarrassed by the incident, he said, and he thoroughly disapproved of Number Three, whom he had disliked from the start. He said the other cabinmate, whose name was Phil, was from Argentina, he was a nice fellow and he and Jim had become good friends. Although he was from Mississippi, Jim said he had nothing against black people; in fact, he had been a classmate of James Meredith when they had all the trouble at the University of Mississippi because of Meredith's presence on the campus. Now he was on his way to France to study at the Sorbonne. Scarecrow wished him success.

"Well, I, eh, just wanted to let you know how I felt. Nice talking to you," said Jim.

29

A strong wind had come up. The ocean waters had gotten turbulent. The ship was now rocking back and forth quite forcefully. Although Scarecrow's head had begun to feel dizzy, he liked the feeling, which was similar, he remembered, to that of being pleasantly tipsy. No one of their party, including Maria, had yet arrived in the Lido. He sat there sipping his orange juice, never putting it down for fear it would slide off the table from the seesawing of the ship. Then he saw that girl, Reggie, sauntering toward him. She still had an armful of fashion magazines but she was dressed differently from when Scarecrow had seen her earlier with Dr. Yas. Now she wore a silver-colored blouse with silver-colored bell-bottom trousers to match; her black hair was swirled around her head and arched upward from the front into what he thought was called an "upsweep." Her lips were painted orange and her eyes were highlighted with pastel mascara, just enough to suggest, what with her delicate and extremely pale face, that charmed theatrical look of Japanese actresses. Reggie was a neatly but voluptuously built woman. Men and women were glaring at her.

101

"Hello," said Scarecrow.

Without acknowledging his greeting, she sat opposite Scarecrow. He asked if she wanted a drink and she did not act as if she heard him. She hugged the magazines to her magnificent breast and stared transfixed as if she was hypnotized. "Fuck her," thought Scarecrow, and contented himself with his orange juice. Then he heard her whispering.

"Listen to the wind. Feel the ship rolling over the big waves of time. There ought to be trees on the ocean."

Sipping from his orange juice, Scarecrow studied the strange girl.

"Crescendo. Crescendo," she softly wailed, as the ship rocked her trancelike back and forth in her seat. "I hope it does not storm, I would not like a storm. But I want it to rain and rain and rain and the winds to blow and blow and blow, *crescendo*, *crescendo*. I would like a piece of chocolate. Do they have chocolate up there?"

Staring straight into her face, Scarecrow gave no sign that he had heard her. He'd give her the same treatment she had given him.

Again she wailed softly, "Oh, wild west wind from whose unseen presence the leaves dead are driven, *crescendo*, *crescendo*. The elements are singing to Shelley tonight. Would you like a joint?"

Scarecrow had recognized that she was reciting from Shelley's *Ode to the West Wind*. But her last remark caught him off guard.

"What?" he said.

"A joint, man, some grass, tea, weed, you know, a *joint*," she said, searching in her bag and, cupping it in her hand, she gave Scarecrow a very slim tightly rolled cigarette. He took it and put it in the pack with his Pall Malls.

"I'll have one of those, please."

He gave her a Pall Mall and, after she accidentally blew out two matches, he managed to light it for her. Then he asked her if she was coming with them to the *Dom*? The word had rolled right out of Scarecrow's mouth without any forethought whatever. Quickly he looked around as if to see who had said the word.

"The what!" exclaimed Reggie. It was the first time she had shown any signs of real life.

"The Dom. The place where the jukebox is," explained Scarecrow. "I didn't intend to call it that but the name fits. Have you ever been to the Dom, the discothèque on the Lower East Side?" he asked her.

"She gave him a sad look, and said, "Yeah, Mr. man, I been there. Once!"

Maria entered, wearing jeans; she saw Scarecrow and Reggie. Although the ship was rocking and people were stumbling about, Maria did not make a false step. Scarecrow thought she walked like some kind of predatory animal, a panther, or a tigress, or something. She came right up to them and started explaining to Scarecrow why she was late, she had been listening to some folksingers. Then she appeared to notice Reggie for the first time. "Who's the honkey?" she asked.

Scarecrow introduced Reggie. Reggie nodded. Without saying a word to Reggie, Maria turned back to Scarecrow and started telling how great the singers were. There were three of them, one white and two blacks. They were really far out, especially the big-lip blackest one whose name, she said, was Bendrix. The singers were taking a break and Maria had come for Scarecrow. But instead of getting up, he moved over and asked her to sit beside him. Instantly he felt guilty, inhibited. There was really no reason why he could not have gone with her. He drew his breath and said, "Baby, this ship has made me dizzy. Why don't you go on, I'll wait for you here."

"Suit yourself," she snapped. Then to Reggie she said, "Nice outfit." Before Reggie could acknowledge the compliment, Maria, like a temperamental actress, had turned and strode away.

Several minutes of silence passed between Scarecrow and Reggie. Suddenly, but still in her trancelike manner and speaking as if to no one in particular, Reggie told Scarecrow that she was a dope addict, and was on her way to Tangiers where Heroin was cheap and easily obtainable. Scarecrow looked at her now in her state with an eye of recognition. He also knew now why he had not gone with Maria. He had wanted to find out about this utterly beautiful and yet utterly strange-acting girl. She told him further that she was from a very wealthy family who was glad she was leaving the States, so their daughter would not embarrass them. Then, without the slightest warning, her manner changed, she opened up to Scarecrow and recited the story of her life to him. At least she called it the story of her life, but it was mainly about the relationship she had with her mother.

Reggie's mother was always fondling her. Reggie was nineteen years old and her mother still tried to treat her like a baby. She insisted on purchasing her daughter's underwear, which consisted of nothing but flimsy transparent garments. Before she left home, Reggie burned a trunk full of such stuff. She was never able to keep a boy friend, because her mother always played up to him and he would get scared and leave Reggie alone. Her mother bathed her until she was in high school. That was when Reggie caught on to what her mother was really up to. She had a habit of pretending she was angry with Reggie's father and would come into Reggie's room at night and get in bed with her, crying, hugging and rubbing herself against her daughter. What about her father? Wasn't he concerned? Well, he was one of those successful businessmen who had been totally castrated by his wife, powerful in his business and weak in his home. "The faggot didn't have any balls!" Anyway, Reggie finally got fed up. All right, she said to herself, if Momma wants to turn me on, well, groovy, I'll let her. One night she went to bed completely nude, and when her mother came into the room sobbing and carrying on like always, Reggie flipped the covers back. She knew she was sexy. Her breasts were well-developed, her mother had seen to that, the way she had always massaged them in olive oil so they would develop healthily. When her mother saw her like that she quickly came out of her act. She wanted to know what was her daughter doing sleeping in the nude, where were the nice nighties she had bought? Reggie told her that it was showdown time, she was not an innocent child any more, she knew what was going on, and that she had gotten tired of it all. "Get out of those pajamas," said Reggie to her mother. "Come on, you want to hit the sheets or do you want me to hit them first?" Reggie told Scarecrow that by this time she knew what women did to each other; she had slept with both men and women, she had done everything, and some of it, unbeknownst to her mother, was with her mother's society friends. Which was more or less natural, since from the time when Reggie had been quite a young child her mother would summon her into the room where she and her society friends were having their meeting, and the mother would pull up the daughter's dress to show her friends the new drawers she had bought her daughter. "You know what I mean, man!"

When Reggie confronted her mother, the mother pretended she was shocked, she froze. Reggie jumped out of bed and began tearing off her mother's pajamas, which were nothing much anyway. The mother tried to fight off the daughter but the daughter was determined. She knew nobody but they were in the house that night, and if her mother screamed nobody would hear, because the mother wouldn't dare scream that loud. The daughter had the mother trapped. And it felt good, she told Scarecrow, because she was souped up on heroin and pills that night and she got carried away with revenge. She got worked up sexually also. You know, she thought she understood how a rapist felt, or any man, when some woman got him all heated up and then tried to wangle out of it. But Reggie was not going to stand for anything like that. She fell to her knees and grabbed her mother around the buttocks and started making oral love to her. She could not relate to Scarecrow all of the different things that she felt and thought as she was on her knees before her mother, who broke free and started to run. Reggie caught her, however, and knocked her to the floor, whereupon she had flashes of being her father, the sissy! That was what her father should have done years ago, whipped that woman's ass. She grabbed her mother's hair and twisted her head back and drew her mouth close to her crotch. Eat it, she told her mother. Then she began to laugh and she could not stop. It seemed as though she laughed for years, centuries! Her mother looked like the picture of hell. It was the first time in her life that she had been forced to face what she was and what she had done to her own daughter.

"Then," said Reggie, "I was overcome with sorrow. There was my own mother naked before me, naked outside and inside. I pitied her. I slumped to the floor beside her and started making love to her for real. The junk must have been working on me and I got mellow with love for my mother. But shit, I guess by that time I was a full-fledged homosexual myself, I remember that most of my friends were dikes, they were models, you know. So I kissed her and tongued her and blew my breath into her mouth. I caressed her body freely and honestly. I took her hand and rubbed it against my breasts like she had always done herself, but with no pretense this time. It was for real, man. And I rubbed her hand between my thighs. I called her sweet names and whispered in her ear and told her that everything was going to be all right. After all, she *was* my mother. And I made her come. Yes, she did, she came. She clung to me and wiggled and shrieked from the thrill of it. But when it was over, you know what that woman did?"

Reggie's mother claimed that her daughter had assaulted her because she had gone insane, and she had Reggie committed to an institution. Reggie told the doctors the same story she told Scarecrow, but the doctors chose to believe her mother; and, according to Reggie, they gave her a battery of tests to prove that her mother was right. Reggie escaped from the institution, she said, in order to keep from really going mad. It was not her but her mother who should have been in the nuthouse, she declared. "They ought to let out all of the people in the nuthouse and put all of those outside inside, including the doctors, especially the doctors!"

She asked for another cigarette and wanted to know Scarecrow's name. "I've been watching you," she said. "You turn me on. This is the first time in a long time that I've felt sexy. Smack is no good for sex, but right now I really feel it. I want to make love to you, Mr. man. Wow! What you say? I'd make it good to you."

Scarecrow pulled off his dark glasses and boldly scrutinized her body. She could have been Miss America, easily. Then he looked at her dazed eyes. She did not flinch. He drank the rest of his orange juice, and said, "Sorry. In the past, maybe yes. But it's too late now."

"Yeah," she said, matter of factly. "White chicks are out of style, aren't we. Black is beautiful. White is ugly. You got that spade chick, Maria. I like her. She's nice people. You all are nice people, even the poet, what's-his-name, Krane. I dug y'all yesterday, I knew y'all were groovy people. But just because I'm a honkey, your chick can't blame me for wanting to make it with you. Nobody can. Here, let me give you a joint."

After she slipped Scarecrow another reefer, she slouched down in her chair and swayed with the rocking of the ship. "Oh, wind, drive my dead thoughts across the universe and quicken them into a new birth, *crescendo, crescendo*. But," she interrupted herself, "If you change your mind between here and Europe, let me know, Mr. man."

With his eyes Scarecrow saw Reggie clearly, but in his mind she had begun to shimmer and blur and change into someone else. The ship was rocking now with a fiercer momentum and it became a ship of time, a ship of biography, and Scarecrow was no longer with Reggie. He was with another woman, his high school sweetheart, at two different times in their lives, and in two different places.

30
NEW YORK CITY, 1962
Juanita said, "Let me have your belt."

Scarecrow pulled it off and gave it to her. Tightly she strapped it around her arm, tighter! Then she shoved the needle into her skin, her pale arm looked like a long bone with dead veins in it. She pulled the needle out and shoved it into another spot. Her hand shook, saliva dripped from her lips, blood leaked from her dry skin onto the floor. She pulled the needle out and, fumbling, pushed it into yet another place. The stuff emptied into her vein. She sighed. She seemed to come alive, her frail face grew calm, she smiled, her eyes grew enchanted, she looked elated.

"What the hell you gaping at!" she snapped. "Haven't you seen a junky take a fix before?"

Scarecrow lowered his eyes.

CHATTANOOGA, TENNESSEE, 1950

It was the opening of school. Not only was Scarecrow an honor student but he was also a basketball star. He had become a star overnight; in one game against Pearl High from Nashville he had scored forty-two points, a thing that was unheard of in those days, and his school had beaten its arch rival for the first time in ten years. Because of this and his academic record, he had been selected to aid the teachers in registering the incoming students. They were in the gymnasium. When Juanita came in, a chill ran over him.

Quickly he learned her schedule and made certain he was at the right places when she came along. After school in her home room he would often sit in her seat and examine her notebook, her papers and the personal things she left lying around. He wanted to approach her but she was such an angel that he was scared to say a word to her.

Then for an entire week Juanita did not come to school. Her home-room teacher informed him that the girl was ill.

That Sunday, having put aside his shyness, he went to see her. His grandmother had encouraged him. Juanita was sitting up in a big chair with a blanket around her. Scarecrow thought she looked so beautiful being sick like that. He gave her the flowers and stammered out some words. When her mother went out of the room for a second, Juanita slipped him a letter and whispered that all year she had been waiting for him to ask her for a date, and since he hadn't she decided to take the initiative by writing him a letter. A pity she had to get sick before he would make a move.

NEW YORK CITY, 1962

"Give me a cigarette," she said. "I guess you want to know why I bothered to contact you after all these years?"

"It hasn't been that long," ventured Scarecrow.

"It's been a lifetime." She puffed on the lengthy Pall Mall, enjoying it. "I kept seeing your name in the papers. They kept calling you a controversial writer and announcing where you were speaking and all that kind of stuff. I didn't believe it was the Scarecrow I had loved, the honor student, the basketball star, and yet I knew it was. Then your picture was in the *Times*. Well, I just had to call. I see you got my message."

She crushed out the cigarette and went to the sink, where there was a cabinet. Sauntering across the floor she looked like a gangling tree, still in fruition but nevertheless withering. She opened the cabinet and brought out a box of chocolate. "Want some?"

Scarecrow shook his head, no thanks.

"It's been a long long time," she sighed. "So much has happened. You look great, a little older, a little slimmer, but handsome as ever. And you're really a writer, a controversial writer. That means people talk about you and argue about you. I always knew you had something in you, I used to tell you that, remember? That's why I loved you so," she burst into tears.

Scarecrow went over and embraced her. She had always been lean and trim, but now she was bone and skin.

Juanita recomposed herself and pulled free of his embrace. "I didn't get you over here to cry on your shoulder," she said, standing back, scrutinizing him. "I wanted to have a look at you. You must have a life of your own now. That woman who answered your phone? Your wife, eh. She didn't sound like a Negro. Got yourself a white woman. I could have predicted it. Well, I can't say that I'm sorry I didn't wait for you. I regret it, I *have* regretted it, but what good would it do to say all of that? I've got my own life now too, if you can call this life. I'd gotten used to being loved, and when you left for college I felt alone and I was afraid you'd meet some attractive educated girl and forget about me. You didn't want to get married then anyway, did you? So I left Chattanooga and went to Chicago and married the first no-good nigger I slept with. I got pregnant in one of my tubes and had to have an operation which nearly killed me. The nigger went to the Army and never came back, took up with some Japanese whore. I lived with his folks, I was sick, almost dead, I had to. They hated me because I was light skin. Hell, it wasn't my fault. But they treated me like a dog."

CHATTANOOGA, TENNESSEE, 1953

Juanita and Scarecrow grew incensed with each other. When they walked the street Scarecrow felt that people could tell everything they had done. Secretly He was the king of the world. The men who hung around on Ninth Street in front of the Lucky Chance Recreation Parlor would whistle and make catcalls when the couple went by on Sundays on their way to the movie. Juanita would blush and squeeze Scarecrow's hand in a very intimate way; or, feigning arrogance, she would laugh and shake back her long black hair just like a white woman. Scarecrow knew that that was one of the things that made the eyes of everybody, white and colored, turn and stare as they walked down the street. Juanita could have passed for a white girl.

NEW YORK CITY, 1962

"So there you have it," she said, sitting on the bed which was unmade. "I don't want anything from you, I do pretty good, I'm in the trade, you know. Sometimes I make as much as five bills on weekends alone. But my monkey is expensive. I have a little money saved up if you need some. I understand writers don't do so well until they make a bestseller. I'll keep an eye out for your bestseller. I ain't going to lie, I don't read much and I haven't read your book and probably won't. Come here," she said. "Don't sit over there like you're afraid of me. I won't contaminate you."

He went to her. She reached out for him. "Junk makes you sexless ordinarily, but when you do get worked up it comes on powerful, and I want to give you everything that's left in me. For old times' sake."

She cried the whole time he made love to her.

A week later Scarecrow returned, thinking he would persuade her to come see this beatnik psychiatrist by the name of Dr. Yas who had recently moved downtown to the Lower East Side and was doing a lot of work with dope addicts for free. He also brought a hardback copy of his book, since the paperback edition had not yet been released. The superintendent of the fancy apartment house, a big West Indian woman, told Scarecrow that the lady he was looking for had been found dead alone in her flat the day before, apparently from an overdose of drugs.

31

Gradually Scarecrow became aware of being nudged in the ribs. He looked around and saw Reggie there. Her eyelids were drooped over her eyes as she said, "Hey, man, what you been taking? I been trying to tell you for some while that your woman, your black woman, is standing over there by the door watching over here."

When Maria reached the table she made a motion with her head for Scarecrow to follow her. He walked behind her for a short distance. Then she stopped and said, "Do you have a compulsion to sniff that Viking's behind too!"

"Who? Reggie!"

"*Who? Reggie!*" she mimicked Scarecrow. "Who do you think I'm talking about Fats Domino? I can look at that girl and see she's hot in the drawers for you Women can sense these things Is that who you been hiding out with leaving me alone all the time claiming you been writing in your journal Where is it anyway? I haven't seen you with it I thought when we left New York things were going to be different You haven't spent any time with me You don't talk to me I never know what you're thinking about But I know what's getting your goat buddy and I can play the same game you're playing! You just wait and see You're up to no good If it isn't that damn Viking over there in that silver costume then it's someone else A boat full of Vikings! I know you've got to have one of them You can't stand being around them without getting all aggravated can you I'm no idiot! I understand that book of yours You're psychotic over white women Aren't you! There's that Hellos I caught her sneaking around down there by your cabin But just you wait black boy I can play the same game you're playing Just you wait!"

Maria's voice had risen to its highest pitch, and it seemed to Scarecrow that everybody in the place was staring at them, staring at Scarecrow. What did she want him to do! Hell, she was the one who was psychotic about white women. That's why she kept attacking him. Couldn't she see that. Goddamn her. Women were so paranoid. They accuse you when you haven't done anything, as if to push you into doing something. Yet, for the life of him, Scarecrow felt on the defensive, he felt guilty. He was not guilty, so why did he feel guilty! *I love you, Maria, I am faithful to you and I really need you, beautiful black woman, and I'll prove it to you. But stop crowding me, please give me some goddamn slack!* He started to say something like this to her, but Dr. Yas interrupted.

"Hey, baby! Where you been hiding?" He put his hands on Scarecrow's shoulders and started talking into his face. "You should've been there, man. Groovy folksingers, baby, I mean they can wail, two black cats and a hillbilly. You missed one hell of a set."

"He's been too busy contemplating the cosmos!" said Maria.

"Where you been keeping yourself, son of a bitch?" said Rex, the novelist, maneuvering his way around to Scarecrow's side. "Want a swig?"

"Give me some of that Pussyfoot don't drink!" Maria jerked the bottle out of Rex's hand.

To Scarecrow Rex whispered, "What's the matter with her?"

"Whole lot of whispering and intrigue going on on this boat ride!"

"Yeah, baby, speak louder, scream! Haw, haw!"

Hellos entered the bar. She stood just inside the door and started gazing at Scarecrow. He flicked his eyes around at Maria and saw that she was watching everything. Scarecrow was torn between a feeling of wanting to evaporate and a feeling of wanting to strike out. But he controlled his emotions. Casually he walked over to Hellos and found that he could not speak a word of what he had planned to say to her.

To him Hellos said, "Well, is everything all right?"

Get out of my life, bitch, you're rocking my boat, he thought. But, over a fake smile, he said, "Wonderful."

"I mean, have you broken with Maria?"

Scarecrow looked back over his shoulder at Maria. He was glad that Hellos always spoke in a whisper, because Maria was staring at them and was no doubt straining to hear what they were saying.

Krane burst through the door. "It's started to rain," he announced. Then, seeing Maria with the bottle, he made his way to her. "Give me some of that," he said, shaking the rain out of his hair.

Maria told Krane, "Take the bottle pig But you don't have to give me a shower in the process!" Then she made her way over to Scarecrow and Hellos. Looking Scarecrow dead in the eye, and in a cocky manner, she hung her arm around Hellos' sumptuous hips. Scarecrow was shocked, instantly his hands began to sweat. Still looking him in the eye, Maria said to Scarecrow, "Kiss me sweetie!" It was an order.

Scarecrow looked at her, he looked at Hellos, then he looked back at Maria. So this is it, he thought, both of you. Goddamn it, this is war. He put one arm around Maria and with the other hand he caught Hellos by her hair and pushed her face close to Maria's face. He kissed both of them fully on their mouths at the same time.

Maria laughed, loudly, in his face, and strolled away, letting her arm slide slowly from around Hellos, brushing her buttock in the process. Hellos moved away also, singing in a shrill voice, "Listen to the rain, listen to the rain, it's going to storm, fantastic, we're going to have a storm, fantastic, fantastic, wheeeee!" She spun round and round, and tears were leaking from her eyes.

Krane came over to Scarecrow. "What's the matter with these wenches? Hellos's been whining and carrying on all night and Maria just now jumped salty cause a little water out of my hair got on her. Bitches!"

Scarecrow slipped him the two reefers Reggie had given him. "Wow, hot jig a-damn!" exclaimed Krane.

"Well, all right, let's get out of here!" yelled Dr. Yas, looking around, asking where was Reggie.

"Here she is," said Krane, putting his arm around Reggie. "Pretty little thing." He kissed her.

Someone opened the door. The wind and rain rushed in.

"A storm, a storm, fantastic, fantastic, Wheeee!"

Rex whispered to Scarecrow, "A motley crew."

It was difficult walking because the rain had made the deck slippery and the wind blew the rain into their faces. It appeared as if they were really going to have a storm. Inside, they found the discothèque relatively empty. They pushed tables together up near the dancing area and gathered chairs around them. Scarecrow took a seat at one of the ends near a large window. Maria sat on his left and Rex on his right. Dr. Yas was down at the other end of the tables; he was flanked by Reggie and Krane. Krane was petting and kissing and cuddling Reggie, who sat there limp, sleepy-eyed, nonresponsive.

Then out of the blue, Maria said, "Hey! You! Honkey Viking! Come up here and sit by your maker."

Everybody looked.

Reggie rose and sauntered up to the other end of the tables.

114

All eyes followed her on her slow journey. Maria reached back and pulled up a chair for Reggie to sit beside her. When Reggie sat down, Maria said, "Where did you get that outfit?" Then she laid her hand on Reggie's thigh, and kept it there.

Hellos picked up a chair from down by Dr. Yas's end of the tables and floated up to the other end also. They all watched her make her journey, Scarecrow in particular. To him she appeared to be walking as if in a dream; as if in slow motion, Scarecrow watched the movement of her long legs, he observed the swishing of her skirt just above her large knees. When she reached them Hellos placed her chair between Rex and Scarecrow, and plopped down in it. She looked first at Scarecrow, then at Rex, then around once at everybody, then she looked back at Scarecrow. "Everybody is mad," she cried.

Despite having just come from out of the cold, wind and rain, her face appeared warm, too warm; her eyes were shining, the thick strands of her hair lay wetly on her head and about her shoulders; her lips were moist and vibrant-looking, her cheeks were reddened and Scarecrow discerned a few freckles beneath her skin.

Dr. Yas said, "Sometimes madness is the only true road to sanity, haw, haw haw!"

Rex put his arm around Hellos and said, "Take it easy, my child. Have a swig."

Hellos took the bottle and poured liquor into her mouth, most of it wasting on her face and chin. "Why does everybody want me to take it easy? We must be strong and we must be calm, but I am not strong and I cannot be calm, and I don't want to take it easy," she whined, swinging the bottle around in the air.

"Ho, ho! Cry all you want, but don't spill the booze," said Rex, and took the bottle away from her.

"Don't spill the booze, don't spill the booze. You act as if the booze is your life. Everybody acts as if everything is their life, except their life."

"Why don't you shut up, woman!" shouted Krane from the other end of the tables. "You make me sick with that whining of yours."

"I make you sick, ha, ha, ha. I make him sick, make *him* sick, ha, ha, ha." Tears were streaming down Hellos' profile.

Dr. Yas put two bottles of whisky on the tables. "Let's get drunk and maybe we'll love each other for a change," he said.

"That's for me!" shouted Krane, grabbing one of the bottles.

Beer was also ordered. Scarecrow got his usual. Reggie wanted Coca-Cola.

Then the jukebox was blasting.

Krane rose and started popping his fingers and gyrating his hips. "Flip, flop, fly, don't give a damn if I die!" he sang, grabbing Reggie's hand. But Reggie refused to move. Krane looked at her evilly; he then looked to Maria, she gave him the evil look; Krane went dancing onto the floor alone.

Hellos rose and extended her hand toward Scarecrow. Heat rushed through him. He wanted the closeness of her body in his arms, and at the same time he wanted to blot her out of his sight. She flopped back down in her chair, picked up her drink and started singing along with the record.

Maria had begun to bob her shoulders and wiggle in her seat to the music. She was divine. Scarecrow's heart went out to her. But why don't she take her hand off of Reggie's thigh! He was about to ask her to dance, but she said, "Black boy I bet you want to dance with me But guess what I don't want to dance with you because I don't want my face scarred up by all that barbed wire you got on your chin Why don't you shave? That Viking gave you all that fancy shaving stuff and you don't use it Why? Another thing I been intending to ask you What's that trunk doing in your room It wasn't there before What you got in it Another woman stored away?"

Scarecrow was mortified. She had seen the trunk! She had been to his cabin. Tonight! Tonight! He had to get rid of the contents of that trunk. He sat dwarfed, glued to his chair.

Now the ship was seesawing, the wind was blowing, the rain beat down, the music blared out, the noise got louder, each record seemed to get longer. Scarecrow's head began to spin. The frenzy of the crowd took on the aspects of some kind of weird rite. Hips were gyrating, feet were stomping, buttocks were jiggling, grunts, groans and yells. It was just like the Dom, Saturday night on the Lower East Side.

There was a lean twig of a girl, yet very shapely, in a red-and-black peppermint skin-tight dress. She did a few snakelike movements with her body and a few jiglike steps. Then she reached down and peeled the dress up over her head and threw it away. She was stark nude. Her bare feet began to splash against the tile floor, her body became an electrified reed of naked skin. Her face, which was strangely pretty, fumed with perspiration; it held the expression of supreme ecstasy. A blond lad, dressed in tight white pants, jerked his body to her movements like an effeminate flame. A short African, wearing what looked like silk pajamas, danced along with them. Their energy was exasperatingly sexual. Everybody stopped what they were doing and watched. There was a fierceness, a savagery and wildness about the lean naked girl that could have come only from her innocence, her terrible youth. Or maybe from something else, thought Scarecrow. He saw Jim, his cabinmate, in the crowd of onlookers, holding a beer a few inches from his mouth as if he had meant to take a drink and had suddenly forgotten what he intended to do. Then Krane moved in on the naked girl and started jumping around frantically with her.

As if to herself, but aloud, Maria exclaimed, "That bitch is terrific! Terrific!" Then, pointing over heads toward the door, she shouted, "Look! There's Joe Hey Joe!" she called, waving her hand above the heads of the crowd.

He was a mediumly built, boyish-looking, handsome white fellow dressed in a red suit. Smiling, he pushed his way to where they were. Maria introduced him. He was one of the folksingers.

"What's happening?" he spoke to Scarecrow.

"Nothing," said Scarecrow.

"You missed the set."

"I didn't know about it."

"Well, that's cool. There'll be more," said the white boy, smiling.

Maria said, "You like to dance Joe?"

"Well, yes, I mean, if—" He looked at Scarecrow.

"Don't mind stone face he's got more important things to think about!" said Maria, giving Scarecrow a glance out of the corner of her slanted eyes. She took Joe's white hand in her black one and switched away with him. A new song had begun.

Rex Temple, the drunken novelist, leaned over to Scarecrow and yelled above the noise into his ear, "Damn booze too cheap on this ship. Getting bored drinking it. Good booze should cost more than fifteen cents a shot, a dollar a bottle." Observing the crowd, he said, "There's something disturbing about all this pop dancing. It's sexy but it's too sexy. Bet there're more perverts out there than you can shake a finger at."

Someone yelled out: "HEY! THERE'S ANOTHER SHIP OUT THERE!"

Another ship!

My God!

Look at it!

Beautiful!

It's all lit up!

Let me see!

The dance floor was abandoned. Rex got up and shuffled to where he could see. Scarecrow remained in his chair. Fuck it! He was fuming mad. He saw Dr. Yas and Hellos, who had been dancing together, scuffling to get to a place where they could see the other ship. Krane and that naked girl, who had retrieved her dress, were among the crowd. Sitting there, Scarecrow got a glimpse of Maria and the white boy squeezing their way to the window. They were holding hands. Their little behinds jiggled as they tiptoed to look over the heads of others.

Two ships far out at sea, from different places and going in different directions, were passing in the night. Anger, rage, hurt, and jealousy ate Scarecrow up inside.

32

EXTRACT FROM SCARECROW'S JOURNAL

I got to my cabin as fast as my legs would carry me. No one was there. I fell upon the bunk beneath my own, Jim's bunk, and I cried. Maria had hurt me. I cursed her out loud. I cursed Hellos. I cursed that red-suit-wearing white boy. I cursed them all. Dr. Yas, and Krane, and everybody. I cursed them all.

When I finished cursing them I felt much better. I sat up on the side of the bunk and stared at the trunk with my wife's chopped-up corpse in it. I got the key out of my front pocket, unlocked and opened the trunk. Then it hit me. Why not throw away the whole thing at once and be done with it! But on second thought I just couldn't run the risk of lugging that big yellow plastic bag through three corridors up three flights of stairs to the deck; someone would undoubtedly notice me. I had better stick to my original idea of disposing of the corpse piece by piece as I had packed them in the smaller individual bags. Not knowing precisely how much time I would have, since at any moment one or both of my remaining cabinmates might return, I took the attitude that I had no time at all. I opened the large yellow bag and gathered up several of the smaller ones. Then I got the distinct feeling that the parts in the bags were singing.

DHEM BONES! DHEM BONES!
DHEM BONES GONNA RISE AGAIN!

But I knew it was not my wife's dead bones singing. It was the refrain of a song that the old black sisters used to sing in the Baptist Church where my grandmother was a member.

DHEM BONES! DHEM BONES!
DHEM BONES GONNA RISE AGAIN!

Then I got frightened. I dropped the bags back into the trunk and took one of them with a hand in it over to the washbasin. I ran water in the basin, put the bag in the water and it did not sink. All of those bags would float on top of the ocean! Instinctively I hurriedly searched through my things and found a safety pin and punched little holes in the bag. Then I put it back into the water, which seeped inside of the bag through the holes. The thing sank to the bottom of the basin like a torpedoed submarine.

Now I became aware of a most foul odor. The smaller bags were transparent and I saw that my wife's parts were beginning to decompose. The bags were airtight, but having punched holes in several of them, the cabin now reeked with the stench of decay. I went to get my deodorant and spray the cabin and the inside of the trunk. That's when I discovered that the wash-up kit Marlina had given me had been slashed to pieces, as if by a razor blade, and the milky liquid and lotion and stuff were running all over my clothes in the closet. I knew who had done it. The racist bastard! Number Three, to get back at me for the run-in we had yesterday. But wait—I'll catch up with him before this voyage is over!

The hacksaw and butcher's blade went first. I didn't want them lying around until the end. I carried several bags of bones and entrails at once, hidden in various places on my body and concealed by my overcoat. There were other means of carrying the bags but I would get to them when and if I needed to. I had made three trips before I returned and found my cabinmates preparing for bed. But all had gone well. In two more nights, three at the most, I'd have disposed of everything, and only the books, manuscripts and mothballs would remain. I went to sleep with a smile on my face. Yet I was a little disturbed. Each trip I made I got the feeling that I was being watched. Each time I involuntarily jumped. Once I made a deliberate search in the dark but nothing was there. I was jumpy, that's all.

Although my cabinmates, Phil and Jim, didn't say anything, I could tell that they were aware of the lingering stench in the cabin mixed up with the deodorant. They looked at me with their noses all twisted up and they turned away as I got into bed. I'm sure they thought it was me—a Negro—smelling that way.

Earlier today it was announced that the ship had been unable to secure a docking space at the port of Southampton on its scheduled day of arrival. So instead of going directly to South-ampton as planned, the Castel Felice would sail first to Flushing and then on down to Le Havre and then back up to Southampton. This is going to take two more days at sea than planned, and it'll give me more time.

CHAPTER SIX

Friday, September 10 (the third day)

33

He came awake. At first he thought all hell had broken loose. Then he realized what it was. Somebody pounding on his door, a woman, screaming like a hyena. Goddamn. What the hell's the matter with her now? "All right, all right, I'm coming," he said, tumbling out of bed, still not fully awake.

He staggered to the door, opened it and was shocked at what he saw. He had expected it to be Maria, but it was Hellos looking like she had been in a train wreck. She leaped upon him, beating his chest with her fists, crying and screaming.

"He's mad, mad, mad! He beat me and he knows I'm not well. He beat me like I was a man! Look at me!"

"Take it easy, take it easy. Who beat you?"

"Krane! That's who. Goddamn him! I wouldn't give him my money. He beat me up. He knows I don't have much money. I don't know what's going to happen to me. Goddamn him! If I were a man I would kill him!" she cried hysterically.

Scarecrow held her in his arms and stroked her back gently. He had to calm her down, or else everybody on the ship would soon be in his cabin. Holding her, he kicked the door closed with his foot. "Shhh, shhh," he whispered. "It's all right now, it's all right."

She nestled down in his arms and before he knew it she was kissing him. Her lips were soft and wet, she breathed heavily through her nostrils, *kissing* him and *kissing* him. Her body was sumptuous and hot, and she pressed and wiggled herself against him as he held her in his arms. He had never been kissed this way before, he had never held so sensuous a body in his arms before, never! But he was afraid, paranoid; there was something else behind all of this, she was playing some kind of game, and he had to get loose from her. He untangled her arms from around his neck and pushed her away. Her eyes were glassy, her skirt hung loosely on her hips, her sensuous presence filled the room.

"I'm sorry," he said. "But you had better go. You shouldn't have come here in the first place."

"I had to talk to someone," she pleaded. "And you're the only one. I'm in love with you and you want me, you know you do. I told you we are destined, me and you, Scarecrow."

Scarecrow pointed at the door. "Get out of here!"

Instead of leaving she walked right up to him. "You're a sickening fool!" She spat the words in his face. "You're trying to be faithful to Maria, not because you really love her but because you are *supposed* to love her. Why are you supposed to love her? Not because she is a woman who loves you and whom you find to be lovable, but because she is a *black* woman. You are fooling yourself! You can't love *anybody* just because of their *color*. If you really loved her because of herself, it wouldn't be hard at all, you wouldn't be so uptight around me. For it is me you want, not because of my color but because I *suit* you. Maria doesn't love you either. All she wants from you is your *manhood*. To her you're nothing but a tool. She's using you to carry on her perversion. That's right, *perversion!* She tried to pick a fight with me. The fight was just an excuse for her to malign my body. She's a fox."

She was lying. She was mad. She was making it all up. He wanted to wave his hand and wipe her out. "Get the fuck out of my room before I stomp you into the floor, you honkey ass bitch!" he screamed at her.

Whapp! She hit him in the mouth, hard! She caught him totally unaware, and he went tumbling back against the trunk. Instantly, instinctively, he regained his footing and started toward her. Damn her, he was going to beat the breath out of her, he was going to kill her. But Hellos made him draw up short, stopped him dead in his stride.

"I know what's in that trunk," she proclaimed, pointing at the trunk and holding her bag out in front of it by its drawstring in the other hand. "You know I know what's in it, don't you. I can *see* it. I can *smell* it. And look at your face, you look like a scarecrow, Scarecrow." As she left the room she slammed the door behind her.

Scarecrow stood where she left him, frozen in his tracks, rigid, with the sweat dripping off his hands onto the floor. Hellos was a *dead* bitch, she was a *dead* bitch, that's all there was to it!

Doggedly he stripped off his pajamas. He couldn't massage his skin in the milky liquid because Number Three had destroyed it, but he would take a shower, he'd shave also. He went to the mirror over the washbasin, he looked weird, he looked like a scarecrow.

After he showered and shaved he thought he looked a little better. He dressed real nice and went roaming through the ship. He hoped to run into Number Three. Instead he ran into Dr. Yas, who walked up to him and asked Scarecrow how did he feel. What did he mean, how did he feel? Dr. Yas smiled at a woman who was with him but whom Scarecrow had not seen before. Then back to Scarecrow, Dr. Yas said, "You appear to be coming down with severe seasickness. It could linger in the symptomatic stage for a couple of days before it gets worse or acute. You had better come with me. I'll give you some medication."

The sudden detached professional manner of Dr. Yas caught Scarecrow completely by surprise; so he went with them to Dr. Yas's cabin. But when he started to enter behind Dr. Yas, Dr. Yas turned and said, "Wait here."

Somebody was in Dr. Yas's cabin. Scarecrow got a glimpse of them but he couldn't tell who it was. Something was going on that

Dr. Yas didn't want him to know about. He stationed himself by the door so he would be able to see into the cabin when Dr. Yas came out. While waiting, he took a good look at the woman, who also remained outside. She was middle-aged, dressed in a dark-gray coat suit. She was a little on the heavy side but not fat. She was extremely beautiful and intellectual-looking, and she had an abundant crop of blond hair which was done up on her head like the hair of a queen. She did not speak to Scarecrow.

"Take two of these in water every four hours," said Dr. Yas. "If you don't feel better in the morning, you'd better report to the ship's hospital. Incidentally, where were you last night? Where did you disappear to?"

"I was minding my own business."

Dr. Yas said he got the message, and he and the strange woman went away. Scarecrow pretended to walk away in the opposite direction. As soon as Dr. Yas and the woman were out of the corridor, he went back to Dr. Yas's cabin. Dr. Yas had tried to block Scarecrow from seeing into the cabin, but he was too fat and Scarecrow had seen who it was in there. He tapped on the door. "Reggie. It's me, Scarecrow. What's going on in there?" He waited a while and tried the door, which swung open. He was startled. There she sat in Dr. Yas's comfort chair, naked. She had a blanket around her, but he could tell she didn't have on anything under the blanket. She was totally rigid, her eyes were walled up in her head with only the white showing. She looked dead, really dead! *Overdose!* was the first thing that leaped into Scarecrow's mind. Oh, my God! He went to her and slapped her face. "Reggie! Reggie!" He slapped her back and forth. She tumbled out of the chair and onto the floor. The blanket fell away. She showed no signs of life. Her body was fantastically beautiful and proportioned, as if she had been made by a master sculptor. It lay on the floor drawn up in the same position as when she was sitting in the chair. Scarecrow put her back in the chair and got some water in a glass. He dashed the water on her face and began slapping her again rapidly back and forth. Suddenly she let out a yell! She bent over, wrapped her arms around her stomach and tumbled again onto the floor. There, on the floor, she tumbled about, screaming and yelling at the top of her lungs in horrific agony. Scarecrow was at a total loss what to do. He stood gaping like a man locked in a cage.

The door opened and Dr. Yas rushed in. Without saying a word, he knocked Scarecrow out of the way, grabbing up his black bag and coming out with a hypo needle. He sat astraddle Reggie and held her still as he injected something into her arm. Shortly she grew quiet and still again. He had put her to sleep. He lifted her to the bed and wrapped the blanket around her again. Then he turned to Scarecrow and went into a cursing rage. Goddamn you, Scarecrow, why can't you mind your own fucking business. Sonofabitch, she could have died! Trembling, sheepishly, Scarecrow explained that he thought she *was* dead. Calming down, Dr. Yas explained that Reggie was under his treatment for withdrawing from heroin. Unlike all of the other methods of treatment, Dr. Yas did not use any drugs to ease the pain of withdrawal, nor did the addict have to suffer the pain—his withdrawal treatment was hypnosis! No other drugs, no side effects, no pain.

34

Scarecrow felt like a fool. He was embarrassed, sorry and angry at himself. Poor Reggie. He could have blown the whole thing for her, he could have blown her life! He felt worse than ever, maybe he *looked* worse than ever too, for just before he left Dr. Yas's cabin, the doctor had studied him carefully and inquired as to whether or not Scarecrow was taking the pills as he had instructed. Now, as he roamed through the ship, he did not know for whom he was searching, Number Three, Maria, Hellos, or maybe he was searching for himself? One thing was certain, a pressure was boiling in him, mounting and mounting in him until he didn't know any more what he felt in relationship to anybody or anything.

"Scarecrow!"

Somebody was calling him. He was standing outside the snack bar. He looked in and saw Krane seated at a table and beckoning to him. Besides the attendant, Krane was the only person in there. Scarecrow went in.

"Goddamn!" exclaimed Krane as Scarecrow sat across from him. "What's done happened to you? You look like homemade sin."

"Hellos said y'all had a fight."

Krane bent forward, said, "Wasn't no fight, man. I beat that bitch's ass, that's all."

Scarecrow hit him hard enough to knock him out of the chair, but Krane caught hold of the table, then he had an empty Coke bottle in his hand. "Watch it, big black motherfucker!" he shouted. "I may not win but I'll fight your black ass. Fighting is my middle name!"

Scarecrow apologized. He didn't want to fight Krane, he wasn't even mad at him. He didn't know what came over himself.

"I know what's eating you," said Krane, feeling his chin where Scarecrow had clobbered him. "You're fucked up between two bitches, ain't you. Maria and Hellos. Well, I can tell you right now, man, if you want Hellos you can have her. I got me another pussy, young and groovy. But if you knew what I know you'd tell Hellos to fuck off. She's nutty as a fruitcake. Take that bag she carries around, once I tried to look in that thing and she had a fit. I mean, what's she got that's so precious in there. She might seem attractive at first but that woman is sick. She's a Jew, you know, and is all hung up about sex and money and centuries of persecution. She thinks she's the reincarnation of somebody or another. Her mother died in the loony bin."

Scarecrow remembered that Hellos had said that her father died in an institution and her mother in a plane crash.

"That's what I mean, man. You can't tell when she's lying or what. That's the way she relates to people, by mystifying them!"

Listening to Krane talk about Hellos made Scarecrow think about Maria. How much understanding did he have of her? What did he know about her background, her parents, what had she done before she married Simon? Scarecrow did not know as much about Maria as Krane seemed to know about Hellos. It was Maria who mystified him, not Hellos. He knew what he had to do about Hellos. But thinking of Maria made his chest feel empty like it was going to collapse.

Krane was saying, "But dig it, man. What I want to see you about is some bread. I'm flat broke and I'm hungry. I wonder if you'd lay some dough on me, just a little to last until we get to Europe?"

Scarecrow reached in his pocket and gave Krane the loose thirty-five dollars that he had there.

Krane's face lit up, "Oh, wow, man! You're great. Really great. Boss!" He raced up to the counter and returned with a ham sandwich and a plate of french fries. He looked around for Scarecrow but he was not there.

35

"A bottle of gin."

The bartender smiled, triumphantly.

A group of Americans entered the Lido, the women sat down, leaving the men at the bar. One of them said, "I ain't seen a nigger with a body like that since I left Georgia. I sho would like to invite her to my cabin."

"What would you do with your wife, Fred?"

"Why, hellfire, make her watch! Maybe she'd learn a thing or two."

They laughed. One of them saw Scarecrow standing there. He nudged the others and they grew quiet. They would never in their lives come close to knowing how deeply Scarecrow hated them.

The bartender returned with the bottle of gin and Scarecrow went to the table where he had seen Rex sitting.

Rex turned up his nose at Scarecrow's gin. "You must be sick," he said. Then noticing Scarecrow's face, he said, "Jesus, what's the matter? You *look* sick."

"Don't look at me, then."

"Take it easy," apologized Rex, leaning forward and asking Scarecrow if he'd seen the woman with Dr. Yas, who was she?

Scarecrow did not know, he was curious about her himself.

After taking a large swallow of scotch, very pointedly Rex said, "I'm not curious about her or any woman. I merely asked, that's all."

Singing came into the Lido. One of the Americans sitting on the other side of the room said, "It's that beatnik and those two niggers again."

Through the glass wall which looked out onto the swimming pool, Scarecrow saw two Negroes with guitars and a group of people sitting around the pool. Maria and Reggie were among them. That white fellow, Joe, was out there with a guitar. Scarecrow went over to the wide picture-glass window. Rex stayed where he was.

A very handsome Negro with a beard played a smooth guitar, plucking it softly, and his voice was sweet. He knew how to smile too, just like he was on television or in a nightclub. He sang a very romantic song. The crowd clapped loudly. The Negro looked pleased, he knew he was good. Then the younger Negro moved into the center position, tuning up his guitar, looking out at the people, frowning, looking ugly, taking his time. Silence prevailed.

This Negro's feet were too big, his trousers were too tight and they revealed everything about his gangling body, and his jacket was up around his bony arse. He was blacker than coal and had an elongated nappy head. His lips were oversized and his mouth was wide. Finally he gave the eye to Joe, the white boy, who then swung his fist up and down across the strings of his silver instrument. *Wraaaannngg! Wraaaannngg! Wuuuuuuunnnggg!* The Negro threw back his head and opened his big mouth.

> I ain't scared of the grave!
> The grave better be scared of me!

I got mo jo dust in my jaws!
I got fire and lightning in my brain!
Look out! brother death—
I'm coming to git chu!
I'm gonna live while I can
And die when I git ready!

When he finished nobody moved, nobody clapped, you could hear a pin drop. Then they gave him a ten-minute ovation! The Negro gave Joe a big hug. Scarecrow lit a cigarette. It was the white boy's time to sing. He sang in a heavy southern accent; his voice was earthy, rich, fluent, and it was no mystery now why his guitar playing had enhanced the singing of the Negro. He sang a song about a "mean woman." Maria went and plopped down by his side and, goddamnit, she grabbed that cracker's leg and smiled up into his fucking face. She sang along with him and sounded as good as he did. Together they were a team! Scarecrow didn't know she could sing too! Seeing her there that way with the white boy made Scarecrow so sick that he was nauseated by his own emotions.

He was in his cabin before he realized. He took several of the pills Dr. Yas had given him and got into bed without taking off his clothes. He groaned and rolled from side to side, sick, sick, sick, sick.

Someone was knocking again. Well, let them knock, he didn't give a shit who it was. The knocking continued. "Hey, it's me, Joe. Sorry to bother you but it's important. May I come in?"

The white boy came in and Scarecrow got out of bed and stared at him, and kept on staring at him, hatefully. Joe stammered, terribly self-conscious—he managed, however, to invite Scarecrow for a drink, saying that it was on him.

No one was at the bar. Joe got himself a beer and asked Scarecrow what he wanted. Scarecrow went over to Rex's table, got his bottle of gin, returned to the bar and plunked it down.

Joe said, "It's about Maria."

Scarecrow just looked at him. Secretly he was preparing his moves.

The white boy sighed, "Look," he said, "I know you're a right dude, so I ain't gonna beat around the bush. Me and your woman made it last night."

He was looking straight into Scarecrow's face and Scarecrow was looking dead into his blue eyes. Scarecrow's knee went up. But the white boy turned slightly, blocking the intended knee to his groin. Scarecrow's reflexes were lightning, his fist was almost in Joe's face. But Joe's open palm was there to catch the intended blow and he caught it and held onto Scarecrow's fist in midair. For a while they stood there frozen in their poses, like a snapshot. Damn, this boy is fast or I must be losing my grip, thought Scarecrow. Then he relaxed on his stool, took the gin and drank nearly a third of it.

"But it's over, it never started," said Joe, taking a sip from his beer. "I wanted her, I won't lie about that, she made me want her, she's aggressive, you know. But what I'm saying is she don't want me. Not even last night she didn't want me. She talked about you, called your name, when she was with me."

Scarecrow, who was still staring straight into Joe's face, said, "You told me what you had to say, so what the hell are you still standing here for!"

Joe said he wasn't through yet. He wasn't trying to tell Scarecrow what to do but he believed that Maria needed something from Scarecrow.

"Why don't you tell me what it is she needs, white boy wonder, since you seem to know so damn much!" Scarecrow shouted with such bitterness that saliva from his mouth sprayed Joe's face. He did not mean to do that but he didn't care once he had done it.

Brushing the spit from his face, Joe said that he knew how Scarecrow felt, and that he thought he knew how Maria felt also. He didn't know exactly what it was but Maria was expecting something from Scarecrow. Maria had been terribly upset. She saw Scarecrow through the glass when they were singing by the pool, and she did what she did not for Joe's benefit but for Scarecrow's. "She's in her cabin having fits over you right now," he told Scarecrow. "She drove me out of the room. I thought I ought to come tell you. I mean, to apologize. I'm sorry. I hope you'll forgive me." He paused, drank the rest of his beer, then said, "I'm through." He walked away.

"Hey! What was that all about?" yelled Rex from his table.

He was in his cabin again, fuming! Jim came in and went right back out. Scarecrow knew last night what Maria had on her mind. He was through with her! She didn't need him. What's she having fits about? It was a game, that's all, a damn game with her. Maybe there was something in what Hellos had said after all! But to hell with Hellos! That white boy had nerve or else he was crazy. But Scarecrow couldn't be mad at him. The white boy was a man. Maria seduced him, he said so. Scarecrow fought to keep it from entering his mind but it leaped into his thoughts uncontrollably: *wonder if she made love to the white boy the way she made love to me*. Bitch. Whore. Slut.

36

Scarecrow heard her sobbing before he entered her cabin. She was in bed with the blanket pulled over her head. He went to her and told her that it was him, Scarecrow. She peered out from under the covers and started weeping like a grateful baby. She clung to him. She did not have on any clothes. Her body was hot and trembling. She told him that she loved him and had missed him and she wished she was dead for having been such a bad girl. She had been so miserable. She wanted to make love, she was hurting for his loving. She pulled him down on top of her.

Scarecrow could barely contain himself, but he had to hold back. They couldn't make love in Maria's cabin with all her roommates, any number of whom were liable to come in at any moment. He glanced around quickly. She told him that the cabinmates were at the costume dance. "Lock the door, fix the latch, they can't get in," she whispered.

He did as she asked. Standing there he still felt wrong somehow. He suggested that they go to his cabin, since he had made friends with his cabinmates and they would stay clear of the cabin if he asked them. She buried herself down in the bed and shouted, "NOW! I WANT YOU NOW!"

Their passion was uncontrollable. The noise they made, the grunts and groans and sighs, especially Maria, who screamed all sorts of enticing vulgarity. God knows Scarecrow had missed her. Maria's cabin was on the very bottom deck of the ship. The sound of the engines and the thrusting of the waters against the hull of the vessel below the surface of the ocean, drove them down and down and buoyed them up and up, until at last they lay like two sea-wrecked creatures cast up on an uncharted beach, spent and serene, with nothing between them but the panting of their hearts. Maria had never spent herself like this before. Were there no limits to her passion! Then Scarecrow heard a distinct noise. Earlier he had felt or sensed a presence. Now it was a noise! He jerked around.

On one of the bunks in the rear of the cabin there sat a girl in the dark with a sheet around her. She was busy manicuring her nails.

CHAPTER SEVEN

Friday, September 10 (the same day)

37

"Don't be slamming doors in my face!"

Back in her cabin, when he had discovered that girl, he could have killed Maria. But he kept his cool. He had scurried into his clothes, rushed out of her cabin, up three flights of stairs, down the corridor and into his room, slamming the door behind him. Maria had grabbed her robe, getting into it all the while she chased behind him, clutching after his shirttail. She was at his door when he slammed it, but was unable to lock it, as she instantly kicked it open and told him not to slam it in her face.

Now, in his cabin, he pointed his finger in her face and said, "If you don't get out of my room I'll slam your face into that door!"

She cocked her head to one side and stood back on her legs. "Do it," she said.

He socked his fist in his palm. Damn this woman! He slammed the door closed, it made a noise, *Blammm!* Turning from her, he went to the sink and dashed water into his face. The seasickness pills were on the shelf, he threw several of them into his mouth, the rest dropped to the floor. He was shaking all over. He looked into the mirror above the washbasin and saw Maria standing there by the door. Without turning from the mirror, and trying to keep as much of the rage out of his voice as possible, he said, "Maria, what was your cabinmate doing in that room? You told me they were at the dance."

"Wasn't my cabinmate," she spoke up.

Scarecrow wheeled around. "Who in hell was it, then?"

Maria said it was just a friend.

"*Friend?* My ass! You told me nobody was in there. Nobody!"

Maria said she didn't know the girl was there.

Scarecrow stared her dead in her eyes.

She faltered. Gesturing, she said, "Well eh yes I knew she was there I mean *before* but I fell asleep I thought she had gone to the costume dance with the others She must have fallen asleep too back there on that bunk and I didn't know she was in there I mean I forgot she was back there."

"Oh, shit, woman. If she was asleep you made sure you made enough racket to wake her up while we were fucking!" shouted Scarecrow. Then, shaking his head and running his hand over his hair, he said, "But you're lying, Maria, lying all around. That girl was not asleep and you hadn't been asleep either. Joe told me you were down there having fits. You were crying, or pretending to be crying, when I got there, and Joe didn't mention no girl friend to me, he said you were alone. That girl came after Joe left. I'll bet you planned it with her like you planned it with Joe. That girl was naked. If she didn't live in the cabin, what was she doing naked? I been wondering about you and now I'm beginning to figure out what you are. Hellos told me you accosted her."

"That bitch! That bitch! I haven't put a hand on the wench I haven't seen her I haven't said a word to her she's lying but." She walked over to him with her robe swinging open down the front, and said, "Why don't you stop pussyfooting around black boy Be a man and tell me what you think I am!"

Scarecrow raised his fist. But Maria had fallen to the floor before he could swing out. She had anticipated his blow, and it made him feel helplessly defeated; everybody was outflanking him. Maria struggled to her feet, steadied herself and stood there with the muscles of her legs arched back, sneering at Scarecrow. He stepped toward her but then wheeled around. She had left her robe lying on the floor.

With his back to her, he said, "For God's sake, Maria, put on your robe and get out."

"I'm not going anywhere until you *make* me."

He faced her and, in an almost pleading voice, said, "What are you trying to do to me!"

She raised her fist in his face, and said, "I want you to be *real* with me You've got a wall of glass between yourself and me I want to crack that wall You never let yourself go with me You keep holding back like some sissified white boy Be a nigger nigger I want SOUL! I want attention I want raw affection That way I'll know you love me and not just my pussy."

She had begun to tremble. The sneer had vanished from her face, and now she looked like a child on the verge of panic. Scarecrow could feel the warmth radiating from her jet-black body. The magnetism of her hot personality filled the cabin. He felt himself giving in. But he knew what she was capable of, and he had to get her out of there.

He walked past her, picked up the robe and put it around her. Standing in back of her, he held her by the upper part of her arms. He spoke very softly, tracing their relationship from the time they got on the ship, how easy it should have been, just the two of them, lovers, leaving everything behind with no problems, not even a money problem, he had enough money to last them for ten years, even if he didn't write another book and she didn't have to work. Now here they were fighting and eating at each other's hearts. What happened? What's gone wrong? Maybe she was right, he didn't know, but he felt like she was wrong. At least he was unable to think straight any more and he wished she'd leave. Their relationship needed a rest, he needed a rest, he hadn't slept since before yesterday. The pills Dr. Yas gave him didn't seem to be working. Why not let him get some rest and later, tomorrow, perhaps they could sort things out without fighting.

She broke into sobs. "You want to get rid of me so you can have that Jew witch don't you that Hellos Why don't you have her on the side? I mean I'm willing to let you try her cause I know she's nothing but a fake."

Scarecrow released her and turned his back to her back. She wheeled him around, raising her fist in the air, and said, "You have never *seduced* me! Look at you standing there now calm and collected Can't you ever show any feelings Why do I have to carry the whole load? Are you so damn scared to let me see that you are a damn nigger just like me?"

"Lower your voice," whispered Scarecrow.

"Fuck you!" she exclaimed. "You care more about the passengers on this boat ride than you do me Fuck these people!" She had tied the cord on her robe and was stalking him. "You don't have to back up in no corner I know you ain't scared of me You just want to get me out of here all right I'm leaving but this boat ride ain't over I'll never let you go as long as I live You got what I need and I'm going to get it if it kills me You know it I know it Later black boy." She reached for the door.

"Maria," he called. She turned and faced him. She was standing in the open doorway. Scarecrow wanted to know something about her, like where was she born, what did she do before she met Simon, had she ever been to college, and so on.

She threw back her head and laughed. So he wanted to know the vital statistics. After she told him a few things about herself, she said, "And for the record I did not seduce that Caucasian boy He seduced me He crawled and before this boat ride is over you're going to do the same You're going to beg See you around sweetie."

38

EXTRACT FROM SCARECROW'S JOURNAL
Today I learned, not all, but a few interesting things about Maria's

background. She is the daughter of Dr. Charles Du Paul and Madam Angelina E. S. Du Paul! I was shocked to hear it but it is true. Dr. Du Paul is a famous man, known all over the world. On two occasions he has been offered by the United States Government the posts of ambassador in Ethiopia and Haiti, both of which he turned down, preferring to remain in Union, Louisiana, as president of the historically renowned black university, Filmore Institute, a position he has held for twenty years. He is a pure black man and Maria is his daughter, for she looks exactly like him. Maria is twenty-five years old. She has a degree in law from Columbia University. That is where she met her husband, Simon, while he was studying art. She has also been a striptease dancer in downtown New York nightclubs. Maria hates her father, she referred to him as "that bastard." I wonder why? Maria's Mother, Angelina, is, or was, as famous as Dr. Du Paul. She is a concert pianist virtuoso. She has been retired for some years now and some of the younger generation might not know of her. The mother looks like a white woman. Maria has a brother, Everett Sarttaire Du Paul, who looks just like the mother and is an ambassador. I forget the country, somewhere in Africa, I think.

39

The blues is a feeling born of many ingredients. It is born of loss, frustration, loneliness, disappointment, defeat, and it makes you tired and weary. Yet the blues is more than any one, or any combination, of these things. At the core of the blues is a sense of having been hurt, of having been wronged, about which in the meantime one can do nothing except endure. The blues, then, is not only the inner feeling but the attitude taken toward that feeling. The blues is born of all those things which in turn are borne. The blues is deeply spiritual, it is experienced in one's soul. The blues is melancholy and depressive, but the inward pain is often sensualized and given artistic or creative expression. While the blues is misery, its expressions can be, and nearly always are, beautiful. The person who is blue feels the urge to *sing* the blues.

After Maria left his cabin, had Scarecrow been gifted with any kind of singing voice at all, he would have thrown back his head, opened wide his mouth, and bellowed the blues. For the blues was what he had.

He soon tired of writing in his journal. He tried to write a couple of poems. But it was no good, he had to get out of that tight, stuffy cabin. He went out on deck and stood near the Dom. He heard the music and gaiety coming from there, he saw some of the crowd lounging outside in their costumes, necking and petting, and all of this made his blues bluer. Everything seemed unreal, the scantily clad women around the swimming pool looked like sensuous figurines. He gazed at the women, at their thighs, their breasts, their pelvises, and was overcome with a loneliness that he had been trying to conquer all his life. Maria had been right, he wanted every woman on the ship. But she had been only partly right, he wanted every woman in the world. Fighting it, he turned his eyes out to sea, the hot sun glistened upon the water, great sheets of clashing foam suffused the ocean. Flashes of his grandmother raced through his mind. He was haunted with the feeling that she might be dead. He wondered if her spirit was out there somewhere in the deep of the waters. Thinking that he would never see her again, he wept for the comfort of her bosom.

A slap landed on his back and someone was shouting, "Joy! Joy! Joy!" It was Wantman Krane. He peered around into Scarecrow's face. "Hey, man, what you crying for?"

Scarecrow turned around and what he saw should have made him laugh, but the blues had such a hold on him that he couldn't. Krane had his clothes on backwards, and the girl with him wore an old-fashioned sleeping gown similar to what Scarecrow's grandmother might wear. But Scarecrow's imagination stripped the gown from the girl and he saw her naked as he had seen her the other night in the Dom, for it was the same girl.

Gesturing to the girl, Krane said, "Kiss him, pussy."

The girl brushed her lips on Scarecrow's cheek.

"Mushy-mushy him in the mouth," Krane told her.

140

She pressed her mouth fully to Scarecrow's.

"That's enough!" said Krane; then to Scarecrow, he said, "There, man, that ought to make you feel better. This is Putsy, my new dream. She's a famous model, ain't you pussy. She's already been in Vogue and a whole lot of other magazines."

When they strolled away, each one had a hand on the other's backside. How happy they were! Scarecrow could not bear his loneliness any more. He went into the Dom, looking for her, but she was not there. He went to her cabin and she was not there either. Where could she be? She had mentioned, he remembered, something about meeting a crippled fellow and spending time in his cabin. Where was his cabin, what was his name—Scarecrow did not know. There was a slight chance that she might be in the Lido. Outside the Lido he noticed for the first time a glass case containing snapshots of the ship waiting in harbor back in New York. There was a large close-up photograph of a well-dressed Negro coming up the gangplank with what Scarecrow took to be his wife and two little daughters. He stared at the photograph, he just stared at it, with a blank mind and an ache in his heart. The case was full of snapshots of people waving good-bye and boarding the ship. Lo! In one of them, along with a crowd of others, was a picture of Maria. In another one he saw Dr. Yas and Krane. In still another there was Reggie, and finally he saw himself. But it was all meaningless to him. It seemed so long ago. He felt as though time itself had passed out of existence. He tried thinking of his life in New York and he could not focus on a single thing. He felt as though he never had had a past.

She was not in the Lido. Rex was standing at the bar, or rather, he was leaning there. He was really drunk, plastered! Scarecrow walked over and asked Rex if he had seen Hellos. Between hiccups, Rex wanted to know if he looked like a missing persons bureau. "About twenty minutes ago Dr. Yas asked me the same question," he said. "And while I'm at it, I'm tired of playing nursemaid to this gin bottle for you." Rex plunked the bottle up on the bar.

Someone judged Scarecrow from behind. It was the singer, the one with the romantic voice, the handsome one. "Hey, brother," he said. "I been looking round for you. I thought we should meet, being brothers and all. My name's Archie."

Scarecrow returned the introduction and offered Archie a drink of gin. The singer thanked Scarecrow but no thanks, he didn't touch the stuff. Then he said, "Well, look, brother, haven't seen you round on any of our sets. Guess you been busy writing."

Scarecrow told him that he had heard them once. They were good. He wondered how long they had been together?

"Well, yeah, brother, thanks, but, I mean, we just met on this boat. I'm from Philly. Well, I was born down home, you know, Georgia, but I been in and out of Philly for five years. My man, Bennie, is out of down home too, Nashville, I think. But he's got an old lady from the Big Apple, Miss Ann, and they got a chip off the block, Miss Ann's block, if you dig what I mean. The ofey's from down home too, Mobile. He just broke up a country rock band. I'm headed for God's country, you dig, Stockholm. Bennie's headed for London. I don't know where the white boy's bound."

Scarecrow offered Archie a cigarette.

"Never use nicotine, brother." Then, looking over Scarecrow's shoulder, he exclaimed, "Dig it! Here comes my main man, Bennie. What kept you, baby? I been hanging here a good little bit."

Bennie said that he had to mind the baby. His wife had a bad headache and he was getting domesticated in the meantime.

"Dig it," said Archie. "Meet the brother here."

Bennie stuck out his big hand and said, "My name's Bennie Bendrix, I need a haircut, I been working on the chain gang, I got a son named Bennie Junior, I'm twenty-one years young, I'm ugly, I got a hundred dollars to my name, I smell good, I sang bad, the womenfolk call me Candy Man, I'm a mean motor-scooter rider and I'm gonna make it!"

For a moment nobody reacted. Then the ethnic warmth exploded between them. They rocked the bar with laughter. Scarecrow laughed so hard, and was so glad to laugh, that he forgot he had the blues. Bennie was laughing at his own down-home wit as hard as Archie and Scarecrow were.

"Hey!" called Rex, from the table where he had retreated when the threesome first got together. "Why don't you fellows come and join us."

They looked over there and saw Dr. Yas and that blond woman at the table with Rex. All of them were looking in their direction.

Bendrix whispered to Scarecrow, "Wait a minute, baby. I been intending to ask when I met you about them people you hang out with. I know they must be artists or intellectual or something, but this boat's crawling with all kinds of off-the-wall creeps. Me and the old lady can't walk through the ship without feeling like we gon be attacked or lynched or something. I don't hate all white people, just most of them, and I'd rather lay dead if I'm going to embarrass them or they going to insult me. That drunk chubby joker, who's he? And that sloppy loud-mouth dude with the beard and fish fingers, and that Nordic dame over there. I mean, what kind of bag do they be into? Where they be coming from?"

Scarecrow ran it all down to them. He didn't know the blond woman, but if she was a friend of Dr. Yas she must be cool too.

"Dr. Who!" They both said it at the same time.

That was his name, Dr. Norman Yas, psychiatrist.

Bennie said, "You mean like opposed to Dr. No! Well, I'm gonna write home and tell Momma."

Archie said, "Well, if this cat's a doctor, does he live up to or down to his name, brother?"

Scarecrow had noticed that Archie held his eyes like Reggie held hers. So he did not reply to Archie's question.

When they got to the table they looked at them, especially at Dr. Yas. Then they exchanged glances among themselves and burst into laughter again.

"What's all the fun about?" inquired Rex.

"Yeah, baby, pray tell me too. Haw, haw, haw!"

Winking at Bennie and Archie, Scarecrow said, "We've been standing over there looking under this lady's dress."

Silence fell over the table. Awe registered on their faces. The skin on the face of the woman jerked involuntarily. She looked down at her dress, which was well below her knees, nothing could be seen. Everybody, all of them, broke into cathartic laughter.

When they regained their breath, Rex said, "Sit down. It's about time we had some fun."

The woman was looking at Scarecrow now and smiling fondly. It was the reaction Scarecrow had planned on. Her first name was Kerstine but Scarecrow wanted to know more.

Dr. Yas said, "She is Dr. Kerstine Wentworth, anthropologist. She lectures, back and forth, in New York at the New School and in London at the British Museum. She's not for screwing because she's married. At least that's the line she shot me. Now go to hell."

To Scarecrow, Dr. Wentworth said, "I've always wanted to meet you. I've read your book several times, and it's an astounding piece of literature." She smiled, sort of knowingly.

The honkey bitch queen! Scarecrow held a stone face, at least he thought he did.

Archie drew his chair up to Dr. Yas, and said, "Dig it, man, look here . . ." His voice trailed off into a whisper.

Bennie said to Dr. Wentworth, "Do you be one of those people who dig up dead bones or is you one of those who be snooping among the savages?"

Rex started chuckling.

Somebody touched Scarecrow from behind. He was a tall middle-aged man with graying hair, in a nicely pressed suit. "May I speak to you," he said, politely. "Over here, privately, please."

As Scarecrow went with the man, he felt as though he had seen him somewhere before. The others watched until the man and Scarecrow disappeared out the door.

40

The man said that he had singled Scarecrow out because Scarecrow seemed to be a man of responsibility. Scarecrow appeared to be the leader of the group, and the man thought he would appreciate what he had to say more than any of the rest.

"What's your name again?" Scarecrow asked him.

"Handson. Martin Handson," replied the man. He chewed on his cigar. Then said, "Now here's the deal. Putsy claims she's in love with this Wantman fellow and that he's so wonderful, writing her poems and all that foolishness. I think it's a shame for a grown man to act like that. He's old enough to be her father. If he was a sensible man I'd talk to him, but can you imagine what it would be like trying to reason with him!" He took his cigar stub out of his mouth and began gesturing with it. "I'm Putsy's uncle and manager," he went on. "She's all I've got and I'm all she's got. Her father, my younger brother, was killed in the war, the Korean War, shot to bits by the gooks."

Scarecrow was astounded, his mouth dropped open. Putsy's father! Shot in Korea! Oh, my God, no, no! Scarecrow had killed Putsy's father, Sergeant Orvil Handson. Poor Putsy! Poor nothing. He had done her a *favor*. Orvil was a fascist racist hung-up pig! How in the world could a man have a daughter, who must have been but a baby at the time, and go around raping and slaughtering the young daughters of other men, like Sergeant Orvil Handson had done in Korea. Scarecrow had done Putsy a favor indeed. Now here was that man's brother. Scarecrow recognized the similarity in their features, and he wanted to strike out. But he closed his gaping mouth and maintained his cool.

Martin Handson was saying, "My sister-in-law, Putsy's mother, poor thing, died a year later in a car crash. I've had Putsy ever since. I got her into modeling. It's a rough racket, you know. I was a civil servant, a few more years and I could have retired with full benefits. But I resigned and put her talent before my welfare. I made her what she is now. She had nobody before me, she'd been in and out of foster homes and orphanages all her life, until a year ago when I took over. She's got it coming big in the future. She's headed for the movies, she'll be a star for sure. But she needs me to deal with the cutthroats, the nasty old men and wormy old spinsters, the pawing photographers and thieving Don Juans. Suppose your friend makes her pregnant. I can't have that. There's plenty of time for that when she gets older and her career is secure. I'm not old-fashioned, not a bit, but the way she's going now with this Wantman, she'll be in the gutter two weeks after she's in Paris. Do you know that that character has wormed his way into going to Paris with her? That cannot happen. You've got to do something to break it up, to stop that Wantman, he's your friend."

To keep from grabbing hold of Handson, Scarecrow grabbed hold of the railing. He had to suppress so much rage until, when he spoke, his voice sounded like a frog's croak. "I'm nobody's keeper. Can't do you no good, Mr. Handson. Sorry," he said, and started to walk away.

Handson pressed Scarecrow's chest with two of his fingers. "Just a sec," he said. "There's something about you that women go for, even Putsy, once they get to know you. I'm a good judge of human character. You could intervene between Putsy and Wantman, whatshisname, Krane, and once you broke them up, you could bow out. Understand me? I could make it worth your while."

Scarecrow grabbed the man by his collar and bent him backwards across the railing. Handson's eyes popped out in his head, he strained to speak, to yell perhaps, but Scarecrow had him so tightly he could hardly breathe, let alone speak.

"Motherfucker, I ought to kill you like I did your goddamn brother!" slurred Scarecrow between gritted teeth. "I know what happened. You just told me. You let that girl stay in institutions until she got of age and came out and started making it good in modeling on her own. Then you stepped in to clean up the gravy. You bastard! I know you won't believe this, but I'm going to give you something to think about for the rest of your rotten life. *I'm* the *gook* who killed your fucking brother, Sergeant Orvil Handson. See, I know his name! I filled him full of holes and said the *enemy* had done it. And if you ever come close to me again!" Scarecrow was so full of his own emotions he could not go on. He spit in Handson's face and slung him hard against the side of the ship, and left him there looking like a man who had been struck by a hurricane from out of nowhere.

Back in the bar, on his way to the table, Scarecrow stepped on a man's foot. He was so mad that he didn't realize he had done it. But the man apologized to him. Scarecrow did not like the looks of the man. He had a smile that was plastic and greasy. When he got to the table he reached over everybody and picked up his gin bottle by the neck and downed half of its remaining contents. They wanted to know who was the man and what had gone on outside? Scarecrow told them who the man was and nothing else. Then he realized that the reason he was standing was because another person had joined the group and was sitting in his chair. He was relieved and glad to see Hellos but he was still too enraged to express it. He put his hand on her shoulder, bent down and whispered in her ear, "You're in my chair, bitch." His lips brushed her ear as he said it to her. She smiled and kissed him on his cheek. The rest of them were watching.

Scarecrow drew up a chair, placed it close to Hellos and sat down. Hellos laid her hand in his lap and he put his palm over it, then he eyed her all over. Her legs were crossed and her large knees were bare. The carnality of her body *occupied* the chair she sat in, which was alive with the richness of her sexuality. At least it seemed that way to Scarecrow. He took his eyes off of her because he could not stand the fire that was now ablaze within his chest. He glanced at the anthropologist and she was staring at him with a look of abandoned disapproval. What did Scarecrow care what she felt. It was such a thrill to sit with Hellos beside him, especially with the secret knowledge of what he was going to do running all through his body. Bennie Bendrix and Dr. Yas were having some long discussion and he caught the phrase, "mark of oppression," but for the most part he missed everything, because his mind and emotions would not keep still. He drank from his gin bottle like gin was going out of style. Over the heads of the rest he saw Krane and Putsy coming toward the table, they were holding hands. Thank God, Putsy did not look anything like the Handsons, she must have taken after her mother.

"Krane, Putsy!" called Dr. Yas. "Got a wild psychedelic discussion going on."

Grinning? Or was he blushing? Krane got two chairs, holding them over his head to avoid hitting anyone. He made it through the crowd and placed the chairs next to Dr. Yas, who was on the other side of the table from Scarecrow and Hellos. Krane reached for two beers, the table was full of them. He gave one to Putsy, drank out of one, plopped down beside Putsy, blushed, laughed, then said, "Proceed! Keep on keeping on."

Bennie took up from where he left off, "I mean, I can't be staying in that country. My music is too far out and it's gonna get more far out. But it's my son I'm thinking about. I don't want them racist pigs screwing up his mind like they did mine with that shit they run down on you."

"I hope young man that you are not under the illusion that you and your family are going to escape racial hatred altogether by going to another white country, or, for that matter, by going to an all-black country."

Bennie batted his eyes at Dr. Wentworth the anthropologist, and said, "No, Mam. Eh," he snapped his fingers. "Excuse me for calling you 'Mam,' but you look like you be a high-class-type white woman and I keep forgetting your name."

"Call me Kerstine."

"Well," said Bennie. "I mean, no! I don't think that. But I can go where there ain't so *much* racism. I can leave America. And when it gets like America wherever I happen to be, I'll split from that place too."

Rex said, "In other words, you'll keep running."

Bennie started to reply but a man interrupted him. The man

148

had knelt down beside Bennie and was resting his hand on Bennie's thigh. He was whispering.

Bennie said, "What? Can't hear you, man, talk louder. We be among friends, I think."

The man continued to whisper. Scarecrow recognized him. He was the one on whose foot he had stepped, the one with the unctuous smile.

A big grin appeared on Bennie's face. "Hey, y'all, dig this!" he exclaimed. To the man, he said, "Go on, tell them."

The man stood up, his posture was perfect, his hands were by his sides. "I'm the Reverend Kenneth McIntoch. It seems that I'm the only minister on board. Therefore, the Captain has invested me with the duty, and privilege, of conducting the service in the ship's church day after tomorrow, which is the Lord's Day, you know. The only Sunday we'll have on this sojourn across the Good Lord's ocean. We should all give thanks for the safety we've enjoyed so far, and offer up our hearts to Him so that our journey will continue in peace and good fortune. I have just asked Ben here if he would be so kind as to sing for us day after tomorrow when we pray."

The minister knelt back down beside Bennie. They were silent at the table. Other people in the bar were looking in their direction, and those nearest the table were listening.

Dr. Yas raised his hands in the air and began to clap. "Yeah, baby, how bout that! Crazy psychedelic worship on the day of the Sun, haw, haw, haw!"

"Wait a minute, wait a minute," said Bennie, waving his hands around, trying to stop the cheering and clapping in which everybody had joined, except Hellos and Scarecrow. "Y'all must be stoned out of y'all's mind," continued Bennie. "I don't be grooving in no church, none of that it'll-all-be-over-in-the-sweet-bye-and-bye. I used to listen to my Momma sang that junk when I was a kid and it used to turn my stomach. You, too, Reven, you must be off your rocker. I mean, do you be knowing the kind of songs I sang?"

The Reverend said, "Why, yes. I heard you earlier today out by the pool. Frankly, I understand your hesitancy. But I'm not what you think I might be. I like the way you sing. It's what you call *ethnic*, rich with soul. I don't know what kind of messenger of the Lord I would be if I didn't reserve a place in my service for soul."

"Haw! He's one of them s-o-u-l-ful preachers!"

"Have a drink?" said Rex.

"Thank you," said the minister, taking the glass and bending back down beside Bennie.

Bennie screwed up his face and said, "But you still don't understand. Sir, eh, I mean, minister. Say, what should I be calling you anyway? I don't know how to talk to no preacher. I always want to call them officer, cause they be reminding me of cops."

The minister smiled and said, "Relax, just call me Ken."

Bennie rubbed his big black hand over his nappy head and said, "All right. If that's what you want. But Sir, I mean, Ken, I ain't going to sang in no church service. Look-a-here, tell me why you want me to sang? Why not somebody else? Joe. Or him. Hey, Archie, wake up, some cat, eh, minister Ken cat be wanting me to sang in church."

"Aw, my man, don't bug me with that crap."

The minister said, "I want you because you're natural. There's too much artificial worshiping going on in the church nowaday."

Scarecrow saw Maria and Reggie come in the Lido. They glanced over at the table but went to the bar instead. Reggie looked different, younger, even more beautiful, her eyes were open and alive. Perhaps she had kicked the habit, or at least she was recovering from the withdrawal successfully. Evidently Dr. Yas knew what he was doing with his hypnosis. From the bar Maria motioned to Putsy, who got up, over Krane's protest, and went to the bar. Maria put her arm around Putsy and started talking to her.

Scarecrow's attention was drawn back to the table by the loudness and the hostility in Bennie's voice. His long finger was pointed in the minister's white face. "Man, I ain't dumb," he said.

"I been around, and I ain't getting up before a lot of square whiteys for them to say, oh, how natural that nigger sangs. How sensuous and all that junk, when I know they don't give a damn about me. They don't understand me or my songs. They don't know where my songs come from. Preacher or no preacher, you go to hell."

"No, no, my boy, I really appreciate your music," said the minister, patting Bennie's thigh.

"Baby," someone spoke to Bennie, a hand rested on his shoulder. "What are you arguing about now?"

It was a frail, timid-looking and yet rather attractive white girl. She was standing behind Bennie slightly to his left, the minister was kneeling on the right. The girl held a baby in her arms that was white-looking, except for his black curly hair.

"Sugar dumpling!" exclaimed Bennie, embracing the girl. He took the baby from her and rocked it in his arms, going *tooo, tooo, tooo,* in baby talk. To the table, Bennie said, "This be my main nigger. Eh, see there," he scolded himself. "I'm so brainwashed. I got to get all of that mark-of-oppression crap out of my system too. This is my son!" he said proudly. "And this is my wife, Maryann Bendrix."

Everyone started marveling over the baby and making the wife welcome. Bennie looked down for the preacher but he was not kneeling there any more.

"Oh, here you be," said Bennie, facing the minister, who was now standing, gaping at the baby in Bennie's arms. Holding the baby in one arm, Bennie extended his other hand, and said, "Let's be friends. No time for arguments when the family comes on the scene. But forget the sanging. Okay."

The minister had a very pale complexion. But now he had turned red as a beet. Scarecrow noticed his hand. The minister moved his hand toward Bennie's hand, but something happened and he could not raise the hand higher to meet Bennie's hand, whereas before he had not been able to keep his hand off of Bennie's thigh. The minister's reddened face began to twitch uncontrollably. His small bee-bee eyes got like marble. Out of the blue he started singing at the top of his churchlike voice:

> MINE EYES HAVE SEEN
> THE GLORY OF THE COMING
> OF THE LORD
> HIS TRUTH IS MARCHING ON!

Witnessing the one-man choir, and gazing at the redness of his face, which was in a jerking spasm like the skin of a horse twitching away flies, Scarecrow felt as though his own face was twitching like the minister's. And he was transported back in time. He was waiting for his wife outside the bank in midtown Manhattan. His daughter, Oriki, was in his arms. Two construction workers from the street, wearing those hard hats, came up to him and wanted to know what was a black nigger doing with a white baby in his arms. Several more of them gathered around and a struggle developed. "Daddy, daddy!" Oriki cried, clinging to Scarecrow. Fortunately his wife emerged from the bank in time and screamed for the police.

The minister sang two choruses. He was insane with singing, his head thrown back like Billy Graham, his mouth working like a psychopath who was no longer in control of what he was doing. Everybody, at the table as well as in the bar, was spellbound as they listened and watched with incredulous eyes. Somebody from the crowd yelled, "Lookout! He's going to throw up!"

Bennie, with the baby in his arms, jumped back just in time to keep the filth from landing on them.

"Let's get out of here," said Scarecrow to Hellos. But Hellos was already going out the door.

Outside, Scarecrow found her slumped against the railing. "That man is ruled by unspeakable evil," she whispered.

Scarecrow had had too much gin. His seasickness had gotten worse. Then there had been that mess with Martin Handson. His stomach churned, his head was spinning, his sight was fuzzy. But the preacher had lit the fire to the fuel. He wanted to explode, he could hardly stand up, and *he* felt like vomiting. "Let's go lie down," he sighed.

He put his arm around Hellos' shoulder for support. They turned and collided head-on into a man. The man's image was blurred in Scarecrow's eyes, and darkness had fallen. But Scarecrow thought he recognized the man as being Number Three.

"Sonofabitch!" Scarecrow cursed him.

"Excuse me," said Number Three. "But I've been looking for you. I saw Jim and he told me . . ."

Number Three was advancing toward Scarecrow with his hands up and out. Scarecrow's head was whirling, clear perception failed him, he was weak and he felt defenseless. But somehow his karate reflexes went into play automatically.

"Oh, Lord!" screamed Hellos.

Scarecrow heard her and checked himself. Instead of throwing Number Three overboard, he dumped him on the floor. Number Three groaned, rolled over, crawled to his feet and limped away.

"What made you do that?"

"He used to be my cabinmate. He tore up my shaving kit and smashed my medicine."

"But you were going to throw him overboard!"

"I'm confused, I'm mad, I'm tired, I'm sick."

Hellos took his feverish face in her hands and kissed him. The touch of her lips was soothing. But he could no longer stand up. "Help me to my cabin," he muttered, holding on to her now with both hands.

In the cabin he fell upon Jim's bunk, the one below his own, he did not have strength to climb up. Phil was there but he excused himself. Scarecrow felt his shoes being taken off. "Hellos is so sweet," he thought. "Perhaps . . ."

Then he heard hostile voices. Grabbing hold of the ladder running from Jim's bunk up to his own, he pulled himself up and strained to see what was going on. It was Maria. She and Hellos were arguing.

"I got something interesting to tell you black boy," said Maria.

153

"When's the last time you looked in the inside pocket of your jacket?"

Scarecrow rubbed his hands over his face. He didn't know what she was talking about. Maria got his jacket, searched in the pocket and threw something on the bunk. Scarecrow peered at it. It looked like a puzzle, yes, it was a puzzle.

"It's a photograph," said Hellos, standing beside Scarecrow, gazing at it also.

The puzzle was indeed a photograph, a torn photograph. Miraculously the pieces assembled and the picture was clear. It was his daughter's photograph. But the meaning of why it was torn was still a puzzle to Scarecrow.

"I did it," said Maria, standing back in the muscles of her legs. "Yeah me! I did it all Why do you think I asked you to shave that night when you know I don't give a damn about that sort of thing Yes I chewed up that shaving set and smashed everything in it because that fancy-talking Viking gave it to you and I ripped up that damn picture of your honkey baby you kept looking at and brooding over All of that shit was nothing but part of the glass wall that kept me from getting closer to you So I destroyed it black boy like I'm going to do anything else that keeps us from getting down with each other."

Like a wildcat Maria tore into Hellos, hitting and clawing and kicking and biting and pulling her hair. Hellos did not do much fighting back. She doubled up in a knot and tried to protect herself as best she could, kicking Maria away from time to time. Scarecrow did not do anything to stop them. He was beyond where they were. He stood there glassy-eyed. He felt his face twitching again, and he began to shake all over. The muscles in his neck were choking him, his eyes pained. Somewhere in his mind he saw himself hoisting Number Three up over his head and dumping him into the ocean. He realized now what Number Three had been trying to say to him with his hands up in the air. Had it not been for Hellos, Scarecrow would have killed the wrong man! It was then that his hands reached out and locked themselves around

154

Maria's throat. He was not trying to protect Hellos. By doubling up into a knot Hellos had done pretty well at that herself. Scarecrow was trying to blot a nameless thing out of existence.

"Scarecrow! Scarecrow!" screamed Hellos, and got between them and wrestled with them until Maria was free. Scarecrow felt heat rushing inside him at a terrific speed and he could not breathe enough of it out to keep it from suffocating him. Then he was on the floor. But no. Somehow, as though in a dream, he was trying to run. An object appeared out of nowhere and he crashed into it.

"Hey, look out, baby! What's going on here?"

But Scarecrow was on his feet again and running through the corridors, up the stairs, air! He needed fresh air. Freedom! He needed release, and he was running out on the deck. The air felt good on his face and in his lungs. He kept on running until he reached the railing, where he leaped over and his body splashed into the sea.

CHAPTER EIGHT

Saturday, September 11 (the fourth day)

41

They were in Scarecrow's cabin. Scarecrow was sitting up in one of the lower bunks, the one that Number Three used to occupy, a pillow was propped behind his back. Dr. Yas was sitting in a chair, his stethoscope hanging around his neck. A queasy feeling was in Scarecrow's stomach, his head was slightly aching. Dr. Yas had spent several hours nursing him back to consciousness, or, as Dr. Yas had phrased it, nursing him back to "life." For Scarecrow had not been unconscious in terms of fainting or anything like that. Rather, according to Dr. Yas, he had been in an acute schizophrenic state, and Dr. Yas had lectured Scarecrow at length on the nature of that state.

Despite the widespread use of the word by common people as well as by doctors, nobody knows what schizophrenia really is. Let's begin by saying it is a label placed on a person called "patient" by another person called "doctor." The patient is placed in the inferior position and the doctor is in the position of authority. Ancient people thought of what we now call schizophrenia as a spell cast on a person. The person was possessed by some supernatural power, usually of a demonic character. A person can be thrown into such a state by undergoing prolonged vexation and intense hysteria. Freud made the biggest error of the century when he said that hysteria was most peculiar to women. Men are just as susceptible to hysteria as women are, declared Dr. Yas. Hysteria stems from fear and frustration. In order to escape this fear and frustration, a part of Scarecrow had split off and "frozen." It is a survival trick that the psyche plays on its enemy—to separate that part of the self which is threatened by harm or extension from one's consciousness and pretend that it is "dead," and yet go on acting out the fear and hysteria unaware of what one is doing. Dr. Yas called this phenomenon "cataleptic schizophrenia" or "schizophrenic catatonia." One part of the self is capable of doing almost anything while the other part will be totally unaware of what the former part is doing. This, according to Dr. Yas, was the state Scarecrow had been in when he dove into the ocean. Had Scarecrow ever experienced anything like that before? No. Furthermore, he denied having been in that condition when he jumped into the ocean, asserting that he was well aware of what he was doing but that he was helpless to stop himself, as though some more powerful force had entered his body and had compelled him against his own will. Scarecrow had remembered everything, and he related it to Dr. Yas in detail, or so he thought. But when Dr. Yas explained how he had jumped into the ocean behind Scarecrow and how the Captain had been alerted that they were overboard and all about the crew rescuing them, and how Dr. Yas had convinced the Captain that Scarecrow had accidentally fallen overboard, and how Scarecrow had sat there in the ship's hospital being examined and confirming the story concocted by Dr. Yas, and how Dr. Yas had recognized that Scarecrow was in a trancelike state by the fixity of his glassy eyes and had taken him to his cabin and nursed him back to "life." When Dr. Yas related all of this to him, Scarecrow had but the faintest recollection, and he changed the subject by asking about Maria and Hellos. They were fine and had been gravely concerned about Scarecrow's attempted suicide. Hellos, however, had cried and said that she was to blame for everything. No, no. After denying that his intentions were suicidal, Scarecrow had exonerated Hellos, saying that Maria had caused it all, for it had been she who had deceived him. Upon hearing the word "deceived," Dr. Yas looked at Scarecrow intensely and made a gesture to comment. Instead, raising an eyebrow, he inquired about the sores on Scarecrow's body. When Scarecrow had explained the sores—that is, when and how suddenly they had occurred and about having gone to Bellevue Hospital and being given the milky liquid —Dr. Yas pushed back his chair and stood up, then paced the floor in a pondering mood. Then, sitting abruptly on the trunk at the foot of the bunk opposite the one in which Scarecrow was sitting, he went into a lengthy speech.

"Okay. Let's say that you were possessed last night, possessed by a demon that drove you to do what you did against your will. I can deal with that. I'm a psychiatrist and psychiatrists are historically very close to exorcists, who drive evil spirits out of people who are possessed. You dig? But where do evil spirits come from? How do they get inside people in the first place? That's the question, and I'm going to answer it. You've left New York, right. I don't know anything about your background and all that. I've read your book and it impressed me. But you can't really judge a man by the knowledge he puts in a book. Anyway, there is a big difference between knowing something and being able to live by what you know. I don't know what the deal was but I know you had a wife and baby, and you must have left a whole lot of memories and things back there too. The trouble with people, though, is that they can't seem to leave things behind psychologically! What I'm getting at is this. To be possessed is to be mad. The life of a person is made up of all the experiences he has ever had, including those he may have forgotten, along with those which may have never happened in what we call real life, such as in dreams, fantasies and other (for lack of a better word) phenomenological experiences. But even dreams and fantasies are real to the person who has had them, inasmuch as they happened in us and influence our behavior even if only the way we sleep or twitch in a certain place on the face or, say, break out with sores that can't be medically diagnosed. Ninety-nine per cent of our life stems from the relations we have with other people. And if we go mad, or insane, or become possessed, it is because other people have driven us to it. They may be people who are with us at any time or who we have known in the past. Shit, they may even be people who are dead. Whichever way it happens, madness, or possession, like murder, is a condition visited upon people by other people! Scarecrow, you're involved with two women on this ship, physically and psychologically involved in a triangle with Maria and Hellos. I don't know much about Maria, I never met her before now. I'm getting some impressions but, you know, I can't be sure, not yet. Hellos is a different matter. She is not what she seems. Wait a minute. I take that back. Hellos is precisely what she seems! Can you get to that? And if I may say so, you ought to cool it with her. I mean, dig it, baby, you need a rest. I'm making this little speech to you now, well, because I can't babysit for all of you people on this ship. I have my hands full with Reggie and Hellos. Reggie is groovy, she's co-operating. But Hellos is another matter altogether."

At that point Scarecrow broke in. "I thought you said Hellos was all right. Where is she anyway? If she was all right, she would be here now. Why isn't she here?" he quizzed Dr. Yas.

"I don't know where she is," said Dr. Yas. "I advised her to stay in her cabin but she's not there. She's disappeared again. Nobody's seen her."

Scarecrow ventured that Hellos was with her friend, the little man, the cripple she had told him about. Dr. Yas grew irate. "There's no cripple on this ship," he asserted. "Nobody's seen him. I ain't seen him. You haven't seen him. The cripple is another one of Hellos' phantasms."

Phantasms! What was Dr. Yas alluding to? What was the matter with Hellos? Dr. Yas dropped his head and mumbled that he didn't know. Scarecrow told him that he thought he was lying. All right, he admitted it, he was lying. But he was a psychiatrist, a doctor, and he would not break the professional confidence of anyone under his care. If Scarecrow wanted to know anything about Hellos he should ask Hellos. "Now, I want you to take these pills," said Dr. Yas, bringing the session to an abrupt halt. "They're barbiturates to make you rest and sleep." He went to the sink and ran water into a glass. As Dr. Yas watched, Scarecrow took the pills. But he had already made up his mind to keep awake no matter what kind of pills they were.

42

Scarecrow supposed, if the story was accurate, that he owed Dr. Yas his life, and he was grateful. He also appreciated Dr. Yas's concern and now had a greater respect for him. Dr. Yas had covered for him with the Captain and had offered to psychoanalyze Scarecrow free of charge, but Scarecrow had said he didn't think it was necessary; he really didn't favor psychoanalysis, he thought it was useful for other people but for himself he was diffident about it, almost superstitiously so. On the other hand, there was this secret business between Dr. Yas and Hellos, which irritated Scarecrow, made him curious and anxious. He was further unnerved by the fact that his trunk with his wife's bones in it seemed to draw people toward it. Maria had wanted to know what was in it, Dr. Yas had sat on it, Hellos had said she knew what was in it. Well, what was in it wouldn't be in it long. That was for certain.

After Dr. Yas left the cabin Scarecrow had climbed up into his own bunk and pretended to go to sleep. Dr. Yas had stuck his head back in the cabin, smiled, then eased the door closed again. Scarecrow took the pillows from the other bunk, Number Three's bunk, and lined them up in his bunk with the blanket over them. Then he went to Hellos' cabin.

No one answered his knock, so he tried the door. It was not locked. He went inside, it was dark in there and he felt for the switch and turned on the light. It was a railroad cabin, sort of like a dormitory, with a half-dozen bunks or so. No one was there.

Hellos is with that cripple, he thought. In spite of what Krane and Dr. Yas had said, Scarecrow still believed such a person was on board. He had to believe it. How else could Hellos' "disappearances" be explained. Standing there in the cabin he grew anxious. The bunks and other furnishings were arranged similar to the way they were in Maria's cabin. Thinking of the incident in Maria's cabin made him want to get out of there.

He switched off the light and started out but he bumped into a dresser by the door. Something fell. He turned the light back on, this time having trouble finding the switch in the dark. He knocked over something else, it sounded like glass. Yes, some pills and cough drops and a large framed photograph lay at his feet. In the photograph he recognized a very youthful-looking Hellos, standing between a big muscular man and a short plump woman. Carefully he slid the photo back into the glass frame and placed it on the dresser. He then scooped the pills and cough drops back into the jar. There was a lifesaver among them which he casually threw into his mouth. He headed back for his cabin to put on some clothes, he couldn't search for Hellos in nothing but his robe.

Near the ladies' room where he and Maria had made love, his legs began to grow weak and he leaned against the corridor wall to rest. He gasped for breath and massaged his chest with his hand. His heart was beating so forcefully that he felt as though it was going to break through the walls of his chest. He slumped to the floor. The walk from Hellos' cabin to his should have taken no more than five minutes, ten at the most. Yet he felt as if he had been traveling over a vast desert, fatigue consumed him. But he was starkly awake! Now he *had* to get out of the corridor because he heard footsteps approaching.

He struggled to his door. Leaning there, he did not have the energy to reach out and turn the knob. The word *pneumonia* leaped into his mind. He had had it when he was a child, and at the onset he remembered everything had gotten blurred and confused. But now he knew he was not coming down with pneumonia because his mind was so clear and awake that it frightened him. It was those pills Dr. Yas had given him, the sweet-sour taste in his mouth.

He opened the door and saw Hellos sitting on his trunk. She frightened the hell out of him! For a split moment she flashed on him like some kind of weird creature, sitting there with her legs dangling over the side of the trunk, her hands folded in her lap, and the broom from the closet leaning by her side.

When she saw him she jumped down. "You all right?" she asked.

Now he saw her as looking more divine than she had ever appeared before. The loveliness of her face glowed brighter than the fluorescent bulb hanging from the ceiling. The radiance and carnality of her presence flooded the room. Scarecrow wanted her. Oh, God, how he desired her! But his body, his flesh, felt completely numb. He crept to the bunk and fell upon it, the one below, Jim's bunk, he did not have energy to climb up to his own.

Hellos bent down to him. "Are you sick?" she asked. She wanted Scarecrow to forgive her. She felt terrible about last night. There was so much she had to tell him. But where had he been? And why the pillows lined up in his bunk beneath the blanket? She had been waiting for more than an hour.

An hour! What was she talking about? Scarecrow had been gone only a few minutes, and why was she yelling like that? He wanted to ask where *she* had been, but he found that he was without the strength to open his mouth.

"I'll massage you," she yelled, pulling the robe down from his shoulders. What were those sores? Scarecrow must do something about them. Hellos had cried all morning about how terrible she had been to Scarecrow. She had tried to use him and Maria. She'd lied to Scarecrow, and to Dr. Yas, and to Krane, and to herself. She'd lied to everybody all her life, she told him, because she had been afraid of everything and everyone.

Her hands on his body felt mellow. Scarecrow felt like a baby being caressed by a nymph. His flesh seemed to have been melting into jelly. Then her touch was suddenly electric, erotic, and a hundred thousand cells in his body dissolved into warm soothing liquids.

Hellos was telling him that she would not stand between him and Maria. Hellos loved Scarecrow but Maria loved him too and she had found Scarecrow first. She admitted that she despised Maria and envied her. But Maria was young and strong and black, and Hellos was old and weak and white, and she, Maria, loved Scarecrow with such desperation!

She kissed the back of Scarecrow's neck and lay upon him. He felt that every cell in his body was being activated from the sheer weight of her resting on his back, a weight as heavy as the ship itself and yet somehow as delicate as dew. Lying there with her on top of him like that, he was acutely aware of every curve, crevice and muscle in her body. He felt the heavy softness of her breasts pressing down on the bones and veins of his flesh; he could smell the scents from every pore and organ in her body; and his sex rose up hard like steel, more intense and powerful than he had ever experienced in his life. He rolled over, pulling free of the robe, and took her in his arms and pressed her to his nakedness.

"Don't hurt me!" she shouted.

"Take . . . clothes . . . off," he said, shocked at the incoherence in his speech.

She broke away from him, stood up and saw his black nakedness like that. Her face turned to a mask of vomit. She wheeled around, shielding her eyes from the sight of him with her hands. Scarecrow got up and grabbed the back of the neck of her blouse and ripped it off. He was in agony to feel her breasts in his hands. He yearned, and pained, to press them against his face and to feel them all over his body.

"Don't touch me!" she screamed, still shielding her eyes and kicking backwards at Scarecrow. "You can't touch me. I've thought of you as my father." She was standing in one corner of the cabin with her face to the wall.

Scarecrow said, "Father . . . not . . . color . . . bald . . . mustache." He had tried to say, "Don't hand me that father shit.

164

I'm not old enough, I'm the wrong color, I'm not baldheaded and I have a mustache." Then he noticed that a glass on top of the closet was about to tilt over and strike Hellos on the head. "Look . . . glass!" He pointed.

She looked up and moved just in time. The glass fell and shattered on the floor, barely missing her.

Scarecrow heard Phil coming through the corridor, he recognized the sound of Phil's effeminate walk. He stepped into his trousers and threw the robe around Hellos, for she was bareshouldered and still facing the wall. Phil came in, mumbling pardons, asked how Scarecrow was doing, got his overcoat, said he and Jim were spending the night on deck, noticed the broken glass, gave Hellos and Scarecrow another quick glance, then left.

Hellos turned around and faced Scarecrow. She extended both hands out, and said, "Stay back! That glass didn't look like it was going to fall, but it fell, and you saw it falling before it fell! My hearing is excellent but you heard that fellow coming and I didn't. The way you're talking too? How did you know my father was baldheaded?"

"Photo . . . loose."

"Photo? You been in my room," she yelled, much louder than ever before. "That photograph! Did you take anything out of it?"

"What are you going on like this for?" said Scarecrow, and looked around, startled at the sudden return of clarity in his speech.

"Listen," whispered Hellos, mysteriously. "Do you hear anything?"

He heard the jukebox playing in the Dom, the noise from the Lido, the engine of the ship, a baby crying . . .

"The light. Look at it."

Scarecrow looked up and could not stand the light. In fact, he had been plagued all the time by the flood of light rays, not only from the bulb overhead but from everything in the room, spectrums of color bouncing off the walls and chairs, the washbasin, and even from Hellos' clothes.

"You took something from my cabin," she said. "THINK!"

"A lifesaver, a stale one at that," said Scarecrow, smacking his lips, for the taste of it was still in his mouth. Right! That's where the taste had come from and not the pills Dr. Yas had given him.

Hellos slumped into a chair, folded her hands in her lap, sighed. Then said, "You are under the influence of—" She stopped, looked up at Scarecrow, and started anew, "I don't know how to tell you this but I know I must. Listen carefully. You are hearing and feeling and seeing things, all out of proportion to ordinary. You must not have had LSD before. That's what that stale piece of candy was, a sugar cube of lysergic acid."

She paused, drew a deep breath, and said, "Now you must be calm because you are going on a trip. You have been on it ever since you stumbled into this cabin. But it ain't really started yet."

From somewhere in the ship Scarecrow distinctively heard the sound of the flushing of a toilet.

43

But if the thing wasn't a lifesaver, why did it have a *hole* in the center of it!

The hole had been put there deliberately to throw anyone off who might have discovered it. Hellos had not considered that someone might eat it. It was hidden in back of the photograph and would have been safe if Scarecrow hadn't knocked it off the dresser. The one Scarecrow ate was the last she had. She was done with that stuff now, thanks to Dr. Yas, and was going to throw it away, but she just hadn't gotten around to it.

"What's Dr. Yas going to say when he finds out I lied about that too?" she said to herself. But didn't Scarecrow think it was odd for one lifesaver to be among all those pills? Just *one!* She started for the door but Scarecrow stepped in front of her. He did not think he was Superman but he was Scarecrow! Hellos was not going to get away. She needn't worry about the LSD. He was not going to turn into a raving maniac. He was going to make love to her.

Hellos' eyes grew large. Scarecrow didn't know what he was saying. That was one of the effects of the drug, to make a person think he could do anything. Scarecrow could actually hurt himself and Hellos and he wouldn't even realize it. A shrillness was in her voice that had never been there before. "Listen to me," she intoned. "Anybody who takes LSD for the first time needs a guide. I'm not strong enough and I don't really know you. You've got to let me go get Dr. Yas."

Scarecrow detected that she was afraid and was trying to hide it, and that appealed to him. He reached and touched her hair. He let his fingers play with her nose and cheeks and her lips, which were wet and slippery. He took the robe from around her and sent his hands over the top portions of her body, which was bare. He felt and squeezed her naked breasts. Sinking to his knees, he threw both arms around her hips and pressed his face into the softness of her crotch. He began to cry, fitfully. He didn't know why but he could not help it. With his face pressed to her belly like that, he became aware of a pulsing from within her sounding in his ear.

No! Don't! She pushed him and he landed against the closet. Standing in a half crouch, like a frightened animal, she gaped down at him. Seeing her like that, it dawned on Scarecrow that Hellos had a fear of sex! A fear so unreasonable that it had made her frigid. He *had* to have her now. He had to liberate her from the nameless spell that had been put on her, for although her body was sexy she was not sexual. Such a sensuous body with no feelings!

Playing it cool now, he got to his feet and apologized. "I'm sorry," he said, "I didn't mean to be rough."

Hellos was sorry also. She shouldn't have lost her head. But that was what she had been trying to tell him. She was not strong. Shifting the weight of her body, she stared straight into his eyes and said, "You listen to me now and listen carefully. I'm going to walk out of here and get Dr. Yas and you're going to stay in this room until we get back. It might seem like hours to you but I'll be gone for just a little while. Remember that. Just a little while! I'm taking the key so we can get back in. You might not recognize what it is when we knock or call to you. Don't say a word! Sit down and be still."

Somehow Scarecrow understood without knowing precisely what he had understood. While Hellos had been instructing him she had been waving her bag very slowly in a circular motion in front of his face, and for the first time Scarecrow perceived that there was something about her which was more than a spell, something far more uncanny, something not of this world. It was this nameless something which had so lured Scarecrow to her in the first place. He had been wrong. Hellos was not scared of him; she knew him, her gaze was riveted to his face, and he could not meet her stare because he had glimpsed that the blue was running wild in the roots of her eyes. Eyes which were not only Hellos' eyes but the eyes of generations and generations of other similar women who had preceded Hellos in many lives that had gone by and who were her spirit relatives. Scarecrow did not know who the women were, he could not summon their names, but he knew the places where they had lived out their fates, England, Ireland, France, Salem. So when she told him what to do, he had obeyed because it was Scarecrow who feared Hellos.

44

Alone in the cabin her absence haunted him. He was filled with utter loss, a loss so deep and total that it was as though he and Hellos had known one another intimately down through the centuries. Who they were, Holy Nuns of Satan, cloaked in shawls, crept at sun's hourglass to that Calvary where Whose wretched effigy primordial darker assemblage stood in fear's primeval stead, and pressed to parched lips the red wines of their urine, as wind and drought and sand and thorns picked and thrashed Whose flesh to rags! Despair consumed him. He dissolved into sorrow. He felt his face expanding so that now it saturated the cabin. But he no longer remembered what his sorrow was about.

So many years had dragged by. He wept like an infant, because he longed to be delivered from the burden of time.

Suddenly he found himself vomiting in the washbasin. The dregs of his stomach were insects and maggots. He turned on the faucet, the water roared forth as if from a turbulent waterfall, and he was trembling with fear, because he was drowning! At first he was fighting. He was a good swimmer but no one can swim the ocean. He yelled and the salty water rushed into his mouth. He spat it out and kept on fighting. But now his legs and arms were getting tired and heavier to move. His lungs were bursting. The currents were casting him back and forth and lashing his flesh with their icy tongues. *Help!* he cried. But no more, for now the water was taking him. The water entered his lungs, his belly, his intestines, his bloodstream, and he felt it bursting into his brain and pressing against the walls of his heart. Consciousness surrendered him. But he was not dead yet. He felt a cell burst in his brain, his lungs exploded, his eardrums collapsed, and the walls of his heart gave way like the walls of a dam before the onslaught of an unconquerable flood. The water animals, fish, sharks, snakes, octopuses, tore his limbs asunder and scattered his entrails in a galaxy of directions, where days later the undercurrents of the waters buoyed up his remains on the surface of the ocean, and the carrion birds swarmed in the air overhead.

Death by water! He put on a lifejacket and crouched in one corner of the room. He shook uncontrollably. His fear grew stronger. His teeth dropped out. His eyes turned into huge bubbles of slime. His tongue was on fire. Inside his body, in his lungs, kidney, liver, in his veins and muscles and tendons, in his stomach, loins, bladder, flames were burning him up! Oh, Jesus, his *heart* was on fire! His heart, his heart, why was it taking so long to go from one beat to the next beat? BOOM! He grabbed his chest. His heart was going to kill him, if not from giving out on the way then surely from the terrible thrust of its bursting labor. *Help me, God, help me, somebody! Help me, grandmomma! I do not want to die, I can't die, not now, not here, not this way, I want to see*

*my daughter again. Help me, Hellos, Maria, anybody! P-l-e-a-s-e,
don't let me die . . .*

Now his eyes revolved like targets in a shooting gallery. The
room was spinning, spinning, spinning, objects: beds, closets,
doors, broken glass, the floor, the ceiling, the porthole, the trunk,
spinning, hundreds of objects, spinning, fusing, revolving, spinning, the washbasin, how many washbasins, and a million mirrors, faster, faster, faster, the MIRROR! above the washbasin,
if he could get to it he could escape GO AWAY DON'T
BOTHER ME! He started crawling, but which way? There were
so many mirrors, so many washbasins, a thousand beds, ten thousand chairs, a million merging fusing trunks! He feared his psyche
would explode and the words, thoughts, would scatter there on
the revolving floor like numberless pieces of shattered glass; and
now his stomach was cramping, his entrails were being sucked
away by the force of spinning and pulling and ejection. Yes, ejection! Everything was being ejected out of him. He folded his arms
around his stomach and doubled up there on the spinning floor.
Then it got worse, the cramps, the pains, the gasping for breath,
and his brain, his brain, the heat in his head, the millions of
thoughts, images, symbols, machines, wild, images, mother, sen-
tence, words, cats, wind, structure, fox, mailbox, jungle, milk
washing bag lemon Hellos faces, doll civilization, Maria, rejection
slip, lift line phrase, mouth blood semicolon, drunk civilization
masks, birds sound onion trains yield witches, rocket child park-
benchBessieSmithlovelightscolorssignalsimagessensespatternsproc-
essesfasterstarintensityfasterintensitydensitywheel/OH/OH/
STOP/CAN'T/STAND/MORE! He reached out blindly and
grabbed the first thing that came through his psyche. Luck was
with him, it was the washbasin. He pulled himself up and looked
into the mirror. That was when he discovered that he was inside
somebody else's body.

Two fangs of barbed wire hung in each corner of his mouth.
His mustache was of muskrat fur. He had four eyes. His head was
bald. Three stalks of corn grew out of his skull. He had no nose,

and across his face his name was written in blood. Goblins were perched on each of his shoulders, but they had the faces of screaming gargoyles. The one on his right shoulder had the face of Maria, and the one on his left had the face of Hellos. In the mirror he saw over his shoulder, over the heads of the goblins, the lid of his trunk open and the nude body of his wife rose up, singing: DHEM BONES! DHEM BONES! DHEM BONES GONNA RISE AGAIN! He screamed and banged his fist against the mirror.

The mirror did not break. But the face he saw in it had turned into the face of a rag doll. *Rita!* He yelled his sister's name but the doll did not respond. He leaned his head against the mirror and moaned. Through his moaning he heard a voice call. It was his grandmother's voice. He looked up and saw in the mirror that his black face was beautiful, and he began to weep and laugh at the same time. On and on he cried and laughed. A great rush of optimism swept over him. He was a great poet and one of the greatest novelists in the world. He possessed everything he had ever wanted, including the very goodness of God. The next thing he realized was that he was standing on deck gazing up at the stars.

45

The moon was in its place, the stars were dancing, the planets were fixed in their orbits. Far out beyond the planets, beyond the stars, beyond the last signposts of light, sound and motion, stretched the domain of endless dark where time was still and stillness was the only reality. But the stars made him know what humility was. Eons ago fires had blazed in the universe. Now, a million years hence, when the fires themselves had long since turned to ash, their sparks populated the heavens and shimmered in the night like clusters of virgin jewels. Scarecrow realized how small a fraction of the cosmos he really was. How foolish and ungrateful he had been to complain about the burden of time, when the duration of his burden was more brief than a drop of rain in the sea. He was accosted by the immediacy of his singularity. There was no time for fretting and complaining. Live while the sun is shining, for we are here today and gone tomorrow. That's what his grandmother always said. He headed for the Dom.

It must have been past midnight, the Dom would be closing at three. The doorkeeper, a big Negro who pimped for white women, recognized Scarecrow and let him squeeze inside without paying the door charge, which was a courtesy he received for being a notorious black poet on the Lower East Side. As always, but especially on Saturday nights, an orgy was going on. The Dom had originally been an old Polish meeting hall, back during the days when the Poles first immigrated to New York. It was a huge building in the center of the block on East Eighth Street between Third and Second Avenues, on the Lower East Side of Manhattan. Six months ago, Stanley Tolkins, who was a good man and who already owned two neighborhood bars that catered to artists, writers, poets, and far-flung scene mongers, purchased the Dom and renovated it into a discothèque. Now Stanley had to turn the crowds away.

He pushed his way through the mob, looking, as best he could in the crowd, for some of his friends, for David Henderson or Ishmael Reed perhaps. He saw no one. Then he realized that he was not in the Dom on the Lower East Side but in the "Dom" aboard the *Castel Felice!* What was he doing there? Everything seemed unreal. But now he realized that unreality was the most real of all reality. He thought to catch a girl and dance, but he could not dance and he discovered that he had fallen down. Lying on the floor an urgency for nudity swept over him. He started to pull off his clothes but was unable to hold still long enough to unbutton a button or even loosen his belt. Some girls helped him to his feet and he tumbled into their midst. He kissed one and then the other. He felt the wonder of their presence and his hands were full of the strangeness of their bodies. He wanted to make love to them, *both* of them, he yearned to spend a lifetime with them, sharing the processes and functions of their carnality. He ran his hands up the front of their miniskirts and felt the hairy diamond nestling in the fork of their jewels. A man stuck his head in their huddle and said, "There is a time and place for everything."

The man's head was on upside down but Scarecrow recognized him, Reverend Kenneth McIntoch, he smiled that greasy smile. The preacher pushed one of the girls aside and threw his arm around Scarecrow. "I hope you don't have any hard feelings because of the little incident yesterday," said the Reverend.

"I don't want you puking on me," Scarecrow told him.

"We've got to love one another," spoke the preacher out of the top of his head.

"Your goddamn face is on upside down."

"That's because I'm a messenger of The Lord."

"You're a fascist freak!"

"Let's not call each other names."

"You're the perpetual reincarnation of universal evil!" shouted Scarecrow.

The minister turned sideways and said to somebody, "See. What'd I tell you. The nigger's dynamite."

(A WOMAN, *blond, thin features, good-looking, pink dress, neat figure.*)

THE REVEREND

(*Introducing the woman to Scarecrow*) This is Miz Snow White.

SNOW WHITE

(*Extending limp feminine hand*) Kenny's been talken boutche so muuch. Says yall's rite mean but I don't blieve him. Yall's not mean, is yall?

SCARECROW

You're from the South.

SNOW WHITE

(*Drooling*) Yhas. Bone and reared in dear Ole Dixie!

SCARECROW

You're not prejudiced, are you! You believe that Nigras are people same as whites. There's good and bad in both races. Nigras should have their civil rights. But they should be educated first.

You don't know about eating together, though. That might lead to abusive vomiting between the races. Then there are the chillun to think about. You've the highest esteem for Martin Luther King Junior as a dead leader of the Nigra race. Your favorite novel is *Gone With the Mothersucking Wind*.

SNOW WHITE

(*Blushing, leaning toward Scarecrow*) My lands! How did yall know!

THE REVEREND

(*Leering, grinning, unctuous, lecherous*)

SCARECROW

Fuck *how* I know. Just be comforted *that* I know.

THE REVEREND

(*Ejaculatingly!*) I told you. This one's mean, black, bitter, militant, and revolutionary, but intelligent!

SCARECROW

Mister Messenger of The Lord, you've pimped things up just fine. Now why don't you stuff your tongue back into your head and hat up! (*Wheeling him around and kicking him in the rump*)

THE REVEREND

(*Landing on all fours, but rising, arms extended up toward heaven, singing out of the top of his head*) We Shall Overcome! Right on! We Shall Overcome! Right on! S-o-m-e-d-a-a-y!

SNOW WHITE

(*Admiringly*) Land's sake! Yall sure do make life exciting.

SCARECROW

(*Clutching Snow White in the crotch of her pink cotton dress, jerking her forward*) Come on!

SNOW WHITE

But I wants to dance with yall. I wants to dance! When I Was In Dixie! (*Throwing her arms up in the air, stretching her frame, prancing, jumping up and down with no rhythm at all!*)

SCARECROW

I play basketball and swim a little. But I can't dance or sing. (*Jerking her, forcefully*) Now come on, ho!

174

SNOW WHITE

But yall can't. I got on the rag. Honest to God. Li'l ole me is dripping wet. Can't yall feel it!

SCARECROW

The bloodier it is the better it is. (*Reaching under her dress, pulling the Kotex, with the image of J.C. on the cross on it, from between her legs, blood dripping on the floor, flinging it over the heads of the crowd*)

THE CROWD

(*Dancing, singing,* IN THE MANNER OF SEVEN DWARFS, *throwing the Kotex from one to the other, festive! Dancing! Singing!*) The Bloodier . . . The Better . . . The Bloodier . . . The Better!

SNOW WHITE

(*Standing wide-legged, free! Radiant! Blood splashing to the floor*) Yall sure don't have none of them inheebitchions, do yall!

THE CROWD

(IN THE MANNER OF SEVEN DWARFS, *dancing, singing, festive, eating pieces of the Kotex*) I Am The ResErection . . . I Am The Life . . . The Bloodier . . . The Better!

THE REVEREND

(*Fighting his way through the crowd, clutching Snow White by her neck*) Anything but this! Not when the blood is flowing! It's too much! I cannot stand for it! Sin! Sin! Sin! Sin! (*He drags Snow White away and he and she go into a huddle, whispering, nodding to each other, pointing, plotting.*)

Scarecrow said, "All right. Let's play a game. Let's play scarecrow figure of time!"

"Who's that?" she asked.

Outside he shoved her in front of him. "Walk four or five steps ahead of me, ho!"

"But why," she cackled, "my lands, I do blieve yall's scared t'death a me. We ain't down home now. We're in New Yoke! Anyhow, I ain't shame t'walk sides yall. I ain't prejewdish. I been with two black bucks down home who work for Daddy, he, he."

A few feet from David's apartment Scarecrow got a glimpse of Maria and Simon, walking hurriedly in Scarecrow's direction. Damn her. So she had told Simon about them after all. Simon's face was white as cotton, his long nose was red as fire; he was going to put Scarecrow through King Alfred's solution! Scarecrow stood erect like a piece of architecture on the sidewalk, pretending to be the Smithsonian Institute. Maria and Simon rushed on by, their mouths full of Scarecrow's name.

"This is the ladies' room," observed Snow White, looking around. "Won't it be dangerous in here?"

"This is the shit room," Scarecrow corrected her. "All shit should take place in the shit room. How do you like mirrors?"

She threw herself against Scarecrow, shivering. "I'm scared t'death."

"Get off of me, ho!" Scarecrow pushed her away and ordered her to strip.

"I just mightn't do that," she said, glaring at him, prancing, flexing her figure in the pink dress. "Why don't yall strip me? Yall's big and black and revolutionairy."

Sadness fell upon Scarecrow. He wanted to wave his hand, to scream, to give his life to make the world all right. But it was far too late. The world would never be all right. WAPP! he hit her. "If you don't do what I tell you I'll kill your daddysucking ass!"

Snow White turned red as her menstrual blood had been. She undressed. Her body was lean and well-proportioned. She came to Scarecrow crying. He was sitting on the ironing table, pensive and alone.

"I'm ready," she choked. "But ain't yall gon take off your clothes too?"

"Who are you?" said Scarecrow. "What do you want with me? Leave me alone, go away!"

"But! I thought! Saaay, what is this?"

"All right, a game! Go over there and let your bowels move."
"What!"

"And don't flush it."

176

"But I can't. I ain't got to. I swear!"

WHAPP! He knocked her to the floor.

Hours passed. The sounds she emitted came into his ears as if they were in a doomed world. Every grunt, groan, every sigh of agony, comfort or discomfort. The sound of her whimpering rose and fell, sometimes bursting into spasms of violent sobs. When she emerged she was a frail and sickly-looking thing. She climbed upon the ironing table and laid down in back of Scarecrow.

Looking over his shoulder at her lying there like that, he wanted to take her and shake her until she *realized*. He jumped down and turned on the showers, all four of them, but not full-blast. The sound of the water was the sound of spring rain splashing on the trash-littered pavement of every ghetto in America. He went back and gazed down at her lying there like that trembling. His heart grew heavy, as though there were a dead body buried inside of his body. He rocked back and forth to get a sense of his own existence. When he spoke his voice sounded like the voice of a ghost, the voice of a dead man whose mouth was stuffed with rotten rags.

"I have always wanted a sister. There must be a reason, think of a reason, any reason. When I was a boy down in Tennessee I wanted a sister so badly that I used to study my mother's belly when she was not noticing. She never got pregnant. But I got me a sister anyway. I named her Rita. Everywhere I went I took Rita with me. Do you understand what I'm saying! I loved Rita more than anything in the world. The world was full of loneliness and deception! Then a redneck cracker boy raped my sister. Not in the vagina, not with his penis, no! He mutilated her from behind with a goddamn stick and she died."

Snow White jerked around. "What you gon do t' me! You're mad! Lemme outa here!" she screamed.

WHAPP! He knocked her off the ironing table onto the floor. Her pale flesh screeched as she landed on and slid over the green bathroom tile. Steam from the showers had begun to vaporize in there. Sweat oozed from under Snow White's armpits and it ran down her body, which was getting sticky and slimy. Breathing, Scarecrow was aware of the warm mist entering and leaving his lungs.

He said, "I used to have an uncle named Beechum who was on television, he made commercials, soap, toothpaste, cleansers, deodorants, and products like that. He did an act in his commercials, that's why they let him stay on television as long as they did. He used to take a tube of toothpaste or soap, or whatever it was, and he would scrub this huge monument. Sometimes it would be one of those monuments in Washington, D.C. Other times it would be somebody's grave statue, one of America's national heroes. And he would wash it with the product and the monument would get white as snow. Just like that! Then a voice would say: USE SUNSHINE BRIGHT AND KEEP AMERICA SPRIGHT! Nobody knew that the man was Uncle Beechum, because he always wore a full-size suit of whatever product he was advertising. But one time he got carried away in his act and over-did it. The suit ripped apart, right on television in millions of white people's homes. That same night a mob gathered outside the television station. They ripped Uncle Beechum to threads. Then they made a fire, roasted his body and ate it."

Snow White looked up at Scarecrow with what he thought was a start of recognition, blood leaped in the veins of her eyes. "LIAR!" she screamed, and fell prostrate on the floor, which was now covered with evaporating steam.

He yanked her up by the hair. "Can't you get anything through that thick skull of yours!" he said. "I told you about my sister. What do I have to do? Draw pictures! I never had a sister! I told you plain as day that my mother never got pregnant."

"Well, who did that boy do that to? Why would anybody want to eat your uncle? You're making all of this up. You're crazy, mad!" she moaned.

Scarecrow dragged her over the floor to the mirror. He picked up her panties and wiped some of the mist away. The nylon screeched on the glass like her flesh had screeched when he dragged her over there. He shoved her before the mirror. She looked. Her face stiffened like a piece of granite. Looking over her shoulder into the mirror, Scarecrow saw himself grab her, wheel her around and bulldoze her over to the toilet enclosure, the one that she had used. She put on brakes. "Naw! Please! Anything. But please!"

Although he was moving at breakneck speed, something inside him was standing still. A *presence!* Somebody was looking on, a *third* person, watching! He had to move faster. He forced Snow White to her knees before the toilet bowl. She closed her eyes and shook her head. Her little hands were balled into tight fists and she held them in the air. Her body shook like an epileptic. Scarecrow whacked her across the head, just enough to sting her. He tightened his grip around her neck and forced her head into the bowl, but not all the way down.

"Open your eyes and face it, or I'll choke you to death!" he threatened her.

She looked into the bowl. "N-I-G-G-U-U-R!"

Her body went limp. Scarecrow fell back against the side of the stall, his body was wringing wet. He staggered out of the ladies' room and leaned against the corridor wall. All his labor had been for nothing! He rubbed his face in his hands. He strained his brain trying to connect anything with anything.

CONSOLIDATED EDISON
MEN AT WORK

The sign on the door of the ladies' room made him remember that he had forgotten to pay his utility bill before leaving New York. He would pay the hardhat workmen now. He searched in his pockets for some money, but then he spied them coming to get him. Krane and Putsy, Dr. Yas and Kerstine Wentworth, Maria and her husband Simon, and Rex Temple with a barrel of scotch in his hand. But not Hellos. What had they done with Hellos! No

179

time to worry about her now, though. He flattened himself against the corridor wall. He had to run, escape! But where? how?

I PROPOSE A TOAST TO THE AFRICAN
BULL WHO PISSED IN THE RIVER THAMES
SHIT ON THE GREEN GRASS OF RUSSIA
WIPED HIS ASS ON THE AMERICAN FLAG
JUMPED OVER THE GREAT WALL OF CHINA
AND HAULED ASS BACK TO AFRICA

He slipped back into the ladies' room and started running in there. Running, a thousand legs and feet, ten thousand fingers and toes. Yet time was moving faster than he, so that he was actually going backwards, backwards, backwards. Time eclipsed him! Spiders, roaches, fleas, two-headed dogs, cats with lizard bodies, fish walking on hoofs, mean-eyed babies eating salamanders, witches and warlocks fornicating with pigs, and screaming lambs puking out vaginas and laughing fetuses. He had just been born. Old black sisters with aprons covering their loins, Lawd, child, born with a veil over his face, gonna see varmint and belong to the haunted.

I AM THE MAN YOU THINK YOU ARE
WHAT YOU SEEK TO DO TO ME
I WILL DO TO YOU
ONLY MORE OF IT

Then joy folded him in her bosom, ecstasy saturated his soul and he was floating through layers and layers of jelly tissue which opened up and sucked him down into the processes of his own organs. Soft swamp of elemental bliss. He knew everything and he knew nothing. He felt everything and he felt nothing. He dissolved. He. Innocent. Unborn.

REGGIE

(*Standing in doorway of ladies' room, motioning to Dr. Yas and the rest, but IN THE MANNER OF SNOW WHITE*) Here! Quick. In here.

MARIA

(*Entering*) Oh my poor sweetie!

KRANE

(*Pointing*) Dig that position he's in.

HELLOS

(*But IN THE MANNER OF SIMON, MARIA'S HUS-BAND*) Ooooh! . . .

DR. YAS

(*Rushing in*) Great! We found him. How long has he been in here, Reggie?

REGGIE

(*Still IN THE MANNER OF SNOW WHITE*) Thirty minutes at least. I found him in the Dom arguing with that preacher. I tried to calm him down but he broke away and ran down here. So I followed him. He's been going through changes, screaming and crying and carrying on about Snow White or somebody. I turned on the shower so people wouldn't hear all the racket and put that 'Out Of Order, Men Working' sign on the door to keep people out of here. He scared shit out of me with all that Snow White business. Glad you got here.

REX TEMPLE

(*Ten-gallon barrel of scotch in hand*) I'm an old fogey when it comes to these avant-garde psychedelics, but I'd say he was sloppy drunk if he wasn't doubled-up there like a fetus.

MARIA

Well don't stand here peering at him Do something! (*Then to Hellos*) You did this bitch leaving that drug lying around like candy It's all your fault.

HELLOS

(*Still IN THE MANNER OF SIMON*) I'm sorry. I'm sorry. I'm sorry.

MARIA

(*Going over, approaching Scarecrow*)

DR. YAS

No, Maria. Don't touch him. Wait. (*Bending down, steth-*

181

oscope, examining pulse, heartbeat, etc.) He's all right. But he must have leaped into total regression.

KRANE

(*With childlike wonder*) He's in the womb again. Wonder how it feels?

MARIA

That's horrible.

HELLOS

(*IN THE MANNER OF SIMON*) I'm to blame. Ooooh! . . . (*EXIT: runs out, hysterical*)

DR. YAS

(*To Kerstine*) Go see after her. (*Then*) He must be in the Fourth Level, and he'll be getting into the Fifth Level soon. Better move him to my cabin. It's safe there. Rex, see if the coast is clear. Maria, get his clothes and turn off the shower. Krane, get him over there. I'll take this side. Easy now.

Violence! Momma, baby needs some lov-ing. Of lies pledge a flag ellation One Nayshun divisible, milk, breast Momma (1) baby twelves years Under God. Eat me lots of salt sword into your body I could have been what they wanted Love me. After all could have been born dead but I was born a man! Dig it, If I ride this underground railroad fifty thousand dollar morgage on your navel cord Momma, please. Fed me from the breast of Dhe Nayshunal AssOateshun For Dhem Colord Peeple gemme some pepper could have been *what?* There goes our e bon y fag i zine Neero cesspools of history SUICIDE stockdale junebug mule head billy slaton street nineth street smoldering pretty Juanita injecting poison Miss Ann Meri Moloch Ca! from slime we live in to slime they live in Milk! Praises be to Massa less we go laboring in de same old ligion liquor jes a-closer walk wit dhee for no thing delusions vicarious sleep in a hollow log. Momma I needs some love-in now Maria you Ma real Momma Black loving good pussy W oman, a split le vel X is tense monkey suit strait-jacket round the back and above the arse perched amongst plastic figurines indigesting dogshit Department of Defense Offense dispatch

182

Civilization. Violence! Sociologists report suffocating womb suck suck release my throbbing heart NOW, oh, please let me out Maria, I don't want to be born dead Hellos!

DR. YAS

(*Fat body struggling, breathing heavily out of the nostril*) Open the door, Rex. Over there, on the bunk.

KRANE

Phew! He's heavy. Somebody give me a cigarette.

MARIA

Is he going to be all right?

DR. YAS

He's having hallucinations and memory fantasies. If things get too rough it might be better to put him to sleep.

MARIA

He's already asleep.

DR. YAS

I mean, Maria, I might have to give him an injection, deactivate his brain impulses.

Dispatch Civilization. What am I doing here? Eager minds. Lawyer, preacher, long slick lemon queen sucking genitals of butchers, liars. moved. drunken wretch gutter wallowing dark night HOW SHALL I SEND THEE human being curled out undead puking rotten slime decay summer winter nothing to salvage. What am I doing? Defenders Truth, Harriet, Fred the Lion, Dubois C L R and X X X still more NIGGURS RUN AMUK PERPETRATING CRIMES AGAINST *PROPERTY!* Generations chulluns donchu git weary! Moved: Korea, Viet Nam, Nigeria, the Congo, Trinidadd, maan! makebelieve dip low mates sin a tors moved: poor sit ions of a point ment and colord mens of bus I ness, parents of parents progenitors of progenitors, chullums floating in alleyways of folkways—dispatch TROOPS JETS TANKS GUNBOATS NEW YORK BOSTON DETROIT WASHINGTON DEE SEE niggurs run amuk perpetrating crimes against PROPERTY! Sociologists reports HAIL TO DOCTOR SKINNER FOR HE'S A WINNER dispatch the wine the pluck, baby! clawing at jagged tongues pants leg slit, NAME written on gangreen thigh. Dispatch: this is DownTown BOWERY UpTown walk beef markets vaginas beggards peeless penises in cunt less Advertisenues—HARLEM, miss ass sip pee, Jack Johnson *vs* the power structure, help me! Miss you great after the fall, guilt, Johanna! Coltrane Elvin Jones Spots of Five REMEMBER REMEMBER Johanna! suckercess mad schizophrenic spade stand, bright eyed tourists feed on corpses turned muck for maggots, my child, my Oriki, I love you I miss you but I am lost! Take it back Joe Louis knockout Tojo jap save America brown bombers *vs* yellow peril for missa charline give you a metal made of rope, boy! Jughead I something need you love makes me weep.

DR. YAS

(*Extending his long arms, gathering the others and directing them toward the door*) I think everybody should split now. Too many people might be too much for him to handle. Not you, Maria. Stay. He might need you. (*ALL EXIT, EXCEPT DR. YAS AND MARIA*)

MARIA

Dr. Yas look! He's got your stethoscope.

DR. YAS

Don't go near him. He don't know you from nothing. We're just atoms to him.

MARIA

(*Ducking*) He's smashing the mirror! and he's got your cigarette lighter He's setting fire to the bed Dr. Yas!

DR. YAS

Don't interfere. Maria! Do as I say. Get some water quick. (*MARIA COMES WITH WATER IN REX'S EMPTY SCOTCH BARREL AND DR. YAS PUTS OUT FIRE. Then*) I'd better give him the injection now. Hold his arm, Maria.

MARIA

(*Trembling, holding arm*) Oh sweetie don't hurt yourself over some no-good dope It ain't worth it S-w-e-e-t-e-e. (*Weeping*) Dr. Yas he's collapsed He may be d-e-a-d.

Psycho Ana List Report. Sick laying hands on sick heal my wounds mad trying to cure mad promoting mad sanctioning mad devolving mad. Trapped now here and trapped there everywhere in wellsfargoland set upon by rats and roaches at the house of birth before and after ambushed between definitional montanas between no place and some place everywhere within and without the gate Civilization will three veiled sisters Dispatch! Motherrages auditioning main characters horror Capitol empire blowjob ing state the bomb. People of the planet Earth, disunite! Looking for the class struggle in all the dry ice middle ass dike nigger honkey pussies of the known world! strident sons sleep with doorknobs between their deoderized rumpy di dumps, yaas, yaas. Blackjacks lurking in alleyways of the mores. Look! Up in the sky. It's a scarecrow. No hell it ain't neighbor. It's the son of liberation coming out of the first nation nal with a roll of green in his fist, estranged from *what* reality? Every man's gotta suck some filthy prick, theologians black and white report in different language but it's the same shit. I ain't got to suck nothing! Dhis Nigger Will Run Amuk First! I don't say Furst, I said First! departing mirrors departing: listen to the don of the wolf ticket of black noise! by any means whatever! Go on shot me, shot me, shot me, Nietzsche is dead: this dope is killing me: KILLING me.

DR. YAS

(*Sighing, putting hypo needle back into black bag, standing, looking on*) The cat's having phenomenological nightmares of a profound genealogical nature. But he's cool. (*Getting his jacket*) He'll be tripping out for fifteen hours or so. Can you stay with him? Good, that's hip. I'm going to Kerstine's cabin. Be there all night. Check by first thing in the morning. Dig it, don't let anybody in, understand, nobody! Later.

MARIA

Dr. Yas Ah well I take back all those ungroovy things I said about you.

DR. YAS

Haw, haw!

CHAPTER NINE

Sunday, September 12 (the fifth day)

46

organic drama molecular memory
silvaticus

. . . Scarecrow lay now upon the red-hot anvil of infrastructural time. An image danced in the museum of his genes; it was a little boy, only Scarecrow himself was that little boy.

YOUR DADDY IS THE SANTA AND YOUR MOMMA IS THE CLAUS. PUT THEM TOGETHER AND THEY MAKE SANTA CLAUS.

IN HEAVEN THE STREETS ARE PAVED WITH GOLD, ANGELS FLY IN THE SKY AND BABIES LIE IN THE FOREST CRYING FOR THEIR MOTHERS.

The little boy stole forth into the black night, asking himself why people deceived him.

ONCE UPON A TIME THERE WAS NOBODY IN THE WORLD EXCEPT GOD.

Then he realized that he himself had been first forced and then fooled into becoming a part of his own deception, and he descended willy-nilly into the forgotten bowels of atavism, and through the protean fluids of ancestral blood he discerned the figure of another little boy, and he was also this little boy; more-

187

over, he was every little boy and every little boy knew who he was and to whom he belonged and ran naked through Bush, and he was furthermore every man and every woman in full knowledge of who they were, and they all lived in Bush and beat Drum and sang Song and danced Dance, who were all gods who spoke Word and Word was Oracle of all Gods in the land of First Creatures in which Black gods dwelt not in blue horizons but in black bodies of Water Mama and Earth Papa, and at the same time all of his people, and every man and every woman and every child who had ever lived and who were living and who were yet to be born, were all contained in and possessed by Water Mama and Earth Papa and were never unconscious of consciousness. Thus, Scarecrow grew old and took wives and sired sons and daughters; and through successive generations of sons and daughters, he experienced himself being born and living and dying and being born and living and dying again and again and again. Two hundred centuries of Agwe and Ezili and Ogon and Legba and Song and Dance and Drum and Word came into his being . . . Laughter. Thunder. Fire. Iron. Flesh. Fertility . . . and he understood all of these things.

DEMBALLAH!   DEMBALLAH!   DEMBALLAH!

Then suddenly he doubled up and cried out in agony to all his gods, but Dumb had captured Voice and a cat-o-nine leash lay hot upon his tongue. The sea boiled flame and over the horizon's rim Scarecrow saw grotesque vessels creeping toward the land. Oh, what a fearsome sight! Snarling wolves and white dragons foamed at the mouth, spewing out Carnal Sin, Monotheism, Monogamy, Silver Lie They Shun.

JAHWEH!   JAHWEH!   JAHWEH!

Oh, yes, he saw them and heard them, and he began to run; but they had captured Thunder and split Fire and sold Iron and stole Flesh and banned Fertility, and Scarecrow was shot down and bound and gagged and thrown, along with millions of Himselves, into the festering bellies of grotesque vessels which were manned by snarling wolves and before whose mast stood Three Dragons

188

of Unspeakable Evil: one held a white cross and had the face of
Reverend Kenneth McIntoch; one held a piece of flaming iron
and had the faces of Orville and Martin Handson; the third held
a python in its foaming mouth and had the face of Hellos. Scarecrow, yet a little boy, and being at once thousands of Himselves,
began to wail and rave and struggle and fight and throw Himselves overboard into the shark teeth of man-eaters who swam the
seas and stalked the blood-bathed vessels as they sailed westward
to where more snarling wolves and evil dragons threw dice for
his soul, took away his name, ate his father, violated and defe-
cated on his mother's beautiful black body, and finally stood him
in a field where rags were glued to his flesh and forced his sister
to turn foxy tricks before his very eyes while the wolves and
dragons snarled and foamed at the mouth, which caused his sister to despise him, and Scarecrow who, in his own land, had been
the son of seers and forgers of iron and carvers of wood and givers
of word, was now driven mad because he could not understand
any of these strange things that were happening to him and Himselves in the land of evil dragons.

47
I'LL BE YOUR WITNESS
WILL YOU BE MINE

. . . there was scuffling of feet, a murmur went through the mul-
titude, someone was tugging at his legs, he looked down and they
were lifting him up. Somebody else threw chains around him, he
heard clicking of locks, handcuffs were fastened around his wrists.
He was taken down and stood in the center of a crowd, which
now formed a ring around him.

"What's going on here?" he asked.

A hand slapped him. "Shut up!" he was ordered. "You've
had your say. You're now on trial before the Black People's Court
of the Neo Republique of Acirfa in the South Deep."

"The what!"

He was slapped again. "Do not blaspheme this court. Another outburst and we'll hold you in contempt. How do you plead?"

He looked around. The one who had slapped him and who was doing the talking was standing there in front of him. But Scarecrow could not tell who it was because his face was covered with a mask of solid sapphire. The voice sounded, from behind the mask, like nothing he'd ever heard before. He looked out at the crowd and spotted many people he recognized. They were people he had known in his past. Some of them poets and writers he had been friends with on the Lower East Side. And there were Jomo Jones and Uhura Samson, who used to drink and smoke pot and chase more women than you could shake a stick at. Also he recognized Bettye Snakejohn, who was never seen anywhere without her fat blond roommate from Vassar. They all looked different. They wore African clothes, which was all right, but the real difference was that now they looked mean and evil and were herded together like a pack of crazed beasts.

"Get on with the trial!" they howled. "Get it on and over with!"

"How do you plead?" asked the one with the mask on.

"Are you crazy! Plead to what?" he said, struggling to get free, but the chains were real. He did not feel real.

A big, handsome, black-skin man stepped forward. "I'm your lawyer. You plead guilty. Throw yourself on the mercy of the court."

Scarecrow recognized that man. It was Reverend Spikes. He remembered Spikes and his plane trips and his new Cadillacs every year and his two-hundred-dollar suits and twenty-dollar shoes and his deals with the white cops, and he remembered that when he was really in trouble how Spikes had come to court that day and wasn't able to do a damn thing for him among those white people. And he remembered Spikes had baptized him and was so drunk that Spikes had called him "sister."

"I'll defend myself," Scarecrow told them, still not believing it was real but merely going along with the game until they'd reveal the joke.

The one with the solid sapphire mask, the prosecutor, said, "Suit yourself! Let's have the first witness. Reverend Spikes. Is this traitor guilty?"

"Guilty!" ejaculated the preacher, with pious revenge in his moldy eyes.

"Wait a minute!" yelled Scarecrow, getting a little frightened. "What am I supposed to be guilty of? What am I on trial for? It is Spikes who should be on trial!"

WHOOP! The prosecutor gave him a blow to the head. "Tell this fiend what he's guilty of."

Spikes leaped forward. "Guilty of using the Lord, eh, I mean Allah's name in vain. Guilty of coming to church because he liked the singing and not my preaching. Guilty of begrudging my Cadillacs and my fine clothes and my beautiful light-skin wife and her impeachable chastity. Guilty of going off to college and coming back all biggity and uppity. Guilty of writing in the white man's language!"

Scarecrow made a motion to knock Spikes down, but the chains were too tight for him to move a limb. Before he could speak the next witness was called.

"Guilty of thinking he's better than we is."

"That's a lie," he managed to say before the masked one knocked the words back into his mouth.

The next witness stepped forward. "Guilty of fornicating with the bitches of the enemy!"

A howling roar went up from the mob.

"Guilty of not becoming a doctor."

"Guilty of not becoming a respectable representation of his race and nation!"

"Guilty of being counterrevolutionary!"

"Guilty of going crazy."

"Guilty of sleeping in too many beds."

"Guilty of whoring!"

"Guilty of rebelling against the wishes of those who loved him."

"Guilty!"

"Guilty!"
"Guilty!"

The accusations were coming so fast that he could not keep track of them or from whom or which part of the crowd they were being hurled. He recognized the raspy voice of one dude, though. Jake the Rake he used to call himself, and used to beat up black women, get them hooked on heroin and pimp off of them. Juanita had told Scarecrow about Jake the Rake. How he had tried to pimp off of her and she had threatened to cut his throat before he had left her alone. Scarecrow got so mad at the dude that he forgot he was in chains and he actually began to wiggle and move toward him. But the pack had surged in on him to the hilt now. His head was spinning from the howling and blows that the masked prosecutor kept banging on him. They were also beating and kicking him, many were spitting in his face. His temple was bleeding, his arm had been cut, his legs pained. Somewhere in the crowd, to the left, he got a glimpse of his grandmother, she was crying and struggling to get to him. "Let her through! She'll tell you I'm innocent!" he shouted.

But it was no use. They had gone wild for his blood. Between the blows and kicks and slaps and scratches (yes, the prosecutor was *scratching!*), he spied out his mother. She looked much older, and wore the same expression of sorrow, melancholy and long-suffering on her face. Goddamn them! He was not going to accept this without a fight. He started rolling on the ground, tripping some of them, and biting as many legs as he could dig his teeth into. He'd outdo them and bring them to their senses. For their enemy was his enemy and his enemy was their enemy. A flurry of kicks from the masked prosecutor made him double up and gasp for breath. He was stood up again, his clothes were ripped off, leaving Scarecrow naked in his chains.

"A mirror!" demanded the prosecutor.

A huge mirror was placed before him.

"Look at yourself. You are full of sores!"

He made a leap for the mirror, to dash into it. Once in the

mirror he could conquer this madness. But the prosecutor shattered the glass into a hundred pieces with his fist, which now, Scarecrow noticed, resembled a paw.

"Bring the portfolio!"

He knew his portfolio. Where did they get that? The prosecutor opened the portfolio and began ripping up the contents.

"Don't destroy my manuscripts!" he pleaded. "Not my *journal*. Please!" But he pleaded in vain.

"Exhibit Z!" howled the prosecutor.

An old battered trunk was brought out and placed before him. The lid was ripped open. There was nothing inside. Panic seized Scarecrow. "Rita!" he yelled. "What have you done with the body of my sister?"

The masked one pointed a stark finger into Scarecrow's now cringing face. "He cohabited with his own flesh and blood. Then he murdered her to keep her from squealing on him. To hide the evidence he chopped up her body and threw the pieces into the mirror. He put a rag doll in the trunk to cover up his crime and burnt it up. His crime? His *sin!* He ain't got no sister. Never had one. It was his grandmomma he screwed!"

The pack went wild. "Guilty! Guilty! Guilty!"

"He is guilty of being Guilty!" The prosecutor flipped off the mask of solid sapphire and stood back proudly. A job well done.

When Scarecrow saw the face of the prosecutor, which was the face of a snarling wolf, spasms jerked inside his brain. Whole sections of his psyche uncoupled, flipped, went haywire. He yelled so strongly until his bowels broke loose. He went on yelling, and he could not stop . . .

48

. . . now in the cells and genes and molecular spheres of his body and mind there came a great cataclysm. Darkness and harassment prevailed. Confusion, famine, riot, bloodshed, disease and malcontent gripped the people. Millions stood on soup lines, in the cold, in the heat, year after year, suicide for the rich, starvation for the poor, and the finance institutions of the land vomited up sawdust and debris, while the grain shelters and milk dairies went forth and leaped into the seas. The fields lay barren and dust and sand from the entrails of the wasted earth blew willy-nilly with the unscrupulous winds of social erosion into the eyes of the figure of time on the hill, who stood alone and wept in his dire and sore need. Father! Father!

WE HAVE NOTHING TO FEAR BUT FEAR ITSELF

Then there was at this time, in the time before the birth of the body, the legend of the man, the man from Le Grane, Georgia. Handsome, daring, drinker, gambler, liquor runner, woman handler. Now historical time and biographical time merged, and the man begot the boy and the boy became the man, but the man did not become the boy, while neither boy nor man ever set eyes on the face of the other. Scenes of feet washing and betrayal. Wild scenes! Cursing, jitterbugging, dice shooting, three-card molly, drunkenness and low life along the eastern coast of the Tennessee River. Bessie Smith singing muddy water in her shoes. Bessie Smith dying on the Alabama pavement. Bessie Smith singing empty-bed blues and Lady Day singing strange fruit hanging from the poplar trees. Working on the WPA, T-i-m-b-e-r in the woods, working for the TVA.

Oh, Mothers, keep your daughters tucked under your dresstails! Hide them in the closet! Cover their faces with the darkness of virginity! Forbid them to stray when the moon rises! When the moon rises the gambling man from Le Grane comes a-singing and a-whistling and a-tap dancing and a-finger snapping and a-jelly rolling! Flashing green money, smiling a gold tooth in a mouth filled with gin and sex and sin! Oh, Grandmomma, hide your only Magnolia flower among the gossiping trees! Fool, fool, fool.

Whose little boy are you? Name him son of woman. Whose little boy are you? I'm my momma's boy. Name him child of Magnolia! Who's your momma? I'm my grandmomma's boy. Name him? Whose little boy are you!

NOTHING TO FEAR BUT . . . the legend from Le Grane,

fear him and love him and hate him. Life loved and hated, life gainsaid his name and took it away without a gravestone . . . search the cities dead, set aside and beautified. Rip the pages out of the telephone directories. Oh, census taker! A NAME.

Who's your daddy? You got his eyes! Four men in black from Memphis Town with mean black faces going around Chattanooga Town, REPRESENTATIVES FROM BOSS CRUMP. Gotta message for your old man. Where is he? You got his mouth. Spit out venom like a snake. Shake it out of you. Bastard!

No, no, Grandmomma, don't send me to the store. I'm afraid to go out and play. Those men. Why won't they leave me alone? Who are they talking about?

Billfolder. Green money flying. Red nigger eyes flashing. Strong cigar smoke. Gold tooth. Brown limbs walking. Black and white two-tone shoes. Easy manipulating fingers. Birth certificate. Bulls and Chrysanthemums. Bring forth, bring forth

FEAR ITSELF!

BREAK

METEMPSYCHOSIS

ENVIRONMENT

LIGHTS OUT!   DIG

The *name* . . .

Bang!

Bang!

Bang!

First in the hip, second in the neck, third in the back! Running, now falling, now weeping, crawling, now choking, dying . . . Oh, Lord . . . don't let it happen . . . in this swamp . . . my seed . . . my child . . . in her belly.

CHAPTER TEN

Monday, September 13 (the sixth day)

49

Scarecrow threw up his hands. "Wait a minute, Maria. Let me catch up," he said. "Whose cabin is this? What time is it?"

Maria looked at him disgustedly. She had been talking very seriously to Scarecrow about their relationship. She had wanted his strict attention, but evidently he had not even been listening to her. She told him where he was and gave him an estimate of the time, since she did not have a watch. He wanted to know what day it was.

"Monday," she said.

"Monday!"

"That's right You tripped all day yesterday What's the matter I told you already Weren't you listening? After all I'm trying to be honest with you The least you can do is pay attention to what I'm saying As I said I don't hate you sweetie I still like you maybe even love you and I hope you don't have any animosity towards me."

"Slow down, Maria. Go back. I don't know what you're talking about."

"It's over between me and you!" she shouted. "That's what I'm talking about And I might as well tell you now I'm not going where you're going That's out too I'm leaving this boat ride at Le

Havre and going to Paris with Reggie and Putsy. Reggie ain't going to Tangiers now that she's almost kicked the dope habit And I'm going into modeling with Putsy Anyway I did some fashion modeling once in New York."

Scarecrow gazed up at her with his mouth open. He was shocked, bewildered. Of all the things he might have expected from her, this was not one of them. Something had happened. He noticed too that she had risen from the bed where she had been sitting beside him and was standing back aways. A strange, or perhaps a rather frightened, expression was on her face. She had begun telling him about her parents. Scarecrow listened intently now and observed her closely for any sign as to what had possibly happened.

She told him that her grandfather on her mother's side was named Everette Sarttaire. He was a musician with a mixture of French, Italian and African blood in him. He played mostly in and around New Orleans for the ritzy set of white people. This man met a very black woman who was a gospel singer of the times and he fell in love with her. Although they never got married, Everette Sarttaire impregnated the gospel singer, whose name was Mabel Hamilton, and she eventually gave birth to a female child by the name of Angelina, who was to become Maria's mother. Angelina never knew her parents. The gospel singer, Maria's grandmother, died shortly after childbirth from pneumonia, and two years later Everette Sarttaire died also, mysteriously it was said. Anyway, some New Orleans white people took the child, Angelina, and raised her, sent her to the best schools in the North and then later to Berlin, where she studied music. Maria was certain that the white people were relatives of her mother's father, Everette, because he was very light complexioned and was officially classified as a "gent of color." Which was the way mulatto Negroes were distinguished from the rest in New Orleans during those times. On her father's side of the family, Maria knew next to nothing about her grandparents, she didn't even know their names. Charles, Maria's father, was the son of slaves whose family had been broken up at the auction block, the mother had been sold to one master and the father to another, leaving their son with still another master. After slavery was abolished, the son adopted the name of his former master as his own, that's the way he got to be Charles Du Paul. Nothing is known about what Charles did or where he was during the Reconstruction period. Around the turn of the century, though, and in his early twenties, he appeared in Charleston, South Carolina, where he was known as a preacher of the firebrand type. Later he entered the South Carolina Institute for Negro Boys. Graduating from there, he then attended Oberlin College in Oberlin, Ohio, being one of the first few Negroes to graduate from that school, which is famed for its abolitionist and liberal tenets. Fate would have it that Charles got a scholarship to study theology in Germany at the University of Berlin. That's where he met Angelina, who was there studying music and giving piano recitals by this time as well.

Of course, Angelina fell in love with the tall, black and handsome Charles Du Paul, who possessed such a powerful speaking voice. Maria wanted to know if Scarecrow had ever heard her father lecture or make a public address. Before an audience Dr. Charles Du Paul was a black Pericles! People used to tell Maria that they could hear her father's voice in her voice, and she hated that. Anyway, Angelina and Charles got married. Charles was offered a post at Boston University, the first black man, and maybe the only one, to teach theology there. A year later he became president of Filmore Institute in Union, Louisiana, where he remains to this day. Maria was not saying that her father was not a brilliant man. He *is* brilliant, and cunning! But no matter how brilliant a black man was during those times he could not advance like Charles Du Paul did without the help of the white man or without the white man's permission. Did Scarecrow agree? Well, yes, he agreed, more or less, and he understood also, but he didn't quite see why she was going into it all.

"You don't see because I haven't gotten to it yet," she said. "So just hold your horses."

There was a knock on the door. It was Krane and Putsy. They wanted to see if Scarecrow had come down off of his trip and how he was doing. Putsy was wearing a psychedelic multi-colored miniskirt and a green sport jacket. She was a model all right, the modern lean long-legged vintage. Krane looked tormented, the lines in his face seemed constricted, especially around his eyes. He tried being his usual jovial self and made a few jokes about LSD, but he was not convincing. Maria showed signs of annoyance. Occasionally she smiled warmly at Putsy, but she deliberately ignored Krane, who held Putsy's hand all the while, as though he was afraid to let go of her. Something was brewing.

After they had gone, Maria went and locked the door. "Can't get a damn thing said for people running in and out of here," she said, puffing on her cigarette. "The point is this My father fears white people and I know he would have never married Mother with her as white as any cracker woman unless he wanted to *use* her You know the connections she had with her white aristocratic relatives down in New Orleans Mother wanted to forget those people but Father wouldn't let her so he could become what he is and he forced Mother into retirement which was the worse thing she ever did except marrying his black ass He's a caculating snake He came to Union penniless and powerless and now he's the great Nigger Educator and owns a million in real estate and three years ago he turned down an offer to become United States Ambassador at the age of *ninety-one* The sonofabitch is going to live forever! My brother Everette named after my grandpa got the job I like Everette a little He's docile like Mother Looks like her too But my father is the Big Nigger He needs nothing loves no one he's everything himself and everybody got to bow down and kowtow to him."

She crushed her cigarette in the washbasin, perspiration had risen on her shiny black forehead, her lips were dry, her face was tense, her blouse had gotten wet under the armpits. Scarecrow watched her as she bent down and ran water into her mouth from the faucet. She was tired and her breathing was like the panting of an animal. He wanted to take her in his arms but he did not dare. She brushed the water from her lips, which now possessed a sensuousness that Scarecrow had never noticed before.

She screwed up her face as though she was going to burst into tears and said, "You want to know something? My father has never touched me! I mean that literally He has never put his hands on me in all of my life not even to beat me which would have been better than nothing None of us ever got any love any affections from that man never got no attention He turned my brother into a sissified weakling and he treats my mother like a rag you throw in the corner Yes I'm talking about the great Negro humanitarian educator When I got busted in Alabama on the Freedom Rides and organized the jail on a hunger strike he accused me of embarrassing his name and he was the regional president of the NAACP at the time Hell it was *my* name too *Was* my name Good riddance! I loathe Charles Du Paul so much until it makes me sick That's why I've done so many idiotic things to get back at him Like when I started burlesque dancing I sent him a close-up snapshot of myself And when I got married I sent him a color photograph of me and Simon kissing! Charles Du Paul fears white people He hates Jews even more But I can't go on forever letting what that man's done to me fuck up my life."

She broke off. The tear clouds had cleared from her eyes. She lit another cigarette, puffed on it awhile. "Now," she started anew. "I don't know what all you experienced from taking that drug I can't say but I feel like I've been under it too I mean I've been here in this room with you for the last twenty-four hours and I think I got some insight into you and into myself You got your hangups and you don't have time to get all messed up with mine I mean you can't do anything for me and I don't think I can do anything for you After the first day on this boat ride I got aggravated with you because I wanted all of your attention *All* of it and you wouldn't give it So I reverted back to acting towards you like I acted towards my father Which was wrong You didn't do anything to me He did I did those mean bizarre things for the

opposite reason than what it seemed I came on like a nympho-
maniac because I am frigid And that frightens the hell out of me
because frigid women either come on like raving nymphos or
they end up out-and-out dikes Did you ever catch yourself imitating somebody you hate? I'm like my father If he would have given
me some love and affection I wouldn't be like I am I'm no dike or
lesbian or anything But I do feel cold inside and I don't want to
be this way I hate it but it was the only way I could live with my
father and not go crazy I had to compete with him understand
every man I've ever known I felt compelled to dominate him and
I knew that was wrong It wasn't what I really wanted But none
of them were strong enough to subdue me I thought you were
going to and when you didn't I shifted the blame for what my
father had done to me and the animosity I have for him onto you
I was trying to escape from my father through you Secretly I wanted
you to make me over to help me to become what I'm supposed to
be My life with Simon did nothing for me He is weak and sexless
and I wore the pants even around other women just like I've always done Even in bed he was the sissy and I was the butch shit
He needs a black nanny That's what he wanted from me and I am
nobody's damn nanny So I set my eyes on you because I thought
you were a strong black man who would make me into a black
woman No lie that's why I fell for you I wanted you to manhandle
me dominate me even beat my black ass because I thought it
would make me into a girl But you are too far ahead of me
sweetie and all the while I was relentlessly hanging on to the
hangups I have about my father Some fucked-up shit eh!

"But the same goes for you What's good for the hen is good for
the cock I mean hanging on to hangups that hang you up ha ha!"
she laughed good-naturedly at the play of the words. "Check it
out: the very things that have formed you are the things that have
deformed you I saw it last night You don't love me All right all
right Maybe you do love me but you can't do anything for me and
that's what counts at this stage of the game And although I think
you need love more than any man I've ever met I doubt seriously

if you are capable of giving a woman the kind of love she needs I know you got some kind of thing about that Hellos honkey and you're free to have her She's feminine and pussified and all that But it ain't going to work out because she is a false woman False I say And there's something strung out about you too when it comes to women and it makes you a dangerous man! Until you deal with all of this you'll never be ready for a meaningful relationship with any woman black or white You'll never be able to help a woman Not really Not much Not even help yourself let alone a high-strung broad like me actually."

50
EXTRACT FROM SCARECROW'S JOURNAL

They must have been waiting outside. Immediately after Maria left, Dr. Yas along with Kerstine and Rex came into the cabin. Dr. Yas examined me and gave me a clean bill of health. I noticed that while he was examining me, all of them, including Dr. Yas himself, were glaring with grins on their faces. All right, so I was nude under the blanket. Why couldn't they be as mature about that as they were about everything else.

I noticed something also about that woman Kerstine. She was wearing pants, and although from her waist up she possessed the beauty and aristocratic looks of a queen, the bottom half of her body, from the waist down, was nothing. She had no shape, her pelvis was like a box, straight and square, like a man. A woman's torso and a man's body. I was disappointed. But nature is often strange. If you look closely at the most beautiful person in the world you can always find an imperfection somewhere. Everybody, I mused, is deformed in some way or another.

Dr. Yas wanted to know what was an acid trip like for a black man. Kerstine expressed disdain at the implication that LSD affects Negroes differently from the way it affects anyone else. But Dr. Yas pointed out that no two trips are identical, and since black people have separate background experiences and different problems from what most "ofeys" have, why shouldn't these dif-

ferences be reflected in an acid trip. He wanted to know if I had seen King Kong, haw, haw, haw! I told them what I wanted them to know, leaving out the bit about Snow White. Dr. Yas ventured that I undoubtedly didn't remember all that had happened, especially while I was "out," so to speak. But, he said, for the next few days, or even for the next week or so, certain thoughts and feelings and perceptions would suddenly pop into my mind. "Instant enlightenment!" He recommended that I get some rest, because a trip burns up as much energy as an all-night football game, even if one were out as I had been for a good portion of the trip. "Dig. Looks like all of us are going to make it in spite of ourselves," concluded Dr. Yas, as they vacated the cabin so I could dress.

"Hellos!" I called after them. "How is she?" I asked, surprised at myself, for I had not been thinking about her.

Dr. Yas gave Kerstine a look. She told me that Hellos had been "upset" about me having taken the sugar cube, she had felt responsible. She was all right, Kerstine thought, although she had not been seen since yesterday. Then they went out, rather nervously, I felt.

I dressed and went to my own cabin. Dr. Yas was right. Jesus, I was tired. On the way I noticed that my vision was more sensitive than usual. I was aware of lights and color patterns along the corridor to a degree that I had not noticed before, brilliant rays sprang right out of the colors and danced in the corridor before my eyes. It was not that I was still under the effect of the drug, I reasoned, but that by having undergone the trip I was now more open to certain perceptions than I had been before, like the difference in looking at a painting before, and then looking at it again after, you have taken a course in art appreciation.

In my cabin I undressed again and went to the shower. For some reason I felt that I would really enjoy it, and I was right. Stepping from under the water I glanced at my reflection in the mirror across the bathroom. Good Lord! My skin was smooth! The sores were gone, vanished, not a trace! That must have been *what they were grinning about while Dr. Yas had been examining me.*

I went back to my cabin. I noticed that there was hardly anyone in the corridors. I checked my watch, nine o'clock. It was night. Yes, I would risk it. If people were scattered all over the decks, well, I'd just turn around and come back to my cabin and put the bags back into the trunk and wait for the next opportunity. I was fortunate. I made three trips, getting rid of everything except the head before something happened, or I imagined it happened. When I made the last trip, the third one, just as I was throwing the bag overboard I felt a definite presence behind me, and when I turned I heard, or thought I heard, footsteps running away from the area where I was. Maybe not footsteps but a sound as though something was being hurriedly dragged along the floor. I pursued the sound to a set of stairs where there were lights but saw nothing, no one.

Anyway, real or imaginary, my nerve was lost for the night. Before falling off to sleep, I remember thinking of Maria. I simply could not believe she really meant what she said about us being through. She had revealed a great deal about herself to me and it made me feel closer to her now. I believed she was serious, but I felt also that if I could resolve this thing with Hellos, Maria would come back to me, or she would consider coming back. Yes, that had to be it.

CHAPTER ELEVEN

Tuesday, September 14 (the seventh day)

51

Scarecrow woke with a start!!! He looked around in the cabin. Jim was sleeping quietly, Phil was snoring. He wondered when had they gotten in. The green fluorescence of his watch glowed in the dark. Five A.M.

He sat up in bed and shook himself. But the feeling persisted. He was sweating, his throat was dry. He got down from bed and drank lots of water, his thirst astounded him. He turned around and stared at the room. Something was haunting him. The cabin door creaked open. He jumped.

It was Krane. "You wake?" he whispered. "Come outside."

Outside in the light a worried expression shone on Krane's face. "You seen Hellos?" he asked.

Instantly it came to Scarecrow why he had waked up the way he did, sweaty, thirsty, and jumpy. He had had a dream. He had dreamed of Hellos. But he could not recall what the dream had been about.

"What's the matter with Hellos?" he asked.

Krane looked at him with the face of an ant. "She is dead," he said.

52

In Scarecrow's vision Krane grew small, and still smaller until indeed he dwindled into an ant. The ant started receding farther and farther away. The ant ran down the corridor on a thousand mechanical legs. Then it came back with a piece of paper in one of its tentacles. But now the ant was clinging to Scarecrow and crying hysterically. He took the piece of paper and tried to focus but it was littered with snakes, hundreds of them, and they were crawling onto his hand, up his arm and over his body.

53

The snakes were not as many as Scarecrow had imagined. There were maybe thirty of them, sketched on the piece of torn notebook paper. Some were huge with gaping mouths and long forked tongues. Others were small and looked rather like worms. They were all over the sheet of paper, lying, standing, crawling, flying around, almost like ornaments and yet somehow terribly fierce. Some of them were combinations of snakes and other animals, dogs, rats, birds, cows. At the bottom of the paper there was one with the outline of a human fetus in its belly. Another one, which extended from the top of the paper to the bottom, had the head of Hellos herself. On the belly of this snake, which was in the center of the page, the following words were inked over and over in capital letters:

WHEN   I

I AM   AM

NO LONGER ALIVE

DEAD AGAIN

"What the hell is this!" Scarecrow demanded.

"It's from her notebook she carried around in that bag on her shoulder. Look at the page, it's torn out, I saw the notebook once. I found this in my bed. I know she's dead."

Krane was in hysterics. Scarecrow took him by the shoulders

and shook him. He calmed down and told Scarecrow the rest of the story.

Krane had been with Putsy all day and most of the night. After they left the Dom, he and Putsy wandered around on the ship. Then he walked her to Maria's cabin. That's where she spent most of her time lately. Reggie and some other girls were in there also. Krane left Putsy there and went to his cabin and found the piece of paper under his pillow. That was about four-thirty this morning. But Krane had no idea when the piece of paper had been put under his pillow, since he had been out all day and night. When he found it he went straight to Hellos' cabin. He woke her cabinmates and they shrugged him off sleepily, mumbling that Hellos seldom stayed in the cabin anyway. Her bed had not been slept in, a broom lay on top of it. Krane returned to his cabin and quizzed his cabinmates, but they knew nothing, had seen no one entering or leaving the cabin. That's when Krane came for Scarecrow.

"Let's go find her," said Scarecrow. "She's on deck somewhere. She's always disappearing. You know that. She could be anywhere. Maybe with Dr. Yas, or Rex, or with that crippled man, or anywhere."

"There ain't no crippled man," declared Krane. Then he pointed at the torn sheet of paper Scarecrow still held in his hand. "That's the suicide note. It's from her notebook. She wouldn't let anybody touch it. She blew her top once when I stole a peep in it. She wouldn't have left that if she weren't dead."

"This piece of paper don't mean a thing!" Scarecrow balled the paper up and flung it to the floor. "Hellos is *alive*."

"She's dead," lamented Krane, getting to his knees, retrieving the paper, opening it and staring at it. "She left this behind for me. It's my punishment. She's dead, dead, dead."

Scarecrow drew him up and shook him again but he kept on moaning, "dead, dead, dead." Scarecrow pushed him against the wall and slapped his face back and forth. Krane looked at him with sober eyes.

"Let's go find Hellos," said Scarecrow.

54

They woke Dr. Yas and Kerstine, who was sleeping with him, or rather on top of him, in the small bunk. Then they collected Rex, Maria, Reggie and Putsy. All of them, except Krane, were confident that Hellos was on board somewhere. She had disappeared several times before only to reappear as if from out of nowhere. Krane kept staring at the piece of paper and mumbling about his "punishment."

In the corridor outside Maria's cabin they stood in a huddle. Dr. Yas took control. "If we split up we'll find her much sooner. First we ought to check out her cabin."

"I done told you already she's not there," said Krane. "She ain't nowhere." He gestured the piece of paper toward them.

"She may be there *now*," Dr. Yas told Krane. "And lower your voice, we don't want to alarm the whole ship." He tried to take the sheet of paper from Krane, but Krane would not part with it. "All right," said Dr. Yas. "Keep it but put it out of sight. I'll go check her cabin. Everybody wait here."

He started away. Krane and Scarecrow followed after him. "Okay. You two come along, but the rest of yall wait."

Hellos shared a cabin with five girls in their late teens. They were asleep, so Dr. Yas woke them up. They said that Hellos seldom stayed in the cabin day or night. The little time she had spent there she slept or stayed curled up on her bunk in the corner, writing in her diary or messing around with the stuff she kept in her bag. She never talked, had not even introduced herself. They liked her but were hesitant to approach her. Hellos was older than us, said one of them, so beautiful and distant at the same time. Kind of gave you the goose pimples. They did not know exactly when they had seen her last. Sunday? Maybe Monday? Yes. One of them, Kaisa, the one who did most of the talking, said that she had wakened early Sunday morning and seen Hellos entering the cabin wet with rain and carrying that broom. What broom? That one, there on her bunk, they had seen her with it several times.

Hellos' absences meant nothing to them. Why were they looking for her? Was something wrong? No, nothing wrong. Just wanted to find her, that's all.

Back in the corridor, Scarecrow suggested that someone should be stationed there in case Hellos came while they were searching elsewhere.

Krane said, "We ought to tell the Captain. Show him this note. Get it over with."

Dr. Yas ordered Krane to put the paper away, saying, Suppose they report Hellos missing and then she turns up? Suppose they had reported those other times?

Krane insisted that this was not like the other times. Scarecrow said that he believed Hellos was alive and that they would find her. They had to!

Krane slumped to the floor. "I'll stay," he mumbled. "Yall go on."

They divided. Rex took "D" Deck, the bottom deck, and Kerstine took the one above it, "C" Deck. These decks were the least complicated, comprising only a few cabins and two or three washrooms. Dr. Yas volunteered for "B" Deck; he lived on it and said he was completely familiar with it. Putsy and Reggie were assigned "A" Deck, where there were the dining hall, the Lido, the Veranda Lounge, the library and other gathering places. Maria and Scarecrow covered the "Upper" Deck, the swimming pool area, the outdoor lounging areas on either side of the ship, the fore and aft parts of the vessel along with the Dom and the "Sunshine" Deck, which was atop the Dom. If anyone found Hellos or heard anything they were to report to Dr. Yas's cabin and wait there. In any case, they were to report there immediately after breakfast. It was now six A.M.

55

"I got to be crazy I should be getting my sleep instead of tracing around on this deck before day in the morning looking for a needle in a haystack."

Maria was walking beside Scarecrow, hugging her fur coat to her body and doing no searching at all. From time to time she strolled on ahead as Scarecrow stopped to look around. Partly to get her off his back, Scarecrow suggested that Maria go look in the Dom while he go around back where the bench was, where he and Maria had first made love.

"The Dom is locked," she snapped. "And if Hellos was in there do you think she'd be alone?"

"Will you stop nagging!" shouted Scarecrow. "Let's go on top."

"You go That wind is hell up there."

Actually there was no need for both of them to climb up to the "Sunshine" Deck. It was a small circular area of the roof of the Dom, containing a few deck chairs and some benches. But Maria had aggravated him and he grabbed her arm and goaded her up the stairs atop the Dom. It was the highest point and the wind was rough. Maria fumed as she grappled to keep her hair tucked under her coat collar.

No one was up there. Cigarette butts, paper cups and napkins lay crumpled on the floor. A blanket hanging across the railing blew in the wind. The waves were huge and the ship rose and fell with every thrust forward. One cup, still intact, rolled up and down the floor with the seesawing of the ship. Scarecrow guided his eyes along the entire length of the vessel. There were the rows and rows of seagoing chairs on either side of the deck, the water sloshed about in the swimming pool as if it were a miniature ocean. There were the beams and cables and other apparatuses, and at the opposite end of the ship the lifeboats were stacked higher than where they were standing. There, where the lifeboats rose high, the Captain and his officers were sleeping in their quarters. But no. For now it was getting daylight. Those sea birds, whatever their names are, were hovering above the ship; their bullet bodies, their long drooping motionless wings effortlessly expanding and riding the air. There were a few lingering overhead where Scarecrow and Maria were standing. Scarecrow looked up at them, wondering how they were able to sail as fast as the ship without flapping their great wings for such long periods at a time. Just as he was thinking this, the birds made a great dip upward and sailed away. Scarecrow felt goose pimples run over him, for the sudden departure of the birds seemed to have been connected with their sight of him. The paper cup, as it rolled back and forth, made a hollow scratching noise on the floor. Scarecrow slumped against the railing and sighed, "Oh, God, she can't be dead."

"Dead! That bitch ain't dead She ain't even lost If you ask me she's laying up somewhere in somebody's bed what she's been doing all along *disappearing* How hung up can you be I mean? You're so possessed over that woman until you think she's some kind of goddess It figures She's Caucasian But you never carried on over me like this Suppose it was me lost or missing or hiding None of you would be poking in every hole and corner trying to find me That dope must have dismembered your brain I mean she's been missing before black boy Why panic now!"

Scarecrow asked Maria to please stop calling him "black boy," and he mentioned the note Krane found in his bed. Maria wanted to know what the note said. He told her that she would have to see it herself.

"Why do I have to see it? Didn't you read it? Can't you tell me what it said?"

"It was full of drawings, snakes and things. The words were: *When I am no longer dead I am alive again* or maybe *When I am alive again I am no longer dead*. Because the words were written in a jumble like a puzzle. Krane thinks that Hellos tore the sheet of paper from some notebook she kept in that bag she carried."

"Sounds nutty to me I knew that all along But if anybody's to blame it's that crazy Krane She left him the note didn't she? Where is he anyway? Probably somewhere trying to seduce somebody's child What's the matter with him? Can't he get it up for a woman! But Hellos is no woman I'll bet you haven't made it with her yet and you never will All she wants is to keep you dangling until she gets Hell I don't know what she's trying to get out of you All

213

I know is she's false through and through and if she wasn't white she'd be whoring in Harlem for a fix of dope at a time Honest you aren't the nigger I knew back in New York You ruled those honkey Vikings with an iron hand But look at you now You look terrible sweetie and all because this bitch keeps dangling her rump in your face and won't give it up because she ain't got nothing to give and she knows her power over you will evaporate soon as you start demanding what she has not got which is WOMANHOOD I hope to God she stays wherever she is . . ."

In order to keep himself from bashing Maria in the mouth, Scarecrow turned and leaped down the stairs, ran through the ship, down more stairs and through the corridors. He stopped in front of Dr. Yas's cabin and leaned there, breathing heavily. He opened the door. Krane was sitting in the middle of the floor, alone, gazing down at the sheet of notebook paper lying between his legs. He didn't so much as glance up when Scarecrow walked in. Scarecrow started to ask him why he had left his post outside Hellos' cabin, but he realized that Krane had given up completely.

56

They had two meetings in Dr. Yas's cabin. During breakfast they had stationed themselves at various places in the dining hall, all except Krane, who remained in Dr. Yas's cabin.

Hellos did not show at breakfast. What is more, the people at her assigned table did not seem to know who she was. They said that a girl fitting Hellos' description had eaten at the table once, they thought, but they were not absolutely certain of that.

After breakfast they checked Hellos' cabin again. Then they gathered back in Dr. Yas's cabin. Krane still sat Yoga-fashion in the center of the floor staring at the piece of paper which, by now, everyone had seen. It was obvious that he had already taken upon himself the burden of mourning. The rest of them were grim, silent. Tension filled the room. Dr. Yas kept prancing in his tracks and rubbing his fingers over his bearded face. Maria sat on the floor in front of the door, staring straight ahead, her face was set like stone. Reggie and Putsy flanked Maria on either side. Rex leaned against the sink with a glass in his hand, fumbling with it more so than drinking from it. Kerstine sat on the bunk with her eyes on the floor; from time to time she glanced over at the paper, which lay between Krane's Yoga legs. Scarecrow could not keep still, and he kept stepping across Krane's legs to pace up and down in the small, now crowded, cabin. They could hear people in the corridors and noises throughout the ship.

Then there came a knock, a rather delicate knock. Maria was up and had the door open instantly.

There he was, standing there as they all stared down at him, and then back around at one another in stark astonishment. It was the mysterious cripple, the one Hellos had spoken of and whom no one believed existed, except possibly Scarecrow.

"Hello. May I come in?" he said.

They stepped aside. The little cripple had a teddy bear in his arms, it was as large as he was. Peering around, he said, "I have been thinking about your companion, Hellos. We have talked a great deal, or rather, I have talked and she has listened. She is a sweet and lonely child, something like I was once. With all deference to you, she told me so. And of course, being what I am, I knew it the first I saw her."

They were amazed! And now hopeful! But then he told them that he had not seen Hellos in three days, since Sunday when she last visited him. Before then Hellos had visited him all the time, spending hours and even an entire night, holding him in her arms as he sat on her lap and told her of the many many things he had seen and learned since he first took to the seas fifteen years ago. On Monday he had purchased the teddy bear because he wanted to give Hellos something to remember and cherish. But after her visit on Sunday she had not returned, and the little dwarflike man with the large head and short arms and the huge feet on tiny legs, his torso twisted and deformed, had grown fearful that Hellos had flown away and he would never see her again. That's what he said, *flown* away.

He placed the teddy bear on the bed and bowed to them. "If she does not return to the ship before I disembark, please tell her that I understand," he said as he left.

They watched him shuffle out the door, for he could not really take steps; instead, he sort of pushed one foot out front and dragged the other one forward. Scarecrow had grown uneasy about the little man. Secretly he now regretted that he existed. But he couldn't quite put his finger on why he felt the way he did. One thing he was fairly certain of, though, is that all the while the little man had been in the cabin he had refused to look at Scarecrow.

Maria closed the door and wheeled around. "All right," she said. "That crazy talking little freak proves it Nothing means a thing the so-called searching we've done For all we did was run around and look in obvious places She could be in the engine room or in any one of the two hundred cabins and other places that are locked That man proves it Hellos is somewhere aboard this ship."

Everybody agreed except Krane, who sat there in silence, out of it. They hit upon the idea that none of them knew very much about Hellos. But they all knew a little, and if each one shared what they knew perhaps a composite account would point to where Hellos might be. There was a frenzied exchange of glances. But no one said anything. Finally Maria said, "All right let's take it the other way around Suppose just *suppose* she is dead? Does anybody know anything or have a guess? I mean why would she kill herself?"

Dr. Yas laughed, involuntarily, for it was not his usual guffaw.

Krane reached over and took the teddy bear left by the cripple in his arms and began to rock back and forth with it.

Putsy began to sob. Reggie put an arm around her.

Kerstine rose and said, "We must tell the Captain. We have to."

"No!" said Scarecrow.

Maria looked at him. "What then?"

"What about her things, her clothes and stuff, and that bag?" said Dr. Yas, twisting up his face and gesturing both hands out toward them.

Krane told them that most of the stuff he and Hellos brought on board belonged to him, his poems, his typewriter, his writing material and his model airplanes. Hellos had only a small suitcase plus the clothes she had worn, and of course that bag. They went to her cabin again and found nothing, not even the framed photograph Scarecrow had knocked off the dresser. Strange, he had not noticed the absence of the photo before or how deserted her corner of the cabin was. One of the cabinmates was there, the talkative one, Kaisa. Like an actress she kept screwing up her face, twisting her mouth, frowning, widening her eyes, now smiling, moving her lips, pressing her finger to her cheeks as she took time out to concentrate. All she told them was that now that they had brought it to her attention, she seemed to remember that she had first noticed the absence of Hellos' suitcase, along with the empty dresser and the missing photo, last night, Monday night. She wasn't sure but she thought, or it seemed, that Hellos' things were in the room up until Monday night.

Everybody left the cabin in a rush. Once more they scattered throughout the ship, Maria trailed after Scarecrow. It was well into the day and passengers were everywhere. In the Lido they ran into Bennie Bendrix and Joe the guitarist. They had not seen Hellos but they would help them find her. This time Scarecrow and Maria went all over the ship. They kept running into people they had gotten to know or those they had seen so often that their faces had become familiar. Scarecrow felt that at any moment Hellos would appear among the faces. But she didn't.

At lunch the first and second shifts came and went. Hundreds of pretty girls but not Hellos. The third and final shift came. Maria said, "Sweetie you might as well sit down and eat I have a notion we're going to need it."

At the table College Joe Gentry went into his spiel, grinning, his eyes made larger behind the thick lenses of his horn-rimmed glasses. He wanted to know where they had been, he thought they had jumped into the ocean, aah, ha, ha! And who was Reggie, was she French?

217

"Welcome back, stranger," said Sue to Scarecrow, smiling at him.

The redhead pregnant one just stared at Reggie. Then she focused on Maria. "Your hair!" she exclaimed. "What have you done to your hair?"

"Thinned it," replied Maria, half-heartedly.

Right, thought Scarecrow. He knew there was something unusual about Maria's appearance. It was her hair, which used to be thick like a horse's mane but which was now thin and stringy like the hair of a white woman.

After lunch they found everybody in Dr. Yas's cabin, including Joe, Archie, Bennie and his wife and baby. That man Handson, Putsy's uncle, was there also. As Maria and Scarecrow entered the cabin they looked toward the rest expectantly. But no one had anything to relay.

Scanning the room, Maria said, "I wish I was a mind reader For I have a feeling that somebody here knows something and Hey!" she exclaimed, peering around. "Where's Dr. Yas?"

WHEEEE!
WHEEEE!
WHEEEE!

Silence in the cabin. Then everybody reacted, including Krane, who jumped to his feet. It was the emergency alarm. The ship was coming to a full halt.

CHAPTER TWELVE

Tuesday, September 14 (the same day)

57

"You mean to tell me this passenger has been missing all this time and you are just now reporting it? Didn't you read the instructions that were handed out when you boarded this vessel!"

The Captain was a giant, nearly seven feet tall. He was addressing Dr. Yas, who stood now like a reprimanded child before his elder. In addition to his size, the Captain had a powerful face. The lines under his eyes and around his mouth and down his cheeks were as though they had been chiseled by a sculptor. He must have been in his mid-fifties. His eyes were stern.

Dr. Yas shuffled in his tracks. The Captain looked past him at the rest of them in the background. "Who are these people?"

Krane came forward. "She was my girl friend, sir." He lowered his head.

A frown moved across the Captain's face. "What's that?" He pointed at the teddy bear which Krane held in his arms. Before Krane could reply, the Captain waved his great hand, "Never mind." He turned to his men, there were four of them. "You, you and you, come with me," he said, and to the fourth one, "Mr. Salveretti, see that these people fill out the appropriate forms. Check their credentials."

The Captain wheeled back around. The floor cracked as he moved. His shoulders were humped and his head lunged forward. "What is your name?" he addressed Krane.

Krane told the Captain his name and the Captain ordered Krane to come with him and his men.

They were not gone long.

There were three chairs and a small couch in the Captain's quarters. Kerstine and Putsy sat in chairs; Bendrix, his wife Mary-ann and the baby sat in the third chair, which was at the Captain's desk. A nameplate was there: Captain Joseppi Bonascalco. Rex and Dr. Yas occupied the couch. The rest of them were standing. Maria and Reggie were in a corner by themselves. Joe, the white boy, offered cigarettes around but no one accepted. Mr. Salveretti, the officer left in charge, moved among them passing out the "appropriate forms" and explaining how to fill them out. He too was a big man, six feet, but with a broad smile and a pleasant manner. He looked to be in his early forties. Even though he was not as big and did not move with as much weight as did the huge Captain, there was something about him, in his cap, gloves, and officer's uniform, that inspired respect and obedience. This man, thought Scarecrow, will be the Captain when the Captain retires.

58

Shoulders towering above everyone, the Captain threaded his way back through the crowd which had gathered outside, and opened the door. Mr. Handson, who was leaning there, jumped out of the way. As the giant stepped inside, Scarecrow noticed that he walked with a slight limp in his right leg. Krane's face was twisted, he still hugged the big teddy bear close to his chest, but tighter now than before.

Gesturing toward Krane, the Captain said, "This man says the missing young lady is pregnant."

"I knew somebody knew more than they were telling!" said Maria, impulsively, then, looking at Krane, threw her hand to her mouth.

Everybody looked at each other quickly, shock was on their faces. Rex stood up and then instantly sat back down. Putsy rose and burst into sobs. "Oh no," she cried. Mr. Handson took her in his arms. "I warned you about getting mixed up with these . . . people," he said.

Confusion had its way. Everybody talking back and forth. Why didn't she tell somebody? Whose baby was it? They looked toward Krane. No wonder she cried and carried on so much! But she didn't look pregnant. Some women are like that until the last month. How far was she gone? Who What When Where How? Kerstine was babbling something into Dr. Yas's ear, but he didn't seem to be listening. Scarecrow felt far away from it all, too far away.

The fist of the Captain banged on the desk. "Quiet!" Then he turned around, hump-shouldered, and said to Mr. Salveretti, "This is serious. Wire the authorities at Flushing. Tell them to come immediately."

Mr. Salveretti disappeared behind a curtain into an outer room, a room which no one had noticed was there before. The Captain said to the group, "I want all of the people who were traveling with the missing passenger and who knew her to remain in this room. The rest will please leave. If I need you I will call for you."

Bendrix, Joe, Mr. Handson and Putsy, along with Maryann and the baby, all left. Scarecrow found himself walking toward the door unconsciously.

"Not you," said Captain Bonascalco.

"I was going for this chair," Scarecrow lied.

As Scarecrow sat down Dr. Yas rose. "Sir," he addressed the Captain. "It is not true that Hellos was pregnant. She was a terribly frightened girl, extremely confused about herself and everything else. But one thing is certain, she was not pregnant."

"He's lying!" declared Krane, holding the bear in one arm and searching his pocket with the other hand. "He knew she was pregnant, he knew it back in New York. She went to him for help, we both did, but he turned out to be just like all the others. He wouldn't help her. He didn't lift a finger even when she said she would kill herself if she couldn't get rid of the baby."

"You don't know what you're talking about," Dr. Yas whispered across at Krane.

Krane, however, would not be hushed. "You killed her!" he accused Dr. Yas. "And I did too. I deserted her when she needed me, I admit that, I'm to blame. But you killed her too, because you're a doctor and you could have gotten rid of the baby but you wouldn't!"

"I take it that you were the father of the baby?" interjected the Captain.

"Yes," said Krane. But then corrected himself. "No! I mean, she tried to blame it on me but I did not do it. I don't know who did it, I don't think she even knew. She was like that before I met her. I tried to help her. I took her to Dr. Yas but he lied to her. Look, look!" he said to the Captain, finally having found what he was searching his pockets for. "This is what she left in my room. It's the note. It's full of symbols but look at it, these snakes, and this one with the words written across its belly. 'When I am no longer dead I am alive again!' It means she was pregnant. But Dr. Yas kept trying to psych her out of it by telling her she was *imagining* it. That's why Hellos is dead now."

Captain Bonascalco was standing in the middle of the room. Quietly he was studying Krane and carefully observing the rest of them. While Krane had been talking, Dr. Yas had slowly, almost cautiously, moved across the floor and placed his hand on Krane's shoulder and pressed him down into a chair, so that now Krane was sitting in the chair with Dr. Yas's hand resting on his shoulder.

"He's right about asking me for an abortion," said Dr. Yas to the Captain. "But first of all, I have not practiced medicine in sixteen years. I'm a psychotherapist. When I was a surgeon I performed one abortion and it was legal. In the second place, when I talked to Hellos I discovered that she was in an unbelievable psychological state and was keeping herself going by taking drugs, some of them extremely dangerous if taken without the advice of someone who knows about them. But the main thing was that I found she was not impregnated! I examined her several times myself, using the most up-to-date sophisticated tests. But I did not settle for my examinations alone. Two other physicians, one a gynecologist, ran pregnancy tests and certified her as *negative*. The certificate was mailed to me and I gave it to her. She still insisted that she was pregnant. True. She showed all the psychological symptoms and some physical ones too. But there was not a real material fetus. So I began psychiatric treatments with her. I did help her to some extent with the drugs, and I tried to help her work through her (for want of a better term) *pregnancy psychosis*. I advised her not to come on this voyage and referred her to a colleague when I departed. But she took this as a hostile attitude toward her on my part, and he, Krane here, agreed with her, which, incidentally, did not help at all."

During the time he spoke Dr. Yas had not made a single gesture with either of his hands. He held one at his side, and the other lay on Krane's shoulder.

Krane looked up at Dr. Yas with the face of a pleading pup. "You're l-y-i-n-g, Dr. Yas. You confused her with all your psychological jargon, you mixed her up more than she really was at first. She was pregnant! I *heard* it kicking in her stomach, she let me listen. I asked her about the tests and she said you lied, you made it all up. And the certificate? She said you made that up too. There was never no such thing. If so, where is it now?"

"I do not know," said Dr. Yas, as if to himself. "She could have torn it up. For all I know, it may be with the rest of her things, the few clothes she had, the photograph and the bag, wherever they are. But a duplicate of the certificate can be obtained quite easily, since it's on file with the health board in New York."

59

The chief officer, Mr. Salveretti, returned from the outer room and took Captain Bonascalco aside. They whispered. From the expression on the Captain's face, he did not like what his officer was telling him. Finally he slapped his palms together and said aloud, "All right, we'll do what we can until they get here. Take some men and round up her cabinmates, check the list of people eating at her table and get them up here too. Instruct the desk to inform the passengers of what has happened and that we'll be anchored here probably until morning. I'll make my announcement from the address system here."

He turned back to the group. "The weather is too bad for the authorities to reach us before morning probably. I want to sound a general alert to the passengers as well as to the crew. But how will anyone know she is the girl we are looking for if all we can give is a verbal description? I need a picture, a photo." He looked at Krane.

"There's an artist on board," said Rex.

Maria walked over to the Captain. "I'm an artist," she announced. The miniskirt she was wearing had stuck to her behind, and in front it was riding high between her thighs where the straps of the garter belt held the tops of her expensive fishnet stockings. Everybody was taken aback by Maria's claim to be an artist. Expertly she brushed the skirt free, stood back on her long legs, and stared up into the Captain's face. Maria is a statuesque woman, nearly six feet tall, but the Captain peered down on her as if she were a midget. Looking up at him out of her slanted eyes, she said, "Got any paper and pencil Captain? I'll make some sketches of Hellos for you."

She did two sketches freehand style. One showing Hellos from the front view and another from the side. They were not sketches. They were full-size portraits, from head to feet, with Hellos' shoes and stockings and that loose-fitting skirt and blouse she wore, and the bag on her shoulder. Maria did both of them in no more than ten minutes! Reggie had wormed her way up next to her, so had Krane on the other side. All of them watched as Maria swiftly stroked the pencil across the paper.

"Is *that* the young lady!" exclaimed the Captain. "I know her. I've seen her."

"That's her all right," lamented Krane, and slumped back down in his chair.

The Captain requested Maria to draw more portraits so that he could post them around the ship, a request to which Maria responded with obvious pride. Scarecrow found himself loathing her, and yet feeling a little proud of her, which in turn made him loathe her even more. Maria flaunting her ego over the drawings of a girl who, for all they knew, might well have been on the bottom of the ocean.

Having obtained a dozen exact portraits of Hellos, the Captain thanked Maria and told everybody that they had best go to supper.

60

The dining hall was in an uproar. Passengers with wild looks in their eyes, groups of them standing around nervously, some were interrogating one another and making speculations as to what had happened, others were wandering listlessly back and forth through the crowd picking up whatever they overheard, and still others, mainly women, were gossiping about some horrible shipwreck tale they had read in this or that magazine. Everybody was bombarding the waiters and dining-hall crew with questions. Coming through the crowd Scarecrow heard one irate waiter tell a group of old ladies in blue dresses and white bonnets that the Captain had spotted an albatross. When one of the ladies screamed and admonished the waiter that the poor bird must not be harmed, the waiter stood stone-faced for a few seconds, then he deliberately moved his hand from underneath his tray, splashing food and dishes to the floor, and walked away.

Before they reached their table, College Joe Gentry spied them coming. "Sit down and let me tell you what's happened," he said, standing over the table.

"An albatross has been sighted," said Scarecrow.

College Joe laughed that college-boy, ugly-American, business-man's laugh, and proceeded to correct Scarecrow. "Good joke. But we may be stuck here for days. Aah, ha, ha," he peered around delightfully from behind the magnifying lens of his horn-rimmed glasses. "A turbine has gone faulty in the engine room. A new precision part is needed and there is not one on board. The Captain has wired ahead. But with the bad weather, not to mention how rare the particular part is that is needed, why, we may be standing here for two, three, four days, maybe even a week!" Gentry forked a hunk of meat into his mouth.

Sue, the round-faced homely girl, was cuddling the pregnant redhead in her arms. Perspiration covered the redhead's face, bubbles stood on her forehead, her neck was oily with sweat, under her arms and around her full maternal breasts the thin flowery blouse she wore was soaking wet. She cuddled in Sue's arms and her large protruding eyeballs stared blankly at the untouched plate before her. She was holding both sides of her impregnated belly with her hands, which were tiny and wrinkled.

Maria told Gentry, "Why don't you shut your mouth You don't know what you're talking about anyway A passenger is missing She was traveling with us We've been in the Captain's office all day."

That did it! Even the redhead glanced up in surprise. But Gentry went wild. The news that Hellos was missing was undoubtedly the most exciting thing he had heard in his life. He beamed, made faces, took off his glasses, pointed with them, chewed on them, put them back on, stood up, sat back down, analyzed, speculated, improvised. In his excitement he knocked over a glass of water, much of which landed on Sue, who sat next to him. In one breath he apologized, but continued in his reverie over the missing Hellos with increasing asininity. Scarecrow felt that this boy, if he was not already, could one day become a threat to the human race. But Maria was really at fault. She should have kept her mouth closed. Now she had gotten into a free-for-all, know-it-all babbling session with not only Gentry but with Sue and one of the Canadian fellows at the other end of the table. Scarecrow hated them. All of them. He got up and left.

Maria trailed after him, Reggie trailing after her. Outside the dining hall Scarecrow turned and said, "What the hell are you trailing behind me for? Don't you have anything better to do, like broadcasting the news among the passengers that Hellos is missing!" He started away.

Maria caught his arm. "Don't you speak to me in that tone of voice!" she shouted. "Can I help it if Hellos is missing?"

"Maria, the girl was pregnant and she may be dead. And you sitting there at that table babbling with Gentry like you were talking about a baseball game. You're no different than Gentry is."

"Gentry is a ballbreaker but what harm is it to talk about it? Everyone's going to know when the Captain sounds the alert What's the matter with you anyway? You know that woman wasn't pregnant She was nutty and that Krane is too I believe Dr. Yas But I mean why are you acting so touchy like you know something you ain't telling!"

"Reggie!" Scarecrow shouted over Maria's shoulder. "Get your mistress away from me before I do something I'll be sorry for!"

Reggie, like a hurt child, balled both fists up to her eyes, screwed up her white face and burst into a crying fit. Scarecrow was shocked at her unrestrained outburst.

"Goddamn you!" Maria drew back to strike Scarecrow, but a voice came over the public address system just in time. ATTENTION . . . PASSENGER REPORTED MISSING . . . DESCRIPTION AS FOLLOWS . . . PASSENGER MISSING . . . ATTENTION . . . ETC. . . .

Maria held her intended blow in midair, Reggie calmed down. Then it registered in Scarecrow's mind what Maria had said: *Why you acting so touchy like you know something you ain't telling!* And he had had a dream . . .

He leaped up the stairs and was presently running through the ship. He was aware of bumping into people, and for no apparent reason images of his wife and daughter flashed in his mind.

On his way—to where?—he remembered catching sight of himself in a mirror and mentally he hesitated there, but he did not actually stop running until he was in the Veranda Lounge, standing, gazing out of the huge glass window overlooking the stern of the ship and far ahead to where the waves in the ocean rose and fell like sheets in the wind.

He stood there for a long time. It was night now. The ship was lit up from fore to aft and bottom to top. The portraits of Hellos had been posted throughout the vessel. There was nothing to do but wait.

He went to his cabin. Phil and Jim were there. He got the feeling that they were avoiding him, for after they mumbled something about being sorry in reference to Hellos, they soon went out. Which was fine for Scarecrow. It gave him opportunity to get rid of his wife's final remains, the head. But no. The ship was lit up like Times Square and people were roaming everywhere. Not a chance. All right then, he'd get some rest, it had been a most taxing day, to say the least. He climbed up into his bunk, not intending to sleep but merely to rest. Soon, however, he was fast asleep and again he drifted into a dream. It was the same dream he had had before, but he had been unable to recall what it was about.

61

. . . Scarecrow had come from the shower and had been elated because the sores on his body had disappeared. He went to bed and fell asleep. No. First he made several trips and got rid of everything in the trunk except his wife's head. Then he went to bed. Early in his sleep he dreamed that Hellos appeared in his cabin. Where had she been, Scarecrow wanted to know, since no one had seen her for some time now. She told him she had abandoned her cabin and was now living in the sky with the big-winged sea birds. They sing to me, she said. Scarecrow took off his pajamas and asked her to come to bed with him. He reached for her but she jumped back, closed her eyes and began to weep and laugh at the same time.

WHAT'S THE MATTER WITH YOU WOMAN! OPEN YOUR EYES AND LOOK AT ME!

Don't touch me! Don't touch me! she screamed, handing Scarecrow a very worn notebook. You don't know me. Read this. She cried, still with her eyes closed and her back turned from Scarecrow's black nakedness.

He took the notebook and thumbed through it:

WEIRD SINISTER DRAWINGS SNAKES AND BIRDS AND FISH AND BIRDS AND RODENTS AND HUMAN BABIES AND BIRDS ALL MANGLED AND MIXED UP TOGETHER . . . WHITE BODIES AND BLACK BODIES HEADS OFF FLESH TORN AND BLOOD DRIPPING FOR-NICATING AND DEFECATING WORN OUT DIS-CARDED CONFEDERATE MONEY . . . THIN BLACK LEGLESS DOGS AND HUGE GEESE ASTRIDE FLESHLY WHITE MARES WITH NEGROID FACES . . .

Scarecrow continued to flip through the notebook, reading snatches of what was scribbled on its pages:

I AM NOT THE CHILD OF MY MOTHER AND FATHER! *Mother:* a word meaning death, mother used to hang herself on a RACK in the basement of our house in Florida for hours on end PENANCE: fucked by a passing stranger, RE-LIGION: the name of GUILT, my mother was so goddamn re-ligious and my brothers raped me one at a time against that very same RACK, I was so beautiful, how could they resist me, too sexy, the bastard daughter of a passing stranger, all my mother ever taught me was SIN, and father beat me with his cane from the slick seat of his wheelchair whenever he happened to catch sight of my bare legs, and the MASK, father made me wear the mask over my face and heavy black gowns which covered me in darkNESS father was a Jew, JEW BASTARD! Beat me with your ROD Moses go down SNAKE filthy snake . . .

Scarecrow slammed the book closed. He went to Hellos and

embraced her from behind because she still would not turn around and face his nakedness. He did not care about her background KILL THE PAST, he said. Whereupon she broke from him crying F I L T H, and her eyes still were closed tightly. Read on, ODYSSEUS! she yelled, pointing back at the notebook which Scarecrow still held in his hand.

He read more:

I am the cause of the death of my poor helpless mother—she tried to teach me French, she was French, *of* French *descent*, that's important, one's DESCENT. But she was evil, mean, she stuck her finger up my vagina and lectured me on the evils of men, she deserved to die in childBIRTH with me, Oh, Father, I blame myself for BEING BORN. But you loved that evil harlot so much until her death, my birth, drove you OUT OF YOUR BODY! *Letter To My Father:* Dear Pappa, send me an omen from the Holy Pulpit of the SandUsky Valley Methodist Church, send me some LOVE today, Oh, how I yearn to love my fellow man, and my fellow woman. I Know you are a Godfearing minister of God, you make me puke, you are evil and now since your paralysis you want your wayward daughter RUTH to come back into the cave with LOT, you send me money order Western Union, and you hold nothing against me, I'm your only child, Oh, prosperous father, sometimes when I used to be the abusive child, I wanted to take your genitals into my mouth and have my brothers and sister for you! I loved you that much. I wanted joy joy joy joy!

Scarecrow began to feel sick to his stomach. But he read on:

PORTRAIT OF MY MOTHER: Dear, such a wonderful tiny little lady, so helpless, so beautiful, Irish Catholic—LETTER TO MY MOTHER: Dearest Darling: I, Third Child, am so happy to be one of your many daughters, and if I were my brothers born after me, whom you love beyond all life, beyond sanity, beyond manhood womanhood and madness, I would still be thankful to be your sonofabitch. Thank you for the nice presents, especially the doll with pins in its orifices, but I just can't get over the fact that you did what YOU did! How, tell me, please, could you do that with a scarecrow IRISH CATHOLIC POOR WHITE TRASH WITCH BITCH THEY SHOULD HAVE BURIED YOU ALIVE IN 1781 INSTEAD OF HANGING YOU AT THE STAKE IN 1859. So there!

Once more Scarecrow slammed the notebook closed. He had had it. He would not read any more. But then somehow Hellos was leading him by his hand. He had on his robe and they were moving along deck in the darkness and it was windy and raining. Her hand in his hand was soft and warm but it sent a strange chilling sensation up his arm, which then distributed itself throughout his entire body. He felt a feeling that something of their destinies was going to take place, and he realized then where they were going, to the lifeboats; Hellos had insisted that he accompany her up there.

Reaching the lifeboats, Hellos said, look this is where I live now, look at the birds, she pointed up at them hanging there in the air above the ship not minding the rain and the wind. They are singing, listen, can't you hear them? Scarecrow heard nothing but the wind and the splashing of the rain against the sea and ship. All of my things are up here, she went on, my clothing, my photograph of me and my parents who are not born yet, and my bag here—I live here now, this is my home, the birds sing to me at night, can't you hear them?

Her eyes shone like blue rubies in the dark. But it is lonely here too, she continued, nothing is here but sky and wind and bird. Oh, my God, I forgot my broom, without it how can you and I possibly fly together? I can't live with nothing, I am not strong, I am old, I am dead, all of my brothers, my father too, used to nestle around my thighs as I sat weeping from my womb on the stairs of my mother's great house! They made me die, my sisters. She started crying. They made me go out and earn money in low-life pubs and taverns on the squalid streets of Ulster. They made me into a whore, the drunken farmhands, cart drivers. Once I fell in love but that was several lifetimes ago.

Scarecrow noticed that she was throwing her things into the

ocean. He tried to stop her and some of them, her bag and some of its contents, scattered on the deck. LEAVE ME BE, I HAVE BROUGHT ENOUGH MISERY INTO THE WORLD, she screamed. HELP ME, HELP ME, KILL, KILL, KILL!

Scarecrow jumped around. He thought he heard something but there was nothing. Turning back to her he saw that Hellos had taken off her clothes. Was she beautiful! Scarecrow embraced her. Look at me, he said. If we can forgive each other we will be freed forever of what has cursed us.

ONLY DEATH BY YOUR HAND SCARECROW CAN FREE ME! THAT'S WHAT WENT DOWN IN 1593 AT THE LAST ASSIZES AT HUNTINGDON! She screamed again and clawed free of Scarecrow's embrace. I must die once and forever, she intoned. Scarecrow jumped between her and the railing. Hellos relaxed, folded her hands in front of her, and said, I am the bastard child of a German woman of ill-repute in Maine and a mysterious fieldhand. At birth I was carted away to a distant relative and my mother never learned the truth about what had fathered me, but the other children of the family hated and scorned me because they envied my beauty, they were an ugly family they were, uncultured farmhands, and somehow they, my "sisters," found out about me and told me what I was, which was a thing more despicable than Original Sin—NIGGER BLOOD is what they called me. I ran away from there because I was never really strong, I wandered everywhere seeking my true mother. In my wanderings I hit upon the idea of passing. I became a light-skin Negress and lived for several hundred years with an old black woman in the slums of Boston, but then I ran away from there because I was nothing but a body toy for every black nigger buck in the vicinity. Later I discovered my true mother, she had a heart attack when I told her I was her lost-found child, the wretched harlot! I came to New York on the Lower East Side and got pregnant, but Krane did not make me pregnant, for he imagines me a little girl. The child in my womb belongs to that Negro woman in Boston, she put it there, it is not my child, no little black rascal

COMING OUT OF MY WHITE WOMB—NEVER! For I am my own true mother, that nigger woman in Boston voodoo cultist stripping naked her black body hanging nightly upon the RACK of sin witchcraft and DEATH. Do you understand what I'm telling you? I have done everybody wrong. Get out of my way, for I must surely die.

Scarecrow banged her face with the back of his hand, but she shook her head and refused to look at him. Her long brown reddish hair was soaking wet and now it blew in the strong wet rain like the mane of an untamable horse. The lids of her eyes were pressed so tightly that the veins throbbed with blood from the pressure of the muscles. SNAKE! she yelled. FILTHY SLIMY SNAKE REPTILE! NEVER! NEVER! NEVER!

Scarecrow reached and tenderly putting his hands around her neck he squeezed. She sank to her knees. He choked her until the only thing which held her there was the strength of his hands around her throat. The lids of her eyes fell apart, her tongue hung out; warm water mixed with the rain leaked down her flushed but lifeless face onto Scarecrow's hand; he saw deep behind the blue of her eyes the blood-vein map of death. A scorpion leaped from between her teeth and scurried across the deck. He flung her into the ocean, kicking her skirt, blouse, shoes and the rest into the water behind her, everything except the bag, which he was just about to kick overboard when his reflexes caused him to jump quickly around.

Yes! This time somebody was actually there. He was about four feet and had a huge head with the face of a small child, a girl child, his body was twisted and his little legs were like bent sticks; he looked like an s with dangling arms. And he was just standing there in the rain with his mouth open, gazing at Scarecrow. No doubt he had witnessed it all. But Scarecrow had no desire to kill him. Had he wanted to he would not have been able, for he was too beautiful and he had been born that way. So Scarecrow looked *into* him and made him *know*. The little figure shook his monstrous head from side to side and backed away, dragging huge feet with his tiny legs wobbling like bent spokes in a bicycle.

62

When Scarecrow woke from the dream he felt the same as he had felt yesterday morning when he had come awake with a start, knowing then that he had had a dream but unable to recall what it was. Now he had dreamed the dream a second time.

He climbed down out of his bunk and drank from the tap and splashed some water on his face. The mirror was above the wash-basin. He looked terrible. But who wouldn't after such a dream. It *was* a dream. And yet, now that he knew what it was about, the dream he dreamed yesterday morning was now somehow more vivid, more alive than the dream from which he had just awakened, although both of them were identical up to a point.

He sat on the side of Jim's bunk. He looked at his watch, five A.M. He gazed at the wall. Let's see. Today is Wednesday, Wednesday morning. So then it was day before yesterday, Monday, that I woke from the LSD in Dr. Yas's cabin with Maria talking to me. Later Dr. Yas examined me, and we discussed my trip. Kerstine and Rex were with him. When they left I got up and went straight to the shower, yes, and found that my body was clean, the sores had vanished. So I slept the whole night through until I woke that morning, Tuesday morning which, now, was yesterday morning. I was troubled when I woke because I had had a dream. Phil and Jim were fast asleep. Then, like now, it was five A.M. I had not been out of this cabin all night since I went to bed. I spent some minutes just standing here in the cabin trying to recall the dream. Krane came and said that Hellos was missing. No, he said she was dead. We spent all day yesterday, Tuesday, looking for her. Now it is Wednesday morning, and here I sit.

But how could you dream of that little man Monday night or Tuesday morning when the first you saw him was Tuesday *afternoon* when he came to Dr. Yas's cabin with that teddy bear! How could you do that, unless, maybe, you conjured him up in your dream from the description that Hellos gave of him that day she told you about him in your cabin. Yes, that was it. But, damnit, she hadn't really said that much about the man. Why, too, did you feel that the little cripple was behaving strange because of you as he stood in Dr. Yas's cabin? Oh, to hell with it! thought Scarecrow. He remembered that he still had his wife's head in the trunk, and that was definitely more important than anything else. Now might be a good time to throw it in the ocean, since he figured that most likely everybody was still asleep.

He unlocked the trunk and raised the lid. A knock came at the door; it was a soft knock but it frightened Scarecrow to the bone. Quickly he shut the trunk! Whoever was at the door had opened it and was coming in.

It was Rex. He looked like he had been up all night. His eyes were puffed, a bottle was in his hand. "Couldn't sleep," he said. "Figured you'd be awake too. Let's go up and wait until they come. It's getting light outside."

CHAPTER THIRTEEN

Wednesday, September 15 (the eighth day)

63

Rex insisted that Scarecrow take a drink from his bottle, it would do him good. The liquor burned Scarecrow's throat. He felt it going down hot to the pit of his stomach. After he had recovered from the spasm and returned the bottle, he told Rex that Hellos was really pregnant. He remembered that Hellos was with him when the LSD had first taken effect. Scarecrow had gotten on his knees, put his arms around her hips and pressed his face close to her belly. That's when he heard the noise coming from inside her, a knocking or thumping sound, just like Krane had said.

Rex said, "She came to me a day or two after we sailed. She wanted me to use my influence with Dr. Yas and get him to perform an abortion. I told her that she should wait until we get to Europe. She was aboard a ship and Dr. Yas hadn't practiced medicine in years. It was in the morning, in the Lido, we were alone. She got upset and started crying and carrying on like a child. Well, I got this father streak in me. So I told her when we got to Europe I'd help her with the abortion, I'd give her the money and help find a doctor. And I meant it too. The strange thing about it, though, is that later on I spoke to Dr. Yas about it and he assured me that Hellos was not pregnant, you know, saying what he said up there in the Captain's office, and I believed him. Despite what you just said, I still believe him." He handed Scarecrow the bottle.

No, thanks, one drink was enough for him.

Rex sighed. "I was on a ship once before and an old lady jumped overboard during the night. We don't know when Hellos went. We've been traveling at about thirty miles an hour for the last two or three days. That's a lot of ocean. They can't drag all that water. They'll just have to certify she's dead. Jesus, wish they'd get here. Weather looks fine this morning."

More people had crowded the decks. Tension was among them and some complained of waiting up all night and now they had grown even more anxious. Glancing around, something caught Scarecrow's eye. "Keep my place, Rex. I'll be back in a minute."

He went into the ship, mounted two flights of stairs and came out on top where the lifeboats were lined in rows of twelve and stacked higher than Scarecrow was tall. The boats were roped off and a PASSENGERS NOT PERMITTED sign was there. A vague feeling of familiarity stirred in him. He went under the rope, took a few steps and found himself standing in the spot where he dreamed he had killed Hellos. It felt real, yet not real enough. Something was missing, something that Hellos had said in the dream, but it would not come to him. Perhaps something of hers was lying around there? In the dream she said she lived up there. There had to be some sign, a clue, a scrap of food or something. He looked good and peered into several of the boats but there was nothing. Then he heard something move, he felt a presence behind him, just like in the dream. His heart pounded, he leaped around.

"Not permitted, sir," said the lanky sailor with a toothpick hanging in one corner of his mouth.

When he returned he found that Rex had failed to keep his place vacant at the railing. He squeezed in beside him anyway. "Rex," he spoke softly, "I think I killed Hellos."

238

"We all killed her," said Rex, taking a powerful gulp from his bottle. "She needed help and we failed her. All of us."

"But I had a dream!" Scarecrow was talking too loud, he lowered his voice. "I dreamed I killed her up there where the lifeboats are."

Rex said, "I dreamed she was floating in the ocean screaming for me to save her and I threw her some money instead of a rope. Ask the rest, bet you they've had dreams too."

64

A PT boat and a helicopter brought four men, two dressed in blue uniforms and two in civilian clothes. They were international marine police operating out of the Dutch port of Flushing. The oldest one, with gray hair, was the Chief Inspector. He had a rough face, chalk white, and was of average height but fat as a pig, fatter than Dr. Yas. He was immaculate though, his charcoal one-button suit fitted him perfectly; his shoes were spic and span. He was pleasant and took his job in the manner of a detached scientist. The Chief Inspector's name was Cederberge. His assistant, whose name was Poole, was a bulldog, ugly in the face, balding on top of his head. His drab wool suit did not fit him, he spoke English with a guttural Dutch accent, insulted people, smoked in chains, and wore an expression on his face like a man with a perpetual stomachache. It was he, Bulldog Poole, who introduced the notion that foul play might have been involved in Hellos' disappearance. Despite repeated warnings from his superior, Poole's entire approach toward the case persisted along the lines of foul play. The other two men in uniforms merely stood by and did not say a word during the whole investigation.

The group—Krane, Reggie, Maria, Kerstine, Rex, Dr. Yas, and Scarecrow—were with these men all morning in the big room with a long table, through the curtain leading from the Captain's office, with only a few minutes off for lunch. Putsy, at the behest of her uncle, had for the time being disassociated herself from the group. All of them were exhausted, especially Krane, who had gotten the worse of it from Bulldog Poole.

First, they called the group in. But then Cederberge and his men spent more than an hour alone with Captain Bonascalco while the group sat sweating in the larger room. Finally they came out and started asking everyone questions. Poole interrogated Krane. He wanted to trap Krane, due to Hellos' pregnancy, or her alleged pregnancy, and get Krane to admit that he killed her and threw her body overboard, or that he pushed her and she drowned. Krane freely admitted that he and Hellos were not happy, that he had broken off with her, leaving her despondent. But he repeatedly denied that Hellos threatened him with her pregnancy and that he disposed of her. At several points Krane broke into tears, once he yelled poetic obscenities at Poole. "You arse belching inter cunt i nental mother fuzz!"

The rest told their same stories. Dr. Yas insisted that Hellos was not pregnant. Scarecrow told them simply when he had last seen her, saying nothing about his involvement with Hellos or anything about the dream.

Poole was not satisfied. The ship had been thoroughly searched, every cabin had been looked into, and Krane's cabin along with Hellos' had been ransacked. When nothing was found, nothing of Hellos' things, not even a hairpin, this made Poole "abzolukely kertain" that foul play was involved.

"Vhaire iz hur passport!" he ranted.

Then, without the slightest warning, Inspector Cederberge asked Scarecrow personally whether or not Hellos and he were involved in a clandestine relationship. The question jolted Scarecrow inside but on the outside he remained as calm as the inspector. But his mind began to work furiously because he then realized that the Captain, or somebody, had told the inspector everything he knew or thought he knew, about all of them. Before Scarecrow could reply to Cederberge's question, Maria spat out, "That man is my man! He wouldn't be carrying on any kind of thing with any woman except me."

240

The inspector smiled, nodded politely toward Maria and thanked her. Back to Scarecrow he repeated his question, to which Scarecrow said, "No, sir."

By midday the investigation was still going on. The inspector summoned Hellos' cabinmates, all of them. They were questioned separately one at a time. They said that they knew nothing. Hellos was mysterious, never talked, remained aloof, and they seldom saw her since she was hardly ever in the cabin. The talkative one, Kaisa, who used her face like an actress, said that she last saw Hellos early Sunday morning coming into the cabin wet with rain and carrying a polkadot drawstring bag and a broom, and that she had not seen her since. All of them agreed that since Saturday night Hellos had not slept in the cabin. Concerning her belongings, the photograph on the dresser, the bag, the couple of skirts and other clothes, the girls first noticed that these were not in the cabin on Monday night.

"But maybe I should tell you something else, Captain, sir," said the would-be actress. "Now I don't know this for a fact but, Captain, I think I saw her Sunday night talking to a sailor."

Cederberge said, "Excuse me, young lady, but I am not the Captain of this ship. This is your Captain here. I am Inspector Cederberge."

"Oh, yes, I know, sir. Anyway, as I was saying, I think I saw her Sunday night at about half-past eleven. I was coming from the snack bar, it was closing, and she was with or was standing beside a sailor. But as I say, I'm not sure, because both of them had their backs to me and I didn't see either of their faces. I wouldn't go around and stare at them. I'm not the nosy type."

The people who ate at the same table with Hellos were brought in one at a time. None of them knew anything. They were not even certain that Hellos had ever eaten at their table.

After they left, one of the men in uniform, a smooth-faced boyish-looking man, parted the curtains, and in walked Reverend Kenneth McIntoch with that smile on his face and looking eager. Piously, he narrated the sermon he had preached on Sunday, finally telling in pulpit dramatics how he had seen Hellos come into the congregation and take a seat in the very rear. He told how, from the podium of his pulpit, he had seen Hellos sitting back there with that funny colored bag, waving some kind of object around in the air at him! The inspector listened patiently, leaning in the corner with his hands in his pockets. Bulldog Poole paced up and down.

Next came an old man and his wife, passengers, both in their sixties. They claimed that they had seen Hellos yesterday, Tuesday. She had been standing on the bridge looking alone and dejected, poor deary, they said.

Poole wanted to know how they knew it was the same person they were looking for. The couple knew it was the same girl because they had seen her posters, such a dear, lonely child. Poole rammed his hands in his pockets, walked over near the porthole, took his hands out of his pockets and held them by his sides. "Vhat am I doing vith my haands?" he asked the couple.

They told him that he had them in his pockets.

Furiously Bulldog Poole went to them. "You're blind as bats, both of you!"

The old couple left with sadness on their faces.

Poole turned to his chief. "If ve continue this vay every nut, freak, and sympathic passenjer on this ship will be in hair soonar or lator."

"We shall see," said the nonplussed inspector, inserting a stick of chewing gum into his mouth. Slightly leaning where he stood, he gave a nod to Captain Bonascalco, who, in turn, left the room and re-entered with a tall lanky sailor. Scarecrow recognized him instantly, and instantly he looked at Cederberge to discover that Cederberge was watching him. A heat wave went through Scarecrow. *This man is a super cool sleuth!* He and his bulldog were no doubt playing a game, they were a team. Yes, that was it, for things had been too easy. Scarecrow had expected an individual, secretive, third-degree type of interrogation. But this fat, charming, unassuming man had a technique all his own. Look how he chews that gum, his lips closed, his jaws working easily. Fright gripped Scarecrow. But what the hell should he be frightened of! He had done nothing. But he had been involved with Hellos. He had had two dreams, one of which might not have been a dream at all. And there was the dead head of his wife down there in his trunk. Scarecrow's hands began to perspire.

The Captain questioned his sailor, who, it turned out, had been carrying on a love tryst with Hellos. On Thursday night last, two days after leaving New York, the sailor had been going about his duty of checking the lifeboats and had found Hellos lying up there in one of them with a broom beside her. She was undressed, he said, embarrassingly. He made love to her, only once, he insisted, in return for letting her come and go up there as she pleased.

"She was a strange one, sir, like something out of a storybook. She said she flew with the birds at night over the ocean and knew many secrets and mysteries of the world."

The sailor spoke in an Italian accent that was impossible for all, including Scarecrow, to follow except for a few words here and there. The gist of what he said was that Hellos was up there at various odd times day and night, but mostly at night. He had been the sailor Hellos' cabinmate, Kaisa, had seen with Hellos on Sunday night. He said that he had tried to stop Hellos from going up to the lifeboats because it was windy and looked like rain. But he let her go after all due to her crying and getting angry and saying bad things about him. The sailor broke down now and started crying himself. He stopped trying to speak in English altogether and reverted to his native tongue. Captain Bonascalco translated. The sailor confessed to dereliction of duty on Monday night. He had been drunk and he could not say if Hellos had come up there or not. He said that on Tuesday morning he had seen some things that might have been clothing floating in the ocean but that he could not be certain because he had no reason to give it much thought at the time. Then Hellos was reported missing and the sailor had gone up there thinking he would find her, but there had been no one. Furthermore, there were no traces of her ever having been up there. Guilt had gotten the best of the sailor and he had voluntarily come to the Captain.

The huge inspector moved a few steps out of his corner toward the sailor, the legs of his trousers were perfectly creased, he was a big fat man but he was comfortable and cool. "Did you ever see anyone else up there?" he asked the sailor.

"Inspector," Captain Bonascalco intervened, "I'm afraid any member of the crew can go up there."

"I saw *him* up there," said the sailor, pointing at Scarecrow.

"Vhen vas he up there!" Bulldog Poole came alive.

"Today, before you arrived."

Scarecrow spoke directly to the fat man. "That's right. I had a dream."

"Yes," said Rex, "I was with him when he went up there."

Inspector Cederberge stopped chewing. "A dream?"

"I dreamed she jumped from up there."

"From up *there!*" exclaimed Poole, accusingly.

"Aw man why don't you cool it," said Maria, inching her chair closer to Scarecrow. "You're uptight because us black people are traveling with these honkeys That's what's eating in your crank racist!"

Poole looked at Maria and snorted. Maria stared him down. He strode away to the other side of the room. Cederberge smiled. Scarecrow glanced at Maria and wondered about her. It was the second time she had come to his rescue. Was she still in love with him? Did she still care? He put his arm around her.

Dr. Yas said, "It's quite simple, the symbolism. A person drowns, you dream of lifeboats."

"That's all," said Cederberge to the sailor, lifting his hand to hush up Poole. To Scarecrow, he said, "There is nothing incriminating about a dream necessarily. I dream about most of the cases I investigate." Then to the young man in uniform standing by the curtains, Cederberge said, "Let's have the last one."

65

When he came in a quiet fell over the room. His wiry legs wobbled as he dragged his heavy feet across the floor, his miniature arms flopping about. Everybody was staring at him. Scarecrow gazed at him the same as the rest. He had to act natural because he could see Cederberge's eyes darting from one person to the other. What is more, the young officer who had brought him into the room was carrying a knitted drawstring bag which he handed to Cederberge, who took it and plopped it down on the center of the table with an air of no concern at all. *So they have the bag. They've had it all the time.* Now, finally, Scarecrow realized that Cederberge could not be trusted whatsoever. He was more than clever, he was more than unassuming, he was a tricky, sly, crafty bastard! When the bag landed on the table a stir went over the room.

"That's her bag!" exclaimed Maria.

"That's it!" yelled Scarecrow, and instantly felt that he had overreacted. Then the urge gripped him to look at Cederberge to see if Cederberge had noticed his reaction. Fearing that the fat man had done just that, Scarecrow looked at Maria, which he felt was a more natural move to make, after all.

Krane reached for the bag first, then Dr. Yas, then they all reached. But not Scarecrow. To hell with it. He wasn't going to play any cat-and-mouse game with anybody.

"Don't touch it," said Poole, bending over the table.

Cederberge strolled the length of the room, taking his own good time, and placed one half of his mammoth rump upon the corner of the table in front of Scarecrow and all but blocked his view. The little man was seated at the opposite end of the table.

"Please state your full name," said Cederberge. His manner was the same as always, but Scarecrow thought he detected a slight change in the fat man's tone.

He gave his name as Euston Peters Winslow-Davis. He spoke nervously, his neck twitched, his small eyes jerked in their sockets.

He had no shoulders to speak of, his tiny arms lay on the table with the big hands folded, and his face was the face of a female doll. Scarecrow sat back in his chair and did not strain to peer around Cederberge's huge rump to look at him.

Euston began by telling them essentially what he had said that day he came to Dr. Yas's cabin looking for Hellos. *Pretending* he was looking for her, thought Scarecrow. He had been standing on deck last Friday watching the sun set when this young lady from out of nowhere approached him. She told him that he was beautiful. Subsequently she visited him in his cabin a number of times. That first day on Friday; then twice on Saturday, once at noon and again in the evening. The last time he saw her was on Sunday after breakfast. She had come to his cabin wet with rain and exhausted from crying. Unlike what he told them that day in Dr. Yas's cabin, he now said that Hellos always did the talking. She told him that she had no mother or father. She had spent seven years as a child in an orphanage in Berkeley, California, and another three years in a sanitorium in Boston. She had been an airline hostess for a year. She got fired because she falsified her credentials. She then took to traveling like a hippie or a beatnik. Men had always used her, women had always envied and hated her. She was pregnant by Krane and was on her way to Europe to have an abortion, after which she was going to enter a convent. She hoped to eventually become a painter. She cried all of the time. She always sat with the little man on her lap, cuddling, hugging and kissing him.

Concerning the bag, he said that Hellos had forgotten and left it in his cabin on Sunday. He told of having come to Dr. Yas's cabin on Tuesday after he had gone to Hellos' cabin and found her not there. He had also searched the ship and come to the conclusion that she had "flown away." He was a keen observer. He knew, for instance, the names of at least a hundred passengers, where they lived, with whom they associated, plus their day-to-day habits aboard the ship. This was all he had to do, travel and observe. During the last fifteen years he had been to every country in the world and had not once set foot on land. He had been a lonely outcast all of his life. His father was *the* Howard P. Winslow-Davis, director and principal stockholder of FEROLITE UNLIMITED, foremost multinational corporation, which enjoys a virtual monopoly on the battery industry throughout the world. When his father died, young Euston became the sole heir to this fortune. But his mother and sister went to court and claimed that because of his physical deformity Euston was mentally incompetent and incapable of exercising control of such a huge chunk of corporate empire. The sister and the mother, along with sundry assorted psychiatrists and corporation lawyers, eventually succeeded in what Euston called "the most nefarious act of legal piracy of all times." The courts were gracious enough, however, to award Euston ten thousand dollars every month for the rest of his life. Guilt money! But Euston did not hate them; he pitied them, he said.

To the crucial question, he answered, "No." He did not kill Hellos. He had searched her bag but he had not taken anything from it. He was sorry Hellos was gone. "She was an angel," he said, tears leaking from his pea-sized eyes. "She begged me to kill her once, but how could I do that when she was the only person in the world, in all of my forty-nine years, who ever treated me like I was a human being?" He lay his head on the table and wept.

All the while he had been talking, with the inspector sitting on the table in front of Scarecrow, not once did the little man look in the inspector's direction, for that would have meant looking also in Scarecrow's direction. True, to some extent the inspector was blocking Scarecrow, but Scarecrow had the distinct feeling that Euston was deliberately avoiding his eyes. In fact, he *knew* it.

66
CONTENTS OF HELLOS' BAG
1. 3 rabbit's feet: 1 white, 1 brown, 1 pink
2. an ugly sad-looking rag doll, a male with pins stuck in it

3. a plastic doll with the face of a frog

4. a pair of Siamese dolls, made of cloth and joined by their sex, which was of the human male and female but which had the legs of birds and the bodies of goats; the faces of these Siamese dolls were human, one held the expression of ecstasy while the other held the expression of pain

5. a small woodcut of a haggard woman stirring in a huge black pot

6. a piece of a dog's tail, or maybe a cat's

7. a pinch of red soil or earth in a gold container with a moon's crescent on the top

8. some kind of blue powder in a small tin container

9. several strands of finely cut weeds

10. a photograph of Hellos as a child, along with a balding man and a stout hard-faced woman, the one Scarecrow had seen in Hellos' cabin

11. a tiny box of assorted different-colored pills

12. an animal tooth from a horse or mule or maybe a tiger or a lion

13. a pencil drawing of a scarecrow with a woman's face and long flowing blond hair

14. a pencil sketch of Hellos astride a broom

15. a used sanitary napkin, molded, years old

16. an ink drawing of a baby in the womb, apparently dead, and a fat woman dancing, with the word HATE inked over at the top

17. a crayon drawing on white paper of a dove eating an elephant, three human eyes looking on from above, with the word LOVE inked over at the top

18. a front-view drawing of an opened vagina with a snake crawling out

19. the wishbone of a chicken

20. a jar of Vaseline

21. a long strand of coarse black hair

22. a typewritten poem

"That's my poem!" exclaimed Krane, and reached for it.

"Let it lay," ordered Poole.

23. a small edition of the Bible

24. a paper edition of *The Wisdom of the Buddha*

25. a poem by William Blake, "Little Girl Lost," torn from a book

26. an African comb

There was no notebook and no passport.

Dr. Yas reached, over the protest of Bulldog Poole, and grabbed the official-looking document. "See," he said. "This is the pregnancy certificate I told you about. It says 'Negative.'" He passed it around.

Poole jerked it from them and plunked it back down on the table.

CHAPTER FOURTEEN

Wednesday, September 15 (the same day)

67

Never before had Euston Peters Winslow-Davis been as frightened as he was when Inspector Cederberge dismissed him from the inquiry. He had not waited around to see what the outcome would be. At first he had been shocked that the inspector had let him go. Then he was relieved. Moments later, however, fear swept over him once more. As fast as his little legs could carry him he had scurried through the ship to his cabin. He had to do some serious thinking.

First of all, he had not been put through a rigorous cross-examination. He had been questioned all right, but no one had questioned his answers. Cederberge had simply accepted Euston's entire story without any third-degree tactics to see if he might have been lying at any point. Euston knew he had lied about, for one thing, how he came to possess Hellos' bag. Something was wrong. It had been too easy. Euston knew that that fat man could not possibly be as easygoing and nonchalant as he had appeared. It was a trick. It had to be. What Cederberge had in mind Euston could not guess, but he was convinced that some scheme was being laid to entrap him. Euston was deformed, and if life had taught him anything at all, it was that normal people were prone to look upon people like him as psychopaths and potential criminals.

But if Euston was fearful of Cederberge, he was terrified of Scarecrow. He had been terrified from the very first night he accidentally saw Scarecrow throwing those packages overboard. Euston, in his many years of wandering, had seen some strange things, but when he first saw Scarecrow he thought he was having a nightmare. Later he thought he was going out of his mind. It wasn't until he had met Hellos, and she had explained Scarecrow to him, that he came to accept the existence of Scarecrow as a walking, talking, living creature. After he had first seen Scarecrow and after Hellos had explained, Euston had monitored Scarecrow's every move, partly out of fascination and partly out of fear. Fear and fascination went hand in hand. Also, Hellos had come up with an explanation as to what was in the packages that Euston had observed Scarecrow so secretly throwing overboard in the dark of night. How Hellos came by her knowledge was a mystery that Euston did ponder. Surely, if she could mix a potion that enabled them to fly out across the ocean on a mere broom, then nothing was beyond her conjure, nothing was beyond her knowing. Whether or not he and Hellos actually flew or that the potion she concocted caused him to hallucinate that they flew, was not a thing for Euston to question. One thing was certain, with his very own eyes he had seen Scarecrow kill Hellos. He had witnessed the whole episode. That was how Euston came to possess Hellos' bag, it had been left lying on the deck. When Scarecrow had looked Euston in the eyes that rainy, awful night, Euston had been pierced to his heart with fear. He had vowed to himself, and in a sort of nonverbal manner to Scarecrow as well, that he would never reveal what he had seen. Then that detective had come aboard and summoned him as a witness. But he had kept his vow.

Now, though, sitting in his cabin, he had to rethink the entire affair. Euston knew that Scarecrow knew. He not only knew that Scarecrow knew but he knew that Scarecrow knew he knew. Euston reasoned that it had been a mistake when he went to Dr. Yas's cabin with the teddy bear. The bear had been a decoy. He had really wanted to reassure Scarecrow that he intended to keep his vow. None of the group had seen him. Nobody knew that he had ever actually met Hellos. He should have laid low and he never would have been brought into the affair. Now he was exposed, not only to Scarecrow but to that detective as well. Scarecrow, however, presented the greater danger. With Scarecrow, Euston's very life was at stake. He had to think of something. He had to think of some way of protecting himself. He could hide but he could not hide forever. He had to do better than that. He had to come up with a plan of action. The best defense was an offense, he thought, remembering now something else that Hellos had told him.

68

The *Castel Felice* set sail again. Soon the vessel would anchor in its first port, Flushing, Holland. Then on to Le Havre, France, and finally back up to Southampton, England.

Scarecrow along with the rest of the group had been obliged to sit through the whole of the inquiry. In many ways his reaction to the investigation was similar to the way Euston had felt. He was suspicious of the outcome, it seemed too easy, and most of all he knew that there was much more to the case than they had ascertained. He knew, for one thing, that he had killed Hellos, or if he had not done it, then Euston had been the one. The official statement had said:

"Sometime during Sunday or Monday nights, September 12 or 13, a young lady passenger, American, en route from New York to Europe, of apparent Caucasian descent, distressed and tormented because she thought she was pregnant with a child she did not want and whose father she did not know, and known by the name of Hellos, jumped from the *Castel Felice* and ended her life."

As for her age, birthplace, her family and so on—these would be checked out with the authorities in New York and subsequently entered on her death report. Evidently, it was deduced, that Hellos' passport along with whatever else she possessed had been on her person when she leaped. No mention was made of Hellos' notebook by anyone, and they all knew she had such a book. The group seemed satisfied and indeed relieved with the outcome of the inquiry. It was further stipulated and agreed by the Captain and Cederberge that Hellos must have jumped on the night of Sunday or Monday, September 12 or 13, because first of all she was last seen on Sunday by the sailor (she could have jumped that night), and secondly, although she was not seen on Monday, the search did not begin until Tuesday; so she could have actually been somewhere on board all day Monday and jumped sometime during the night. It had to be at night, because had it been during the day, somebody, a passenger, a member of the crew, would have certainly seen her.

69

The whole thing sounded fishy. Scarecrow was loath to believe that they had dismissed the matter in this manner. Secretly he wanted to know how Hellos came to know how his wife looked. Item thirteen in her bag was a drawing of a scarecrow with his wife's head, her face, her features, her hair! Another item bothered him also. Item twenty-one, a coarse strand of black hair. Hellos' hair was brunette. Could that strand of hair have been Maria's hair? It looked like a black person's hair. Then, too, Scarecrow knew that all three of them—he, Euston and Hellos—had been up there among the lifeboats the night Hellos was killed. According to the dream, Scarecrow had put the fear of death into Euston. But why rely solely on the dream? For some unknown psychological reason, perhaps the dream was distorted in Scarecrow's mind. Could it have been Euston himself who killed Hellos? If he did not kill her he certainly had the key to *why* Scarecrow had killed her. Scarecrow knew also that Euston had seen him throwing away his wife's remains; he recognized the scraping sound he had pursued that night as being the same that Euston's feet make when he walks. But Scarecrow was safe on this account because he was secure in his knowledge that he had made it impossible for anyone to know what he had been throwing away. So it was the missing notebook that troubled Scarecrow more than anything else. If Euston had the bag he could also have the notebook. After all, nobody really knew what went on between Euston and Hellos. All they had was Euston's word for it. The case might have been over for the officials and the rest, but for Scarecrow there were still some crucial things that had to be dealt with, and Euston was at the core of them.

Scarecrow had wanted to leave the room as soon as Cederberge and the Captain had come to their decision. He had wanted to go see Euston. But the group had been instructed to remain until every detail had been taken care of. Now, finally, after having extricated himself from Maria and the rest, he hurried to Euston's cabin. He had gotten the cabin number from the passenger list posted in the main foyer of the ship. Euston was not there. Scarecrow banged and banged. Either he was not answering his door or he was hiding somewhere. The little weasel. But Scarecrow would find him, and when he did he would get the whole truth, or else!

Failing to find Euston, Scarecrow rushed to his own cabin. If his cabinmates were there he'd just have to find some way of getting them to leave. It was dark outside and he probably wouldn't get many more opportunities to dispose of his wife's head. He tried the door, it was locked. Good. They were not there. They wouldn't be asleep. It was night but it was not that late. If they, or either of them, were in there sleeping, well, he'd just have to bide his time. He turned the key in the door and went in. The cabin was empty. Yet he felt a little peeved that his cabinmates were never there. He was certain that it was because of him, not exactly because he was black, but just because it was him!

Inside he shut the door and turned the latch. All right, he'd get this over and that would be that. He already had the key to the trunk in his hand. He bent down slightly to open it and discovered that the heavy-duty Yale lock was not locked. But that couldn't be right. The trunk had to be locked. He had the only key. He had taken it out of his pocket a few seconds ago at the same time that he had gotten the key to open the door. The trunk was locked all right. Sometimes, because of the way they were made, those Yale locks had a way of *appearing* to be unlocked when actually they were really locked. Holding the key in his right hand, he bent all the way down to his knees this time and cupped the lock in his left hand. He aimed the key at the keyhole in the bottom of the lock. But that was useless. He saw plain as day that the thing was not locked. Then he snapped his fingers as a wave of relief went over him. It had been him. *He* had left it unlocked. Early this morning he remembered that Rex had nearly caught him with the trunk opened. He had managed to get it shut but in his haste he had forgotten to lock the thing. Yes, that was it, he assured himself as he rapidly took off the lock and raised the lid of the trunk.

The trunk was empty. The head! It was not there. It was not in the trunk. He grabbed the lock up off the floor, hitched it onto the trunk and locked it. He went and sat on one of the bunks and stared at the trunk. He had not thrown away the head and forgotten it, it was there this morning. He went and unlocked the trunk, feeling as he went through the motions that somehow this time things would be as they should be. But they weren't. Nothing was in there. He felt a sharp pain in his chest, a boiling sensation stirred in his stomach, effluvia rushed up in his throat. He lunged for the washbasin but the vomit broke loose before he got half-way across the cabin. Holding his mouth, the stuff running out on his hands, he got to the basin and slumped over it. At first he was aware of how foul it all was. But after a while he felt a mounting relief, a relief that was so all-encompassing and gratifying that it was as though the vomit had been building up in him day by day and night by night ever since he had boarded the ship. He was leaning there this way when he gradually realized that his door was being banged on and someone was frantically calling his name.

Half blind from having heaved as he had and with tears in his eyes from the strain of such all-consuming spasms, he stumbled to the door and opened it.

It was Kerstine. She too was in a state and had started to fall upon him, but the sight of his condition brought her up short. "Jesus! What's happened to you?" she said, taking his arm to assist him, for he was still coughing and jigging around on his feet.

Kerstine caught sight of the floor and the washbasin. "Good Lord, you're sick!" she exclaimed.

Between coughs Scarecrow managed to tell her that he was all right, his stomach had just been upset, he'd be fine in a few minutes, once he got his breath back. But what did she want? he asked her, as he seemed to get better and the coughing spasms began to subside. She told him that Krane could not be located and that they were afraid for him. She wanted to know if Scarecrow had seen him or knew where he might be. Then Putsy and Dr. Yas came running in, saying that they had found Krane, he had been in his cabin all the time. But he would not open his door to them and they didn't know what he might do. They wanted Scarecrow to come with them and talk to Krane. Since they both were writers and had known each other for years, they thought Scarecrow might be able to make Krane come to his senses more so than anyone else.

Krane opened the door for Scarecrow and Dr. Yas, but first they had to send Kerstine and Putsy away. He did not want to see "no sonofabitching bitches!"

Krane was in his shorts sitting in the yoga position on his bunk. His face looked as if he had aged by ten years. He went into a sorrowful monologue about his relationship with Hellos. She had wanted Krane to marry her, he said. But he couldn't do that. He had only met her a month before. He had liked her, though. Oh, man, the way they made love, "sixty-nining," all over Krane's junky little flat. He wasn't going to lie, not now, they had enjoyed themselves. All the while Hellos was staying with some other guy, a painter, according to her. But she wouldn't tell Krane the guy's name or where he lived. She even refused to let Krane walk her home. Then after three weeks she told Krane that she was pregnant and wanted him to marry her. Well, shit! How could he marry her when he didn't know if the baby was really his, and she was supposed to be living with some other sonofabitch. That had been when Krane brought her to Dr. Yas. Krane had believed Dr. Yas at first, that Hellos was not pregnant. But she kept telling him that Dr. Yas was lying, that he was trying to blackmail her into going to bed with him. Who was Krane supposed to believe? On the ship Hellos had started whining and crying and carrying on. So Krane had said to hell with her. But now he admitted that he had been wrong.

"I should have married her and she would be alive today," lamented Krane, repressing a sob. "I wanted to marry her, and I would have if I had known that she was not pregnant. I swear I would have. But she kept saying she was pregnant. Shit! I still could have married the wench. Now she's gone and I'm alone. I killed her, man, I know I did. I forced her to jump. I killed her just as sure as I'm sitting here." Krane threw his head in his hands and broke into sobs.

Dr. Yas sat down beside Krane and started trying to console him. Scarecrow eased himself out the door, he had no time for Krane. He went back to his cabin and looked in the trunk again, it was empty. He locked it. On an impulse he went to his bunk and felt under the mattress for his journal. He had been careful to hide it there since it contained his most intimate thoughts and deeds. The journal was still there. He went to open it but something dropped out. It was a small composition notebook. He opened it. It was Hellos' missing notebook. Page after page: the drawings, the writing, the "letters" to her mother and father. It was all there the same as it had been in the dream. What was her notebook doing in Scarecrow's journal? Who put it there! When had they put it there! The *dream*. Scarecrow thought of Euston again. Hastily he started out the door and met head on with Maria. Reggie was by her side. Quickly Scarecrow shoved the notebook into the inside pocket of his jacket. Maria told him that she had come to fetch him to a meeting in Dr. Yas's cabin. Scarecrow wanted to know the purpose of the meeting.

"How should I know man? Wow, I mean it's just some meeting, Dr. Yas probably wants to talk or something."

70

Dr. Yas was standing in the center of the cabin, talking and waving his hands about. As Scarecrow, Maria and Reggie entered, the psychiatrist was saying:

". . . even after the certificate she still persisted in her pregnancy mania. It was a mania, as you all now know. But I knew then, back in New York, that there was no word or concept in psychiatry or any so-called scientific discipline which could depict Hellos' condition, let alone diagnose it. She thought she was possessed, bewitched, hoodooed and, most of all, she thought she was a whole lot of other people, some of them living and some dead a long time ago. Inasmuch as she thought and believed these things about herself, then for her she actually became and was these things. Within her being there was no-being. Within her no-being other beings, powerful and supernatural, were locked in raging conflict for the hegemony of her soul. She told everybody she ever met conflicting things about herself, for her soul was plagued by demons that have haunted mankind from the very dawn of creation down to the precise moment of this hour. Was she goddess or devil, angel or witch, utterly mad or merely super sane? And at the vortex of these warring dualities, fear and guilt drove her Out There where but few men and women have ever been."

Scarecrow scanned the cabin. All of them were there—Putsy, Reggie, Maria, Kerstine, Rex, everybody except Krane. Scarecrow moved past Dr. Yas and sat beside Rex on the edge of one of the two bunks that were on either side of the cabin. As he sat down he felt the notebook pressing against his heart from within the left breast pocket of his jacket. The faces of everyone were

259

solemn, their heads were lowered and their eyes were on the floor. The words *black sabbath* echoed in Scarecrow's mind as he looked on with impunity.

Perspiring heavily, Dr. Yas spun around in an effort to get them to look at him. Scarecrow was looking but the rest kept their eyes downcast. Dr. Yas slapped his palms together and continued, "Nevertheless, once she was on board I tried to do what I could and in the best ethics of my profession. But she continued to lie to me. I trusted her but she never trusted me. She never trusted anyone because no one had ever trusted her. I knew this, it is classic. So I went on trusting her in spite of herself, hoping that she would finally recognize this trust and then find it unnecessary to lie to me. But I could not hold or control all of the other forces of darkness and light that were affecting her. Hellos did not need all of us, she definitely didn't need to be on this ship among thirteen hundred other human beings! Alas, I could not help her because she refused to let me. She was not a pathological liar, no. She could not tell the truth because she no longer knew the truth. She was totally mystified. She made up parents, relatives, and her background according to whatever fears and guilts she felt toward whoever she happened to be talking to at the time. Most of the time she conceived of herself as a phantasy. All of her language was symbolic. Her obsession with being pregnant and not wanting the child, her fear that the child would be born dead, meant that she conceived of herself as *already* dead! In her mind when she leaped from this ship she was not killing herself, she was merely disposing of the already dead, the alien spirits inside of her dead body. But I am most responsible. If anybody killed her it was I. I am the doctor. I have practiced medicine for twenty years and psychotherapy for almost sixteen. I took too much into my own hands. I failed. I failed myself. I failed you. Hellos, oh, high priestess of heaven, earth and hell, I failed!" Dr. Yas's voice cracked. He threw his hands to his face and wept like a woman.

Now everybody was looking at him, and weeping with him. Scarecrow saw it in their eyes, in the way they swallowed, forcing down their tears. But not him. He felt the pathos in the room, but at the same time he was fighting an urge, alien, to throw back his head and laugh out loud. He lowered his eyes to the floor.

Dr. Yas stopped crying, blew his nose, mopped his hot wet bearded face, and said, "But the doctor is neither God nor Satan! Let's hope that her tormented soul is at peace at last. Now," he took a self-composing breath, "Krane is leaving us. It's his decision. He's getting off the ship at Flushing tomorrow morning to catch a plane back to New York. I've given him the money he needs. That's all I can do about that."

Suddenly the ship began to rock. They heard the winds raging outside, and hard rain began to fall. WRROOOnnn! WRROOOnnn! WRROOOnnn! The winds were furious. The huge vessel rocked and cracked more fiercely than it had ever done before. The group looked at the ceiling and it was seesawing like a balancing board on a flagpole. They had to hold on to the bedposts and other fixed things in the cabin to keep from tumbling about. The lights went out. The closet door came open and a broom fell out onto the floor. Rex, on an impulse, reached to pick it up.

"Don't touch that broom!" yelled Dr. Yas.

Too late. Rex had grabbed it, but the thing burned his hand and he quickly threw it back to the floor.

Kerstine stood up and threw her hands to her profiles. "We are being visited," she whispered.

"Visited?" echoed Maria.

Then the cabin door swung open. No one was outside. THUNDER! . . . LIGHTNING! . . . WRROOOnnn! . . . WRROOOnnn! . . . The winds! And the rain. The sound of rain splashing, lashing the ship! And now hail, solid balls of ice bombarded the ship and zoomed in and about it. Then snow. Great flakes of BLACK snow fell with the rain and hail, exhuming soot and black dust throughout the vessel.

"Close the door!" yelled Rex, holding on to the bedpost to keep from being thrown across the room.

SLAMMM! went the door by itself. The broom on the floor rose, levitated and hung in midair before the closed door, which, of its own accord, opened again.

"LOOK!" screamed Maria. "There! There! T-h-e-r-e!" she she cried, pointing steadfastly at the open doorway. Her slanted eyes were on fire!

"What is it?" said Rex, peering at the doorway.

"It's her! It's h-e-e-e-r!" cried Putsy.

"My God!" whispered Kerstine. She fell to her knees, hands in the prayer position before her face, and began mumbling unintelligible words in some strange unknown language, repeating from time to time the name of Helena . . . Helena . . . Helena . . .

Maria likewise sank to her knees. "Oh, Lord, oh, Lord, forgive me, forgive me!"

A gush of wind rushed through the cabin and brought Reggie's skirt up above her waist. "Help! Don't let her get me!" she pleaded, and fell to the floor clutching at Scarecrow's leg. But Scarecrow was transfixed.

"Keep cool, everybody, just be cool," whispered Dr. Yas, in an extremely high-pitched falsetto voice.

On her knees Maria started chanting, not in her own voice but in a perfect imitation of Hellos' voice, "We must be calm and we must be strong but we are not strong and cannot be calm . . ."

The broom before the doorway began to glow and undulate along with the glowing and undulating Hellos just outside the doorway. Rain, hail and black snow had gotten in the cabin and it, along with the soot and dust from the black snow, blew about the floor in the wind.

Then, as suddenly as she had appeared, Hellos was gone. Her illuminated body, her serenely smiling face, vanished. The levitated and glowing broom fell to the floor, lifeless. The wind and hail and thunder and black snow ceased. The lights came back on. Only the sound of heavy rain could be heard.

Scarecrow came to himself and looked around the room. Putsy

had fainted quietly on the bunk. Kerstine was still on her knees, mumbling in that strange tongue. Reggie lay prostrate at Scarecrow's feet. Maria was still on her knees, weeping and chanting in the character of Hellos herself. Scarecrow was not shaken, he had not been frightened at any point. He was Scarecrow. As he looked at Maria now on her knees like that, he truly felt for her, he felt *with* her so deeply and completely that once and for all he knew he would be in love with her forever.

Dr. Yas helped Reggie to her feet. He felt Putsy's pulse. Then he went to Kerstine and took her in his arms, they held each other closely. Scarecrow moved to assist Maria but discovered that he was clutching Hellos' notebook tightly in his hand, there, visible in front of everybody. He flicked his eyes quickly around the room. Apparently nobody had noticed the notebook. Rex! Where was Rex? He was not in the room. When had he gone? At what stage, and why? Had he seen the notebook? No, he would have said something, taken it from Scarecrow perhaps. But nobody had seen the notebook, so how would they recognize it? Should he tell them about the notebook? And the dream which was not a dream? Should he? No, he crammed it back into his pocket. He was not sure of what he had to tell. But now he was going to make sure.

He slipped out of Dr. Yas's cabin and rushed back to his own. As usual, neither Jim nor Phil was there. Should he go look for them? No. He would wait for them if it took all night. Once more he checked the trunk, after which he sat on top of it and instantly thought of Hellos sitting on top of it, her legs dangling over the side, that night he had taken the LSD. If she had really known what was in the trunk, perhaps she also had a way of getting into it. But the head had been there when Rex had come for him, which was after Hellos had "disappeared." Sitting there, he took out the notebook and rechecked it. Everything was exactly the same as it had been in the "dream." The mysterious storm had subsided. Now, though, a storm was gathering in Scarecrow.

CHAPTER FIFTEEN

Thursday, September 16 (the last day)

71

Dawn crept through the porthole and lit the cabin. Fine particles of dust and soot from last night's storm mixed with the sunlight and rode on the spectrums that shone in the room. The engines ceased their toil. The *Castel Felice* was being towed into its first port.

That was when Jim and Phil burst into the cabin. "Oh!" They gave a start upon seeing Scarecrow sitting on top of the trunk. Collecting themselves, they told him that they were sorry about what had happened. Scarecrow said that he had been waiting all night for them. Jim stammered but didn't say anything. He opened the door, revealing two girls waiting outside. Jim introduced the girls to Scarecrow, who spoke to them and turned back to find Jim and Phil hurriedly putting things into suitcases. There was something fishy about these two guys, thought Scarecrow. Why were they in such a hurry? Why were they acting so nervous? Why had they always avoided him? There had been the odor in the cabin, but that was over now. All right, he would confront them head on with it. "I want to ask you about Monday night," he said.

Abruptly, both of them stopped what they were doing and looked at Scarecrow. Jim said, "That detective's been asking us questions. That's why Phil is late packing. Why he's been, eh—" But Jim hushed up quickly. Phil was staring at him disapprovingly.

"Detective!" exclaimed Scarecrow. "You mean, Cederberge is still on board?"

Neither of them responded. They gathered Phil's stuff in their arms and started out. Scarecrow stepped in front of them. Addressing Jim specifically, he said, "What did Cederberge want to know?"

"Well, eh," stammered Jim, "he wanted to know what you got in your trunk there, but we didn't know. Your belongings, clothes, books. We don't know." He shrugged and maneuvered to get around Scarecrow.

Scarecrow braced himself. So Cederberge was interested in his trunk, damn him! "If Cederberge wanted to know what's in my trunk why didn't he ask me?" said Scarecrow, offensively.

"Don't know."

Scarecrow looked Jim dead in the eyes. "What else did you tell him!"

Jim looked back over his shoulder. Phil gave him a half-hearted nod. Jim said, "Well, he wanted to know everything we knew about you and, eh, that girl who, eh, well, jumped. But look!"— he gestured, glancing back at Phil—"we didn't tell him anything, because we don't know anything. That's why he kept us so long, he didn't believe us at first. Now we have to go, we're going to be late, the girls are waiting."

Scarecrow said, "All right. You didn't tell Cederberge anything but you're not leaving this room until you tell *me* something. You said Cederberge quizzed you. Suppose you tell me exactly what you told him. Then we'll see where we go from there."

"We told the truth," said Jim, nervously but with an underlying determination. After all, they knew Scarecrow was no, eh, murderer. So they had told Cederberge about Hellos coming to see Scarecrow on Monday night.

Scarecrow was not shocked, he had expected as much. But

266

he wanted to know certain details such as the time and circumstances, and so on.

They didn't know the specific time but they thought it was about ten or eleven. Jim looked at Phil for confirmation. He and Phil had come to the cabin about that time to freshen up, they had a date, eh, with the girls outside. Scarecrow was in his bunk asleep. They took about fifteen minutes getting ready and then went back out. That was when they saw the girl in the corridor. She wanted to know if Scarecrow was in the cabin. They said yes but that Scarecrow was sleeping. She wanted to come in anyway, so they had let her in. Well, Jim and Phil went on to meet their dates. When they returned it must have been around two in the morning. Neither Scarecrow nor the girl was there, so they didn't know what happened while they were out. About an hour later, about three, Scarecrow came back in. It had rained that night, remember? Scarecrow was wet and kind of noisy. He had waked them up, that's how they knew. Scarecrow had a notebook in his hands, eh, the same one he had now. He was in his robe and looked exhausted. Jim and Phil figured he had been writing all night, like he does sometimes.

"Notebook!" Scarecrow echoed the word, trying to keep the panic out of his voice. "You told Cederberge I had this notebook?"

"Why, no," said Phil, in his effeminate voice, the first he'd spoken during the whole time. "Isn't that your personal writing, your private journal? Mr. Cederberge knows you're a writer. Why should we mention that?"

72

Scarecrow stood there in the room with the door open, disembarking passengers were rushing through the corridors. Euston was definitely in the clear on both accounts. Not Euston, but Scarecrow himself, had put the notebook in his journal after he had killed Hellos. There was no doubt in his mind whatsoever about it now. Yet Euston was still the crucial factor in linking Scarecrow with the murder. He was therefore the only man who knew why, or who knew what had driven Scarecrow to strangle the life out of Hellos.

Scarecrow had to move fast. Everywhere passengers were coming and going. He did not remember if the little man had said he was leaving the ship at Flushing or not. Since he undoubtedly was in fear of his life, he most likely would disembark the first chance he got. But what about Cederberge? The sly bastard! Two things. One: Cederberge was on to Euston, he knew Euston had the key to Hellos' "suicide." Two: Cederberge was suspicious of Scarecrow's trunk. But what was he waiting for? If he had Euston and if he had the head, or if he had either one of them, why hadn't he made his move on Scarecrow. Simple. He didn't have Euston, he didn't have the head, and moreover, he did know about the notebook. But if the fat man was still on board and was questioning everybody all over again, it was just a matter of time. Scarecrow got the feeling now that he had nothing to lose any more, yet this feeling made him know that he had everything to lose.

Scarecrow tried the little man's door, he banged, he called, but Euston did not answer. Had he left the ship already? With the crowd everywhere, Scarecrow rushed up on deck as best he could. Keeping a close watch for Euston, he edged his way through the crowds. But it was impossible. Already the gate and the steps had been lowered and passengers were leaving the ship. Scarecrow stationed himself as near the gates as he could get.

Among those disembarking he saw Archie with his guitar case on his shoulder and waving good-bye back up to Joe and to Bendrix and his wife, holding the baby in her arms. Reverend McIntoch was there. All of Hellos' cabinmates in a bunch and cackling like chickens, including Kaisa, the would-be actress, strutting down the steps, smiling, flipping her eyes around at everybody. There were some of the crowd from the Dom and some familiar faces from the Lido, also the Canadian lads from the dining table, several of the girls who had been Maria's cabinmates, and some of the older conservative crowd from the Veranda Lounge. Finally he saw Krane. Dr. Yas was with him, so was Putsy.

Scarecrow pushed his way through to where they were. Krane looked worse than he ever had. Evidently he had refused to say anything to Putsy, who was weeping. Putsy's uncle, Handson, stood off aways, watching.

"Wantman!" Scarecrow called to Krane, and stepped up to him. Krane threw his arms around Scarecrow and began to cry.

"I got something to tell you," whispered Scarecrow, and pulled Krane off a piece. "Hellos didn't commit suicide. She was *murdered*. I murdered her. *Me!* I did it up there on the boat deck. Monday night."

"I know," sobbed Krane. "The dream."

"But Krane, I—"

Krane would not listen. He had pulled away and was now descending the steps. Scarecrow thought of Hellos' notebook. "Wantman!" he yelled. But Krane was lost amidst the crowd. It was just as well. What good would it do for him to know now? Anyway, he would find out sooner or later, they all would. Or would they?

73

It was way past noon and the *Castel Felice* was still anchored in port. Scarecrow had been to Euston's cabin several more times and he had looked in all of the places he thought Euston might be, and not a sign of him anywhere. If he had managed to disembark and had fled with what he knew without telling anyone, Scarecrow was home free. Momentarily a heaviness lifted from him. On the other hand, Scarecrow wanted to know what had happened, you don't kill people in a dream, or do you! And where was Cederberge? Scarecrow had not seen him anywhere. Perhaps the fat man had given up and had left the ship, after all. But there remained the disappearance of his wife's head. If Scarecrow could only talk to someone, confide in someone, confess to someone.

He had seen Maria, Reggie and Putsy out by the swimming pool. He knew that Reggie and Putsy had moved in with Maria, but now the threesome were inseparable. Maria was busy at that knitting she had been doing for the last day or so, some kind of green garment; Putsy and Reggie were sitting on either side of her, snuggled almost on top of her. Scarecrow had gone over to them and asked Maria to come with him, he had something important to tell her.

She stood up but she did not move. "Speak up," she said. "Anything you got to tell me you can say in front of Reggie and Putsy too." She put out her hand for them to stand beside her.

She was doing it again, damn her! He felt that imploding pressure billowing in his chest. He had turned from them and hurried away.

74

Shortly after sunset the tugboats towed the ship out of port. It was a strange experience, leaving that little Dutch port. It had the atmosphere, the smell, of a clean sewer; the wet cobblestones, the emptiness of the port except for a few Dutch women in wooden shoes, and a blondheaded boy in knickers. There was a slight wind, misty rain was falling.

That was when Scarecrow saw Cederberge. He walked right up to him, because he knew that Cederberge had seen him also. He figured a straightforward approach was best.

"Good evening," said Cederberge, smiling pleasantly. "I suppose you're surprised to see me."

"Yes," said Scarecrow. "I thought you left with your men."

"No." The inspector easily unwrapped a stick of chewing gum and inserted it into his large but thinly cut mouth. Chewing, he said, "I've been with Captain Bonascalco. I slept there. Guess What?"

Scarecrow held his breath.

"I had a dream last night."

Scarecrow waited. What was this man up to? If he knew, why didn't the man go on and arrest him?

"It's funny," Cederberge went on, moving his big jaws slowly up and down. "I dreamed that I saw how the girl died. She was murdered, strangled, up there where you had your dream. I recognized the man who did it, Euston. The strange thing was that he had the face of a scarecrow. The young lady's drawings must have affected me."

Scarecrow felt he had to say something. He ventured, "Hellos' death has affected all of us."

The fat man was not looking at Scarecrow. Both of them had strolled to the railing and Cederberge was leaning there looking out at the moon. Scarecrow had never been in the presence of a man like him before, standing so close to his own executioner. Cederberge did not breathe like Dr. Yas or most men his size, snorting through their nostrils. Cederberge was a quiet breather. His entire composure was murderously calm.

Scarecrow heard himself asking, "Have you told Euston about the dream?"

"We cannot find the little rascal. He is not in his cabin. We have searched everywhere. But he's on board. He has not left the ship. I watched from up there in the Captain's quarters, and his things are in his cabin. We'll find him, don't worry. I might as well tell you," he said, looking at Scarecrow now. "I'm running a check on all of you, especially Euston. He is obviously demented. Data is being wired to me from your places of origin. The authorities will be keeping track. That goes for Mr. Wantman Krane also. It's my job. I like my job. I'm good at it. Incidentally, Mr. Scarecrow, we have been in your cabin, we used the Captain's keys. I wonder if you would be so kind as to tell me what you have in your trunk."

"A few books, sir, and some old manuscripts."

Cederberge looked at Scarecrow with a raised eyebrow. "That is correct," he said. "But why such a large trunk for just a few books and papers?"

"It hasn't always been that empty. Maria brought her furs on board in it. Then she decided to wear some of them, so she took them out. You've seen her in the coat. She hasn't put any of them back yet. Meanwhile, the mothballs are stinking up my books and stuff. Women!"

"I see," said the fat man.

75

Cederberge was getting hot. He was a master fisherman but he had not caught anything of real substance yet. It was not his fault though, it was simply that circumstances had been stacked in Scarecrow's favor. Scarecrow *knew* more than Cederberge did. He had thought he would faint when the trunk question was put to him. But if the man had known he would not have been asking. Would he? Scarecrow had told him part lie and part truth. He had been direct, he had not hesitated, he had maintained his cool. But so had Cederberge. Which meant that Scarecrow had to cover himself by informing Maria. He was sure that she would go along. She had come to his defense a couple of times before. But something more urgent than that was now nibbling at his brain. The encounter with Cederberge had started his sixth sense to working. Everything was clear to him now. He should have guessed it in the first place. Euston had been playing the game of the rabbit: look here I'm there, look there I'm here. Scarecrow's intuition told him precisely where Euston was at that very moment.

This time he did not even bother to knock or call out. He put his shoulder to the door and heaved. It gave way and came open. Inside the cabin he closed the door again and began looking. First in the closet. Next he went to the bunk on the right side of the cabin and bent down. He crawled to the other bunk on the left side of the room and peered under it. It was so low to the floor that he could not see even with the lights on. He felt in his pocket and struck a match. "Come out!" he shouted. But Euston would not move. Scarecrow tried to reach him but there was not enough room between the floor and the bed. He got up and went to one end of the bunk. He took hold of it and jerked and pulled and heaved until it finally broke loose from the screws that held it fixed to the wall. He slung the bunk clear. It toppled up against the other one on the opposite side of the room. Euston was lying there with his deformed body pressed tightly to the floor and the wall. The little toad! In his arms, hugged close to his chest, was the head of Scarecrow's dead wife with her blond hair flowing about his stubby neck and doll-like face. It was a sight to make even Scarecrow scream. But he had expected it. He snatched the head from Euston and wrapped it in the original plastic bag which was under Euston's shoulder. Why had he taken it? Having done so, why had he taken it out of the bag? He was definitely demented.

Euston had now faced the wall as though he thought he could glue himself to it. Scarecrow yanked him up by the belt of his pants and held him in midair. He didn't weigh any more than sixty or seventy pounds. Scarecrow took him over to a chair and rammed his twisted frame down in it. He had so many things to ask him, and such little time to do it in, that he did not know where to start.

76

It took some doing to get it all out. But, using the threat of death, Scarecrow got it out of him in a matter of a few minutes. Euston had been afraid that Scarecrow was going to kill him, to keep him from talking. Euston was not going to talk no matter what, but he had been afraid that Scarecrow would not believe him. Yes, he had seen Scarecrow throwing the bags overboard. But he had not known what was in them. It had been Hellos who had told him about the bones in Scarecrow's trunk. He didn't know how she knew. She just *knew*. After the investigation he had gone to Scarecrow's cabin with some tools. He had knocked in case the cabinmates were there. When no one responded to his knocking, he had picked the lock on the door and had been prepared to do the same with the lock on the trunk, but he had found it unlocked. He took the head and was going to hide it. He intended to make a deal with Scarecrow, that if Scarecrow let him leave the ship he would tell him where he had hidden the head. But Cederberge was so hot on his trail until all he had time to do was hide from one place to another, never getting time to deposit the head in some safe place. Why had he come forth as a witness in the first place, and with Hellos' bag? The night Scarecrow killed Hellos, Euston had picked the bag up and scurried away under Scarecrow's fear-instilling gaze. He still had it in his possession when he reached his cabin. He hid it in his closet, but Cederberge's men found it before he had a chance to get rid of it. The bag had given him away. He feared that they would pin the murder on him, since he was deformed and crippled. He had had to come to the investigation and give evidence, in order to at least clear himself. But he had not mentioned that he had been a witness to the killing of Hellos.

"All right," said Scarecrow. "You saw me do it. But I don't want to know what you saw, I want to know what you heard. Understand. What you heard. Didn't that girl ask me to kill her? Didn't she *beg* me?"

Euston closed his bee-bee eyes and nodded his huge head up and down.

"What happened? Did I kill her then?"

Euston's eyes opened wide and he pointed at his throat. Scarecrow was squeezing it so tightly that Euston could bearly speak. He choked him tighter. "Tell me what we said and I'll spare your miserable life!"

"She was . . . naked," he groped. "And . . . you . . . had her like this . . . round . . . her neck and you . . . wanted her to . . . look at you because you . . . were naked . . . too . . . and . . . she wouldn't open . . . open . . . her eyes . . . and you said . . . free me and she . . . wouldn't . . . and you started . . . screaming . . . and she did too . . . your sister's name."

"Rita!" exclaimed Scarecrow.

"No," croaked Euston, gasping for breath. "Your *sister,* Maria!"

He stood there gazing into mirrors. So that had been it! Zigzag of an old red house, splitting the soul, desecrating the whole-
ness of the flesh, wherefore the crack split, and scarecrow on the
hill nor rose in the garden knew their kin. He stood there gazing
at colors changing, the wall of madness in the hood of his people,
cancer festering on both sides of the ruptured past, gangrene ooz-
ing out like a tapeworm in the personality. He reached out for
those twisted mirrors. He would smash them! He would kill that
wall!

Euston was groaning, "Don't . . . please . . . you said you
wouldn't . . . kill me!"

Scarecrow released the little man's neck. He heaved for breath,
his little eyes flashed like lights in a pinball machine. He passed
out.

77

Once more Scarecrow hurried through the ship but not aimlessly.
He would never go anywhere aimlessly again. It was all so clear
to him now. Dr. Yas had been right, but he had not been right
enough. What was it that Krane had said about the sea? ". . . *containing everything, breathing, living, decaying, regenerating . . .
the eternal unfolding refolding expansion of consciousness!*"
Krane would never know how right he had been. And Dr. Yas
could only speculate as to the degree of "instant enlightenment"
that had taken place within Scarecrow. Because Scarecrow understood everything now. Hellos had squirmed before Scarecrow's
nakedness. She dreamed she walked one inch above earth, and
by day she fancied sleep in a coffin. Everything and everyone she
longed to touch, she feared, because she had been maimed by
everything and everyone. She was *no* body because she had been
made to feel and believe that her *body* was a vile thing. The broom,
ancient symbol of Arab Munkidh, was her totem, a symbol and
rite which the superstition of purity decreed heresy because the
broom represents Copulation, Penis, Vagina, Body, Flesh! Oh,

yes, Scarecrow now understood both Hellos' notebook of apparent confusion as well as his own LSD nightmares. He also realized that having been born with his mother's entrails over his face, *over his eyes*, and the old black sisters soothsaying that he would be a ju ju child, was nothing more than ju ju itself! There was nothing supernatural about him being a scarecrow and Hellos being a witch and Maria being whatever she was. While their agony was extremely personal, it was at once altogether universally founded in historical reality. Scarecrow, Maria and Hellos constituted personages going back centuries in time when the first woman was strapped to the stake and burned as a "witch" because it was said that she had communed with "a beast in hairy skin, with horns, hoofs, claws, and whose fundament bore the face of a black man." Devices of devilish divinity are conjured by communities of sin to purge black on white sabbat diabolique. And Scarecrow knew precisely why Hellos had proclaimed their destiny, and why he had been mystified by her. Both her and his agony could be terminated once and for all only by her death at Scarecrow's hand. No other means of death could spell absolution for Hellos, no other act of murder could free Scarecrow. Yet Scarecrow knew that he had not killed Hellos; because, as Dr. Yas had so aptly put it, Hellos was *already* dead. What had killed Hellos were the mores of the Apostle Paul. This, not Hellos, was what Scarecrow had slain. Indeed, as his LSD nightmares came to light in his mind, he, Maria, Hellos, and the rest of them, were not only aboard the *Castel Felice*, but were at the same time aboard other vessels that stalked the seas centuries ago; vessels loaded with black bodies standing from Africa to the West Indies, to the Americas, dealing in triangular commerce, and vessels standing from Europe to the New World laden with various "pilgrims," "settlers," "pioneers," "indentured servants," and other unwanted white trash. All—or nearly all—a pack of hysterical aliens who murdered a whole nation, imported, enslaved and stigmatized a once naked black body of people, and who literally raped an entire continent, crying "manifest destiny" of the pure white-only race! That they were mad, and are mad, was absolutely certain in Scarecrow's mind. Hellos had been among those insane aliens, and Scarecrow among the black bodies; so too had been Maria! This was when it all had started, the possession, the spell, that was laid on them by the Three Dragons of Unspeakable Evil. They were all aboard: Reverend Kenneth McIntoch was the first dragon, the white cross signifying a religion (superstition) of sin and guilt and hypocrisy; Martin and Orville Handson were the second dragon, the flaming iron signifying lust for power and material possession; and Hellos herself the third dragon, the python in its foaming mouth signifying womb and phallus as dirty, nasty, repulsive things.

Such were the demons that had haunted Scarecrow and Maria, and, although she was unwittingly and wittingly the agent-embodiment of these demons, Hellos was also cursed by them! Scarecrow and Maria trying to make love and finding that they could not, and Hellos with all those heads of people sprouting from her shoulders as she appeared on the ocean and floated toward them like an apparition out of the white foams of hell. Scarecrows, foxes, and witches. Figures in an allegory. Scarecrow had slain the devil.

The night was black everywhere now. Standing on deck, Scarecrow relieved himself of the final remnant of legerdemain that had been visited upon him and Maria; the head of his wife made a *blop* sound as it hit the ocean. And like the black night the sea prevailed far and wide. Those birds that beckoned to Hellos sailed the smooth winds over the *Castel Felice* like creatures of nature's affirmation of her own glory. While the winds themselves rode the snowy horses of the ocean's foam, and the white-frocked waters rolled in liquid supplication to the egoless universe. Scarecrow and Maria were free now; again they would know Drum and Song and Dance, again they would be One with Water Mama and Earth Papa. Scarecrow would now go and tell Maria all about it.

277

78

"Sweetie!" she beamed. "Come to pay us a visit You're right on time I have something for you." She stepped back and made a lavish gesture for Scarecrow to enter.

He could not tell if she was really glad to see him or faking. It did not matter. He walked in, Maria shut the door. Reggie was lying across one of the bunks. He did not see Putsy.

Maria said, "Well this is really something Sit down sweetie You haven't been in this room since the second day we came on this boat ride Right on time though because I have a present for you But first tell me what's on your mind I can see in your eyes you're not here just to pass the time of day."

She was wearing a half-size transparent crimson negligee that, like a loose sweater, gathered just below her thighs and cupped tightly around under her buttocks. The negligee was hand-stitched with gold and black lace about the neck, breasts and hips. She wore red Japanese-style house slippers decorated with crystal-clear imitation pearls. The slippers were in the shape of ancient Viking boats. Her hair, which used to be so thick the wind could not blow it very much, now flowed thinly as the strings of a violin about her shoulders. She wore nothing underneath the negligee.

Scarecrow said, "Maria, I killed Hellos."

"Well yes all right Have it anyway you want You killed her We all killed her So then let's talk about something else."

Scarecrow took her and gently sat her into a chair. He said, "Listen to me and listen carefully. I killed my wife before I left back in New York. I chopped up her body and brought the pieces on board in my trunk. Remember, you wanted to know what was in the trunk? That's what was in it. I've gradually gotten rid of all the pieces and I just threw away the head a few minutes ago. I was in Korea but I never killed a Korean, not personally, I don't think so. But I killed my own sergeant, who was Putsy's father and brother to her uncle Martin Handson. I'm telling you this be-cause I need to. My life belongs to you now. You belong to me.

I love you. Nothing is in our way now. When I say I killed Hellos I mean it literally. Physically, with my own hands, I strangled her to death Monday night up on the boat deck. I'm not imagining it. I have her notebook. I murdered her. I can prove it. Someone saw me do it."

Maria's slanted eyes widened. She was beginning to take him seriously. So was Reggie, who got up and started for the door. Scarecrow pointed a finger at her and ordered her to sit back down and stay there. Reggie obeyed. But Scarecrow could tell that she was poised to run out at the first opportunity. He locked the door and put the key in his pocket.

Maria stood up. "I don't know what you want in this cabin I don't know what your motive is," she said, glaring at Scarecrow defiantly. "But you don't be locking me in my own room I don't care what you've done or who you've killed You don't be making me a prisoner in my own cabin!"

She went to the closet, said, "Now I have something for you A gift!" She wheeled around with a bundle in her arms. "It's a sweater I made it for old times' sake You know good-bye present It'll last forever Look at it." She came toward him, holding up the garment. "It's green It's thick It's virgin wool." Then she pointed up at her hair. "See my hair I thinned it I took out exactly two hundred strands of it I counted them and I have knitted them into this sweater Look at it See how the black strands go zigzagging all through the green wool It's yours for the good times and the bad times we had Put it on black man."

It was a magnificent garment. Scarecrow stood there while she put it over his head and got his arms into the sleeves. It was a turtleneck and fitted perfectly. The wool was a thick dark green and the strands of her jet-black hair sparkled as they intertwined everywhere up and down and across within the weave of the garment.

"There," she said. "Looks good Perfect if I do say so myself Now I'm going to tell you something and then I want you to leave Good-bye It's all over We had a ball while we were having it But

I don't think we should ever speak to each other again It's too late for us or for me whichever way you want to look at it It might have been too late from the beginning I don't know any more and I don't care But I know it's over You and me are now headed in different directions We always were I suppose and our different directions fates if you want to call it that were determined long before we met maybe even before either of us were born you in Chattanooga and me down there in Union Louisiana All right that's it later So long Open the door Reggie."

Reggie's bare feet splashed on the tile floor. Scarecrow stepped toward her. "If you don't sit back down I'll knock you back down!"

Reggie sank back on the bed.

Scarecrow turned back to Maria. She was standing now in her bitch pose, with the weight of her body resting on her leg muscles, accenting her thighs and buttocks, the muscles apparently relaxed and yet inticingly taut, gap-legged, pussy-sassy. She was trying to be hard, detached, cruel. Scarecrow liked her all the more for it. He desired her. He had missed her: her eyes, her black face, her great mouth. He took her in his arms and kissed her passionately.

She was cold, rigid. "Black boy you're extremely prissy," she laughed in his face.

The flood broke through the dam. One fist caught her in the eye, the other one landed against her ear. She flipped backwards to the floor. She didn't utter a sound.

Reggie gave a start. "Oh!" She leaped between Scarecrow and Maria. Scarecrow gathered the neck of Reggie's blouse with one hand and with the other caught her in the crotch of her pants and heaved her bodily across the cabin against the door, where she collapsed.

He turned back to Maria. But he heard Reggie unlocking the door. She must have had another key. She was out and gone before he could stop her.

Scarecrow started beating Maria again. She backed into a corner on her knees. She threw up her hands to shield herself from Scarecrow's blows but he beat her hands down.

"Go on beat me!" she yelled, cornered but untamed. "Beat me That's what you came here for Go on nigger Beat me!"

"You goddamn fool!" slurred Scarecrow between gritted teeth, standing over her. "I told you what I came for. I came to confess. I came to offer my life to you. Only you can save me."

Maria screamed in astonishment, "Me! *Save* you!" She got to her feet. "What about that Hellos you say you killed and your honkey wife What about her!"

Scarecrow's face had become a twisted, distorted mass of black flesh. Everything he had ever thought and felt about women boiled up in him like a volcano on the verge of eruption. He wanted to cry. He wanted to get down on his knees and tell Maria how he felt. He sank before her. He embraced her around the waist. He pressed his hot sweaty face against the softness of her belly and trembled as he held her tightly.

Ever since he had been a little boy he had felt estranged from women. Perhaps deep within he had wanted to be a woman himself. Why had he been born to be cut off from more than half of all humanity! All his life he had been in love with women. Their species awed him and left him lonely. He yearned and suffered for their companionship. He pained for their understanding. He hurt for their closeness. He was obsessed with the way women stand, sit, walk, lie down, the way they smell, the movements of their limbs, gestures, mannerisms, the way their clothes fit them in the cracks, contours, curves and crevices of their bodies or hang loosely about them. He was possessed by their faces, eyes, lips, breasts, asses, the intimacy of their vaginas, pubic hairs and the incomparable beauty of their nakedness. The hair of a woman had always been his passion, his one and only fetish. He had spent the greater part of his life wanting and thinking about and pursuing women. His dreams were filled with women. Their givingness was enough to make him meek as a lamb. Their denial could send him into a torrential rage. He hurt for their closeness. No other sound in the world was as appreciated by Scarecrow as the sound of free and honest laughter from a woman. No torment was as unbearable as a woman crying. Scarecrow's singlemost ordeal in life had not been merely his struggle to break down the wall that prevented him from communicating with women, but on a far deeper level, at the very root of his anguish, was the desire to be in *communion* with them. Why had he created a sister, except that his sister had been himself! But what did women know about how he felt? What did they understand about their own gift, their beauty, their intrinsic value, their love? Nothing. For they were locked inside themselves, hoarding the paradise which is their being, twisting it, wielding it as power, using it as violence that denies and smashes.

He was crying now. On his knees with his face buried into the warmth of Maria's body, he released all of his defenses. He wanted to become vulnerable and place his total being in her confidence. She was the milk brought from the countryside to his parched lips. He wanted to face himself. He would at last give in to what he had always felt. Ever since he could remember himself he had loved every woman he had ever known or seen, black or white, it had not made any difference to him. But black women had always rejected him. Some of them acted like they were afraid of him. Others, along the streets, cut him to the core by giving him the evil eye. He had always tried to be an honorable man. He had never wanted to pimp off of women. He could never rape a woman. He had no desire to dominate. Nor did he wish to make a woman his mammy. All he wanted was to love them, perhaps to worship them. Black women had always been beautiful to him. He had always held them in great esteem and with utmost respect. The bodies of women, their sex and genitals, were sacred to him. He felt no need to prove his manhood by making derogatory and filthy conversation and jokes about women, as nearly all men do. This was one of the reasons he hated working at McFadden's steel factory among those foul-mouthed men. Yet it had been he who was called "punk," not only by those so-called big black virile men but by black women as well. These were the kind of men the women evidently preferred, the ones who beat them, pimped off of them, raped them, called them whores and talked about them like dogs behind their backs. Scarecrow had been a brilliant student but he had not been able to get a girl friend in school. He had had to become a basketball star. Even then the girl he got was as white as any white girl. He did not know why Maria had married Simon, but he had gone with white women because they were the only women who would have him. Because of the spell, because he was Scarecrow, he had loved them and been proud of some of them. But he always knew that he was with them not strictly as a matter of his own free choice; rather, it was that white women were the best that he could do. Then he found Maria. She was black and foxy, she would break the spell.

He had killed those women because he had been born to do so. All three of them, his wife, Hellos and himself, were merely acting out that which had been foreordained by their facsimiles who had written their names in the twisted mirrors of time and biography. He had not killed them because they were white. He killed them because they were cursed. Scarecrow had to make Maria see this. She had to see through into herself as well as into him. For she too was a part of what had been foreordained. If she denied him now they both would be lost.

He got to his feet. He took Maria by her shoulders and looked deeply into her face. He would make her understand. The triangle, the spell, the allegory, the whole thing.

"Listen," he said, as the premature wrinkles grew deep in his forehead. "What I have done I have had to do. I, Scarecrow, was ordained to do it. Just as you were ordained to do what you have done. I have lived within mirrors. I killed for myself. But I killed also for you, for us. I did it to destroy, or drive out, that which would have perpetuated our estrangement. It was the only way. Now you and I are free. You no longer have to snarl and dart about. I no longer have to bear the pestilence of the one who stands forlorn in the fields. But our freedom rests upon a single condition. We are not free to go our separate ways, but free only inasmuch as we love one another, become one another, and protest one another. Just before Hellos died she screamed your name. I screamed your name. Please try to understand and accept what I'm trying to tell you. I killed her in your name!"

While Scarecrow had been on his knees crying and trembling and clinging to her, Maria had been thinking how utterly despicable he was, indeed, how wretched all men were, white and black. Here he was, a big old rusty grown man, a *black* man, down on his knees, whining and cringing and carrying on. Men! They were all the same. To them women were but body toys; at best, they were body comforters, an inhuman collection of anatomical parts and functions. Tits, legs, asses, cunts, mothers, cooks, house servants, fuck machines and sex symbols to sell all kinds of worthless things, even themselves. The black ones were no different than the honkey ones. At first, when she left her husband and moved up to Harlem, she had thought that Black Consciousness would be her salvation in general, and that Scarecrow would be her proud Black Warrior in particular. Gradually she had come to realize that too many black men in the Black Consciousness bag were seeking, under a lot of glorified slogans, to do to black women the same thing that white men had done to white women. Under the guises of Nationhood, Black Womanhood, Black Is Beautiful, Black Familyhood and other such slogans, black men were seeking to put black women on a pedestal where they would be redehumanized and used as crutches to aggrandize the black man's deflated ego or his sense of malelessness at the expense of the woman's individuality. Under the cry against genocide, black women would be kept pregnant the greater part of their lives and thus prevented from doing anything else in life, just so the men could prove to themselves that they are real men and they are the Boss. Who did these men think they were fooling? Any faggot can get a woman pregnant! Secretly the children are not valued in themselves. Despite what the men say, they want a whole lot of children because the children are evidence to the world that the men are virile, that they can get it up! Everybody knows that it doesn't take but one little old squirt to make a baby. Maria had observed that many of the women who had been taken in and enslaved by these men showed no gaiety in their lives. They don't even know how to laugh any more. They are not permitted to participate freely in conversation with men. They are made to wear, in summer as well as in winter, an undue amount of heavy clothing that weighs their bodies down. Africans never burdened their bodies with tons of clothes, at least not before the missionaries came and brainwashed them about how pure and at the same time how filthy their bodies were. Maria often wondered whether or not the women of the "Nation Time" black families were permitted to go swimming. If so, were they made to wear longhorn drawers! But she knew what really lay behind all of this. Black men were envious of black women. Not only in terms of what little progress black women were making in the world. But, more revealing, black men envied the sexuality of black women, the very femaleness of being woman. Now here was Scarecrow, her erstwhile Black Knight, down on his knees, weeping like some helpless eunuch, and clutching at her femaleness. It made her despise him. She was glad when he finally stood up.

But when he stood up and looked into her face the way he did, and said what he said, a chill came over Maria. What he said to her was frightening enough. But what she saw, or the way she saw him, made her know that she was in the presence of a man whom she mortally feared. For the first time she saw him as himself, as at once Scarecrow, a man, and an apparition. What she now saw was ugly and made the skin on her stomach flinch. She knew that what he had said was right. She could tell that he had looked into her and seen her inside out. But she also knew that she could never relax with him again. She could never trust herself to his keep, let alone to his love, for she and he were not merely incompatible but were ontological enemies. The fact that he had proposed such a mortal union between them meant that he was mad, that he was completely out of his mind, and that he thought she was too.

Carefully she took his hands from her shoulders and backed

285

away a few steps. Slowly she raised her hand and pointed a long black feline finger at him. "Scarecrow," she addressed him by his name and spoke slowly for the first time, "I hate to tell you this but you have been completely honest with me so I must be the same with you You are twisted and deranged You don't know what love is Even if you did know you are not capable of giving it You have gone too far out I don't know what's out there where you are and I don't ever want to know I know this though Whatever is out there love is not The sight of you is ugly Your touch makes me shiver with cold You are a murderer and there is no way under the sun to explain it away."

Willing now to go all the way with her, Scarecrow said, "Go on, get it all out. Then we can love each other."

"Never!" she screamed, shaking her fist in the air. "You and me can never get it all out! We are done for and we can never make it nowhere together Never! We have been turned out Nothing can bring us together now Our blackness is such a superficial thing that it cannot do anything for us But if it were as black and thick and rich as the continent of Africa it could never settle what scares the shit out of me about you! It would take a new history or a new creation to do that! Is that clear to you? We can never make it! I don't want to make it! No sir Never! Never! Never!"

Maria had started out controlled enough. But as she continued she seemed to have gotten excited under the spell of what she was saying, and now she had become totally enraged. Scarecrow had been called ugly before. People had said that they were afraid of him before. But now he felt ugly through and through. He felt denied and smashed and tore up all over. He had to stop her. The mere sound of her voice was driving him insane. Her outrage was killing him. Blindly he swung out and knocked her back against the wall. Red streaks flashed in Maria's catlike eyes.

"Hit me again motherfucker and I'll be the last woman you'll ever hit!" she shouted.

But Scarecrow would not be denied. He had committed himself unto her, he had relinquished everything, and he could not go back now. He grabbed her by the negligee, which tore off in his hands. He did not see it coming, he merely felt the hot sting of a slap to his face. His instant reflexes knocked her to the floor flat on her back. It was then that his hand went to his face where she had slapped him, and he felt the blood where his face had been opened up as if from a sharp instrument.

Dizzy in his head, he gazed down at her. She was still flat on her back. For a moment Scarecrow thought he saw the face of the fox tattoo on her belly come alive and make an angry snarl at him. He brushed his eyes with his hand and looked again. Maria was getting up. She had gotten to her all fours and was about to stand up, or so it appeared to Scarecrow at first. But from her position on all fours she sprang and leaped through the air upon Scarecrow. Her legs went around his waist and her arms around his shoulders, so that he did not have the free movement of his arms and hands. Riding him like that, she bit through the turtle's neck of the green-wool hair-woven sweater she had made for him, she bit through it into his throat with all her might and held her teeth there. Scarecrow felt the pain shoot throughout his body like the hottest fire. He yelled in agony. Delirious with the pain, he spun round and round in the room with Maria still riding him. Staggering back and forth, he managed to ram her head against the side of one of the upper bunks and knocked her free of him. A chunk of flesh from his neck was in Maria's mouth when she hit the floor.

She spat it out and crawled back up on all fours. She got to her feet but remained in a crouch position. She leaped in the air toward him again. She made a fierce howling scream as she leaped. She would fight him to the end. She would never give in. She would eat him to pieces and rags.

They fought for what seemed like a long time. The cabin looked like a hurricane had been through it. Scarecrow was not aware of having any thoughts. Neither was Maria. They were raw instincts. Both of them moved and acted on orders directly from the source

287

of their anguish. They were that anguish. At length Scarecrow remembered hearing a long resounding nothingness. Through a haze he thought he once got a glimpse of Maria looking up at him with an expression of admiration, of knowing tenderness in her eyes. He had staggered out of the cabin before he realized that he was ragged and bleeding all over, and was fitfully crying.

"There!"

He heard a voice. He cleared the blood and sweat and tears from his swollen eyes and peered down the corridor. The lights blinded him. But he was able to discern them through the haze. Captain Bonascalco, Reggie, Euston, Cederberge and Dr. Yas. They were running toward him. Cederberge had what looked like a gun in his hand. Reggie was in the lead.

Scarecrow wanted to meet them halfway. But he had lost too much blood. He sank to his knees. He tried to say something. Darkness closed in around him. He collapsed on the floor.

79

Neither of them died immediately. They were put on stretchers and taken to the ship's hospital, where they were laid on examination tables, side by side. What clothes were left on Scarecrow's body had to be cut away. Maria was already nude. An oxygen apparatus was hurriedly set up for her. Scarecrow had to have both oxygen and blood-transfusion apparatuses set up for him.

Passengers had seen the Captain and Cederberge with his gun drawn and the rest of them running through the corridors. Crowds of passengers had assembled along the corridor as Scarecrow and Maria were taken to the hospital. Two officers had been stationed at the door of Maria's cabin to keep people from pushing in there to gaze and cringe at its disheveled condition. One elderly lady had fainted upon seeing the cabin. Three other passengers, a little girl and two young women, had also passed out as they saw Scarecrow and Maria being carried to the hospital. A baby had started crying. Passengers had been instructed, and then ordered, to clear the corridor outside the hospital, but hordes of them remained. They refused to believe that what had been done to the cabin, and to Scarecrow and Maria, had been done by them alone.

Inside the hospital the group stood in a solemn huddle. Curtains had been set up around Maria and Scarecrow. In addition to Reggie and Dr. Yas, Putsy, Kerstine and Rex had joined the group. Reggie and Putsy were quietly weeping. Rex leaned by a porthole and gazed out at the ocean, he did not have a drink in his hands this time. Dr. Yas held Kerstine in a fatherly embrace and gently stroked her back. Little Euston was there. He leaned by the chair in which sat the fat man, Cederberge, with his elbow propped on the arm of the chair and his face hidden in his hand. Behind the curtains the ship's three doctors were busy working, their shadows could be seen reflected upon the curtains. Captain Bonascalco was behind the curtains, standing back aways from the doctors, watching it all. The reflection of his towering body shone on the curtains.

Although he never regained consciousness, Scarecrow lasted longer than Maria. Before Maria died, however, she completely regained consciousness for a few moments. When the doctors saw her eyes open and her battered body move, they stopped everything and gave her their undivided attention. Captain Bonascalco stepped closer to where she lay. The group was instantly aware of the slightest change behind the curtains and they all gathered around back there. No one tried to stop them. Maria looked up at the ceiling. Her swollen eyes were incredibly bright. The oxygen mask covered her mouth and nose. Slowly she rolled her head to her right. She saw them standing there gazing hopefully down at her. Her eyes gave no sign to them. She rolled her head all the way over to her left. She saw Scarecrow lying there beside her with the oxygen mask over his face and the tubes and things running in and strapped to him. Her hand moved. The tip of her fingers touched Scarecrow on his arm and lingered there for a brief while as if in a caress. Her eyes smiled. Then she closed them. Her hand and arm fell limp by the side of the examination table.

Even in his deep coma Scarecrow had felt Maria's touch and recognized it as hers. He could not move for he was paralyzed. *Yet he moved and was moving in and among the other players with the speed and dexterity of a true star. He had scored the first basket of the game. He played the left forward position. His buddy, Beverly Wilson, was in the right forward position. Broad and strong-shouldered Lee Derick was on the right post in the pivot. Big Moose stood out front as the left guard. In the position of right guard was Squat Jackson, one of the last of the last of the two-hand-set-shot artists. They dubbed him "Squat" because when he shot from midcourt, either from left or right or center, he would squat down as if sitting in a chair. Both of his big palms would be on top of the ball. He would raise his palms, swinging his arms straight out and up, releasing the ball in the air. Squat never shot more than a half-dozen times in a game. But you could always count on those points because he seldom missed.*

There they were at the beginning of the game, a two-one-two defense. Big Moose and Squat Jackson were out front passing and dribbling the ball back and forth between each other. Lee Derick oscillated in the pivot from left to right posts, and sometimes he came out above the foul line. Scarecrow lounged in the deep far-left corner of the court. Suddenly he moved a few paces in between two opposing men. Big Moose had the ball and shot a hard two-hand breast pass straight between the two opposing men into Scarecrow's hands, who took one dribble, looked up at the basket and shot a hard two-hand breast pass straight over the shoulders of the man guarding him back into the hands of Big Moose. They repeated the same routine three more times, quickly, snappily, expertly. The fourth time Big Moose drew the ball to his breast to pass straight into Scarecrow as usual. At that instant Scarecrow raced four steps in toward the basket and came to an abrupt halt. Big Moose shot the ball slantwise into him. Although he had stopped momentarily, his previous momentum propelled him quickly forward again, and when Moose's pass hit him he was already lunging toward the basket, up and in went the ball. The crowd went wild!

The opposing team brought the ball down. A scramble ensued at midcourt and Beverly Wilson, who was short and quick, came out of the scramble with the ball. Heading downcourt Beverly tossed the ball over heads to his main man, Scarecrow, who was racing downcourt on the left side. He caught the ball and went into a forward drive, dribbling and side-stepping and snake-hipping with men all around him and arms swinging everywhere. Sensing that he was nearing the basket, he swooped the ball up with his right hand away from the men who were crowding him on that side and were between him and the basket. He slapped the ball into his left hand, which involuntarily went up. He did not have full control of the ball in his left hand. It was floating away from him on the tip of his fingers and was going to fall short of the basket. He was helpless to do anything about it, for he had stretched himself to the limit. Someone touched his arm. A slight push was added to the ball, which now went just over the rim of the basket and slipped into the net. Scarecrow looked around. No one was there. Nobody on the court could have possibly touched his arm. Yet he had been touched! He had felt it. It had not been an opposing touch, not like hacking, but more like a caress. Running back down the floor to get to his defensive position, he was aware of the standing, cheering crowd. They were cheering for him, Scarecrow! Nobody on his team had ever shot a lefthand shot before. It was the first time he had done so in a game. They had an old-fashioned coach who didn't believe in "trick" shots. Scarecrow glanced at the crowd and saw Juanita jumping up and down, clapping her hands and cheering for him. The other team shot and missed. Scarecrow and Beverly had screened the basket area and Big Moose got the rebound. He passed it out to Squat at the center of the court, who handed it to Scarecrow, who had come out to help Squat. Scarecrow drib-

bled circlewise toward the right side of the court, then cut back sharply across the foul line and headed in deep toward the left corner. Again he swooped the ball up with his right hand into his left, warding off opposing men with the right side of his body, and shot the ball. The arch was perfect, even beautiful, SWISH went the nets. It was like magic. He had never felt this way before. He had not been touched this time but the feeling of the touch, the caress, was still on his arm just above his waist. He flicked his eyes around at the coach, and the coach was not frowning any more.

The second half Scarecrow could not miss. Two-hand, one-hand, lefthand, jump shots, drives, lay-ups, hooks, fifteen, twenty, twenty-five feet away from the basket. Each time he went up the crowd leaped and cheered before the ball even left his hands, SWOOP, two points! When he had first decided to become a basketball player he had practiced jumping with five-pound weights on his ankles. He was six-foot-two inches but he was able to jump as high as, if not higher than, a man six-foot-five. Near the end of the game, he leaped up just inside of midcourt, high, high, higher, until he seemed to be level with the rim of the basket. He had not known when he would let the ball go, if he was going to pass off or shoot.

Up in the air like that, his basketball vision glimpsed the entire gymnasium. He saw cheering faces of the crowd. He saw his teammates darting about and jockeying for positions. He saw Big Moose and Lee Derick fix their strong bodies beneath the goal, ready for the rebound or the tip in. He saw Squat waiting like a possum in his favorite position at the far-right extreme of center court. He saw his buddy Beverly hurrying toward him and stopping to set up a screen to protect him so he could get the shot off without interference. Still he did not release the ball, which he held in both palms high over his head like a goldfish bowl. Then he felt it. The touch. The caress, ever so gently on his arm. He knew that the goal was already as good as made. He now recognized the touch. It was Maria's touch. Still higher he rose. He saw the beams and rafters in the ceiling of the gymnasium. He saw *through the ceiling and up into the night, he saw the heavens. He let go. His ears reverberated with the jubilee of the crowd. He was transcendent among the stars.*

London, England
Lund, Sweden
Wilberforce and Oberlin, Ohio
1964–1973